[V] Violence

 [N] Nudity

 [AC] Adult Content

A NOVEL

VINCE PASSARO

SIMON & SCHUSTER

NEW YORK | LONDON | TORONTO | SYDNEY | SINGAPORE

SIMON & SCHUSTER
Rockefeller Center
1230 Avenue of the Americas
New York, New York 10020

The author has made up everything he could in the writing of this novel. However, it should be noted that because this is a work of fiction, any person, place, event, or thing that appears in the story and is based on reality, or seems to be based on reality in name or situation or attribute, in the process of composition has been deeply distorted for the purposes of writing the story.

Portions of this novel appeared in different forms in *Esquire* (July 1994) and *Open City* 13 (Summer 2001).

SIMON & SCHUSTER
and colophon are registered trademarks
of Simon & Schuster Inc.

For information about special discounts for bulk purchases, please contact Simon & Schuster Special Sales: 1-800-456-6798 or business@simonandschuster.com

Designed by Lisa Chovnick

Manufactured in the United States of America

1   3   5   7   9   10   8   6   4   2

Library of Congress Cataloging-in-Publication Data
Passaro, Vince.
Violence, nudity, adult content : a novel / Vince Passaro.
p. cm.
I. Title.
PS3616.A86 V5 2002
813'.6—dc21   2001049362

ISBN 0-684-85726-X

The author is extremely grateful to The Corporation of Yaddo, which generously provided him with the time and space in which large portions of this book were written.

For Beth Passaro

il miglior fabbro

Let my eyes stream with tears,
day and night, without rest—
over the great destruction which overwhelms
the daughter of my people,
over her incurable wound.

If I walk out into the field,
Look! those slain by the sword;
If I enter the city,
Look! those consumed by hunger.
Even the prophet and the priest
forage in a land they know not.

We wait for peace, to no avail;
for a time of healing, but terror comes instead.

—Jeremiah 14:17–19

Love knows nothing of order.

—St. Jerome

Violence

Nudity

Adult Content

PART I

JULY/AUGUST

[1]

From the desk of William H. Riordan. To the files: I would like to tell the truth. I am in my office on Rector Street, looking out at the cemetery of Trinity Church, pretending to work, in this sort of trance just short of being asleep. It's a form of mental break, but to make partner around here you can never look like you're taking a break, you have to look like you're billing time, so I have a deposition open in front of me and my head's down over it, as if I'm reading it. You get into an intensity of work that is like exercise, a zone; time attenuates, you're inside the thing; then you're out again and you rest. My head lowered, my eyes cast to the left, toward the window, watching the light on the blackened stone walls and gray slate roof of the church, I can hear the rapid, soft *pock pock pock* of Anna, my secretary, inputting this morning's draft of a motion I'm supposed to have on Jack's desk by tomorrow night; it's a matrimonial case.

> §¶ Contrary to the specious, self-serving assertions in Wife's Answer to Husband's Motion to Order Compliance, Husband 1) never hit, struck, or slapped, or physically or verbally or in any other manner abused or attacked Wife, 2) never hit, struck, or slapped, or physically or verbally or in any other manner abused or attacked his children, 3) never addressed his children and/or appeared in their rooms either in the nude, in unusual garments, or in any other unseemly manner or condition, either while they were sleeping or while they were awake. The introduction into the proceeding before the Court at this late date of these reckless and false allegations,

when Husband merely seeks compliance with an existing order of the Court rendered four months prior to this proceed-
ing and well after all due opportunity was given to Wife to
present arguments against Husband's parental suitability,
deeply undermines the credibility of the allegations.

§¶ Husband did not, as claimed by Wife, arrive home drunk
on "a regular basis"; Husband became inebriated on no more
than ten occasions during his sixteen-year Marriage to Wife,
each of those in relation to business-oriented social events
such as dinners, dinner-dances, banquets, shows, and other
forms of business-related entertainment.

§¶ Because at the appropriate time, when custody was under
valid examination by the Court, no arguments were made
against Husband's suitability, nor was such evidence presented, the argument is, inherently, without standing and
merit before this Court, as fully described in Part 1, §1 et seq.

§¶ For these and the reasons above stated in Parts I and II,
with special emphasis on Part I, Section C, Paragraph 5,
Wife's Motion for Summary Dismissal of Claim should be
rejected, and immediate compliance with existing, legally
valid and proclaimed custody agreements should be or-
dered . . .

Below me, in the whitening summer light, the gravestones in the
churchyard look like scattered teeth. A woman's voice comes over Anna's
intercom: "Anna, can you please ask Will to see me in my office when he
has the chance? Tell him to bring his Day-Timer. Thanks." It's Sue
Williamson, one of the partners. She refuses to buzz me directly, insists
on using an intermediary, not only as a proper formal exercise of her authority, but because then she avoids the risk of buzzing me, finding me

not there or on a call, and *then* having to buzz Anna—five seconds or so of otherwise billable fucking time.

"Did you get that?" Anna calls out.

"Yeah," I say. "Thanks."

"Hey, glad to help, anytime," Anna says, still typing. "Do you want some pages?"

"Give me some pages," I say. "Give me some precious pages."

"I'm, like, on sixteen or something," she says.

"Fine, whatever you have."

Anna says, "I'm sending it to the printing station."

"Why can't you use the printer you have there?" I say. She always avoids the smaller dedicated printer on her credenza, I've noticed.

"I don't want to be responsible for loading the paper," she says. "There's a right way and a wrong way, where it jams, and I can never figure it out."

"That's ridiculous. Just put it in, see what happens." I look up at her from my desk. "Take some risks, for chrissakes."

"That's easy for you to say," she says. "What risks do you ever take?"

"Okay, fine," I say.

"I'm shooting it to the laser."

"Fine," I say. "Whatever." *I'm shooting it to the laser. I'm setting it on fire and catapulting it over the church spire.*

"Sue?" I say, arriving at Sue's office.

"Will," she says. "How are you on Thursday? I have a client coming in for a preliminary discussion at three-thirty."

"Fine," I say.

"Where's your Day-Timer?" she says.

"I don't use a Day-Timer," I say.

"Are you sure about Thursday? I want to confirm with the client."

"Thursday's fine," I say. "Friday I'm getting a haircut."

"I tell you what," Sue says. "Come to lunch with me tomorrow. I'll fill you in on background."

"I'm kind of tied up writing this motion for Jack," I say.

Sue's face undergoes a series of changes, a surface darkening with underlying tectonic shifts. In law firms, superiors rarely give you shit directly; so finely tuned are the nuances of authority that the mere threat of giving you shit is enough. "I'm not going to be free between now and Thursday," Sue says. This means, if I want to work on the case, or any others she has anything to do with in the future, I have to go to lunch with her.

"I guess I can slip out," I say.

"Good," Sue says. The face as instrument of power: hers softens now; she is warm with rectitude and approval. "It's an interesting case. Very desirable if we can get something going. Deep-pocket defendant, possible press, the whole bit. It's a name case when it comes to partnership."

I'm up for partner in December. Broad hints are now regularly dropped. Offers dangle, bribes and extortions hang in the air flaccid as yesterday's balloons. "Thanks, Sue," I say.

She lowers her voice. "Actually, Jack wanted me to use Carol but I insisted on you."

"Thanks, Sue."

"Carol's a putz. She's smart, I guess, but she's a putz."

"Thanks, Sue."

"So lunch, tomorrow, one?"

"Sure." I turn. "And thanks again, Sue."

"Fine." Sue snaps down the flap on her Filofax. It sounds like small-arms fire in a distant field.

At four-fifteen Sue's secretary, Jeannie, delivers to Anna a Redweld file containing Sue's correspondence and notes so far on the Murray case, the case she's invited me to work on. On the outside of the folder, a little yellow stick-on note from Sue: "Will—please review this material before tomorrow's lunch. S." I put the folder on the floor next to my desk, and don't pick it up again until seven, when I've finished revising today's draft of Jack's motion. It is a rape case. Two men broke into the client's apartment, beat her, raped her, and eventually robbed her before they left several hours later. They were never apprehended. It is obvious that we will propose she make a case of negligence and loss of contracted service against the building, an east side high-rise. According to the police report, there were three security people scheduled to be on duty, but only two had reported for work, and at the time of the attack, one of those was on break. The video equipment, a camera mount in the hallway, had been in disrepair for three weeks. No one was overseeing the displays for the surveillance system at that time anyway, because of the shorthanded shift. The police are pleased to include these details because they like to see the guilt radiate and hum, especially without a suspect in hand.

The file includes a psychiatrist's letter, which describes our client as suffering from "chronic clinical levels of depression, hostility, alienation, and aggravated sexual dysfunction. She has been unable to conduct normal relations, sexual and across her personal life, since the trauma. There is little reason to expect any notable level of recovery in the foreseeable future." It also points out that she was a sexually active bisexual before the rape and that now, though she cannot become intimate with men, she continues to have sporadic, "though not entirely conjugal," relationships with women. I wonder what this means. My take is that this evidence can be suppressed, but that with a New York jury, it need not be; we can manage it to our benefit. Sue's notes are in a jaunty hand.

I get home at eight-thirty, neither early nor late for me these days. The entire front of Ellie's blouse is soaked from giving Henry his bath. Henry is almost two and a half; Sam, our second son, is brand-new, fourteen weeks. Ellie's mother was here for a while helping out, but now she's back at her place on West End. She comes once or twice a week for a couple of hours. Ellie mostly has been trying to take care of things alone—I keep telling her to hire someone, but she doesn't do it.

"What's for dinner?" I say.

"It's eight-thirty," Ellie says. "Cookies are for dinner."

"I like the wet T-shirt look," I say.

"Don't even think about it," Ellie says.

"Very sexy."

"Touch me and I'll kill you," she says.

I reach out for the front of her blouse and she drives a fist into my rib cage. "I haven't had a moment to myself all day, mister," she says, a little too loudly. She goes into the bedroom and I make a tuna sandwich.

Later that night we stretch out on the couch together, me propped up and Ellie lying between my legs, with her head resting on my chest, watching television. Television scares us. *ER* scares us, the news scares us, the wildly exuberant weatherman scares us. Jay Leno commences, with the stupid grins of the lawn-jockey bandleader and Jay's tonnage of false cheer. "Let's try Letterman. He's sure to be depressed and easier to take," I say. Ellie does not reply. The desperate, idiotic faces, Jay looking around after each middling joke, a comedian without a trace of spontaneity left in him. All of it drains our lives of meaning, throws into question the reality of who we are, where we are, our high-ceilinged, slightly crumbly apartment, our chairs from Ellie's mother, our plain white Wedgwood china, our nervous days and windless nights—for a moment our existences seem to be staggering at a cliff's edge of unreality. Letterman has some sort of scene from the street, a Pakistani guy with a thick accent stopping people on Seventh Avenue and asking them how much cash they're carrying. I hand Ellie the remote and she switches to *Charlie Rose:* he's with a painter turned film director who's just published a memoir. Charlie is in a frenzy of interest. The painter's face screams substance abuse. I'm still back with Jay, my mind's eye tracking him throughout his day, all the caution of a middle-aged man in jeans and white sneakers, meetings in the morning, teams of Californians helping craft tonight's jokes. The extinction of personality that is television. Ellie burrows into my chest. I hold her. A slight trembling, it's hard to tell which of us it is. Her head feels like it's trying to push straight through to my heart. She is mumbling something into my chest cavity, I can feel words resonating in my lungs.

"Excuse me?" I say.

"Please turn off the television," she says.

"Are you crying?" I say.

"No, just turn off the television," she says.

"Where did you put the remote?" I say.

"I don't know," she murmers.

I feel around underneath us, look down at the floor. Nothing. I make a small motion to disengage and get up.

"Don't leave!" she says. She pins me with arms and legs, her head up under my chin. I stroke her hair. The top of her head has a smell I think I would recognize anywhere. "See if you can turn it off with your foot," she says. I extend my leg, probe with my big toe. It is a big Sony color set, eight or nine years old, that a cousin passed on to us after we were married and I was just out of law school, doing a clerkship; we've never replaced it or upgraded, we employ a guarded laziness in the face of new technologies.

"I need the remote control," I say, unable to reach the little buttons on the bottom, which are so small and invisible a toe probably can't manipulate them anyway. Finally I rise, turn the volume all the way down, glance around for the remote, don't see it, get under Ellie again on the couch. I am sitting, she is lying. The set flickers in silence, like a flame.

"This is why normal people always have the remote control," I say.

"We're not normal," Ellie says. "And we're not even remotely in control." We stay like that for a while, her on top, rising and falling as I breathe. We pass our different brands of tiredness back and forth to each other through the skin. She shifts, then I shift, and then we are pressed together in a familiar and unmistakable way, we click into place like two pieces that fit. A faint rhythm. My hands are in the area between her ribs and hips, the soft concavity of her waist. I pull up her blouse, still damp, she never bothered to change it, and I put my hands on her skin, cold from the moisture. She kisses my neck; her face is wet and slithery, a mermaid's face. She arches up and our lips meet. Moisture. Salt.

"Henry was conceived on this couch," I say.

Ellie pulls back and eyes me. "Henry," she says, "was conceived on the red chair."

"That's right," I say. "I forgot. We were so wild in those days."

"It was just three years ago," she says.

"Our lost youth," I say.

"I'll show you lost youth," Ellie says. We undress. The sadness of clothes on furniture and floor; the hint of missing human forms. Naked, she stands flat-footed; a child at the beach. We touch again, and I know instantly that the small flame that was in her has gone out; her enthusiasm is quieted now, she is tense and shy, her body and her psyche have endured a three-year battering at the hands of the human sex act and she doesn't know what to do with this. She is at the stage of I'll-submit. I don't want her to submit, I want her to want. Or that's not true—if she truly wanted to submit, we would have that kind of relationship, I would physically overwhelm her, and we would both affirm my power in the act. But this is not what she wants at all—I'll-submit passes into I-resent-submitting. Hard muscles, rubbery skin. My advances come back, no forwarding address. Then we wait. She waits to see if I can reignite her, I wait for her to ignite. I *try* various things, and they have all the awkward, one-way feeling of *trying*. With my fingers, my lips, my tongue and arms and shoulders and legs, I'm pressing, dusting, leaning, and appealing. I'm in court to argue a case I haven't prepared. It's a weak case, in any event. Her body is the jury, slack, unbelieving, diverse, impenetrable. And so we reach a settlement, she and I, because I know I cannot win, and she knows she doesn't want to prove it. Not now. Next time. All politeness.

*   *   *

Over onion soup, in a slightly upmarket version of an Irish pub, new wood and cut glass, Sue gives me more details about the Murray case. This distinctly unfashionable, stock-and-bond-trader-type restaurant is a place Sue would never take anyone else, having chosen it as a reminder to me of where both of us are coming from (she's Long Island Irish, I'm Queens). Sue runs down the case. This is the gossipy voyeuristic side of the law, the personal swamp gases you live in so that you can represent someone else in the eyes of the state, so that you can become the person on behalf of the person. The client, when she works, is a "freelance" writer. As far as we can tell, this amounts to some poetry and a few short story/essay-type things published in small magazines, spread out over the last few years. She is black. When she was younger, she had a couple of years as a dancer. Her father is a wealthy and influential friend of mayors and borough presidents and a force in the Harlem political machine; he owns a black cosmetics corporation that gave rise to a media enterprise: three magazines, a newspaper, a radio station, and two underperforming cable operations upstate, that are on the block. The client grew up in Westchester, studied at a prep school, and attended an all-black woman's college in Georgia, majoring in dance and then switching to literature. Two years of graduate work at Yale and a year at the Sorbonne, all in literature and drama, no degrees. A little over nine months ago, two intruders broke into her apartment on the fourteenth floor of a high-rent building on East Eighty-sixth Street, with intent to rob, held the client captive for six and a half hours, raped her, sodomized her, and threatened her with a knife and with various blunt objects such as a club, the telephone receiver, etc. We sit at ninety-degree angles to each other at the square table, and Sue's leg brushes against mine; her hand ventures down, touches my leg. I put my hand on her dress then, which is a slippery material like rayon or silk. This is how we talk, an old routine with us, a game that never goes anywhere. Neither of us would be able to sustain an interest in the other for long enough to take it any-where, not she in me because I am intriguing but not in any material sense important; not I in her because my small, odd fondness for her is regularly scorched by disgust. She finds this game entertaining; she needs to be titillated at a fairly constant level and good associate that I am, I accomodate. Then I stop.

"They did *everything* to this poor woman," Sue says, working her spoon against the side of her bowl to free a hunk of melted cheese. I bring my hand back to my own dining quadrant. "If you can think of it, they did it to her," she says. "You've seen the psychologist's report. Frankly, I'm embarrassed to talk about it. God knows how she's going to testify." She breaks a pumpernickel roll and peels open a foil-wrapped pat of butter.

"How did you ever make partner, Sue?" I ask. She looks at me over her raised butter knife.

"Ninety-hour weeks and a hint of cruelty," she says. She examines me like a piece of evidence. "Will," she says then, "you're a smart lawyer and a nice guy. But you've got an attitude problem. Major. All the partners have seen it. 'Nice guy, smart lawyer, bad attitude.' That's the rap on you. I *strongly* recommend you straighten up and fly right, if you catch my drift."

On Thursday the client, or *the victim*, as I keep wanting to call her, arrives half an hour late and bristling with hostility, a short, muscular, light-skinned black woman with light brown, almost hazel eyes, thirty-four years old, we have seen the age documented, though she just as well might be an old twenty-five or a young forty-three. She's attractive in a blunt way, mostly through the eyes, but so visibly pissed off you don't notice the good looks right away. Her name is Ursula Murray. Sue brings her into the conference room and introduces me.

"Ursula, this is Will Riordan, he's going to be the associate on the case. Why don't we sit over here." Sue directs us to seats at either side of hers at the head of the long table. Ursula glares at me and sits. In her face the kind of rage that builds cities in the wilderness. She seems to rub herself into her chair, as if it is molded to a shape she doesn't quite fit.

Sue picks up some folders. "Ursula, let me just start by saying—"

"Actually, Sue, I have something I'd like to say," Ursula interjects. "I'd like to say that as I recall, there are a number of women attorneys at this law firm and I wonder why, given the circumstances, a man has been assigned. It borders on the insensitive. It borders on the insulting. It's stupid."

We sit in silence. Ursula and I are looking at Sue. "Well, Ursula, let me just say I'm fully cognizant of your concerns," Sue says. Obviously she has thought of this objection already. "We will go to *any* length to make you feel as comfortable as possible with the representation we provide on this very sensitive case. I think it's obvious in response to what you've indicated that we gave a lot of thought as to who should assist on this case, male, female, whatever, and there are several reasons why Will is the best choice. First and foremost, he is our best associate, a fine legal mind and a superb litigator. Second, we felt having a man work with you becomes important when you realize that this case, because of the extensive size of the damages we will seek if you choose to have us represent you, is more likely than most to go to trial. The defense attorneys will most likely be males. We will request a jury, and they will likely seek to put as many men as possible on it. This is to keep in mind, in the eventuality. The judge also will likely be male. Our case will hinge on your testimony. Your ability to deal with the issues of this lawsuit in front of men will be very useful to you at that time. So that's our thinking. Will is a man. He can't help that. We all deplore the tragedy that has occurred here. I suggest you go through with this meeting, think about these issues, and we can talk about it"—Sue looks at her calendar here—"tomorrow is bad, but how about Monday?"

Ursula looks at me. I look back at her: hazel eyes crowded with conflicting messages. Male. Female. Whatever.

"Why don't you get us some coffee then, Mr. Riordan?" she says. Do I detect a smile?

"That's a good idea, Will," Sue says. She fans open her folders across the conference table.

                              *   *   *

There was a memo from Sue to attorneys possibly concerned with the Murray case on my desk this morning: "For purposes of today's meeting, meetings in the future, and all memoranda and correspondence, unless otherwise indicated, what we might typically in conversation have referred to as 'the rape' will be referred to as 'the attack.'"

Although she has, since "the attack," hardly worked, Ursula, it turns out, still writes; she is collecting her thoughts on paper; she is hoarding bits and scraps of language, taping things up, shoring a few fragments.

This she tells me by letter a week after our initial meeting. We are already preparing the lawsuit; we have, in the case of negligence in the building, until the end of September, twelve months after the tort, to file a case. Ursula's initial reaction to my presence, an ideological position much enhanced by certain maladies of the day, seems to have modified; she now prefers a kind of assaultive intimacy, judging by her prose.

> Dear Mr Riordan: Well, I was not in the best of moods when we met the other day and I was startled by your face. It resides on the unhealthy side of skeptical, that face of yours. In any case I do believe I am a kind of "neccessary participant" in the construction of a legal narrative of my attack. What effect my own thoughts might have on your strategies I do not know or really care much about, but I cannot see you there making something of the incident entirely on your own . . . You have a psychologist's report, do you not? I see myself as adding color and hue to the picture, certain "values" as is said in the world of the painter . . .

Ursula has, she says, been writing down the scenes in her head against her will, or against a significant portion of her will, and as a result their form is ambiguous. At first she wrote notes on napkins, deposit slips, the backs of drugstore coupon sheets and podiatrist handouts. Old habits die hard and for a time she was entering these jottings in longer versions on her computer (file name: flowers), but she soon discovered that this activity, expansive and probing, left her feeling paralyzed, speechless, and finally annihilated; at a certain point, though she continued producing her scraps, she let them remain as scraps, dumping them in a large bowl on a side counter in her kitchen—thoughts, images, electric memories. Added to these were clippings that she found, some relating obviously to what had happened to her, some relating hardly at all. From the bowl all the scraps and notes made their way into a shopping bag. Eventually the shopping bag was filled. The loaves-and-fishes miracle of words. Ursula has been a prolific writer, of half sentences, brief paragraphs. She no longer knows what narrative is; or if she knows, doesn't believe in it. What happened to her was not a narrative, it was a flashing dark sword, a horrifying truth in the present tense.

The shopping bag is delivered to Sue by messenger the next day, a Friday. Sue arrives at my office followed by a clerk carting the bag. "On a Friday," she says. "Can you believe it? I want you to go through these and arrange them and have someone type them up so I can read them next week. Bill your time to legal research, I don't want her to know you've seen these."

I don't tell her that Ursula has written to me about them already, knowing that Sue won't read them: "That woman," Ursula said in her letter, "probably can't get through a capsule movie review, so she will be handing these papers over to you. I will be happy to be shut of them, submit them to the process, such as it is. Do you have an e-mail address, for future correspondence?" She has softened toward me in so far as she believes that whatever I am, Sue is worse. I pull out a few ripped pieces of paper: "Hair," the first one says. Underneath that a list:

Who put this pubic hair in my Coke?
Who put this pubic hair in my Cristal?
Who put this pubic hair in my antifreeze?

Who put this pubic hair between pages 76 and 77 of my Remembrance of Things Past?

Who put this pubic hair in my Crest? In my bed? In my eyes? In my mouth?

Then another piece: *A man tosses a child in the air—brute strength.* Next, typed, across the top of an index card, it says, *The Angry Father, a Tale.* Below it three sentences:

This is a story about rape. This is a story about insemination. This is a story about fatherhood.

On a folded sheet of spiral notebook paper: *In the bedroom. Peach-colored sheets. Hair smelling of Rock Sheen. Rock Sheen: paid for the schools, the house, Mother's Oldsmobile that drove me to swimming lessons, skating, the whole suburban trick, all the places where I was the black girl.*

Inside the fold, written in careful, small, block print: *At first tried, struggled. Every time I pushed away he hit me. Neck, ribs, side of head, face. Arms like iron, hands like iron . . . Those of us not used to being hit can't fight. To fight one must always have fought. Start early, never stop. Fight dad, fight brother, fight the neighbor taunting in the yard. Strike mother, strike sister, flail granny, hit teacher. Be struck in return. A discipline of taking blows. His willingness to hit and intimidate may be greater than mine. My desire to kill may be greater than his. When his tactic works, mine is subverted. Learn to get hit, and learn to kill.*

Uh uh uh uh uh uh uh, jackhammer. Uh uh uh uh uh uh uh uh uh uh uh uh uh uh uh uh uh uh uh uh—

My words in your brain, like a cock in a cunt.

On the gray, mottled back of a panel torn from a box of Total it says: *Kitchen recipe book. Recipe 1. Cut a swatch of cheap brown vinyl, from a cheap pencil case, say. Set aside. Snip little bits of curly steel wool, make pile, and set aside. Spread glue onto vinyl swatch in rough triangular pattern. Gather the steel wool snippets and distribute them over the glue, applying as much of the steel wool as the glue will hold. Carve cock from brown wood. Attach.*

*   *   *

Ursula's papers in my hand, heaps of them like a very sloppy person would deliver to his accountant the day before his taxes are due; I'm not reading them anymore, I can't say exactly what I'm doing. Just sort of holding them, in the break mode. I hear a noise outside on Broadway, which at first I don't pay attention to, but it builds and makes itself known as an event of some kind, a beating of tom-toms and rasping of horns. People shouting. I hear a chant take shape. I can't make out what it is. It sounds like a large crowd, something rare, a big demonstration— a throwback, a seascape of nostalgic memories. I'm excited at the prospect of chaos, anarchy, freedom. I press up against the window, looking for television cameras. My office is a little too far down on Rector Street to see Broadway. All I can catch are fragmented reflections in the angled window panels of the art deco building on the other side of Broadway, figures moving upside down across the glass segments, Eisenstein cinema or magic lantern show. Corners of banners, a sense of hats. I go to my door and peek out into the hall. The secretaries have stopped working, waiting for some signal from their bosses that it will be all right to go into the offices and look out the windows. No such signal comes. Anna looks at me. "What is that?" she mouths. I nod for her to come in—she passes me and I shut the door.

"I can't see out this window," she says, pressed hard up against it. A shelf runs the entire length of the wall under the window, full of papers and transcripts, squared-off mountains of documents. Anna kicks her shoes off and climbs up from my chair onto the stacks of papers. I'm standing behind her, ready to catch her if it all slides out from under her, looking at the backs of her brown, bare knees.

"Careful there," I say. I put a hand on her calf.

"It's the health and hospital workers," Anna says happily. She's leaning forward up there, holding on to the window frame. My head is practically under her skirt. I'm bending backward a little, looking at her thighs, trying with some misgivings to insert at least a symbolic distance between my face and the healthy backs of her legs. The strike had been in the paper and on last night's news. "They've filled up Broadway," she says. "I wonder if my cousin is there. It looks like they're turning into Wall. There are thousands of them. Hey, there's Jesse Jackson. I *love* Jesse Jackson. Hey, Jesse! Hey, Jesse!"

"Shhh!" I say. One hand on each calf. Her feet are planted on the briefs and motions, red-dot toes gripping, like gibbons' feet in the trees. "Why do you paint your toenails?" I say.

"I want them to look like little jewels," Anna says. "You wouldn't believe how big this crowd is. They could take over. I mean, if it were a riot."

"Can you make out what they're saying?" We listen for a bit. The chant echoes in the canyon of Broadway, booming a deep bass. My hands move down Anna's shins and onto the tops of her feet. Delicate, curving bones.

"It sounds like 'Let's be fair, we give the care,'" Anna says.

"How old are you, Anna?" I ask.

"Twenty-five," she says.

"I knew that," I say. The chant winds down, there is some independent shouting, and then another chant starts up.

"'Hey, hey, where's our pay,'" Anna says. Her feet wriggle and shift under my hands. You never can really keep in mind how alive other people are until you touch them, smell them, listen to their breath or their muffled drum-beating pulse; you get electric impulses from the skin— organism-with-hope-and-fear. Identity without language. An absolute and dynamic mystery.

"'Aw shucks, Wall Street sucks,'" Anna says.

Second week of July, height of summer. Heat seems to generate up from the subway platforms, blasts from beneath the air-conditioned train cars as they pull into the stations. It is a mystery to me why as you go underground in this city, it gets so much hotter. I've been led to believe the opposite will occur; in other cities, the opposite does occur. Just one more special brutality in New York.

I get home in time to take Henry to the playground after his supper. Other fathers are there in shirts and ties. Exhausted mothers sit alone on the benches. One kid runs crazily back and forth while his father, in a glen-plaid summer suit, follows with one of those drinking mugs with the straw built in, saying, "Nick, are you thirsty? Do you want a drink, Nick?" Nick doesn't want a drink. He wants to exorcize the demons of his parentless days. Henry is cautious, aware of the other children as predators. I unsnap him from his stroller and he just sits there. I pick him up, stand him on the ground. He looks around, wide-eyed. He grips his shovel in a small fist and begins to move slowly toward the sandbox. He builds a tiny momentum. Older children, gigantic-looking three- and four-year-olds, dash around him. He slants across their path unperturbed, like a blind prophet. At the opening to the sandbox, he waits for me to come and help him take the step down to get inside. I bring him his pail and find him a place away from the entrance. For a while he ignores the pail and sits dumping sand onto his legs. I squat, fill the pail, turn it over, tap it on bottom and sides, and pull it away to reveal a solid-looking cylinder of sand. Henry smiles and attacks it with his shovel. I slip out of the sandbox and find a place on the nearest bench. Children are running around frantically, eyes wide, hair wet and matted to foreheads. We all pause to watch as one mother, in a red silk dress and expensive-looking flats, carries her warrior, howling in frustration and defeat, off the playground proper and out onto the park's promenade, where she can comfort him in private and ready him again for the fray. The intensity of the place comes from its packaging—a very urban experience this, a rectangle about the size of two living rooms, one hour a day in which a child can play with its parents. For many of the children, all the tiredness and heat and longing to show off for Mommy and Daddy are squeezed down to an alarming density, a black hole of toddler energy and will. The sky reddens over the Palisades, the river is molten silver-gray. One by one parents load their children into strollers, where they sit panting and dazed. Henry gets up, stands at the step out of the sandbox, puts his hand in the air and squeals—let me out. I go and give him the hand he's looking for and then follow him to the slide, at the base of which he stands, banging. I hoist him and try to put him at the top but he squirms and cries—that's not what he wanted. He wants to go back to the base of the slide and bang. So be it. Then his hand comes up again. He wants to climb up onto the slide, try to crawl up it, so I help him do that. I push him up by his behind, huffing and puffing to make a joke about how hard it is. He laughs at the top, flops onto his belly, and slides down backward. Every time I go to the playground with him I have to learn his new routines. The ones I know from the last time are old already, rarely of interest to him. He shouts at dogs and birds and buses and trucks. Other than that, he is in a world of his own. His jaw tight, his eyes flaming, he hits most of the kids who come near him.

"Henry, don't hit the other boy," I say. "He's allowed to use the slide too. Now it's his turn." The words as units of meaning have little visible effect on a two-year-old; what we know intuitively, however, is that we must disapprove of these things, strongly, so that he will in his relentless emulation of us build a moral order in which this behavior is wrong and suppressed. The other boy looks on with mild curiosity as I lecture. Much larger, he is not disturbed when Henry reaches around to hit him again.

"Okay, that's it," I say, and I lift Henry off the slide. He kicks for a moment, then wails, head thrown back, eyes shut tight, mouth open wide. Albrecht Dürer's *Self-Portrait at the Playground*, in the popular show "Dürer: The Early Work." As I strap him into his stroller he arches and squirms, until he knows the struggle is over and, relieved, he can calm down. As we wheel onto the promenade, a man passes walking two Great Danes. They stand almost four feet high. I expect to hear "Doggie"—but Henry surprises me.

"HORSEY!" he shouts. "Horsey horsey!"

When Ellie and I were first married, I was in law school and we had an apartment on Claremont Avenue, a big one-bedroom looking north toward the tower of Riverside Church and, beyond it, a square patch of the Hudson. I remember the feeling of having so much *room* in those days; Ellie was at work during the day, I was in the library at night. We'd come together for meals, at bedtime, odd afternoons or evenings when one of us happened to break schedule and be there. We went to movies all the time, movies and then a beer or two in a local bar, where often we'd run into friends; that was what we did, we were never big on restaurants or clubs or theaters or parties. In those days there were still revival houses on the West Side. Double features: Ozu and Mizoguchi, Capra and Sturges, a Wim Wenders or Joshua Logan series. It seems now, in certain rosy memories, almost perfect, a quiet and comfortable form of dating. But we weren't committed to each other then, or devoted may be the old-fashioned and proper word, not without two children and the glue of household and routine holding us together. We've grown into a collection of phrases and clichés from our own childhoods: "we *never* go the movies anymore . . . ," "the kids had a good day . . ." Dinners of bottled spaghetti sauce, frozen vegetables. Power, space, domain. Lately I'm there and not there, I look at the tableau set before me, Henry dirty from supper, the deep moss green of pureed spinach across his face and shirtfront, Sam looking damp in his rocker seat; or both of them, clean and sparkling out of the bath, going gooey as I change them (or more often, Ellie changes them), the powder falling like confectioner's sugar over their genitals and small rounded behinds before you pin them in. It has the quality of cinema, of a documentary film before the sound track has been laid on. Raw footage. Nothing is explained. It seems as if it will go on forever. There's a person there, two people, and small children; the apartment they're in looks nice, spacious enough for now, getting a little down at the heels, in need of some freshening up. The light's not particularly good. Soon there will be a voice, titles, something to tell me what's going on. There are pots on the stove. They don't match. The two people, the couple, look tired. They're doing the usual things.

*   *   *

The next day, mid-afternoon, an e-mail arrives from Ursula. Our in-house network's e-mail software puts the name associated with the e-mail address in quotes, as if all of us are concepts, still in the development stage:

To: "William Riordan" <wriordan@rpjlaw.com>
From: "Ursula Murray" <murray212@earthbird.com>
Subject: the truth in black and white

i say to him, he's undoing his pants, notice you're second on a line of two brother? what are you doing taking orders from a white man? what are you messing with a sister so a white man can get his rocks off? haven't you had enough of that shit? he slaps me across the face. he likes that, i feel his pleasure in it, something rising up like vomit, and so he does it again, lifting me up under the knees and turning my body toward him a little so he could slap my ass and my face, my face and my ass. and then he took out the knife. and i'd known the sister line was bullshit when i'd said it, but i tried it anyway, relying on this orthodoxy, this thing i'd believed in until the moment i'd walked into the apartment and saw the two of them standing there, and they saw me and their faces kind of lit up in tandem, joy and the desire to kill, a couple of dogs on a tree'd coon. i'd understood right then, it was these two against me. that's all there is. black and white don't mean shit. my whole life i thought it meant something but it was nothing. cock and pussy, cock and pussy is everything, cock and pussy all the time. has always been and will always be.

I read it; I reread it. What do I do with it? Print it and put it through the incoming document drill? The words on my screen, their presence there, *cock and pussy, cock and pussy, cock and pussy,* every time I look up that's what I see; isn't there some system administrator, paid to search out and destroy such words on the network? Expose and punish the recipient? They make me nervous; or that's not it: they cause a kind of panic. I hit delete.

Coming home on the subway, almost seven, I am beside an old Caribbean woman with a kerchief tied around her head. She is standing against the door. I am on the end of the row, right next to her. The dusty smell of her. High cheekbones, cheeks sucked in over what must be toothless gums. A cheap blue T-shirt from some cheap hopeless place. She smells like old cardboard. Two shopping bags, one atop the other, jammed into a space between her and what is, essentially, my rib cage, filling the space under the bar. She's mumbling something, praying maybe. The broad toes and painted nails of the other women on the train. Cute clothes, jewelry, all the women look comfortable despite the heat; women like heat, and suffer more in winter. Beside me, this woman in kerchief, mumbling, her arms long and muscular from lugging these bags of terrible, useless things, but hers, *her* things, around with her. We make such severe judgments, so arbitrary and complete. The city, the proximity and danger of contact, force them from us. Observations are too close, too detailed, we know too much about each other in too short a time. The way this woman stands, the way she rocks her head from side to side, a certain intensity and lack of control, suggest madness. I don't know her and never will. Yet for me she is revealed, identified and forgotten. She exists forever now, without hope of mercy, as a madwoman on the train.

At home, almost in time for supper with Ellie, close enough that she has waited for me, I am overcome with that feeling of strangeness. It starts in the bathroom—the shampoo is a brand I don't recognize, there's a baby rattle on the sink that I've never seen before. I glance around and suddenly everything looks unfamiliar—nothing suspicious, just everything looks new to my eye, indications of a life I'm not a part of. It's something like what happens when you stare at a simple word you've seen thousands of times before and suddenly don't recognize it. I feel like a visitor, awkward, careful, in the way.

I find Henry in front of the TV, watching footage of a propane gas fire on the news. "This invisible but deadly gas," the announcer croons. Large-bellied policemen direct traffic, which isn't moving much in any case, as people evacuate the town, emergency vehicles on the side of the road. Henry is standing inches from the screen, a tiny figure before a flickering world. The images change and change and change, they still him.

"Horsey," Henry says.

"There are no horseys there," I say.

"CAR!" he shouts. "Car car!"

"That's right, those are cars."

"Car car," he says, marching into the kitchen, where Ellie is making us two pieces of sole, butter, a little bit of shallot, she'll throw in a few capers after the white wine cooks down. She has Sam in the pouch, his head lolling, stupefied by steam, by his mother's intense odor, by the motion of her swinging body, its warmth and the tight canvas grip of the papoose. The air-conditioning is obliterated in here. I look on from the doorway.

"CAR!" shrieks Henry.

"Do you have a car?" Ellie asks him. "Yeeees," she answers for him. He slowly begins to nod. "Did you go to the playground this morning? Yeeees, daddy. Were you very bad at the playground? Yeeees, daddy, I got into a fight on the slide and I was very bad, I slapped a little girl who was trying to use the slide at the same time I was. Did mommy yell at you and make you come off the slide right away? Yeeees, daddy, and I cried and cried and made a scene until mommy took me away."

"Sounds familiar," I say.

Fishy, shallotty, winey steam rises from the pan; Ellie gently moves the fish. Small potatoes are boiling. Some lettuce and fresh tomatoes are laid out. "Nice-looking supper," I say.

"Yeah," Ellie says. "I thought I'd experiment with some of the upper-middle-class elegance you're always going on about. Don't get used to it." The ventilator fan whirs above the stove, laboring to pull out the moisture and heat. On top of the refrigerator, the most expensive clock radio in history plays something fashionably Cuban—music not far from the Dominican meringue that, I don't bother pointing out, when it was blasted loudly out the back windows through long weekend nights in years gone by, we used to call the police about. That was before poor people were removed from most of Manhattan, while their music and clothes became popular.

"Oh hot," Henry says. "Is hot, Mommy? Is hot, Mommy? Hot. Hot."

"Very hot," Ellie says. "Oh so hot."

"Hot," he says again, smiling. Over the past year or so, language has come to him in two stages: the first thing was the word, tactile, musical, a familiar and thrilling sound. No! he might say, or Car!, in an appropriate moment, the word born into his vocabulary because of its meaning, but once his mouth has mastered the mechanics of it he is often likely to use it anywhere, anytime, broaden its connotations until it applies to everything. No might mean yes or no or now or I want it. Car means car, or truck, or horse, or Father, or everything-I-feel. He does the same with gestures. Handing you a plastic bag from the trash might mean pick me up. Gradually, as words have lost their newness and become less like toys in his mouth, he has narrowed them down again to within range of their original uses. Ellie and I cling to the real meaning of the words, and affirm them as much as possible: right! we might say, that's a car, or the stove is *very* hot, you're right!, and in this way we mean to instruct him, convince him that yes, words have meaning, strings of meaning can be made and followed over time, certain linear relationships are suggested, life can be controlled, a larger meaning can direct it. Yes. We do not question this.

[2]

Things at home go through cycles, get better, then worse, then better again—a week of general satisfaction, a moment or two of happiness. The boys thrive in such times, sunlight and play and early to bed, they eat well, their hair shines. The sense of clouds lifting, the clear breeze of a manageable future. Standing at the kitchen sink, I discover that a plastic seltzer bottle, empty, ready for recycling, when held by the base and bopped against the porcelain, makes a rich and primitive range of sounds, like an ancient drum. I start playing it, getting a rhythm going between the deep resonance of the middle of the bottle and the sharp percussive of the stubby top: *ba-ba ti-ti ba-ba, BA-BA! Ba-ba ti-ti ba-ba, BA-BA!* I'm doing a village dance, standing at sink-edge. Henry comes in and laughs at me. He sticks his arms straight out and twirls and falls on his rump. Sam watches us from the baby rocker, eyes shifting among the moving limbs. Ellie is drawn in from the bathroom, about to take a shower. She's in an open robe. She takes Henry's hands and dances with him. The family, the tribe. I keep the beat going and dance before the sink—a spontaneous domestic happening, crazy-seeming but a genuine and reasonable moment for us right then, and I'm watching Ellie dancing on the tile floor, her strong feet grazing the ceramic, a well-made look to her, and Henry staring up at her and bouncing, literally, a dance of rhythmic half jumps. Ellie's almost-black hair flies around her face. Ritual and play. Other families must have this too although I've never heard it discussed. Soon we'll make up a name for what we're doing and no one else will know what it means.

And then a reversion; nights at the office, lost magazines you're in the middle of reading, doctors' appointments made and missed, bills not paid, letting the answering machine pick up; I am late to the office because I have to run out to the dry cleaner for clothes; we forget to put the bag with the Huggies out at night and so walk in to yesterday's memories of shit.

Sam is screaming, Henry is overturning the trash, or you come into the living room and Henry is calmly removing every book from the shelf, dropping them on the floor, spine open, pages folded over on themselves. Tantrums on the sidewalk. Nights of insomnia, mornings oversleeping, and at dinner hour the steely flavor of distraction and rage.

I'm home one night, working after supper, and at one-thirty, when I finally give up, I go into the bedroom and Ellie is sitting on the far side of the bed, staring out the window. "Oh dark," she says, imitating Henry. "*Very* dark." She doesn't turn to face me. "I want out of this," she says. A common theme, in response to our weariness, my distraction, the gray gap that has inserted itself between us, the separation of two people deeply angry with each other but unable to explain why, simmering as if we're incompatible roommates in an apartment we shall soon lose in any case. We talk about divorce like fishermen discussing distant, dangerous seas. Big fish there. Very far. Weather bad. Sitting on the side of the bed.

A week later Jack and I have a date with Ron Adamson, the client for whom I've just written the custody motion. We call him the wife beater. Of course he isn't really a wife beater; we believe him when he says his wife has suggested this out of vindictiveness and a desire for a more favorable arrangement with the children. Our motion explicitly points out the unusual timing of the claim, made only now, eighteen months after preliminary agreements were filed. Her recent motion states, "Wife has not come forward regarding Husband's violent abuse until this time due to personal emotional turmoil and intense fear and shame." Jack and I talk constantly about Ron as if he were King Kong, we do it in fun, as a hex against the idea, because of his wife's intimations and because he is a

tall, dark-haired, elegantly dour, tyrannical man in his late forties, the
kind of man who gets things done, the kind of man who is successful,
wealthy, and universally disliked. Jack in particular is fascinated by the
guy. It seems pretty clear that this is the kind of man that Jack on his
worst days would like to be. Jack is our headliner, he appears in the pages
of the popular press, mainly attending famous men's wives, whom he
cultivates like flowers. He goes to dinner parties. He spreads himself
around. On this case he is representing the man, so some other lawyer
will get the publicity.

Normally, if Ron were any other matrimonial client, we would meet
him in the office or at best a restaurant, but since he's seemed inclined
lately to throw some of his business stuff our way, we decide on a ball
game. The firm has season tickets, boxes behind third base at Yankee
Stadium.

Before we leave, I see Jack in his office. "You know what this is?"
Jack says, holding up the final draft of my motion. "This is saying,
'Judge, I didn't beat my wife *that* much, and the sick shit with the kids
wasn't *that* sick, so what's the problem?' Will, I want you to know, so you
don't have any illusions, god *forbid* you have any illusions, that this guy
we're going out with tonight is an animal, a fucking animal. He's out of
control."

"I know that, Jack. Guy's a fucking killer."

"Everybody deserves a defense, Will. Best fucking defense the law
allows. That's the law. That's the fucking *beauty* of the law, goddamn it.
The lawyer *never* has to worry about what kind of fucking asshole he's
dealing with. The law says: every side is entitled to representation. It's
beautiful, it's true, and it works."

"Fucking A, Jack," I say.

Jack and I love to curse—it's a thing we have together, alone, behind
the closed door of his wide, river-viewing office—we curse, locker-room
style. I say, "You're a prick, Jack, everybody knows it, you're a fucking
cocksucker. But a great goddamn fucking lawyer. What you know about
working with people you could squeeze into your asshole, but you've

overcome that handicap and become a great goddamn fucking lawyer anyway, that's how fucking great you are." Jack loves that. He laughs. We say fuck and shit and that cocksucker! That fucking prick! Who the fuck does he think he is? Screw that fucking asshole. Fuck him. Jack snickers like a high-strung schoolboy. Fuck fuck fuck. Ursula Murray comes into my mind. *Uh uh uh uh uh uh uh uh. Jackhammer.* The syllables and sounds mingle and boom with an incantatory power; my stomach roils, I feel dizzy. I get a kind of motion sickness from such words.

On the way to the ballpark, in a cab, Jack leans forward and says to no one in particular, "Jeez, I wish I could stop home and change, I hate to go to a ball game in a suit." Ron, the wife beater, grimaces. "When I was a kid," Jack says, "and I'd see people at ball games in suits, I'd feel sorry for them. I always thought, What the hell kind of life is that, that you gotta wear your Sunday clothes to a ball game?"

"It's simple," Ron says. "You go to the game from work, you're in your suit. It makes sense. Nothing wrong with it."

"I'm just remembering how I felt as a kid," Jack says.

"Let's take our ties off," I say, beginning to undo mine. "Let's all take our ties off—that way no one of us is ahead of the others on this. We all won't have ties on."

"I'm going to take off my jacket too," Jack says. "When we get there. I'm going to stuff the goddamn thing into my briefcase."

At the stadium, Jack buys programs and passes them out. He keeps score, consulting the instructions a great deal and following them to the letter. What this means is that whenever a play evolves in a way that is complicated and difficult to capture in the scoring techniques, Jack gets upset. The man is pure lawyer. We are sitting so that Ron is farthest into the row, then Jack, then me. This arrangement means I don't have to make conversation with Ron, whose elaborate connection to the team goes back to 1963, when his father took him to his first game, and who spends the first couple of innings inundating Jack with memories of these other, greater games he attended through the years, and the other, greater players he saw there. With his father.

"None of this box-seat stuff, that was strictly for the big boys," he says. His voice is thick with resentment. He points up and behind us. "We always sat in the upper deck. Obstructed-view seats, behind the pillars, you could get those for like a dime or a quarter, I don't know how much, but it wasn't much. That's where we always sat. Up high. Where the eagles fly."

"Let me get you another beer," Jack says.

"Not like today. All these high-five jigaboos with their eighteen-million-dollars-a-year contracts." This piece of gratuitous racism has its intended poisonous effect. We eat and drink in silence for a while. It is a slow ball game. Each team has one hit through three innings. The hot dogs are soft and cold, you have to tear open the mustard packets with your teeth. The beer is watery. Everything costs six dollars. Yet there is that thing, how good hot dogs taste at the ballpark, a cliché, but there I am and it's true. All around us is the background din, ballpark acoustics, nearby conversations and occasional shouts. I hold my food in my left hand, my beer between my legs, and keep serious score. I want a record I can look back at. I want to reconstruct events, reduce them to ciphers. In the bottom of the third, Williams, the eighteen-million-dollar jigaboo, who in fact is a serious, religious guy by all reports, an amateur musician and all-around family man, hits a long, high drive that looks like it's going to be a home run. Everyone rises except me. I can see the curve of the ball's trajectory, the way it will veer foul, and I have all this stuff on my lap. As the ball tails into the upper deck, not even really that close to being fair, the fans let loose a loud, simultaneous groan. Williams is already back near the box, doing his pace and tick, meticulously checking his bat for dings and cracks.

Ron talks about his father some more, but makes no mention of his own children, I notice, taking them here, showing them where he sat as a kid. He has a boy and a girl. He is the type of man who would be disappointed in a girl, but then, he probably can't just go with the boy and not take her too. So he doesn't go at all. We react to our children with a complex series of pathologies. His have recently been documented. Jack buys him beer after beer, like a guy trying to get his date drunk. I watch the game, keep score, think about bringing Henry and Sam here later, or fantasize really, not taking into account how unpleasant it is now, the blasting insistence of the Mitsubishi screen in right field, playing ads and Yankee hype between every inning, the Diamond Vision scoreboard, with its lame and relentless graphics, the array of bad music that attempts to manufacture excitement for fear the fans following the game will go away wondering what they paid fifty or a hundred dollars for, to see a ball game, something they could watch on TV any night of the week. Everyone who says things were better in the past is right: the things that are worse now were better in the past, and there are a lot of them.

About the fourth inning, Jack looks over and sees that I keep score differently from the way the scorecard recommends, a system I used in my CYO league as a kid, involving rendering a diamond in the box, and then tracing over the lines as the hitter reaches first, second, etc. A completed diamond is a run.

"What the hell is this?" Jack says. "You're not doing it right."

"You're allowed to improvise, Jack."

"Where does it say that? Where the hell does it say you can do any goddamn thing you want?"

"Nowhere, Jack, it doesn't say that anywhere, it's one of the goddamn things you have to discover on your fucking own."

By the fifth, the Yankees, an elegant and reliable team most of the time, are behind 3–1, then 6–1, finally 7–1. Their pitching has gone utterly ragged, everyone they bring on looks feeble and unprepared. The relentless prodding of the scoreboard gradually puts everyone in a rage. Fans around us rise, red-faced, shouting. Rolls of toilet paper shoot down from the loge and unravel in the wind. The scoreboard says: "The Yankees Welcome Citibank! Citibank Is the People Bank!" A paper airplane tails and drifts toward the field, its flight path rapidly becoming of greater interest than the game; fans cheer as it sweeps out toward the mound, groan when it curves back in. It lands softly in the grass near the batter's box, to extended applause. Beer cascades from the ramparts. A fight breaks out in the right-field seats. More cheers. The fighters are removed. Boos, then quiet. The lackluster game continues.

When it's finally over, our Dial Car is waiting under the el on River Avenue. Jack helps Ron in gingerly; he's drunk. Jack deposits him and we go around to the other side of the car.

"Age before beauty," I say to Jack, opening the door for him to enter the car first. He puts his hand on my shoulder, maneuvers me around the door.

"Partner gets the window, fucker," he says.

"Get in the goddamn car already!" Ron shouts. "Let's get the hell out of Soweto." I slide in, Jack follows, the car door closes with a thunk. It's a Lincoln, the biggest one short of a stretch, one of those monster cars they still construct largely from steel. We glide out into the stream of traffic running under the el.

"Gentlemen, you've been fine hosts," Ron says, bleary-eyed, belligerent. "And I want to make it up to you. Driver, take us to Lexington and Fifty-first."

"No, Ron—" Jack says.

"Jack, shut the hell up. One last drink on me. I insist."

"I really shouldn't," I say. "My wife—"

"You shut up too," Ron bellows. "You have to do what we tell you. Wait until you make partner, son, then you can tell old Jack to shove it up his ass. Ha ha. Isn't that right, Jack?"

We ride down on River Avenue and turn at 149th Street, toward the bridge. I am squeezed between Jack and Ron, on a soft hump demarcating the middle of the seat. Ron is a bulky, twitching, steaming presence beside me. We shouldn't be that close together, there's room enough for three across in the Lincoln, but his bones seem to be sticking into me— knee, shoulder, elbow. I try to edge closer to Jack but that doesn't really help. Near the bridge there is some kind of club. The street is filled with kids, some maybe as old as twenty, plenty lots younger, girls in gowns and tight dresses, guys in blowsy pants and silk shirts. Sports cars and open-air SUVs are double-parked along either side of the road, gleaming in the streetlights, engines running, radios on. Glaring, loud, slow-motion, the scene looks like a Francis-Ford-Coppola-bullshit rendition of the ghetto, except these kids are putting it on for real, enacting a vision of themselves that's been packaged and sold on the other side of the continent by white men with toupees. They are everywhere, on the sidewalk, on the cars and out on the street, drinking from large plastic cups. The line of traffic worms through. As we pass, kids watch us with a blank hostility. At five miles an hour, we encounter head after head, staring in at us, a totem of fuck-yous.

"Look at those goddamn kids," Ron says. "Look at the fucking cars they have. Are these kids niggers or spics or what? I can't even tell."

"Why don't you ask them?" I say in a quiet voice.

"That's a good idea," Ron says and reaches for the button to lower the window. It starts to go down, then it kind of shakes and starts going up again. The driver, an Indian guy, turns around to look at us, his face stretched and contorted.

"Doan touch that fugging window or I pood you out!" he hollers. Then he faces front again.

Ron is rank with beer and cigar smoke. Jack's chin is high, he's looking out to the left, toward the skyline. Drunk, Jack is an enormous sentimentalist. "Look at that city, will you?" he says, as the car processes onto the bridge. Harlem is a wall, a fortress spread before us, we move toward it, slowly, in a phalanx of cars, and then we are in it, lights throbbing, lights bouncing off cars roofs, white light on black pavement, the reds and blues and greens of the neon signs doubling in the plate-glass windows of darkened storefronts. Eleven at night and there is traffic everywhere. You get the sense the place is a medieval city, a distant port, a cash-only place, full of action except we'll never know where it is. We turn south on Seventh Avenue, which is grand, with the old, ornate facades on either side and a strip of big trees down the center. At 110th Street we zip into the park and away. The heavy Lincoln swings through the park's long curves like a schooner tacking gently in the harbor. If you're an American, you've got to love big cars. After Harlem we are silent, passing through moods dictated by the landscape. In the shadows and halftones of the park, with a headache coming on from the cheap beer, and wanting nothing more than to be at home and in bed with my wife, I become aware of the open oppression at work here. Pinned in this dark chamber, between two hostile millionaires, I feel for a moment as if I've been kidnapped, except I'm not innocent. And then I give myself up, it's as easy as that, I am theirs, they own me. We are in a car together, nothing more. The thick carpeting, the leather seats, the quiet *whoosh* of the tires in the turns, and the music of forty years ago piping softly from the radio speakers behind us. We arrive at Fifty-first Street, each of us steeped in a private and destructive nostalgia.

The bar is a striptease joint, a long narrow place with no tables, three steps down, thumping with the basso of synthesized dance music. The women on the platform swing and sway, pull skeins of bright material across themselves; they fall heavily to the floor to do leg splits before narrow-eyed customers who give them singles, fives, tens, twenties, each accepted without distinction. I can't help noticing their bruises, their tiny scars, the raw, red lumps on the backs of their heels where their shoes rub. Ron orders three beers to go around plus a scotch and soda for himself.

"A goddamn strip bar," Jack says as we wait for our drinks. "I can't even tell you the last time I was in one of these places."

"Sure, Jack," Ron says. "You never go near the stuff. I've always wondered about you, I've always asked myself, Is Jackie a well-digger? Are you a faggot, Jack?"

Jack laughs.

"Jack's been married to several lovely wives," I say. "As I am now."

Ron looks at me with a kind of mild surprise, as if he is just noticing me for the first time. "Why, that's no excuse," he says. "Lots of people are married. I believe I'm still married, aren't I, Jack?"

Jack looks at his watch. "As of this minute, yes, you are."

"Let's celebrate marriage," Ron says, raising his glass. "A stunning subterfuge."

Jack raises his glass. I do not. Above me, a young woman has her hands wrapped over her breasts, her fingers split to allow her nipples to poke through between them. She passes through zones of tinted light, pink and blue and silver. She moves her hands around in circles, in a lewd massage, and flicks her tongue at me. In her eyes a glinting mixture of boredom and hatred. She smiles and I look away. The best ones keep their expressions aloof, and let their bodies do the work, a rhythmic, twitching exposure that seems involuntary, half-suppressed. Even as a child I was unable to participate in games or fantasies that seemed un-likely to me. I suppose that's it. It takes a certain level of bovine stupidity to flirt with a stripper. It is impossible to believe for a moment that they *want* to be here; the only attraction I can imagine is of finding a woman in difficult circumstances, forced to take her clothes off. The addictive swirl of money and subjugation. I look down the long bar, at the row of men lined up, as at a trough. Jack and Ron and I stand an extra foot or two apart. It would be pointless to talk. Barmaids in low-cut bodysuits and stockings hustle around filling drinks. I like looking at their bodies in tights. Having their clothes on, working, makes them look tantaliz-ingly human and sincere.

Then Jack's hand is on my shoulder, his attitude benign and superior—brother, father, priest.

"Good night," he says. "I'm taking a cab. You drop Ron off in the Dial Car and then take it home yourself. Don't leave him here."

"I won't, Jack."

"I mean it, Will. I know how you like to drop the ball, walk away from things when they turn ugly or difficult."

"The world is an ugly place, Jack."

"Don't leave him here no matter what. I don't give a damn if he stays until four in the morning. You stay right with him. Call me if you have a problem."

"Yes, Jack."

One of the things you notice about the adult world, which you saw as a kid but didn't understand, is how frightened most grown-ups are. Jack goes to Ron and makes his smooth-awkward good-bye. It is obvious from this distance, perhaps six feet, as they pantomime their departure in the consuming beat of the music, that each is frightened of the other, and desperate. Jack's face is tight, tired, pale. His smile looks like someone behind him is yanking back his cheeks, exposing his teeth, performing an examination of the physical properties of a reconstructed, late-twentieth-century skull. His Italian suit looks absurd. He leaves the bar a boy, only a boy, embarrassed and frightened and confused. He will go home to his current girlfriend, or to emptiness and silence, and he will pretend he is otherwise. Above me, a woman is leaning with one arm against a mirror, butt out to the room, slapping her own ass.

Ron has finally had it. His eyes look like somebody spilled red ink in them. I'm feeling it in my stomach, a tiredness that coils around itself, knots itself up into a ball. The women are swimming and swinging in pastel light. My God, they look angry. You sense that if a reversal of positions were possible, and they were to seduce you, they would kill you. Right now, though, they have to strut it.

One of the dancers, an Asian woman, stands on her head and scissors her legs. Ron gives tips all around, passing out bills without looking at them. He wants a kiss from one of the barmaids. I'm surprised she complies. His big, purple, puckering lips, her hand around his head, scratching the hair at the top of his neck.

"Let's go, Ron," I say. I touch his shoulder.

"Right," he says, turning from the bar. His lips are smudged with lipstick, catching the light, bringing to mind, for some reason, a Wehrmacht officer on his night on the town. "Let's get the fuck out of here. Let's blow."

Outside, our driver is upright behind the wheel, staring straight ahead. It's eerie to think he's been like that since we got here. Ron and I slide into the backseat. *Thunk* goes the door.

"Take this young man home to his wife," Ron yells, putting some kind of hostile emphasis on the word *wife*. The driver looks at us in his rearview. Ron lives in the East Seventies, I live on the west side, it would make sense to drop him first, but I don't argue, I give the driver my address. We pull out onto the empty avenue, make a left, go over to Third Avenue and up from there, which makes no sense, Madison would have been better, but I'm too tired for a discussion about it. Third Avenue here is a bit like London or some other city rebuilt after the war, a mixture of the remains of old, sagging tenements and cheap office towers where atriums dominate. As we drive farther north, the shops look nicer. Everything is closed, dark, gated, locked, empty.

"Will," Ron says softly. I turn and look at him. His face is a crumbling, ashy white except for the reddened lips. He's sunk down in his seat and he has the most bizarre expression on his face, it is hard to place at first, looking up at me, eyebrows raised, hint of a smile, hint of a tongue at the back of his open mouth, until I realize that this is his impression of a woman. Then I see the rest of it. His shirt and pants are open and he is wearing a white lacy bra and red panties, both of which are pulled absurdly tight across him, with an obscene profusion of hair all around. The panties are too small to hold his balls, which are spilling out the sides, and the head of his cock peeps out over the top. He's fingering the satin.

"I put these on for you," he says.

"Jesus," I say.

"Tell me what you're wearing," he says.

"Ron, this totally isn't my scene." I'm edging myself as close as possible to the door.

"I bet you have on white cotton briefs." He puts a hand around my wrist and locks on. With the other one he's rubbing himself. "Just touch me. Just—touch me."

"Ron, you're out of line," I say.

"I just want you to touch me, you son of a bitch." He's pulling in earnest now, really digging in. He's strong as hell. Then again, so am I. He pulls on my wrist and I yank back hard, pulling him off his center and dragging his body closer to mine. He starts to half-slide, half-crawl toward me. I'm practically up on my feet in the back of the car to avoid having to touch him. The hand-and-wrist thing has been enough—that surprise again, of encountering someone else's actual physical presence, coming up against skin and muscle and bone. This time the experience is a nightmare, a vision of snakes and rats, of things crawling over you in the dark—the horror of unwanted contact. And I picture Ursula again, and for some reason, my mother. Ron slides down across where I was sitting, still holding my wrist, I can't pry him off me, he's sinking down onto the seat with a kind of whining and grunting noise, an infant. I'm crouched with my back against the front seat. I hit him in the rib cage, hard. He's still making that noise, like one of my children, it enrages me. I hit him again, and again, just bringing my fist down like a gavel on his side. Something seems to crack a little bit. He groans. He's just lying there on his stomach, mostly covered by his suit. The car pulls to a stop and I drag myself out the far door and close it fast. I'm standing on the street in front of my apartment building. A whir as the driver lowers his front window.

"Where you want me to take the udder guy?" he says, gesturing back with his head. I just stare at him for a minute, breathing hard. "Wait a minute, sorry," I say and turn away. I'm starting to get the shakes, I can feel them coming, odd and sickening in the warm night. I lean against the car for a second pulling my mind together—it's hot. Then I give him the address. He writes it on the charge slip. He passes the slip to me, on a small clipboard. "Sign please," he says, and I do, resting the board on the roof of the car: *William Riordan, account number 2298, client entertainment.*

[3]

A slight doubling, a fading into and out of focus, as I slip the key into the lock. The hinges squeak, like rats, like buried children. Ellie has left a light on down the hall but I bump into the closet door anyway, on my way into the bedroom; and then darkness, the thick air around sleeping bodies. Sam is in our room, in a bassinet, one more reason not to make love, and when I've gotten my suit off and hung it up after a fashion and am sitting on the edge of our bed peeling black socks off swollen feet, he commences a quiet fussing, *egh egh egh*. I pick him up, still sleeping, soft warmth, a bundle. I lie down with him on my bare chest. Next to me, Ellie stirs. "What time is it?" she says.

"It's late," I say. She huddles her back against my side, trying to sleep by pretending to sleep. Soon enough it works, I hear her softened breathing.

Meanwhile Sam runts around on my chest, quietly fussing; he squirms and his feet tumble against my cock and balls, like soft little fists. Stirrings. There is no accounting for the sex and sensuality of having children. With Henry once at this stage, perhaps a few weeks earlier, I let him take my nipple into his mouth, just to see how it felt. He came off wailing as soon as he realized it wasn't what he knew, what gave food, his mother, but not before he'd latched on and given a solid savage little pull—it was as if I'd put myself into a Cuisinart or into the nozzle of a vacuum cleaner and a bolt of pain shot down from my chest through my dick to the arches of my feet. Do not touch. Fire.

These are the forbidden superphysical zones of parenthood: the children's soft, wet lips, their intense softness and alluring smell. On a recent Sunday afternoon, Ellie came out of the shower and stood at her closet, dressing; I was on the bed, reading the Sunday *Times*. "Look," she said. I turned my eyes up to her, she was over the bed now. One of her breasts was dripping with milk, white dollops against her nipple, trails down her stomach. Both the boys were sleeping, a quiet time. I moved toward the middle of the bed, making room for her to sit down. We watched this small volcanic event in silence for a few moments. Then she said something about waking the baby, and I said you should never wake a sleeping infant, it's like inviting the IRS to audit you, and she said she hated to see the milk going to waste, it was running in frail lines down her belly, and I decided to take this as a kind of invitation. I bent and licked the milk from her tummy, then rose to her breast and put my mouth over her nipple, pulling at it a little.

"Oh," she said, and then, "Oh," again, and then, "Don't. This is freaking me out."

"It is a little weird," I said, bringing my face away.

"A little? What does it taste like?"

"Like sugar water, sort of." Something seemed odd about this question, it conflicted with some vague memory from when Henry was a baby. "You mean you've never tasted it?"

"I've tasted it," she said.

"Then why did you ask me?" I said.

"Because I wanted to know what it tasted like to you," she said.

"What did it taste like to you?" I said.

"Kind of like sugar water, I guess, but a little milkier than that," she said.

"Yeah, but not as milky as I thought it would be, considering it's, you know, milk."

She took my hand, still under her breast, lifting perhaps slightly but mainly just there in a passive way, a witness, and she tugged it away, returning it to me as if it were my wallet or my keys she'd found there.

"You don't like it?" I said.

"It feels weird," she said.

"I was trying to be gentle," I said. "Nonintrusive in as much as a hand on your breast can be nonintrusive."

"A hand on my breast *can't* be nonintrusive," she said. "Especially after having two babies in two and a half years. Nothing can be nonintrusive after having two babies in two and a half years. My hormones, my psyche, and my will have formed a band and you know what their big hit is? 'Get the fuck away from me.'"

And now here he is, Sam, fussing, *egh egh egh*, his body trembling against mine in need and desire, his little feet kicking and digging into my groin, a bundle of squirm. When the *eghs* elongate into squeaky little cries, soon to escalate, I hand him over Ellie's back and without rousing she takes him, puts her breast in his mouth, and I hear his deep breath, his profound relief, and I realize that, as we boys used to say, he is getting it, and I'm not.

Morning . . . My body oozing tar into a porcelain dish. I pay for these nights through the colon. It seems, as we move dazedly into wakefulness, into our lives, that everything is falling, getting knocked over, toppling and smashing.

For instance: I open closet and pantry and cabinet doors and things fall down, cans, bottles, packets of dried food tumble to the floor. I try to take a dish out of the dishwasher, unhook it from among a jumble of dishes latched at crazy angles onto the rubber-coated wire gridwork inside the machine; I take a dish out of this drainer, a glass, say, to pour myself a glass of orange juice, and there will come crashing to the floor behind it, in its wake, on its trail, a bowl or a cup that has been teetering on the edge of an intricate pile, the dynamics of which I detect only after it has lost its integrity. I pull open the medicine chest, for shaving cream to shave my face, to prepare a face to meet the faces that I meet, and out comes tumbling a small glass bottle of glycerine, which Ellie uses to remove ink stains and the red mark of cherries, smashing into a thousand pieces in the sink.

Or early, early this morning, before dawn, Henry cries out, screams, really, a nightmare scream, and I rise, cumbersome like an injured moose, still drunk no doubt, but too sleepy to know it, knock my glasses off the night table, and going to catch them knock a drinking glass and several books down after them. Henry, hearing the explosive fracture and crash, cries louder, as if all the world is shifting and runting its way to extinction. Somehow the baby, fed now and warm in the zone of mother, sleeps through all this. Rarely are both awake at once, as if they know this is a boundary that is best left uncrossed.

Then later, I am in the kitchen, searching in the pantry for a cereal I remember there still being a little of, perhaps enough for a bowl, sure, enough for a bowl, and Ellie is spraying the refrigerator with 409—Henry's drawings, with all the kitchen magnets that hold them, are piled, edges curling, on the stove. She was raised in a modestly well-to-do apartment on West End Avenue with fairly regular help and now, watching her, I can see that she scrubs the fridge door out of some sort of inspiration, rather than from any internally kept schedule of tidiness. Her eyes show the light of a small, concentrated fascination—this is so interesting, her eyes say, the dirt, and then how it disappears in patterns matching those she scrubs in—and I think, after she has seen it happen for a while, she'll be done, bored now, and move on, and who knows how many months or years will pass before she's interested in this dirt again, and once I would have thought this was funny, kind of cute, appreciating a creative mind over an organized one, but now it just makes me feel a little nuts. It should be forgivable—she is not a clean and tidy person. I might be, but it makes no difference because I, in grand and perfect selfishness, am not going to do it, I have the world to batter my way through every day and my own time is far too important for this. Meanwhile I want someone to do it; hire someone, I don't care. It irritates me to see it. I never wanted the marriage to get to this petty place, but here we are and I have no idea how to turn back. It occurs to me watching her in my moment of willful resentment and immobility that there's probably, over the long run, little difference between this hidden, cheating vanity of mine—which touches on housework, on child care, on the very act of love—and the grander, more devastating male crimes in marriage. Drinking. Credit-card bills sent to the office. Secret accounts, other women. It all seems so accidental and tied to the impervious conviction of the superiority of one's own self-image and desires. So much of marital resentment is a matter of timing and patterns of synapse response. I can hear myself, any man: my wife doesn't understand me . . . The cry of the husband with his dick in his hand. My wife doesn't understand what I need. By this he means, my wife has a personality, and doesn't accede to my moods, doesn't care to cater to my wishes or take care of my unspoken desires or be the great mother-comforter of my dreams, especially not now that she knows me and has seen the best of the possibilities. Once, nearer the beginning, she might have been like a lot of women, romantically inclined to experiment with that kind of love, but that kind of love is a necessary opening fantasy, not sustainable or deep, and this other thing—a respectful, abiding love that comes in the form of prolonged intimacy, that comes in the form of devotion, and that comes most of all in the form of acceptance, an embrace of otherness—this, being the only form of love that can replace it, has not, in fact, replaced it. We were working toward that, but then babies started arriving, and we stopped. It is difficult to imagine a modern middle-class marriage not syncopated by rage. Love interrupted—by confusion, by fear, by resentment.

"When we were kids," I say to Ellie, "people had three, four children, five children, younger than we are now. They coped, they cleaned and cooked and went to work, and they didn't lose their minds."

"They did *not* cope," she says. "They *did* lose their minds." She rises, stops washing, the 409 bottle pointed at me like a gun. "By the time I was fifteen, everybody I knew, all my friends, their mothers were nuts. Most of the fathers were alcoholics. All of them were insanely angry." She bows again and shines the door handle. Out in the dining room she has left behind the *Times* she was reading, wide open, flapping over the sides of the table—this morning's morning's *Times*, I call it.

"If they were so angry, why didn't they separate?"

"Plenty did," she says.

"Yeah, but not enough and not in time," I say.

"Some of them didn't have enough imagination to separate," she says. She takes up her bottle again. "And the women had no hope of making money most of the time."

She goes back to scrubbing the fridge, much work in the shades of gray around the handle, shakes her head to throw her bangs out of her eyes. The sounds of *Sesame Street* from the living room. "And you know what?" she says. "We wait, we plan, we go to therapy, we open 401(k) accounts, we don't drink as much and we probably don't screw around as much, but in the end we're just as bad off, it's just as hard and we're fucking up pretty much the same way they did."

I picture my father, sixty-seven now but looking at least ten years older than that, sitting in his apartment, his arm with the remote control in shaking fingers slowly extending itself toward the television. Different from Ellie's world, working class, no key parties or fancy divorces; in my world sometimes husbands and fathers "ran off" and you didn't see them in church anymore and no one discussed them. In the evenings when I was a kid, we took turns, my brother and I, bringing my father his beer and Canadian Club on the rocks. Little alcoholics in training, eight and ten years old. Every night, dinner stewed in the kitchen until it finally burned. Every night my mother sat at the kitchen table looking over the afternoon papers, like Ellie in the evenings now. My mother didn't read the *Times* or the *New York Observer*, of course, but the *Post* and the *Daily News*. All the newspapers she actually liked had closed already, a decade before: those years of devastation and growth, when everything got bigger and bigger and worse and worse, until finally they weren't there anymore and you were secretly relieved. She never came out to join my father, she had her own Manhattan there at the table, and she didn't watch over the food either, turn it off or put it in a low oven to keep warm, she just lowered the flames and let it cook and cook. She had pronounced it ready at six-fifteen. If he was going to drink a second round, and then a third and a fourth, and refuse to come to the table, *Well*, she said, *let him eat the fruit he's grown.* She took her pleasure, as so many wives must, in a strictly moral victory. Those years Michael and I were hungry by mid-afternoon and we'd raid the fridge hourly, but shortly after five Mom would start to kick us out and we moaned and bitched at my father to please, please let us eat. Every night the long, debilitating battle. Every night he won it, through the sheer force of his passivity and anger. After the first drink he was cheerful: *Another five minutes won't kill you.* But two or three or four drinks in, it varied with the night, he would sit red-faced, twitching, his eyes milky pools of grievance and betrayal. My mother's rage was stone, my father's a clattering bee. *Get the fuck away from me. Leave me the hell alone.* One night he made a major speech, let us in on the heart of his fatigue and resentments, stood from his lounger and bellowed at us: *Go and do some goddamned fucking work—if they haven't given you any at the school, there's plenty to do around here.* We stood together at the foot of the stairs, Michael one step above me. *You kids want nothing but to be catered to and served! It's time you learned about work! That's my fucking life! So just get the fuck away from me, all of you.*

And then, on a descending note: *Rotten little pricks. I'll come when I'm good and goddamned ready.* I had the image, watching him shout that night, of his yellow teeth biting me in half. He was a large man then; he is no longer. He had a nervous tic with his hands, he'd click one thumbnail under the other big, tough hands and wide, tough nails that made a loud *click click*, a kind of torture, a dripping faucet of rage you could never fix. The men were so much bigger then, the women smaller, less muscular. Summer would come and the mothers would wear Bermuda shorts, bright canvasy shorts exposing white, soft legs. Weekend trips to Long Beach. Nowadays we are older than they were—we marry older, have children older—but we look younger, keep in better shape, the skin, the muscle tone, it's different. Eternal youth. We're making sure we have a longer time to be unhappy in.

To us, they were all large men; they had fought in wars and seemed to be fighting in wars still. I remember my uncle Ben one night, drunk as he always was by nightfall, very drunk on weekends by nightfall, outside in his driveway pounding on his car and shouting with profound and frightening incoherence, "*Di-da, di-da, dit, over and out,*" Morse code memories, the sound of his hollering finally interrupted by smashing glass, while inside the women and children strained as always to go on as before, chatting with the television on, pretending nothing was happening. He entered the house with blood running off his hands.

At nine, I haven't left for work yet, I'm going to a meeting in midtown. Ellie, before she went into the bedroom to change Sam, switched the TV over to *Oprah*, they're running repeats in the mornings now because they can't get enough of her. The guests, while I tie my tie: two men and one woman stranded at sea for many days and nights. By the third day, the woman says, the two men were useless, losing it, crazed in fear and salt-edged paranoias. "Elliot thought he was on an airplane and Harry kept threatening to kill him if he didn't shut up and let Harry sleep, which he was doing for, like, twenty hours at a stretch. They were hopeless. I was pretty much on my own." Harry and Elliot, victims of post-traumatic stress disorder or whatever they're calling this (I'd call it terror, pure and simple), sit there with small smiles, giving out no light, no energy for the camera. Their story: victimhood; you can tell the woman is still pissed off though. A doctor arrives to back them up. All agree they were fortunate the woman was able to keep her head.

Dinnertime. The apartment looks as if a tornado has passed through, something on the evening news, a sad one-minute-forty-five-second report ending with the words *as people here try to put their shattered lives back together. Back to you in New York, Dan.* I decide to make a speech. "It would be nice," I say quietly, "if we could just manage a fucking *lifestyle.*" I'm still in my suit, standing a few feet back from all the activity and mess. "A lifestyle is what having a job like this is all about. A job like mine doesn't *mean* anything, for God's sake, you do it for the money to buy things that comfort you and help you manage. Otherwise it's fucking *pointless*." I am louder now.

"Don't shout," she says. "And don't use language like that in this house." She used to curse with the best of them—or did she? I am standing here thinking, Do I know this woman? Is there anything I can say to her that she'll even understand?

And through the rest of the evening, I'm working on a motion, the air heavy with anger and silence. Ellie goes to bed before eleven. At two-thirty in the morning I am still up, watching television, cruising through the channels. An advertorial for phone sex, in talk-show format, where the hostess interviews the "real people" who have called her love line with fantastic success or are now waiting for you—me—to call, all of them models and cheap going-nowhere actors and actresses who won't ever get better work than this. Another channel: an hour-long show (I check the guide) about sunglasses, with a studio audience that applauds, for Christ's sake, after various film clips about how great these fucking glasses are. Is this for real? What country is this? What planet? On the public TV station, some weird nature show for kids being rerun, who knows why at this hour. A sincere-looking woman is saying, "You know, it's hard to believe that the bullfrog we just saw was once a tiny black dot, surrounded by jelly." I flip again. One of those super-cheap late-night ads for a restaurant in Brooklyn. "Every day is pasta day at Kenny's"— and I think of the people I've known named Kenny. A guy who bought cars and fixed them up and sold them, I knew him in high school, he was named Kenny. Another guy I met through a friend, he dealt drugs and bred dogs; he was named Kenny and was unendurable. Later in life, one angelic man named Kenny, a sweet, tortured soul who went from drugs to illness to Jesus and died too young. I turn the set off, lie back down on the couch, stare up at the ceiling.

Remembering the final Kenny makes me sad. I just want to go somewhere different, do something different, be a different person with a different life. At the same time I don't want to move, I don't want to move or do anything, ever again. This is death, this is the end of everything, just lying here. After a while I hear a sound in the kitchen and then Ellie is there, framed in the doorway, in her nightgown, her face a dark map. I am happy to see her, though I don't let on to this, happy at the prospect of a real human voice even if it's going to be attacking me, which it does.

"What are you doing?" she says.

"I'm not *doing* anything," I say, sitting up. "I'm watching television. Or I was."

"Why are you lying there with your pants open?"

"I was scratching the jewels," I say, an answer that will only make her more angry, but I don't care. I stand up and zip my pants.

"It's three o'clock in the morning," she says. She turns and starts back toward the bedroom.

"I know that, I know it's three in the morning," I say. I turn out the two living room lamps and follow her. She stops.

"I don't think you should sleep in our bed," she says. "I think you should sleep out here."

"Why?" I say. She doesn't answer. "Why?" I say again. "What the fuck did I do? I didn't do a fucking thing that should get that reaction from you."

"Don't!" she says then, too loudly. "Don't you talk to me that way. I don't want to sleep with you. I don't want to be near you. I hate you, all right? Is that what you want? I hate you."

"Jesus," I say. I follow her back to the bedroom, grab a pillow from the bed, a blanket from the closet. She gets into bed, her back turned, covers pulled high. I stand there for a minute, looking at her. She sits up.

"What do you want? You're keeping me awake."

"Sorry," I say. "*So* sorry to disturb you. I'm sure we'll all sleep the sweet sleep of the blessed if I just go off now into the living room."

"Will, please," she says. "Please just leave me alone. I don't know what's wrong with you, but whatever it is, take it away from here and let me sleep. The kids don't let me sleep, you don't let me sleep, I'm exhausted, please please go. If you don't go it's going to get really ugly."

"Fine," I say. "Fine fine fine. There's no one I would rather leave alone than you. Good night. You're a fucking Medusa." I go off down the hall muttering to myself like a mad despot, and by the time I get to the living room I see it, or feel it rather, as if I'm living inside the image rather than conjuring it: my father, wandering and stumbling around the house late into the night, sputtering and enraged, working up his Nixonian paranoia. That's why all those guys loved Nixon. It didn't have anything to do with political theory or social values, it had to do with seeing him on television, after dinner, sweating through another one of his insane self-justifying speeches, knowing he was one of them, that he was bad at his job and had too many people on his back, that he was just trying to keep the hounds at bay until he could get to the next fucking drink. They knew, looking at him, that he went through two gallons a week just as they did. They could picture him staying up into the deep psychotic core of the night in some armchair in the White House, lights dim, alone, making involuntary sucking sounds through his teeth and going nuts about his fucking wife, his fucking kids, and the fucking niggers and Jews. They loved him for this. If he went down, so would they. He did. They did.

On Thursday I come in late, carrying a take-out coffee. On the side of my desk, I can see the stacks of documents I left there yesterday, more stacks on the cabinets and shelves. None of it seems very pressing. I stand and look at Anna, who is reading the paper.

"What news?" I say.

"Same old," she says. "The rich get richer, the poor get arrested, the government lies about both. Steven Soderbergh is working on a new project." She folds the paper, turns to her computer. I am standing there then, not exactly ready, holding the coffee and doughnut in a white wax bag from the Korean salad bar downstairs. The coffee cup has already begun to leak. In my mind, I blame the Koreans, for cheaping out on the paper containers. Anna, working on her computer. I watch her back, her bare arms set still beside her as her hands, which I cannot see, work the keys. I can hear the keys, she hits them in jaunty syncopation. Key key key space key key key key key backspace backspace key key space. *Plockety-plock, plock plock plock.* My phone rings. I watch her. She lets it ring once, twice, then reaches to pick it up, having finished some sentence or paragraph of mine and getting to the phone just before the call would slide over to the switchboard up front. I go into my office, set the bag gingerly on a free corner of my desk. She looks in at me as she listens. I sit down and pretend to write on my yellow pad.

"And it's concerning?" she says. Long pause, listening. "One moment, I'll see if he's available."

I look out at her now, as if I've been working the whole time. "It's some broker," she says. "About your portfolio?"

"A salesman, in other words."

"Yes. Correct," she says. "*About* your portfolio."

"I don't have a fucking portfolio. I don't even have a Day-Timer, remember?"

"So I should tell him to call back?"

"No," I say. "Then he'll just call back." I pick up the phone. "Will Riordan."

"Mistah Riordan," the salesman says. I hear his voice and instantly I'm seeing those haircuts the Italian guys have sported forever, kind of buzz cut around the ears and a pile of hair left on top, Elvis meets John Gotti.

"Mr. Riordan, my name is Joseph Ferrelli and I'm calling for Kidder Peabody Smith Morgan and Wardwell, and I wonder if I might speak to you for a moment about our new mutual fund—"

"Not interested in you, not interested in it," I say, and hang up.

Anna is watching me. "That was mean," she says. "I've never seen you be mean before."

"It was not mean. Calling people and bothering them when they don't want you to is mean. Speak truth to power, that's what I say."

"Where's the truth?" she says. "Where's the power?"

"That guy, before he even made the call, he had a book of information on me. Did you know this? They have all kinds of information, it's like *Glengarry Glen Ross*, only electronic. He probably knows where I buy my socks. Where do they get this information?"

"It's all, you know, out there." She waves her arm. "On the Internet and in computer networks and stuff."

"I mean, this is electronic harassment, the phone, the data, the whole thing. It's terrorism."

"You'll survive," Anna says.

"What about my privacy? What about the *libertas civilitas* that has made this fucking country so fucking great, you know, the sustaining hope of oppressed peoples, a light shining in the dark world, et cetera, et cetera? What about your own family, fleeing the newest local tyranny, which always surpasses the last tyranny in its brutal suppressions, making their way to these golden shores?"

"So they know where you buy your socks," Anna says. "So what? They know how much insurance coverage you have, they know who you're calling long distance, what difference does it make? Besides, my family left Cuba because they were worried about their money, not about freedom. Just go about your business. Freedom is in the heart."

"'*Freedom is in the heart*,'" I say. "That's really quite lovely. You know, you're a miracle. You're a genius. You've made me feel better, suddenly. You're the greatest secretary in the history of corporate America. Come here."

"Forget it," she says, turning to her keyboard.

"That elegant sleeveless thing you're wearing, is that a dress, cinched with the belt, or is it a skirt/blouse combo, the joints of which are concealed by the belt?"

"It's a dress," she says.

"Come on into my office," I say. "Take some dictation or something."

"If you want to dictate, use a tape," she says, her back to me.

"Isn't there some filing to do in here?" I say.

"No," she says.

"What about lunch?" I say.

"No," she says. "I gave up eating."

"When?" I say.

"When you asked me out to lunch." She's typing away now, her fingers a flurry above the keys.

"Anna, I want you to know how much I respect you, how grateful I am," I say. "What can I do for you?"

"Let me know in an envelope at the end of the year," she says. "Something computer-generated that I can take to the bank."

"I don't have that kind of power around here," I say.

"You will soon," she says. "Why else do you think I put up with you?"

On my lunch hour, walking down Broadway, aimed at Battery Park, I pass a businesswoman with a cell phone, standing in front of the corporate sculpture outside an office building, singing, "The Itsy-Bitsy Spider." I can hear how the conversation will end: *No, honey, Mommy will be home tonight. Mommy has to work right now. When I come home tonight, I'll read you a book. What book would you like me to read?* I imagine the child at the other end.

After lunch Anna brings in the afternoon mail. A few circulars, two law journals, a request for a hearing that I have her pass along to Jack, after stamping it in and making multiple copies for my files, her files, the firm files. Ursula is in frequent touch by e-mail now; I am some figure of release for her, and under the excuse that she is contributing to her case, she can suddenly write anything she wants. Today is this:

subject: lisping white heterosexuals

a scene came to me today, and i was in london, in a nice flat as they would say, i lived there (all of this comes in an instant, there's no stopping it, it's as if your wires have been crossed into someone else's life, in some other time) and i was standing in the parlor, there was a man there, a lovely man, and i was looking out the window, with an exquisite melancholy, watching an old woman with a cane inch painfully across the square. everything was so green. all of writing can be this, just tapping into other people's images, other writers' scenes. this is some virginia woolf moment perhaps, or forster or james. i have been in london once, for a weekend. in my mind i hear the word the way the english pronounce it—weekEND. there is no reason really, except sense, to limit oneself to a single voice in a single place and time. a hundred narratives, a thousand, all in one.

and the man came up behind me and put his arms around me, his shirtsleeves starched and white. and we stood together, looking out the window. i'm his west indian concubine. late afternoon, long, angled sunlight, an erection, seemingly sizable, pressing into my ass through the elegant hang of his woolen trousers. his hands cupping my breasts. we swayed. neither of us spoke. some jeremy irons type of lisping but vigorous white heterosexual that only the english can produce. this is 1910. we stand and wait for the barbarous century. history is now and in england. our inchoate sense of the coming evil expressing itself in some bit of brutal sexuality—not now but later; he enjoys a good whipping with a leather strop. i can see his white hairless rump, spotted with welts. those men of the english public schools, what they won't think of. his face beet red, his hair matted in strands across sweating brow. dark muffled howls, dank odors. no one bathed then. a foul murderous time, like now.

The coffeemaker in the office's small kitchen, its heating plate laminated with a thousand brown spills baked onto the raw steel. In the freezer there are about nine kinds of coffee, High Andes hazelnut, half-decaf Italian roast, French almond supreme, the treasured Jamaican blue mountain. I sift among them looking for something normal. Jack walks in, watches me. Coffee is a large issue, an ideology with Jack. "We have to get a Braun or a Krups," he says, rinsing his mug in the sink. "Or actually there's this French coffeemaker, Café Xprés. Two espresso slots, two Bundt-style coffeemakers, a steaming nozzle. This American shit sucks, the coffee's always lukewarm and burnt. I mean, we have European clients, we can't give them this swill."

"Jack," I say. "These are ten-, fifteen-, nineteen-dollar-a-pound coffees you've got lined up here in the freezer. I feel like I'm with my dealer, looking at bags of weed."

"You have a dealer?" Jack says.

"No, I'm just saying, a kind of obsessive collection of coffee here."

"Yeah, but, Will, it don't mean a thing if it ain't got that swing. If you don't have a fine machine to make it in, you don't have fine coffee, it doesn't matter what kind of beans you use. This is a law firm, for Christ's sake. The industry is starting to feel our presence. We've been written up in *American Lawyer* and *Crain's New York Business*, we can afford a decent coffee machine."

"Jack, you're in the position to know what we can and can't afford." I pull a bag of Colombian out of the back of the freezer, start to make a pot of coffee.

"You know, Will, there's something I've been wanting to talk to you about."

"Hmm?" I say.

"Ron. He called me yesterday to say he thought we were doing a terrific job."

"We are, we are doing a terrific job," I say. I'm washing out the glass pot, trying not to get my shirt cuffs wet.

"He mentioned you in particular."

"That's so considerate," I say.

"So what's going on?"

"Nothing's going on," I say.

"Ron never struck me as the type to make these courtesy calls."

"Mysterious guy, Ron," I say. "You never know what's really going on in his head, do you?"

Jack gives me a look that says this is now on file, be aware that this is part of the database. Then he goes back to coffee, a subject that really interests him. "Will, look, today, do you have five minutes to do a memo? Circulate to the partners under my name, new coffee machine. Point out the Europeans, et cetera, everything I said, just say for this reason, Preston"—Preston is our chief office clerk—"will be obtaining a new coffee machine within the next few days, if there are any questions contact me, et cetera. Can you do this? Bill the time to firm business, memo to partners, don't put the coffee machine on your time sheet, for god's sake."

"Sure, Jack."

"Better let me see it before you send it out."

"Sure, Jack. No problem."

"Great."

Later I am in David Chin's office, on the Broadway side of the building, looking across at the many-angled facade of the art deco insurance building across the way, pale stone and an infinity of windows. In one of them a woman is visible, standing by her desk, talking on the phone.

"Do you see that woman," I say, making the words clipped, manic, New York. "Do you see that woman, right there, in the window? Do you see that woman? I didn't tell you to turn off the meter, did I tell you to turn off the meter? Turn it on. Turn on the meter. Do you see that woman? Do you see that woman right there? Do you know who that is? That's my wife." David is the only person in the firm for whom I have a personal attachment; this is not true, I have some kind of attachment to a number of people. David is my only friend. He and I do dialogue from movies, throw quotes at each other at odd moments, see if we can catch each other off guard. This particular riff calls for no response as yet. "That's my *wife* up there," I say. "She's up there with some fucking nigger."

"Do you know what a .357 Magnum does to a woman's pussy," David says laconically, without the question's intonation. "*Taxi Driver.* Martin Scorsese as the fare, Robert De Niro, of course, as the driver."

"Ten points," I say. "Do you have the score sheet?"

"Right here, under my blotter, pal," he says. David is a Chinese American who grew up in Westchester and is a pretty-much-out-of-the-closet homosexual. I don't know if his parents know, but everyone else does. He likes to tell witty stories of his failures in love. He pulls the sheet out and marks in his score. If he hadn't known the line, I would have gotten twenty-five for fooling him.

"So the other thing I'm wondering," I say, "is what's with my seeing you going into Trinity Church at noontime?"

David looks at me.

"Are you denying?" I say.

"I'm not denying or confirming," he says. "I'm not commenting at this time."

"Fair enough. If you're going to issue a statement, keep me in mind. What else is going on?"

"The usual," he says. "There's going to be this gigantic meeting of all the dioxin defense counsel in four weeks near Brattleboro, Vermont, of all places. I'm preparing for a committee on invoice histories."

"Not in Brattleboro," I say. "Just *near* Brattleboro."

"Brattleboro, Peterboro, who knows. One of the boros. Some conference center."

"Is there a pool?"

"Ah, actually, there's a lake. It's on a lake."

"A lake? Nice. Do some fishing?"

"I'm bringing my stuff. Who knows?" He stares out his window. "There really is a woman over there."

"Of course," I say. "That's what inspired me."

"Hmm. What are you working on, besides the massive Adamson divorce and the crazy woman who got raped?"

"You really keep up," I say.

"I try," he says.

"Well, listen to this new assignment," I say. "Just in. A memo from Jack to the partners about buying a thirteen-hundred-dollar coffee machine he's got his eye on."

"They give you only the glamour stuff, boy."

"Yeah. That and, you know, photocopying protocols."

"What is this thing he wants, like a coffee machine you can drive to work or what?"

"It's a coffee empire, a coffee continent. It brews, it expresses, it steams milk, it roasts beans, I don't know. It's copper and French."

"Great. So you're going to squeeze this in between your daily efforts to make other people's psychosexual nightmares into coherent social narratives."

"Exactly. The coffee memo is going to be the most sensitive piece of work among the three, you watch. Jack will put me through about five drafts."

"About the Trinity Church thing," he says, looking away. "Have you mentioned this to anyone? Your friend Sue, for instance?"

"Sue's not my friend. And what's the big deal?"

"Have you though?"

"No," I say. "No I haven't."

"Good," he says.

On the subway, going home that evening, I see a boy of dark and amorphous ethnicity. He is a punk skinhead in the meticulous black uniform of the subculture, shaved head with double row of spiked hair running fore to aft, combat boots, laced straight across, steel-toed, needless to say he has a pin through his nose, needless to say he has a series of earrings, needless to say he is playing a radio when this is not allowed and not even the toughest homeys with the toughest ghetto blasters do it anymore. I like the moaning drumbeat music; I like the stylized suggestions of social annihilation. The distinct sour taste of Nazism I do not like. It occurs to me that the skinheads, the Crips and the Bloods, the trip-wire veterans and strange pimply teen gun freaks whose pent-up frustrations find voice in parking lots and schoolyards through the mouths of automatic weapons, the men beating their wives, the women hiring teenagers to murder their husbands, all the lost souls of the syndicated talk-show circuit, suggest a Weimar of the soul, a millennial fever. The century just ended lives in our imaginations not as history but as suppressed childhood trauma, and so we reenact it. Over and over and over—chaos gives its sweet, familiar embrace to the Russians, who respond with their special brand of renewed near-comical tyranny. Germany bubbles with hidden animosities and revives its two-hundred-year search for some world-devouring Idea—so nice to have you back, boys. That part of the globe which hugs the Mediterranean and the Black Sea has spent a decade in the fever-dream of religious and ethnic brutality. We have three thousand troops stationed for all eternity now in the Balkans, strange broadcasts are coming out of Albania, we're hoping against hope that Japan and China don't end up fighting it out over Asia, which is crumbling like a sand castle with high-discipline religions and nerve gas in the transport systems and people who have trouble pulling a meal together but might soon be able to trigger their own stash of tactical nuclear weapons. Worst of all, most ominous, Jerusalem regularly goes up in a storm of bullets and stones, fulfilling the Apocrypha. No one understands anything.

Ursula's right, it is 1910, and we're about to begin again.

[4]

My brother is tall and wafer thin, eyes bright, bony in movement, like John the Baptist. His name is Michael. Through the glass panel beside my door I see him standing by Anna's desk, explaining his presence. I wonder how he's made it through reception—some moment of inattention out there or was it a scene? He looks all right, wearing a brown blazer and khaki pants, hair longish but clean: with Anna he seems to be polite, gentle in his articulations; nothing ragged about him, none of the twitchy pent-up slightly terrorized confusion he can show when he's in his most manic phases. He's a photographer, or a cabdriver, or an apprentice taxidermist, it depends on what month and year you ask him. There was a girlfriend named Bonnie, with a child, not his, in a mobile-home-and-back-to-the-land period in California, which ended about two years ago. I "lent" him $2,800 dollars during that phase. It has been eight months since we last spoke. He was down in Fort Lauderdale for a while. Anna opens the door.

"Your brother is here to see you?" she says as if it's a question.

I stand up, go to the door. "Hey, Will," he says, a mixture of affection and apprehension, like "Hey, Boo" in *To Kill a Mockingbird*.

In response I do my Gregory Peck: "Now, Scout, you say, 'Hello, Mr. Riordan.'"

"Fuck you," he says.

"How are you, Michael," I say. We do an awkward handshake. I want to touch him, not a hug exactly, that would be going too far, we've not been huggers, though I suspect Michael may have been converted to hugging in California, maybe in some twelve-step program. Yet seeing him there, still defiant and proud, I am surprised, I want to grab him, run my hands over him; even just lay a hand on his shoulder.

I pat him lightly on the arm.

"Hey," he says. "I'm sorry to bother you at the office, but I was just passing by, you know, doing some business at the stock exchange. Moving fortunes around electronically and stuff like that."

"Yeah, well, it's good to see you," I say. He follows me into my office and stands by a chair while I move a pile of depositions and motions off of it and onto the floor by the window.

"How are you?" I say again.

"I'm fine, good."

"You look good."

"How are you doing, man? How are Ellie and the kids?"

"The kids are fine."

"Ellie?"

"She's fine. *We're* not so great."

"Ahh," he says.

"Is that 'ahh' like aha, or 'ahh' like ohhh?"

"It's 'ahh' like I'm sorry to hear it," he says. He sounds fairly genuine.

"We're at the hey-would-you-look-at-the-size-of-that-iceberg stage."

"Oh," he says. "That's 'oh' as in oh."

"Or uh-oh," I say.

"*Uh-oh . . . looks like truh-ble,*" he says. It's an old Fred Allen expression and we use it in the Fred Allen voice, the last three words on descending nasal notes. We used to say it when all hell was breaking loose downstairs; a well-faked ironic detachment, in the late teen years.

"Not enough trouble, actually," I say. "I work and go home and watch television or read."

"You're in deep-avoidance mode, in other words," he says. One of his khaki legs is crossed over the other and swinging in an angular off-tempo pendular motion, like a half-broken tree branch swaying in the wind.

"Yeah, basically." My brother is a quick-change artist and something of a con man but oddly direct at the same time, the kind of person—boy, I'd like to say, though he's thirty-three—that you can't help but like, for his obvious decency and kindness, even as he's crushing you with his well-bent emotional needs. I take him to lunch. I watch him; all of his faces are a new angle on pensive, uncertain; he has a vagueness that certain kinds of women are attracted to, women who had vague but affectionate fathers and were never able to pin them down. He appeals to the highly sexual rescuer type, God help them. The face, in my office (pensive polite, the quiet visitor), going down in the elevator (blank but pensive with the populated-elevator blankness), on the street (studying the action, thoughtfully), and then across the table from me at the boisterous old-fashioned deli where despite the noise it's possible to talk in a rather wide-open and warm way because nobody gives a shit what anybody else is doing or saying. Some of the waitresses are Irish and some of them Italian and not many of them Jews. The old-timers behind the counter are Jews, and there is an ancient bald man with dirt-clouded glasses and a red bump on his head, perched on a red stool behind the cash register with all his fat gathered round his hips: years of sitting, nimble-fingered and not much else. The waitresses run around with grim, pissed-off faces, shouting at each other at the slightest provocation. The old countermen intervene only when they have hopes of making the situation worse. The basic complaint seems to be that every waitress is stealing every other waitress's orders; most of the customers are ordering the same six or seven items (pastrami extra lean, French fries, Dr. Brown's sodas), not the esoterica like the herring or tongue, so mixing up the orders must be pretty easy to do. The basic rule seems to be, if you see something at the kitchen window and it matches an order of yours, take it.

Fellow customers are a Wall Street mix, brokers and clericals and one out-of-place fiftyish writer/artist type in jeans and profusive gray hair who is sitting with an executive assistant–type. At the table behind us a head-of-the-messenger-room type with his girlfriend, who looks like a Latina version of one of the young, beaten-up, heroin-chic underwear models, with heavy black eye makeup and an ignorant pout.

My brother, a word similar to "bother," I've often noticed, is edging toward something; or as it turns out, several things. First he asks about our father, how he is.

"I don't know how he is, really," I say. "He's dying of asbestos disease and he's suing a roster of manufacturers and I try to pay no attention to the progress of the litigation because with my professional knowledge I could drive myself nuts."

"Is he mobile at this point?" Michael says.

"Yeah, still mobile. Out for the papers in the morning. I think he plays the numbers. That's it for the day though, then he's shot. He sits in the reclining chair watching television. Watches all the talk shows. He's saving his strength, he says, because he's committed to living to the trial, whenever that is. Now that he's relatively powerless he wants to be nice."

"Is anyone taking care of him? You know, a woman or whatever?"

A woman or whatever. Those who take care of others.

"Helen," I say, "is the woman or whatever. You met her when you were in New York with Bonnie and Clyde. How are they, by the way?"

"The boy's name was *Kyle*," Michael says. "*Not* Clyde. And they're, I don't know how they are. Bonnie's in Florida now, but I haven't heard from her. I miss Kyle more than I miss her, to tell you the truth."

"Didn't she think when she named him Kyle that everyone who ever met them or even heard of them would have to, like, physically restrain themselves from calling him Clyde?"

"I actually tried to explain that to her once. She wasn't having any of it."

I start to laugh.

"No," he says, "really. She was, like, 'Kyle is different from Clyde because Clyde is a *c* word, and Kyle is a *k* word and people don't confuse words unless they start with the same letter.'" He looks at me, he's smiling himself. "I swear," he says.

"I believe you," I say.

"So what about Helen?" he says. "I remember her, she seemed very nice if not that—"

"Bright?" I say. "She's actually brighter than she looks—she's certainly shrewd about him, doesn't take any of his shit. She comes in most days at lunchtime. He pays her, I believe, but they also have some kind of flirtation going. 'My friend Helen,' he calls her, you know, like they're an old lesbian couple or something."

"Well, I'd like to go see him," Michael says.

"Give him a call," I say. I don't want to say what follows but not wanting to say it makes me feel mean and small, so I say it. "Maybe we can go out there together."

"Yeah, that'd be nice," Michael says. He's looking down at his half-eaten sandwich. He eats more tentatively every year.

"Michael?" I say.

"Yeah, don't ask," he says.

"I'm asking, man."

"Look, I need a job. Just a decent job. I'd like to come back to New York."

"You are back to New York," I say.

"Right, well, permanently. The basic thing is, I can't really talk to the women anywhere else but here. I mean, you can't talk to the men either, in that way, but it doesn't bother you. I'd like to start having some kind of active mental life. Physical too. Something simple. A small cell in Chelsea or Clinton. Maybe Queens but I'd rather not."

"'A small cell,' as you put it, in Chelsea will cost fifteen hundred a month and can go to double that, easily. Brooklyn can be very civilized these days. In Carroll Gardens, down from the Heights. I'd also recommend Harlem. Very happening place. In Queens, there are some great neighborhoods coming in, but it's still, you know, Queens, with all that stupidity round and about."

"Yeah, maybe Brooklyn."

Right now he's "crashing"—does anyone really say "crashing" anymore?—at the apartment of a guy he knows in the Bronx. I don't want to know about where in the Bronx, or why. Needless to say, there is no telephone. In other words, as always, I'll be hearing from him at his convenience.

He also claims to have a couple of hundred dollars; this is better than usual.

"I know I can't work at your firm, but I figure you must know some people who would see me. You're plugged into the world." He gestures a little toward the front of the restaurant, and the door—this is the world.

"Strapped in, is more like it," I say. "I'll ask around. There's a lot of illegal construction and renovation going on, you can always hook on with that until something better comes up."

"Yeah," he says. "That's a transportable skill."

A call comes at four forty-five, from Ursula, her first live communication since our initial meeting. "Ursula," I say. "Hello." I modulate my voice between a robust, unsurprised, businesslike four-forty-five sound and pitched-down, friendly encouragement. She says nothing. I say nothing back. Somehow it's not necessary to press her. She knows what she wants and I don't. The silence from her end is skittish, fragile, on the verge of hanging up without speaking. These are the days of phone calls from women who would prefer not to be talking to me.

"Fuck it," she says finally.

"Don't hang up," I say.

"Why not?" she says.

"Waste a nickel."

"It went up to a dime," she says. "About forty years ago. And word on the street is that it's up to twenty-five and soon to rise again. The man is ripping us off. Exploitation. Economic genocide." She delivers this in a flat voice, bored irony.

"Nickel is a better word," I say.

It is very important to find out what she called for, not to let her slip off into a hostile riff; I want to make this case real (I want to make something in my life real, at this point) and I am beginning to like the e-mails, my nighttime companions, the insinuations of a personal literature. I see typed passages in my sleep, underwater texts, almost decipherable.

Ursula has lit a cigarette, I can hear the channeled exhale like a brief, distant wind. "This is such fucking bullshit," she says. "Why should I call you? What can you do for me?" Perhaps she barely whispers, perhaps I almost hear *"white boy"* on the end of that sentence.

"I don't know," I say. "But here we are. Why don't you just tell me why you called, I can respond, perhaps weakly, perhaps trenchantly, we can mutter good-byes, nothing lost."

"I saw him," she says.

"You saw whom?" I say.

"I saw the man. In a coffee shop near here. He's in the neighborhood. It's freaking me out."

"Which one did you see?"

"The tall white one. He has, like, a little beard now, not a goatee but the other kind—"

"Van Dyke?" I say.

"Yeah, Van Dyke, great. Appropriate. Anyway, it was him. I mean, I'd know him."

"What are you going to do?"

"You mean am I going to get a gun and go out and stick it up his ass and blow his intestines across Ninety-sixth Street? Like little bits of bloody snot? I'm thinking about it. Mostly it occurred to me you might come up and, you know, go over there. For a look."

"What about the police?"

"I'm hanging up right now. This is the end of the phone call."

"Don't," I say.

"This is no longer a police matter. I've been to the police, it was worse than the crime. No, not worse, but comparable. I'm not looking for anything involved. I'm not interested in a ten-minute ride in a squad car with two men who are mildly titillated by the sexual interruption. I just want someone else to see him, take him out of my imagination."

"There are women police now," I say. "Every time I see a squad car there's a woman in it. I even saw one recently with two women and no man." Silence from her end. I check my watch. "It will be a little while before I get out of here," I say. "Do you want to meet me there?"

"No. Here. Pick me up here."

I take the train up from Wall Street, at that hour faster than a car, but mined with strange intimacies. I see a woman in red shorts, and her boyfriend, him in blue jeans and sneakers, clean, new, a studied and expensive look masquerading as the casual thing that jeans and sneakers once were. As she sits she pats the seat beside her for him—the gesture doesn't come off as she intended, he isn't looking and he sits down on the other side of her, oblivious. I'm abnormally interested in this small, missed connection. I conclude she did it a little too rapidly, *pat pat*, like a grade school teacher; rather than being nonchalant it had a slightly desperate edge. In any case, he never saw it, she was that far from knowing where he was going to look, what direction he was moving in. In any case, his jaw muscles are jumping. In any case, she seeks his hand, her body gravitates toward his, her limbs hinge toward him, hint at envelopment. The train rattles on, begins its next jolting stop. He appears lifeless, annoyed, and bored. You might call it dread and revulsion. Something about him suggests he despises her and despises himself for needing her. In the proper moment, in bed, suspended over her, he will discharge this need, quickly, with emotions hung between anger and regret. His face will be the face of death in war, the face of grim and violent determination. Thrusts of a mindless dog. And then silence. He will be untouchable and want to remain that way. The dog trots off to the bush, pisses on it. He is the frowning, dirty-faced boy who will not kiss his mother. She, the girl, will be too frightened to reproach him and so she will cling. Man and woman. What God has brought together let no man put asunder.

*   *   *

Ursula's new place isn't that far from the old one, Eighty-ninth Street just off Third. Another glitzy doorman building, overdone and expensive looking, entirely new, lots of security, cameras in the elevator, computer in the lobby, walkie-talkies on the staff. Ursula lives on a high floor, which I picture as flat-walled and large-windowed, not so much an apartment as a protective tank, something Jacques Cousteau would have invented if he'd tried to live in New York. I ride up with a well-groomed, impatient-looking youth in a well-tailored nail-head gray suit, and a thin young woman, perhaps a model or a second wife, makeup done so perfectly you notice it before you notice her. A computerized voice announces the stops, a robot in the walls. As we climb, I am intensely aware of the woman, her long body, its expensive accoutrements. Her legs, thin ankles, and black sandals, the toes painted, her feet fully pedicured—the curious combination of beauty and lewdness of feet, those far sexual appendages; especially when they're cared for, they seem like small, independent animals frolicking at the bottom of the body. The man—one of those overpaid and perpetually angry twenty-seven-year-olds—departs at the sixteenth floor. The woman is going to thirty-one, a floor below my stop. After the doors close on the man I watch her. She ignores me. When I sense her eyes about to move, to see if I am staring, which she suspects, I look away, above, at the numbers. When my eyes go back she is looking forward again.

There is nowhere she can go, nothing she has the nerve to say.

Finally, thirty-one. Our little contest of attraction and repulsion: she leaves as fast as those feet and legs can carry her, shank's mare, my grandmother used to say, galloping down the hall. I have from that floor to the next, plus down the long hallway, to become human again. Unfortunately I don't quite make it.

"It's Will," I say when I hear a soft movement behind the door, and it opens with a sucking implosion, a hundred and eighty pounds of bullet-proof steel and fireproofing. Ursula is wearing sweatpants and a white towel rolled and hung over her neck, like an old fighter. It takes me a second to realize she has no shirt on whatsoever; her large dark nipples peek out from under the bottom edges of the towel like the eyes of a half-hidden child. She turns and walks away from me as soon as the door is open, leaving me to close it. Multiple locks. Her muscled back, striped with sweat. Sweat darkens a triangle of her pants, the stain in the shape of a thong. She goes to a series of mats and weights; there is an exercise bike, a bench, a stand for the free weights. All this takes up half the large open living room. She sits on a bench there; elbows on knees, head lowered, she begins rubbing the towel over her short hair, her shoulders and neck. The purity of tones in African skin. It's a power move, her half nakedness. Thick arms, bulging rib cage, a muscular woman, as I'd thought. I'm left standing in the middle of the room, my bag hanging from my shoulder, feeling like the joke insurance man doing a walk-on in someone else's comedy. True to the character, I check my watch, looking annoyed.

At last she rises and tosses me the damp towel. It settles onto the floor like a failed parachute; she goes into the bedroom and shuts the door. I pick up the towel, fold it, and like a good servant place it neatly on the black bench. I notice an old, dark kidney-shaped stain on the parquet floor.

She's showered and changed and we're at a table having coffee at Ninety-fourth and Madison. Lunch counter, luncheonette, coffee shop, diner, the evoloution of cheap food in the city. Solid tan Formica, vinyl seating a lighter shade of beige. The wallpaper on the long, unmirrored side of the restaurant features a machine-reproduced mural, huge, of Achilles dragging Hector's body around the walls of Troy—it is a fantastic piece of work, really, the sense of the city as an actually round entity quite remarkably achieved. Depth of field, the figures of the women hanging over the top of the walls, twisted in grief. The Greeks, especially Achilles, have a look of grim, heroic vengeance.

I have always been fascinated by these places. The luncheonette, the version of my youth, has almost disappeared. In its stead the Greek diner. One can interpret the counter where one pays—with its small shelf displaying candy, gum, small aspirin packs—as a vestige, the tail stump left over from the luncheonette stage of evolution. Luncheonettes also sold cigarettes, newspapers, magazines, comics, and, occasionally, paperback bestsellers. And cheap stationery. And twenty varieties of cigar. And milk of magnesia, without embarrassment at the suggestion that their own food may have caused the need.

"This is the place," Ursula says finally. "It reeks for me now. It vibrates. I think I'm losing my mind."

"Lunch counter," I say to Ursula. She stares at me with dark irritation. "Luncheonette. Coffee shop. Diner—a history of food methodologies. Jews, Italians, Greeks. Generations of service in thick crockery. Ketchup bottles upturned and balanced on the snouts of other ketchup bottles. Napkins jammed in black metal dispensers, so tight you can't get any out. Minted toothpicks in rows of sanitary paper wrap. Mints in a bowl. How do they get that fold in their aprons?"

"The chances of seeing him again are nil," Ursula says. "We should go. We're wasting our time. I don't know why I called you. I just wanted you to *see* it. Can you *see* how the place is vibrating? Of course not. It's an insane question."

"Have you noticed that mural of Achilles dragging Hector's body around the walls of Troy?"

"What we should do is come back tomorrow, the next day, and the next. Put in some time. Wait."

"It's a murderous rage," I say. "All the pent-up frustrations finally get to him, Agamemnon stole his woman, what a shit that guy was, by the way, sacrificed his daughter for a wind, and then Achilles' best friend gets killed by Hector, so Achilles comes out of isolation and just destroys the poor schmuck."

"I'm going to make this my project," she says. "Track the asshole like he's some kind of animal."

"I love these places," I say. "I love the microphones back to the kitchen." I cup my hand over my mouth. "Cream of mushroom! Special steak!"

"I want you to find him, Will. I want you to find out who he is, where he lives, his name. Vital data."

"Not to bring up a pesky question again," I say, "but if we find him we pretty much have to go to the police."

"Maybe. Maybe not. I'll think about it. What proof is there? My word? I'm not ready to defend my word and nothing more. Wait until they get hold of my *special lifestyle*. There's a lot of stuff they can get hold of. I'll just become another story about women, rape, and the justice system. Good for a paragraph in a magazine article. At best."

"These things have become more civilized, at least in New York. Much time and testimony on hair samples, the structures of proteins. Jockeying over scientific reports, expert testimony from microbiologists."

"Are you saying they wouldn't bring the other stuff up?"

"They're going to do it at the civil trial anyway. Only worse. Public defenders occasionally have a vestige of conscience, that's why some of them took the job in the first place. These insurance defense guys will stop at nothing. There's real money at stake, not just some loser's freedom."

She looks at me, face like dark stone.

In my office there is a large black-and-white photograph of Mickey Mantle, batting from the left side of the plate, just at the end of his swing: my father's favorite ballplayer, a beautiful picture, the closest I will get to memorializing my old man in any way. The photograph is close and isolating, just his body and the clayish dirt around home plate. He is at the end of a massive swing: his head and his legs are in profile but between his waist and chin his body is twisted to a remarkable degree, led, it would appear, by his bat, which he still grips with both hands and which is slung as far as possible behind his right shoulder. His enormous chest, turned far around with the swing, almost faces the lens. He is slender at the waist, thick in the limbs. The pose is classical in the extreme. The blank white span of his shirt is interrupted by a series of folds that radiate from the area of his belt buckle. Similar folds in his pants define the motions of his legs. He looks young.

Other offices, other art: we have a few old men still in the sailing-ship mode, large, heavy, framed pictures, none of which is memorable in itself but taken together, as types, they define a kind of adamant and hypernostalgic WASP-ism. Museum prints framed in chrome, walls of high-quality family photographs, taken while hiking in the Sierra Madre or Alaska, lounging at beach houses, skiing in the Alps. Each partner with his or her unmysterious and carefully cultivated tastes, worn with slight stiffness like new suits of clothes. They feel about art the way Huck Finn felt about shoes and lessons from the Bible.

I must say the firm is very correct, very decent. "Enlightened," it would say if there were another write-up, one of those puffy little profiles and handjobs in the legal press. We have two black associates, a Hispanic partner, an Asian partner, a number of women partners, near parity among the associates. Support staff paid well, decent benefits for a medium-sized firm, medical and dental, etc. Of course, the nonlegal employees have to contribute. Who can afford to carry them at 100 percent anymore? They get two weeks vacation, three weeks after five years, four weeks after seven years. Year-end bonuses on the same schedule as vacation time, two weeks, three weeks, or four, depending on length of service. Raises on a merit basis. There is, nevertheless, something in the names that gives away the new and rigorous social order: secretaries, messengers, and file clerks have names like Jamila, Roberto, and Yvonne. The paralegals are Jamie, Anne-Marie, and Patrick. The attorneys are Jack, Ron, Mary Ellen, Bob, Trish, Sue, Richard, and Gerry. Et cetera. One Clem. One Tim. Two Davids. A different sound, signals of a strict but hard-to-quantify distinction, to which everyone seems to have agreed without rancor.

Sex among staff is tolerated, barely, in uncomfortable silence. One is supposed to keep it secret, though this is gestural in the end, since "secret" has done one of those switches where it has come to mean its opposite, each so-called secret in reality being a titillating public truth, and in the workplace even more so. At a certain inevitable teetering, with the coming of coldness and tension in the corridor, the breakup like the warming of ice in northern harbors in spring, the gun-cracking separations, we all expect something will blow, some big mess with charges and countercharges, with neither party telling the truth, with, God help us, publicity. So far it hasn't happened. When a man takes up with a woman and the relationship lasts, the woman eventually leaves the firm.

Anna. I find myself, after lunch, standing at her desk, idly checking out her stuff. I'm interested in her mail, her personal items. The small, unnameable sexiness of her glasses sitting there on the edge of the blotter, the sense of the stolen intimacy of the moment. Armani knockoffs, delicate reddish-brown frames, quite nice . . . Maybe I should have married someone like her; her stiff efficiency, her quiet ambitions for a good life, would buoy me. The poetry of my early marriage was nice but I have become less poetic by the day, by the hour . . . I like how organized Anna is, and I like how she comes in late too, as if she has a life outside the office and the office is taking valuable time away.

After dinner, Ellie finds a piece of my pornography where I've hidden it under the four-legged tub; I'm in the little room off the kitchen that we use as a study, two desks, three file cabinets, some shelves. I hear her in the hall. "Give this to Daddy," she is saying to Henry. "Give this to Daddy, that's right, he's in his office . . ." He comes waddling in with the magazine in two arms before him, on the cover a girl in leather straps bent over, ass in the air. "Heah, Daddy, heah, Daddy," he says. How happy he looks.

"*Thank* you," I say. "That's so nice, you brought me a magazine." Behind him, Ellie, in the doorway, gives me a look. I'm tempted to drop the magazine in the trash but I don't want to make Henry feel bad and I don't want my wife to win, so I slide it into my top drawer.

"Daddy, I brought you magathine?" Henry says.

"That's right, you brought me a magazine," I say.

"Daddy, I brought you magathine. Mommy told me."

"That's right," I say. "You did a good job. Thank you for bringing me my magazine." Ellie watches—I feel driven with her standing there lording.

"Daddy did I bring you magathine?"

"Yup," I say. "I don't know what I'd do if I didn't have you to bring me magazines. Thank you for bringing it to me. You're such a good boy."

"I am good boy," he says.

"You're a *very* good boy," I say.

"Daddy, I am a good boy," he says. "Dat's right, Daddy." He runs out of the room. Ellie turns and follows him. I go back to work and after half an hour has passed he staggers in with a copy of *Vanity Fair;* later comes *Vogue*, then a magazine with sewing patterns, all of which were on the night tables in our room. He has determined now that his mission is to bring me magazines. All of them have pictures of women on the covers.

The next morning, an e-mail from late the night before, waiting for me, like a hot breakfast.

subject: the café life [written earlier]

i am in a café, i'm through with the coffee shops for now, ruined for me they are. this a rather grand place on the west side, a pretty place with pretty people in it; there is also a lesser group, of people who would like to think of themselves as pretty, or at least of ranking enough to be with the pretty. and i am here. and the waitress comes. and i order a cappuccino.

—i want it dark, i tell her. —i want it unadorned.

she doesn't understand what i am talking about needless to say and i wonder why i talk to people this way. am i insane?

—i mean i don't want cinnamon or whipped cream or any of that shit, i say, by way of explaining.

—the cinnamon's on the table, she says, and she lifts a salt shaker which has been converted to a cinnamon shaker and kind of twirls it in her fingers for me to see, as if she is displaying it as one of the prizes behind the wrong door. from copco international—manufacturer's suggested retail price two dollars and ninety-nine cents. then she puts it down. i can tell, once i said "shit" i became a difficult negro and her defenses went up in typical bourgeois white woman fashion.

—you mean the coffee comes plain just with hot milk? i say. i can't seem to stop myself.

—*steamed* milk, she says and whirls and goes away.

all the waitresses here are beautiful, long, stunning, graceful creatures who are like fine animals on display and give the place the air of a game park. one is asian, one is a latina. the other two are out-of-town white, with long yellow hair, i have one of these. their beautiful friends come in to see them. they exchange the noncommittal kisses and light touches beautiful women use among themselves as currency to confirm their beauty. around me at the tables there are no people of real ambition. it is very difficult to stop listening to the stupid conversations. everyone's face looks just like someone else's face. the place reminds me of another place in another part of town. the dullness of repetition, of having taken in too much, of having known too many people. in the city everything is NEW NEW NEW but then you get to the point where no matter how new it is you've seen it before and you're tired of it. the men in particular are clumsy and absolutely predictable, overconfident and insecure and vulgar in all the same unknowing lifeless patterns. money distinguishes them. each can boast some achievement in the world, some way of existing outside himself that is predictable, comfortable, rarely unnerving. one man at the next table, with a date, says "redundant" three times. he is proud of his words. his hair is arranged in a careful, fruitless attempt to mask its thinness. he should just cut it all off but doesn't have the nerve. —she is SO redundant, he says. i want to lean over and say to the woman, he's a fucking idiot, you know that, right? but of course i don't do that. i'm already the pissed-off-looking, insane, unpretty black chick in the café and who needs more of an outcast status than that?

bach plays on the stereo. overhead large fans turn, slowly, brassily shooting the light. bach. big beautiful white german bach. the fans are elaborate affairs, brass and

chrome and polished wood veneer. marble and pipes. a wall, its bricks left bare. unadorned. the waitresses carry bags of english tea arranged on a plate, like an offering to god. i want it simple, waitress, i want it exposed, something that is what it is
and nothing more. the fans turn. the music builds. bach: to whom every note was a
prayer, every phrase an expanding devotion. across the room, one man's eyes, filled
with hate. he is alone. near him, laughter, brief and strained. conversation rises and
thins like the smoke of ancient sacrifice. the music elaborates itself, two melodies
crossing and crossing again, an idea unfolding. another man, a woman, they are
silent, looking around. marble, chrome, wood, and brick; and outside, out beyond
the cool air-conditioning, the leaves stir with a quick breeze, an early promise perhaps of the end of summer, the end of this astonishing heat. a girl in open-toed
shoes. waitress i want it unadorned. waitress I want. the music. the sound of voices
that ring, like porcelain, and break, like porcelain. everything shattering, breaking
up—let's break up—you're breaking up, can you hear me? waitress speak to me,
speak. the music, bach. the women. the wind. jesu, joy of man's desiring.

i have not stopped thinking about that man.

I learned the facts of life in Dayton, Ohio, from a boy named John. He
lived across the street from my aunt and uncle, whom we were visiting
that year, one of two or three times in my childhood we drove out to
Ohio for a long visit, to my mother's sister's. Like a lot of folks in that
part of Ohio, John had a southern accent and one day with it he an-
nounced, discovering I didn't yet know the score, "Yower father took his
di-yick and stuck it in yower mother's pew-sey—that's how you were
bawrn." It was a stunningly obscene statement, and I said, like any good
red-blooded well-protected American boy of eleven years, "No he
didn't," and John smiled, and he said, "Yes he did, there ain't no other
way to be bawrn," and I said, "No, you're wrong," and he said, "I ain't
wrong, yew know it, too, yew know it" still smiling, a horrible little
knowing smile, and I belted him. We got in a fight that moved into the
driveway, where there was a sandpile for some work that was going to be
done, and I grabbed a handful of sand and threw it in his face. Then I

ran in the house. I knew, though I'd denied it, that what John had said was true; I knew also for some reason that this had happened in their bedroom, in their bed, not, say, in the bathroom, where a child might think all activities involving dick and pew-sey took place, so I must have known more than I was admitting to myself, but don't we always? I tell this story to Chin.

"You didn't know until you were *eleven?*" is his only reaction.

"The Irish-Catholic community was then still insulated against notions of sex as an interesting human phenomenon," I say.

"By the time we were eleven, Jesus," Chin says. He leans back, smiles. "I remember being in the basement with Billy Carroll and a kid named Adam looking at *Playboys*, and then we found this other stuff, really hard stuff, and our eyes were popping out. And that's not all that was popping out. We all jerked off, right there. It's one of my fondest memories."

"Beautiful," I say. "It's a beautiful scene. 'Outside, the snow was general all over Ireland. It fell gently, gently falling.'"

"You're making fun," David says.

"Only a little."

"Meanwhile, you were in your room sobbing your heart out to know what filthy things your mom had been doing all your life. And with *him*. It must have been crushing."

"Hmm," I say. "I didn't have a room, exactly. We were visiting relatives."

"But you cried, admit it. You cried your little Catholic heart out."

"Hmm," I say again.

"Shall I go on?"

"No."

"It's a cruel world," David says. "A cruel, sexual world. Testosterone, murderer of the spirit. I bet your Ohio friend is a little bald fireplug of a guy now, hair running up his back, who beats his wife."

"Nice," I say. "That's a nice image to end the day."

"You want to get a beer?"

I check my watch. Five-fifteen. I have another two or three hours of work I should do. David probably more. But it's summer and nothing's urgent, nothing's today.

"Sure," I say.

We collect our stuff and reconnoiter in the men's room. We urinate side by side, fall into the rich silence of pissing.

Outside, the heat is moist and full of pungencies. We go to a little place up Washington Street a bit north of Canal, a good half-hour walk from the office. Along the way, the smell of garbage from all the take-out Chinese places. In spots around town the private carters have been honoring the sanitation walkout. It appears to be two or three days' worth of fish-stinking mess. There is a huge OTB office, the sidewalk before it crescented with thousands of betting slips. The men gathered inside, black, white, Latino, all look like my father and his generation: canvas car caps, short-sleeved shirts and sans-a-belt slacks; hair slicked back and the Don Ameche mustache, still holding its own; the look says World War II and a lifetime of instinctive misogyny. There is no en-forcement of "No Smoking" signs in there; they wouldn't dare.

At the bar, we settle in, warily make our way into the conversation, joke about the news on the big screen TV, about the two old drunks at the far end ("That's you in twenty years." "No, that's me in six months . . ."). David introduces me to the bartender: apparently David's a regular, an odd one for this place, with the old longshoremen and the young marginally employed downtown straight-boy pool players with sideburns. The bartender is Ronnie. Tall and broad and mustached, in his forties, a professional, with a face that says it has seen some action and is not looking for any more, especially from you.

"Ronnie is the best kind of bartender there is," David says as Ronnie wipes down the area, waits for the order. "He hears everything and says nothing."

"Exactly," Ronnie says. "I know where all the bodies are. Even the swanky ones you've disposed of, Chin."

"I didn't think you specialized in my kind," David says.

"I'm a disinterested observer of the human condition," Ronnie says. "With its many problems. Most of them leading here."

"Two pints of Guinness," David says.

Ronnie goes off, runs the tap, waits for the stout to clear, tilts the first glass, lets some settle, tilts it again.

And then David brings up the Trinity question. "I went in there one day at noon," he says. "About two months ago. They have these noontime performances, music, organ and choir, and something happened, I was looking back toward the choir loft and suddenly everything was, like, louder, more intense, I had this distinct feeling of the music taking me and I was soaring and then, I'm not describing this, really. I was kind of dizzy. I sat there, sweating, I really felt ill, nauseated, and I just wanted to sit and pull myself together and then the concert ended and they had midday Mass, and I didn't want to walk out so I stayed."

"And you've been going back every day since then?" I say.

"Well, not every day at first, but, yeah, a lot. It's been every day for the last couple of weeks."

I look at him.

"I was brought up Episcopalian," he says, "which I always thought of as a colonial vestige, from the British years in China, I guess. I never really asked my father about it." He reaches into his pocket, takes out a pack of Marlboros, and lights one, shocking me. "Something happened," he says, the words coming out on the first pluming exhale. "I mean, it was very weird and believe me I would like to deny such things happen, but it happened, and I had to deal with it. Culturally I don't know what to do about it. It's just there, you know?"

I look into his eyes, which, not to be too ethno-predictable about it, isn't that easy. Black mica behind a half-closed venetian blind. A glint of what looks like private amusement. I am accustomed to parsing out the irony content of David's sentences; but here he is, apparently serious.

"No, I'm not sure I do know," I finally say. I'm trying to answer him directly, although we don't really have a language for that. "It hasn't happened to me, or it's only partially and more ambiguously happened to me, or it's happened to me and I've rejected it and suppressed it. Take your pick. The undeniable thing is what I'm still waiting for, although tomorrow morning I'll deny that." Ronnie puts the two pints down and turns for the other end: I take the first long pull, leaving a series of lacy white rings circling the glass.

"That pretty much describes me too," he says. "Before."

"Are you proselytizing?" I say. "Doing missionary work? Looking to bring nubile belief to the marriage bed?"

"No," he says. "You seemed interested, and I haven't talked to anyone about it before. I just wanted to see how it felt to say some of it out loud, you know, test-drive it in the real world."

"It doesn't sound so bad. You're not the only one, right? 'Upon this rock I have built my Church and nothing shall prevail against it.' Can I have a cigarette?"

He hands me the pack. I light one up. It feels like a bigger crime than adultery, burglary, or murder. The unforgivable. And I suspect, which means I know, that I'm instantly hooked again, after what, six and a half years? It feels insanely good, sucking the smoke down and shooting it back out.

"Like riding a bicycle," I say. "You never forget."

"Oh, God," David says. "Look what I've done."

"How are they, you know, the Episcopalians, on the gay question?" I ask him.

"I'm not really interested in the gay question," David says. "I mean I'm interested, you know, I'm *always* interested, but on my own time. What I'm looking for when I'm there doesn't have anything to do with that. It's more like I'm on a desert island, and I've found an old broken-down radio in the sand, and I'm using bits of glass and paper clips and two C batteries to get it going again. And when you get it working there's a lot of static and you're afraid you're going to lose even that. You're just trying to make contact."

We finish the pints, Ronnie comes around.

"What do I call you, Ron or Ronnie?" I say.

"You call, I respond," Ronnie says. "Ron, Ronnie, Tom, Dick, Harry. Just don't call me Judy Garland." He looks pointedly at David.

"I know someone else named Ron," I say. "You're a much better person than he is."

"You don't know how bad I am," Ronnie says.

"However bad, you don't come close to this guy," I say.

"Two more?"

"Yeah," I say. I put down a twenty and a ten. "You get the next two rounds," I say to Chin, who is reaching for his wallet. I am committing to a major session.

"So," Chin says. "What's going on with you?"

"My secretary tells me I never take risks," I say.

"When, today?"

"No, a while ago, two weeks maybe."

"And you still remember it?" David says. "That's what's on your mind? Was it a come-on or something?"

"No," I say. "It was not a come-on."

"As if you'd know."

"I know in this case."

"So then," he says, "what's the issue?"

"She's right. I take no risks. She says I'm turning mean. She says, 'Freedom is in the heart,' and I realize, I have no idea what that would feel like, if it were true."

"Two children is a risk," David says, trying to be kind.

"Not really," I say. "Two children without a wife would be a risk."

That night I come home happy, for once, slightly drunk but Ellie doesn't seem to mind. I've brought two bottles of beer with me, tall, corked, seven-dollar bottles of Belgian ale, to keep things moving along. I pour them carefully, a mush-drunk pantomime of Ronnie at the bar with expert hands on the Guinness tap.

"Why are you so happy?" Ellie says when I bring her the glass of beer.

"It was nice having drinks with David," I say.

"Are you gay?" she says.

"I don't think so," I say. I take a long drink. "I used to think it would be terrifically convenient to be gay. Leave fifteen minutes early for work and stop in the park for a blow job. Stop in again on the way home. What a deal they had until the early eighties. I could never muster any interest though."

"You walk around wanting blow jobs all the time?" she says, smiling.

"That's only the beginning of what I want," I say.

"Ahh," she says. "Well."

"Is that 'ahh' like aha, or 'ahh' like ohhh?" I say. "Déjà vu all over again."

"What?" she says.

"Nothing," I say. "Just Michael came to see me today, he said 'ahh,' just like that."

"Your brother? He's in New York?"

"Don't be alarmed," I say. "He's staying with some friend in the Bronx. He even has a little money."

"I wasn't alarmed," she says, "*you* were alarmed. I *like* your brother."

"Oh, no, not you too," I say. "Sleep with him and I'll kill you."

"Will!"

"I cannot understand for the life of me why so many women like that guy," I say. "He's thin to the point of disappearing when he turns sideways and he has no money and no ambition. It defies everything I know of the female mentality."

"He's sweet and lost," she says. "Utterly gentle and not threatening. Some women go for that."

"Okay, sleep with him, I don't mind."

"Will," she says. "I like him because he's your brother, please."

"No, no, I want to be big about this," I say, mock tragic.

"Will you please stop."

"First you accuse me of being gay. Sigh when I hint at a sex life. Then you announce you want my brother. What's a husband to do?"

"There is no room in my life for this shit," she says, suddenly angry. "I realize you're just teasing but it's hostile and it's tiring and I don't have an inch of fucking room for it. I'm warning you."

"'You make me soooo . . . ,'" I begin to sing.

"Don't do this," Ellie says.

"'Veeeery happy.'" I give it the lounge-act croon. "'I'm—so—glad you—*came* into *my life* . . .'"

"I want a divorce," Ellie says.

Faster tempo now. "'Sometimes when you touch my soul, you make me lose control . . .'"

"I'm leaving," Ellie says. "Maybe not now, but at some point. Or you are."

"Good," I say. From some kind of unbridgeable mental distance I look on this scene with horror, having so efficiently and relentlessly turned a nice moment into an awful one, full of anger and confrontation. I can't stop; I go on, push forward. I grew up in a world of anger, and in some ways its familiarity is a comfort, yet I have never in my life really understood it, comprehended what it is, taken in its scope and its power to destroy. I'm just seeing it now.

"Good," I say. "That's fine. For a while I was really en*joying* the hostility, the rejection, the sullen looks and knifing comments, but you know, recently, I've got to admit it's getting a little tired."

"It may not be today or tomorrow, but soon," she says. "I'm just going to walk out, or force you out, end it. I can't stand it much longer."

"Why wait?" I say. "Why the fuck wait?" She goes into the kitchen.

[5]

In many offices, one finds a fat person—not just an older secretary or partner grown paunchy with the years—but an immense presence, someone for whom fat is a governing reality. Fat in the office context surpasses social embarrassments and moves into the realm of amorphous power. Size on the animal level, authority, and distance. Our fat man is Gerry Rorjak, quick-tongued, comprehensive, enormous, an observer without prejudice, critic, and occasional prophet. Gerry's suits are tailored in London; his shoes, on the other hand, are designed by an orthopedics firm in the Bronx, specialists in weight distribution and radiating lines of stress. Gerry's legs and feet are axes in a universe of pain, small bones chipped, bent, spalled, calling it a day; not to mention the skin of his thighs, chafed to hard leather; not to mention the red torture marks and hairlessness where the tops of his socks bite into his calves. Gerry has been married to the same woman for twenty-two years, but according to Jack he is on his third wedding ring, each a larger copy of the original, re-inscribed; I picture it as an outward progression, like the circles in a pond when a trout hits a fly. The glories and discomfort of size. Gerry made partner ten years ago, a triumph of substance over substance; he lives in Westchester now, with his wife, captured during a thin phase in his early twenties, three children, and a swimming pool. One imagines him floating across the shimmering aqua plane, wavelets lapping the concrete, neighborhood youngsters diving off him and shouting admonitions.

Like many fat men, Gerry is meticulous and vain. His office is a study in cleanliness, efficiency, and design. He wipes it down with spray cleaner and cloth three times a week. He leaves work with empty desk and barren in-box. All is taken care of, all is put away, consumed. Perfect haircuts from Carlo at the Hotel Pierre. Gerry is situated high above the world, looking down over the beauty and stillness from the mountain of himself. Underwear hand-sewn in Holland, fine umbrellas, exotic hats, antique walking sticks arranged like a petrified bouquet; he evokes Churchill, he harkens to the once proud aristocracy of fat. Never explain, never apologize. Know how to handle the servants. Let your money earn a safe 5 percent, except that portion which you invest in the exploitation of people darker than yourself: that earns vastly more. About his office are sculptures from his three Africa trips, small wooden objects, pieces of cloth in ageless subtleties of color hanging on the wall. Half-Czech, half-Italian, he loves Africa and Africans. Memories of colonization and a natural respect for size. The African can be awed by the regal powers of accumulated selfhood. Immense village doges.

Gerry is on the fourth floor, one above mine, head of our small but effective criminal defense team. We take on special cases for special clients. DWI cases in Bucks County, Ridgefield, the Hamptons; felonies of choice include tax fraud, finagling with stock, embezzlement. Jaguars wrapped around hundred-and-eighty-year-old trees. And occasionally, when the anxiety of meaningless wealth finds expression in the theater of violence, a more serious charge. When I come in at 8:45 I find a yellow sticky note, in Gerry's precise calligraphy, hanging on my chair: "Will—See me on your arrival. Gerry."

I get a cup of coffee in the kitchen and return to my desk. Something tells me I don't want to get involved quite yet this morning in whatever miasma of grief and denial Gerry is working on. I fiddle with papers, make a quick phone call. At 9:20 or so Anna arrives, late again. She throws her things under her desk, jumps into her seat, and logs on to the network so that it looks as if she's been there a while. About a minute-and-a-half later her intercom goes off.

"Anna?" It's Gerry's voice. Anna picks up the receiver, says, "Yes?" and listens. After a moment or two she glances at me. "I think so, Mr.

Rorjak, let me check." She puts her hand over the mouthpiece and raises an eyebrow at me.

"Tell him I'm on my way," I say.

"He says he's on his way, Mr. Rorjak," Anna says into the phone.

I go up the semicircular staircase behind reception. I've made myself a second cup of coffee. I concentrate too hard on holding it still and a coffee tsunami develops in the cup as I climb, a relentlessly building wave, until near the top of the stairs I have to stop while coffee dribbles down my hand and onto my shoe. Why is it I can handle quick stops on the subway but often can't make it up the stairs? I stand and sip. Olivia, Gerry's secretary, is behind her desk near Gerry's closed door. She bends over, puts her handbag in the bottom drawer of her desk, zips it, closes the drawer, opens the drawer again, opens the purse, removes her makeup case, zips again, closes again. I can see the lines of a thong under her jersey skirt. I wait. She locks the drawer—things have been disappearing around here, wallets, bracelets, even a coat. Naturally, the clericals are suspected. Olivia rises, sees me. She straightens her skirt and gives herself a shake, rattling her jewelry. The sound of wood and ceramic, ancient dance of the shaman. It occurs to me Gerry would have given her this primitive jewelry—a courtesy to one's employee or is something going on? I have always assumed you stop having new romances after you hit 320 pounds or so, but who knows?

"Good morning," Olivia says. A pleasant face framed by a bad permanent.

"Good morning, Olivia."

"They're waiting for you," she says. "Gerry said don't even knock."

"They?"

"Jack's in with him."

Jesus, I think. Not good. My face must be showing something because Olivia says, "Is everything all right?"

"Yeah, fine. Thanks, Olivia. I like your skirt."

"I bet," she says. She lowers her voice. "I heard about you and Anna, with her standing on the files or whatever."

"I have no idea what you're talking about, Olivia," I say. "Did she complain?"

"Not exactly."

"I didn't think so," I say. "Because it never happened."

"Right," she says.

"Certain things that you think happen actually don't," I say. "Meanwhile, other things that you never even thought of are occurring invisibly all around you."

"Right," she says. She is on her wheeled seat, pulling up to her terminal.

"See you later, Olivia."

"Right, Mr. Riordan."

I go in, Gerry's on the phone, he points me to a seat. Jack is bent in the other visitor's chair, elbows on knees, palming the shining bumpy surfaces of his head. He's wearing a blue pinstripe Italian suit, a major lunch suit. The pants are wide and elegant looking; his ribbed socks are perfectly straight and taut, his tasseled black loafers are shining. He looks miserable.

"Where are they now?" Gerry is saying into the phone. "Uh-huh, uh-huh. Yes. Yes. My colleague is going to be there at ten-thirty. Right. Tell the grandmother not to open the door, not to answer the phone, not to look at yesterday's mail even. Nothing until my colleague gets there. There'll be a car to take them to Helene's office, service entrance, out through the basement. Right. Call me when you have something. Right. Right. 'Bye."

He hangs up, looks at me. Sydney Greenstreet, Orson Welles, Victor Buono. A package of three cupcakes is open on the desk, cellophane perfectly parted by the seam and lying flat, like a place mat. Squared in the center is the white cardboard, one cupcake half eaten. He picks it up. I hold out my coffee, he slides me a coaster.

"Would you like a Danish? I have some nice Danish." He indicates a white box on top of his elegant, long credenza. I take one. He hands me a pressed cloth napkin from his desk drawer.

Jack looks at me with childish grief. "Where have you been, by the way?" he says. "We're having a crisis here."

"I felt a certain resistance," I say. "A deep need not to respond. I sensed something I didn't want to know."

"I hope all the associates learn your psychic powers," Gerry says. "It'll give an air of this-is-a-quest to getting anything done around here. Every task can be a spiritual journey."

"I just got in," I say.

"Better," Gerry says. "That's not an ideal answer, obviously, but it is a better answer." He presses a button on his phone, shifts himself toward the speaker. "Olivia? Buzz Bill Waverly's office again, see if he's in." Then, to me, "Well, I've had a busy, busy weekend. It involved a friend of yours."

Somehow, I know. It comes to me like a sudden memory of a dream that until this moment I hadn't known I'd had.

"Gerry?" Olivia's voice on the intercom. "Bill's not in yet. I told Ciel to have him buzz up when he's here."

"Playing tennis, the son of a bitch," Gerry says to me. Bill is an associate in the criminal side. "Have you ever seen Bill play tennis?"

"No," I say.

"All energy, no grace. Watching this man play tennis, you think, This is suffering. Why is he doing this?"

"Exercise, Gerry. Exercise. A strange concept."

"Exercise he could get working out, running, whatever. This is social. He wants to be a Protestant. He'll keep playing until his sweat smells clean. He's affected by all these handball commercials."

"Tell me about the weekend, Gerry. No time at poolside?"

"Ron Adamson," he says.

"How did I guess?"

"Did you know Adamson was back with his wife?"

"What?"

"Adamson and his wife were back together. He wanted it that way, the wife resisted but gave in. Good for the children or whatever. Maybe she missed him. Hard to believe, but you never know."

"I knew about it," Jack says.

"Was this before or after the last custody brief I did?" I say.

Jack looks at me. "Oh, after, I think. Or right around the same time. I don't remember." He's lying—I think of the two and a half days writing a brief no one needed. But then I can see Jack's thinking. The divorce would eventually happen anyway, we might even need the brief some-day, and, in any event, Diane Adamson having chosen in the interim to live with her husband certainly weakened her claim of abuse, which was late in the game in any event. In any event, we're lawyers, not psychia-trists. In any event, don't ruffle the client. Plus, it's billable.

"Curiously," Gerry said, "Jack here advised him against it. Rather strong terms, I understand. This is helpful to know in light of this week-end. A little salve for the conscience of the firm."

"What?" I say. I cross my legs, bring both my arms into my lap. I'm going into a modified fetal position.

"The reason I advised him against it," Jack says to Gerry, "is that I was sure, I was absolutely certain, it would lead to something unpleas-ant. Had nothing to do with the firm, law, or anything else. An actual human impulse."

"Will, Ron is now under arrest for the murder of his wife. He's go-ing to be arraigned at noon. United States attorney's suggesting bail of ten million dollars. He'll probably get it."

My head is lowered, my knees are rising.

Jack looks up. "The reason is, to put it bluntly, I knew he was going to do this, planning it even. He didn't say anything, but it was there. I mean, I knew."

Gerry finishes the last cupcake, kind of inhales it, takes a sip of tea. "We don't know that he's guilty, Jack. Please."

"Did you say U.S. attorney?" I say.

Gerry says, "They have a summer place up in Litchfield. Apparently she died there sometime during the week before last. Probably toward the weekend. They were taking that week there, both on vacation. I got from the local cops death by strangulation, probably some sort of cloth, no finger marks, much damage to the neck, some other contusions, we'll know more when we get a copy of the coroner's report. Not that we need more, we need less. Anyway, here's the thing, though. Someone wrapped the body in a Persian rug and dumped it in a rest stop Dumpster on the New York State Thruway, outside Albany. The carpet from Connecticut found in New York makes it a federal case, for now anyway; they've stepped in and taken it. Just inside the border for the Southern District, which the New York people love. They smell the newsprint, which will hit big tomorrow, by the way; Jack has called some of his PR people to assist in handling it. The phone calls are going through there. The police are saying Ron drove upstate with the body and put it in the Dumpster himself, and drove back to Manhattan. They think he had the kids with him, you know, piled them in the back and put Mommy in the trunk and drove."

"The kids?" I say. "He took the kids?"

"The man is an animal," Jack says.

Gerry is up at the white box and just as quickly he's back down again, with half a cheese Danish. It's a cliché: for a big man, so quick on his feet. He cuts it neatly into four pieces, picks one up. "The kids are with their grandmother now," he says, chewing. "Diane's mother. We don't know what they know. Apparently, they haven't been questioned at any length yet because the U.S. attorney's having trouble finding a psychologist. All their people are in the fucking Hamptons. I have someone picking them up in an hour, a social-worker friend of mine. We're meeting in her office at ten-thirty."

All I'm thinking is, Gerry, don't ask me to come. That's all I can think.

"There's more," Gerry says.

"Jesus."

"You said it, brother. Apparently, when they brought him in on Sunday afternoon, it turned out he was wearing some unusual items underneath his sports clothes."

"Ladies' things?" I say.

"Yeah, how'd you know?"

"I'd encountered this special side of the man."

"I'm not going to ask because I don't want to know."

"In the back of a Dial Car late one night, a please-touch-me kind of thing. Red panties. I almost killed him."

Jack is looking at me. "The night of Yankee Stadium? Why didn't you tell me?"

"It was easier pretending nothing had happened," I say. "Ron did the same."

"You should have told me," Jack says. "Christ."

"Look, if I'd told you, we would have had two, maybe three long meetings, we would have composed the obscure apologetic letter, he would have been forced to respond, probably fire us, though he didn't want to, because we'd acknowledged that we knew, or, who knows, worse. Who knows the depths of hate. The man was relying on my silence. I gave it to him. Area of privilege. You can call it work product. I think I broke his rib, I mean, what do you want to do about it? 'Dear Ron, This unfortunate incident where one of our associates beat you senseless while you were drunk in the backseat of a Lincoln, let us assure you, et cetera. I think you will acknowledge circumstances were fraught, et cetera, et cetera.' Come on. Everyone was happier, Jack. Especially you. We have to protect the partners, like children, from knowledge they can't assimilate."

"I knew things were happening," Jack said forlornly. "Who knows what he was doing to that woman."

"Best not to dwell," Gerry said. "We have to leave in fifteen minutes to see the children. Every client is entitled to a defense. If we don't give it to him someone else will. Thank god he called us. I'm estimating a million and a half to two if he pleads innocent, which he is giving every sign of doing, so let's pull ourselves together here."

"How did they get him?" I ask no one in particular.

Gerry fills me in. "Two frat boys from SUNY-Albany found the rug at the rest stop, started trying to pull it out of the Dumpster, saw the body, freaked out, went home. Called from there. Body naked, no identifying marks. Didn't match up with anything in missing persons. Meanwhile, when she didn't show up for work and didn't call—she was a fashion editor at *Men's Journal*—the office called her apartment, got him. He said she was still in Connecticut, he thought she had taken holiday time, like the week before. Two weeks she was taking, he'd been certain of it. They said no, one week. It all seemed very odd. They called her in Litchfield, no answer, tried all that day, no answer. That afternoon they called him back. He said he didn't know where she was. Admitted they'd been fighting and parted. They kind of forced him to go up there, look around, he called the police, told them she was missing and so was a carpet and a bunch of other valuables. Jewelry, paintings, electronics. Missing persons matched it up with the upstate report, or vice versa, we're not clear on this. By the end of the week he was a suspect. He called Jack on Saturday morning, and Jack called me. We started making arrangements to surrender him this afternoon but no, that wasn't good enough. Sunday they arrested him. So far no physical evidence as far as we know. They're going over the car with suction filters for fibers and organic material now, establishing the rug, so they may or may not have a case, they're not saying. Presumably it will be big publicity, so they must have something. It will take a while to bring it to trial if they're going on expert evidence like that—it means they'll have to find everyone who ever knew them to get character testimony, testimony about fighting, violence, whatever. The recent divorce motions will come into play."

It occurs to me, listening to Gerry, that we'll have to use the denials that I wrote, little stories I just made up out of my head on vague indications from Ron. That's what we're paid for in a divorce; no one expects it to go to criminal court in a murder trial.

"What about insanity?" Jack says.

"You tell him he's insane," Gerry says. "Will and I will be on hand to peel him off you. Look, everything depends on the children. The maid was off, he didn't go to work, so there isn't anybody yet who can testify when he was in New York and when he wasn't except them. His story is he and Diane fought that Friday, he drove down to New York, and they didn't speak after that. He assumed she was still up at the house. And one more thing," he says. "It was the federal prosecutor who leaked the underwear thing. They really want front page on this. It's going to be a hot one."

Before we go uptown I have time to move a few files out of my office, throw an assignment at Anna that will keep her busy, and read a new e-mail. Ursula is honing her rage and madness, it's like watching a tradesman with his knives.

Subject: autobiographical notes

i am in a struggle with my church. you didn't know that did you mr riordan? you may remember me from your suburban parish, from your school, the one black family, there were catholics on my mother's side, her momma was from louisiana and my grandfather, my mother's father, was a convert; he'd been in the bread lines at st. francis in new york when the depression started, 1930, they'd gotten him then. he told me once, "i went over because of the latin, i liked the sound of it. it was old and it just sounded right—that high mass, all that singing. i met your grandmother there, so i suppose it was the right thing. do you think it was the right thing, sula? (he would hold me.) i met your grandmama and we married there, and we had your momma and your momma had you. wasn't that the right thing?"

no grandpa.

and now? the same white pricks sticking it up my ass and in my mouth, same as what I've got on the street and in my home, the same bullshit, stinking cock dangling in my face. as a woman, you know, officially, i am too soiled to step inside the sanctuary. you'll notice exceptions are made of course, in the U.S. in fact the exception IS the rule, women lectors, women cantors, women eucharistic ministers. but it's not because they want to stand up to the withered saints of rome and insist on reason and justice, oh no—just look around, who's available? who the hell goes to church anyway? these cynical bastards in aftershave and starched white shirts, they stand in robes and look down over their kingdom from the marble pulpits and who do they find looking back up at them but the black maids that wash the night come out of their underwear and the filipino nurses whose gentle hands slide in their catheters when their hearts and livers finally give out and they go to the hospital to die. that's who they're talking to. that and, when they bother to show up, the irish contractors whose shirt collars pinch at the annual diocesan dinner, where his eminence gives a speech.

i was a dancer. short, powerful; i have a certain kind of African body that he liked. this was one of the few places someone built the way I am could get a chance to dance professionally in any kind of serious dance company. before they went under they had state funding, federal funding, city funding, it was the BLACK-O-CENTRICK dance company we used to say. i was with the robin alter company in harlem and he always wanted me in the pieces that involved nakedness and sweat. I was like a horse to him, a body for grinding work; i think he was turned on aesthetically and physically by the thought of me doing something like pulling a boulder on a rope across the stage. the opposite of dance was what he liked and some of us had the bodies just for that. we fucked a few times but it didn't amount to shit because outside the realm of dance and sex he was incapable of being interesting or engaged with another human being. what really matters now is that for a short time, and only professionally, my body was my own, i lived in it and used it with a degree of certainty and comfort. i would never have been a great dancer or even a notable dancer but I could use my body and expose it in ways I could never do otherwise, because actually it makes me sick, it's not like something of mine but more like some disease, some virus that's been passed along that I can't get rid of. sex now is like this; with women. we do not touch each other. we perform acts over distances, watch each other, order each other to do things. implements are used, but only on oneself by oneself. there is a satisfaction to the brutality and distance, like ordering a killing and seeing in the morning papers that it has been carried out and your enemy is dead.

On the street with Gerry and Jack, we're trying to hail a cab, or Jack is, looking prissy and too rich out beyond the curb on Broadway with his French cuffs in the air. Gerry poses like a statue of some dead statesman, leaning on a superfluous cane, and I'm absorbed in watching a Burger King box caught in a building downdraft tumbling around on the sidewalk, making the sound of horse's hooves on a hard road. The imagining of your own death; not the fear of it, which even the lowliest animals experience and we have known forever, but the calm, newsreel imagining of it, the comfortable sound of the announcer's voice—a man was fatally wounded today when a knife-wielding attacker . . . Seventy-nine people were killed, including six crew members, as a McDonnell Douglas DC-10 attempted to land on a strip of highway near the Boston suburb of . . . etc.

Finally, Jack secures a cab. Driving up to the therapist's apartment along the Westside Highway we are in the left lane when another cab cuts us off and our driver veers toward the low retaining wall—and at that moment I think, This is it, we're going over into the oncoming traffic, and I compose a prayer: "Forgive me, Lord, and help my wife and children." I don't give it a thought, just utter it; the cab humps up over the curbstone, grazes the wall with an unpleasant crunch, and then pulls back into the lane, the driver cursing, hitting the steering wheel, then the horn, four long blasts as he guns the engine and peels into the middle lane to take off after the other cab, and I realize I have just prayed, something I haven't done in—how long? Gerry leans forward over the seat.

"Listen," he says to the driver. "Forget it, forget the other guy, okay?"

The driver turns halfway toward Gerry, jitterbugging in his seat, his face a hypervision. "Do you see what he do? Fucking scumbag." He turns back, hits the horn two more times. He hasn't slowed down.

"Yeah, he almost killed us," Gerry says. He is talking slowly and very clearly. "But forget it. An extra ten dollars in it for you, just drive nice and reasonable and get us where we're going. Very important meeting, okay?"

Gradually the cab rattles down to a more normal speed.

Jack looks at Gerry. "Jesus," he whispers. Gerry's facing straight ahead, imperturbable.

"Nothing to worry about," he says.

When we get uptown, Jack goes out one door, streetside, and Gerry and I go out the other. "I heard that little prayer byte as we went up over the curb," Gerry says. Jack is using his cell to instruct the office to have a Dial Car waiting for us for the return trip. No more cabs for Jack for a while.

They are a boy and a girl, quiet and beautifully tended children, blond haired, near-perfect faces subtly marred, smudged, as if someone has swiped at them with an old pencil eraser. The boy is the elder, four-teen, soon to be fifteen, stretched out and thin, going to be tall, and has about his eyes a look of monastic holiness, the suggestion of hallucino-genic temptations and long vigils in dark rooms. He sits in surreal silence. Gerry has begun by asking gentle and not too loaded questions of him, under the assumption that, being the older, and the boy, he will want to lead. "We are here because your dad is in trouble right now, I won't lie to you, I don't like it when people lie to me and I won't lie to you." He ad-justs his grandeur in the small seat. "He is in trouble and it may take some time to work out. We are his friends and we're going to help him." Friar, the boy, looks around the room slowly, a strange place in the series of strange places that the world has become. He says nothing, he gives no encouraging or discouraging sign. He simply isn't there, he's opted out. It is the girl, her name is Susan, who talks, who fills in the widening hole of her brother's silence. A child perceiving an emotional crisis whose bound-aries she cannot see, though she knows they are large and distant. She is seven—a child drawing on the web of learned behavior, navigating a small dinghy of language through the buck and spray of a terrifying confusion.

"Daddy took us for a ride," she says. The sound of simplicity and shame—*these are the facts and something is wrong with them but I don't know what it is.*

"Where did you go?" says Helene. She is the social worker. Since the girl is talking, Helene will take over. Gerry accepts this and with-draws, sits back in his armchair, a mountain of benign attention.

"We didn't go anywhere. We went home before we got there."

I look up and see Friar. He is staring at me with an encompassing indifference.

"Did you go home to the house in Litchfield? In Connecticut, in the country?" Helene asks. "Is that where you went?"

"We went home to New *York,*" Susan says. "Daddy was going to take us to the beach house."

"Who went in the car?" Helene's tone, to my ears, is too sweet-lilting, too far toward this-is-fun-and-we-are-friends. Susan, who is probably used to being talked to this way, responds anyway.

"Daddy and Friar and me," she says.

Friar hasn't moved, his eyes reflecting like two large pools in the center of the room.

"Was your mommy there?"

"No," says Susan. "Mommy stayed in her room. She was hiding again."

"How do you know she was hiding? Did you see her there, in her room?"

"Daddy said we shouldn't bother her, she didn't feel good. That's what he always says when she's hiding."

"Was she still in her room when you got back from your drive?"

"We didn't go back to *Litch*field," Susan says, as if Helene is being silly. "We went back *home*, like I said. To New York."

"Oh," Helene says, glad to be filled in. "And your mommy wasn't there when you got home? She stayed in the house, in her room?"

"Ya," Susan says, nodding.

"And you haven't seen your mommy since then?"

"Ya," Susan says.

"Do you miss her? Sometimes we miss people when we don't see them. Do you miss your mommy?"

"Ya." Susan is nodding all the way through now.

"And you probably miss your daddy too."

"No," she says.

"It's okay to miss people when they're away from you, everyone feels that way sometimes."

Friar gets up, walks through the living room like a priest. He turns toward the kitchen. I follow. I find him in front of the refrigerator, standing before the notes, the shopping list and recipe clippings magneted to the door. Tiny baseball-helmet magnets with the insignias of every team, many not in use. Friar is twirling a St. Louis Cardinals helmet, one finger at the edge of the visor, turning it round and round, looking at nothing.

"Would you like something from the refrigerator?" I ask him. "Something to drink?" He turns his back slightly toward me. I open the door.

"She's got like various kinds of juice here," I say in a chipper voice borrowed from Helene. This is the voice one wants to use, apparently, with deeply wounded children. "Some seltzer, some old flat ginger ale by the looks of it."

"I'd like some juice," he says. His voice is refined, precise, not at all the voice of the teenagers I'm accustomed to hearing on the street. I search out glasses. The cupboards work, at this late date still a sign to me of rare, middle-class prosperity in New York, the doors click open and shut, echoing well-tooled suburban redecorations. Behind the third cabinet door I find the glasses, columns of them—water, highball, cocktail, juice—a rigid army, silver in the light. This kind of cleanliness and order and insensible optimism always unnerves me. We are in the gleaming kitchen of an Upper West Side psychiatric social worker's apartment. The words "good German" come to mind. I pull a bottle from the fridge.

"Papaya?"

"Yeah, sure," he says.

I pour it as if for Henry, a little bit more than half full, hand it to him. He takes it and I want to say, two hands, hold it with two hands.

"My mother's dead," he says, and takes a sip. His eyes are somewhere to the left of me.

"Yes," I say.

"And my father?"

"He's in jail."

"For murdering my mother."

"That's the charge, yes. But there isn't much proof."

He closes his eyes when he drinks, still a child, and after his long sip he clutches the glass in the forgetful way a child will, having no impulse to put it down until it's absolutely finished. He regards me with his white, ghostly face. "And we're going to live at Grandmother's?"

"For now, probably," I say. "Your father might or might not raise bail, it's very high but he might raise it, and then you might go back with him. Or you might not, it's hard to tell what the courts will say if anyone challenges him."

"The other lawyer," he says. "The big one. Who's he?"

"He's in charge of the case. He's your father's lawyer."

"And what about you?"

"I'm your father's lawyer too. I'm helping."

"I'll talk to you," he says flatly.

"Do you want more juice?"

"No," he says. He puts the glass in the sink. He turns to me in an almost rehearsed way, or a way that signifies he has thought about what he is going to say and how he is going to say it. "When we left Connecticut we drove for a long time and then we got home. I slept in the car. So did Susie. That's all I know."

"Did you stop on the way home?" I ask him.

"We stopped once and got sodas and went to the bathroom. Somewhere on the highway. After that we didn't stop."

"You sound pretty sure."

"I am sure."

"Do you remember how long it took, to get home?"

"No. Like I said, I slept for a while. So did Susan."

"Were you with your father the whole time?"

"I don't know. I mean, yes. Where else would I be?"

"I think you know why I'm asking these questions. I'm not the only one who's going to ask you. And if, when the police are asking you questions, for some reason you find yourself alone with one of them, if Gerry or Helene, she's the lady talking to Susan, or if I'm not there, or a social worker or lawyer assigned to you isn't there, since we probably won't be able to represent you and your father at the same time, then you don't answer them, okay? You tell them you want someone there with you when they're asking you questions. Do you understand?"

"Yeah, sure," he said.

"And that's all you remember about that night? Driving home?

Nothing else, no other stops or waking up and wondering where you are and your father getting in the car when he wasn't there before or anything like that?"

"No," he says. He looks at me steadily, his eyes burning, tough, you can see his father's toughness in them and all you can do is hope it ends up aimed from a purer heart, although luck is not with him at the moment.

"I want to be very clear on this," I say. I wonder if I should say what I'm about to say. I am certain if I do he won't misunderstand it.

"I want to be clear on this not because I believe you or don't believe you but because I want to know that this is your story, the one you're going to stick to." It is an evil moment; I'm not telling a lie, just accepting one, sealing his envelope.

"No," he says. "There was nothing like that, no other stops."

"But you were asleep, right?"

"I think I would have woken up," he says steadily. He's not looking at me now and then he is.

"Okay," I say. "If there's something you remember later, you'll tell us, okay? Or have your grandmother tell us. I'm going to give you my card and you keep it with you and if you ever want to call me, anytime, to talk, that's fine. You promise me you'll use it, you'll call me?"

"Sure," he says. He doesn't move. I open the refrigerator and take out the ginger ale, get myself a glass.

"You're going to drink the flat ginger ale?" he says.

"Yeah, I kind of like flat ginger ale, actually. It has to be really cold, but I like it. Kind of like ginger ale juice."

"Yeah, well, it's probably better than all this papaya and mango and shit."

"Exactly."

"Look," he says. I look. "I, if my father gets out, or when my father gets out, you know? I don't want to live with him. And Susie doesn't want to either. It would be better if we, you know, stayed with our grandmother or whatever."

I finish my ginger ale and put my glass in the sink next to his. "That's understandable," I say. "I'll see what I can do. A lot of it isn't in my hands, do you know what I mean?"

He nods.

"But I'll do my best, okay?"

He nods again.

"Okay," I say. I put out my arm, touch him on the shoulder, he ambles out the kitchen door before me, teen in untied hiking boots and baggy pants, wary and slow. Gerry takes us in as we come back into the living room with an almost imperceptible look. I sit down and watch Gerry; he appears to me as he is—a good man, a decent man with a number of neurotic tendencies who lives in lower Westchester. He has three children. In all likelihood he loves them, he loves his wife, in whatever fashion he can muster. He will work diligently now to free a man who probably murdered his wife and is a danger to his children; Gerry will do this not for money, though the money certainly pleases him, as it makes a number of things around the firm easier, it makes for pleasantness at the end of the year; nor for glory, because no lawyer has glory, at best a lawyer can be notorious, and far more often he is merely invisible; but because he believes that the state cannot imprison or extract compensation or in any other way impinge on the life or the assets of its citizens without adequate proof of liability or wrongdoing, the definitions of which wrongdoing and the tests of which proof have long been established in the rule of law. What happens outside the limits of the law is beyond his control. It belongs in the amorphous world of good and evil; and society's capacity for dealing with those things, which he is thoughtful enough to know is not-very-well, he leaves to moralists, philosophers, and priests . . . Perhaps he goes to church and prays for a better world—his wife and daughter and two sons kneeling in a row beside him, a small battalion in a large fight. If it were his job to shore those fragments against our ruin I'm sure he would turn in a sound and intelligent if ultimately futile performance; but that's no way to support a wife and three kids in Pelham Manor.

I think: That's his story. What's mine?

subject: ineluctable modalities of the violent

mr riordan: this is how violence begins, in fantasy and fever. we'll refer to her in the more neutral third person. she cannot get this man out of her head. not like when she was a young girl with crushes, not like that at all, this is altogether a darker and more nauseating thing. but it energizes in that way; she is not depressed, she is in fact as clear and as sharp as she remembers being in a long time, ready to go off her meds as they say. so she drives to new jersey, just takes her plastic and rents a car and drives herself to mall land. out there, they have whole towns that are just roads and malls. it's been so long since she's driven a car she's dangerous but she makes it, a couple of near misses, a couple of slanting-across-the-highway moves to get to the exit, and by the way have you ever noticed how bad the road signs are in new york? try finding your way onto or off the cross bronx expressway sometime.

so the thing is, she's trying to buy a gun out there. she drives around for a while looking for a sporting goods shop in the malls, it's one big mall down route 17 but what could she see driving like that you can't watch the signs and the road at the same time and every right turn promises ten stores. after an hour she comes to her senses, it's like she's been in a dream, waking nauseated, and she stops and gets a coffee and uses the yellow pages and her maps to find what she's looking for.

but get this, there are all these complications. permits and whatnot. the man at the store is nice, explains everything to her but it sounds like it's going to take a long time.

that's for handguns. for a .22 rifle, no problem, he tells her. a small hunting rifle. he can fit it out with a little scope. it costs her $572 by the time it's over, he's taken her to the cleaners on a .22 rifle she doesn't need and that you would use to kill, like, squirrels, but she has been in a fever, an obsession, and just having the gun tied in a box on the front seat driving back makes her feel electric, makes her feel charged up, turned on. she's the hottest she's been sexually for a long time, a long long time. wetness, blood rushes, shivers. The long barrel, the smell of sulfur, iron, and oil.

now mr riordan the thing about a gun is, once you got it you want to shoot it.

she doesn't know shit about guns. she doesn't know shit about getting lessons with guns. she looks up gun clubs in the yellow pages, let your fingers do the walking through the yellow pages when you have, you know, an urge toward homicide.

if she dares to tell the truth she will admit that she has sat now in her apartment on the windowsill aiming the rifle down at the street, using the scope like a looking glass. how odd all the people look through the scope of a rifle. puts a wrinkle on the voyeuristic side of it, the side of it that is watching people who don't know anyone is watching. don't know that there's no fucking rifle pointed at them neither. this does for voyeurism what salt does for stew.

even with a little training, she realizes, she could be popping people off. could oswald have hit kennedy from a window with a .22? on a lucky day, sure.

okay, a rifle's a rifle, nice to have. she cleans it as the salesman showed her. cleaning your gun. kind of touching, making contact in ritual with all those fathers and sons through the years, dogs before hearths, cleaning rifles together, training their dogs, oiling their boots, letting the soft-jawed labs and retrievers slobber on their hands. killing negroes from time to time, as the need arises. all the leather and cordite and dickery of manhood.

with the gun in the house she has spent some time considering the idea of the Fall, the thing that happened—no, the something humanity did, a choice that now separates us from our creator. the Fall ... something falls, drops, cracks, gets damaged in some irrevocable way, a moment of shock and woe. she can feel it in herself and others, something bent, misshapen.

the gun has unmistakable smells, plus the shaft all oily in your hands et cetera long and hard et cetera et cetera but there's no reason to beat the metaphor to death. to finish the thought: having the gun and not shooting it remains for her a kind of sexual itch, like being consciously horny all the time.

she joins the local gun club. goes to the range. everyone else has a handgun.

shooting, she thinks, one of those profoundly conventional moments of understanding, is like fucking and getting fucked, power boom power boom, piercing the (notice, black) shadow man of the paper target and getting pounded across the shoulder boom boom boom at the same time.

the gun mags: a new, rangy pornography. she wants a handgun. a sleek nine. she lies on her bed with no clothes on and runs the, .22's cold barrel down across her body. little circle patterns on her nipples. she masturbates and comes three times.

we live in a world dominated by fear, mr riordan. fear is the broken part, the bent pin in humanity, the part that repeatedly, over and over and over, across the generations, makes us malfunction.

When I get home Ellie has Sam in a pouch on her chest as she works in the kitchen. He is mildly butting her with his head and wriggling.

"This kid is driving me crazy," she says.

"Why don't you feed him?" I say.

"I just fed him. Before that, I just fed him. All day I've either just fed him or I'm feeding him. I'm going to lose it."

"That's what you said this morning," I say. "He's going through a growth spurt."

"What about this morning?"

"You said, 'I feel like walking out of here,'" I say.

"That's the way I felt."

"And the other night, you said, 'I'm beginning to resent this boy,'" I say.

Ellie works at the stove, steam rising. She says nothing. For some reason, I am furious, looking at her. I am furious at what seems to me a failure of heroism on her part; I pictured one of these divinely loving and competent mothers who take care of everything and have the martini ready for father when he comes home from his long day at the office. The sweat and grease and un-picked-up apartment and lady with the maddened, postpartum eyes I did not picture.

"Aren't these the warning signs?" I say. And I know that part of me is still seeing, or really, feeling, the iron doors and sliding prison gates. Bang, clang, the infernal residence hall. I'm a blind man, I'm on something, only it doesn't have a chemical name. It's too late, I can't stop myself. The anger feels too good, too sweet and powerful after another powerless day. Do unto others: I say, "Isn't this the point where I intervene or fail to intervene? Say or fail to say something like, 'Honey, maybe you should see someone, get some help'?"

"Get some help!" Ellie screams. She throws the wooden spoon she is cooking with; it hits the wall and cracks and falls and sauce goes flying. "Why don't you *give* me some fucking help!"

"I'm just worried it will get to the point, you know, like where you're saying, 'Will, honey, I had the oddest feeling today when I had Sam in the bathtub.'"

"I'm going to kill you," Ellie says. She says it very loudly, and she picks up a fork from the stove. In the living room, Henry, hearing us, begins to cry. Ellie makes a stab at me with the fork, I sidestep her and she grazes my arm.

"I'm sorry," I say.

"You're not sorry, you son of a bitch, I hate you. Get out. I hate you." The fork comes again, I turn away from it, it jabs me in the shoulder.

"Ellie—" I say.

"Get out of here. I mean it. Get out." Her eyes are red, her hair rising around the corona of her raging face. Sam's head in the pouch is kind of flopping from side to side as Ellie prances. Rumpelstiltskin at the fire.

"Watch the baby!" I say.

"Fuck you! Just fuck you!" Here comes the fork again. I go to grab it as she stabs, and, seeing me go for it, she changes its direction, brings it up a bit and stabs harder—it glances off my hand, I go for her arm at the shoulder, but too late, the fork punctures my cheek. I actually hear this kind of grisly *pop!* sound as the skin breaks. I shout, Sam startles and cries, pain rises up through my face, my eyes water. Then Henry is at the kitchen door, wailing. Blood runs off my jawbone onto my suit jacket.

"I told you to get out," Ellie says.

"It's all right," I say to Henry.

"It is *not* all right," Ellie says. "Don't lie to him. Daddy is bleeding because Mommy stabbed him. Tell him. And tell him you're leaving. Then leave."

I go into the bathroom, stand before the mirror. Huffing, puffing, pasty-faced white man with tie and blood, turn of the millennium. From the front of the apartment, the sound of the two children crying, and a spatula scraping the iron pan. I dab at my cheek with a washcloth, clean the surface of the wound. Two nasty purple wounds, blood congealing on stubbly skin. I drench the shoulder of the suit in cold water, mop at it with the cloth. My face, I notice, is a yellowish color, like a blanched almond.

At the hospital, a Latina nurse takes names. I hand her my insurance card, up to date, a clean, sharp-edged plastic ID. A few questions—address, phone, next of kin. The man after me, a tall slender black fellow wrapped in a hundred blankets, has a bad cough. He doesn't have a Medicaid card, no ID of any kind. I stand and listen to the tale. One of those long poverty/bureaucracy stories. "I had it at the men's shelter but a guy stole it, he stole it. I told the social worker but she said it would take three weeks for them to get me a new one, and when I went back she wasn't there no more so I couldn't get it, they didn't have no record. The guy stole it. Just stole it. And no record . . ." The nurse keeps asking him for more information, which is absurd, he hardly knows his name. She sits stolid behind the desk, young, mildly attractive, utterly without imagination. "Well, do you know the number? The nine-digit number that was on the card?"

She asks him four times, in all: "Do you know the number that was on the card?" Mute, he stands before her, his only power his refusal to go away. I look for a seat.

A stab wound can be a semi-high priority but of course I don't tell them I've been stabbed, I tell them I've had an accident. This means a three- to four-hour wait. Why did she have to stab me on a hot summer night? Why not on a Tuesday or a Wednesday in winter, on Thanksgiving, on some form of slow-news day when the wild swellings of urban violence and disease are stilled? There's a pigeon in the room, resting on one of the floodlights attached to the upper wall. Occasionally he moves, his wings beat the air with the sound of paper bags shifting in a back seat, to the amusement of the nurse and cop at the front desk, who look as if they're trying to get something going: the frisson of stupid sex in the face of disaster, illness, and death. The pigeon swoops low, people slide and dip in their seats, somebody shouts. This nurse and the cop, they will fuck someday. I can see it, the cop's white, thick legs and broad, lardy back hovering over her, her cries as he pounds away. *I Tiresius have foresuffered all.* They might consider marrying, neither predicting the depths of resentment each will produce for the other to swim in. The room is crowded with hopeless men slumped on blue plastic chairs, women with children, a scabrous old blind woman with her foot wrapped in newspaper. After a while, an hour and a half or so, I decide to call Ellie. There's no one else to call. I have my cell phone, and step into the foyer, where I hope I can hear my name called if I should get so lucky.

"I'm at the emergency room," I tell her.

"Good," she says. "Stay there."

"The fork you were using, it was stainless steel, right? I mean, I won't need a tetanus shot?"

She doesn't say anything.

"Ellie, look . . . ," I begin. Then I stop. I don't know what I want her to look at. Her phone silence is a palpable challenge. I have nothing to come up with.

"I don't know what to tell you," I say. "I just don't have anything to offer. I have no genuine apology or explanation. I'm working on these cases at work that are, um, bleak. Life isn't what it might be. What can I say? I look at my life and all I see is a black-and-white TV screen with my activities playing across it. The reception's bad and the sound is off. That's the way I feel."

More silence.

"Are the kids in bed?" I ask.

"What do you care?" she says. "Do you know when they go to bed, when they get up, when they eat, when they go to the bathroom? You're exempt, you're just a paying guest, you don't have to know."

"I'd like to know," I say. At that moment I mean it: I can picture a kind of life—participatory, committed, engaged. A life of honor, accomplishment, worth. Minute by minute, heart whole, soul vulnerable and alive. The feeling of flesh and blood raised to a state of graceful consciousness. To love and be loved. Flowing in the stream of human affection. There is beauty in these notions, I am aware that there is beauty but I am not moved by it. I am not moved by much but the face of the white, thick-chinned policeman, the nurse, Hispanic, with a gap between her teeth, nice body, the kind of overlarge breasts a policeman would like, the policeman speaking over his radio, then turning to the nurse, saying, Multiple stab, on the way. You gonna tell them? And she says, I'll tell them when they get here, nobody does nothing till then anyway.

The doctor is a tall round Jamaican man, light brown with a hint of freckles across his nose and under his eyes. The lower half of his face is all beard.

"What happened?" he says, examining the wound.

"A four-pronged domestic object stabbed me in the cheek," I say. "Two prongs penetrated the skin. I suspect contusions must be visible by now where the other two prongs traumatized the epiderm or whatever it is you'd call it. My cheek."

"A fork?"

"Correct."

"How did this fork manage to make its way into your cheek?" he says, turning for cotton, disinfectant.

"It was clenched in a fist and projected at the end of a driving arm," I say.

"Whose arm was that?"

"A loved one's."

"Almost goes without saying," he says. He begins cleaning with a sharp antiseptic. "The wounds are punctured and ripped," he says, working. "And really very small. We won't be able to stitch them." His eyes and hands as he speaks are directed at my cheek, so it feels as if he is talking directly to the small holes there and not to me.

"Good," I say. "I don't like stitches."

"Well, not good if you like your face. You'll probably have a couple of small scars. We can give you consultation on plastic surgery if you like."

"That's okay," I say.

He opens two small butterfly bandages in turn and carrefully places them over the two wounds. "Roll up your sleeve," he says. He opens a package and takes out a hypodermic.

"What's that?" I say.

"Tetanus," he says. "Unless you've had one recently."

"No, but, uh, the fork was stainless. I thought I wouldn't need tetanus."

"Better to be safe than sorry," he says. "That way we minimize the risk of, for instance, death." He straightens my arm, gives it a wipe with alcohol, and stabs. "Won't hurt," he says.

When he's done I stand and put on my jacket.

"That suit has had it," he says, looking at it sadly. "Blood never comes out. I happen to know the subject. This isn't a police matter, I take it? Need to have it for the records if it is."

"No," I say. "Not a police matter."

"Well," he says. "I ain't gonna ask you what you did."

"I talked smart," I say. "And mean."

He nods, writes something on a clipboard. "That will often lead to something hitting you in the face," he says. "Yes, indeed. None of my three wives has really been good about that. Now, I'm giving you a prescription for a topical antibiotic. Watch for infection; keep it clean, use the cream, and if it swells, throbs, turns bright red, or becomes unreasonably painful, use the cream. If that doesn't work, come back in." He shakes my hand.

When I get home, the door is double-locked and the chain is on. I rap on it, peering into the crack. All I can see is a section of the hall; deeper in the apartment, I can hear Ellie moving. She comes into the kitchen, puts something in the sink, a bowl it sounds like, or a glass, with a spoon in it. I rap some more. "Ellie," I say, trying to project my voice without making it loud; the kids' room is just inside the door and I don't want to wake them. She leaves the kitchen and goes back into the dining room or still farther into the living room—I can't tell where she is now. "Ellie!" I say louder, rapping harder. I try the bell, which almost never works, manipulating the button inside its little cup holder, kind of working it around gently, until finally it gives off a cranky buzz. I keep it going. Finally I see her come out of the kitchen door and into the hallway.

Her eyes through the ribbon of open door are glinty and cold; they frighten me. We stare at each other for a moment and then the door closes: a moment hangs: will she lock me out again or unleash the chain? She unleashes the chain. The door swings open.

"Thank you," I say.

She turns and walks into the kitchen, saying nothing.

In the kitchen, in the corner across from the stove, we have a small round marble table with cast-iron legs, the kind of table you'd see at a French café, or so I believed when I bought it, the first year we were married. It had been our only table for a while in the apartment on Claremont Avenue, we put it in front of the window in the living room, looking out at the back of Barnard College. We sat there in the mornings drinking iced coffee and eating walnut bread Ellie had baked. To me these were days of unparalleled romance, days when we were unassailably happy together, but I realize Ellie might have different thoughts about them, having had to fit them into a continuum leading to her present state of mind, the emotional, gull-swiped landfill that our marriage has been for her. She sits at the table, in a blue cotton nightgown, watching me.

"Would you like some tea?" I say. "I'm making tea."

She shrugs. I put the kettle on to boil, open the can of tea, which I will spoon from the tin to the pot after scalding it. When I'm done arranging things, the white cups and white saucers, when everything's ready but the water hasn't boiled yet, I just stand there, my back to her, not wanting to turn around, not wanting to speak again into the muffling pad of her silence. Everything I have to say is dishonest and small, and she knows this and will make sure I know she knows it, such are the webbed communications of marriage, and she will do this because she is beyond cooperating now with the small lies that have recently made our conversations possible.

"You should move out," she says, my back still turned to her. "Tonight. I don't think you should stay here anymore. If you stay I have to go and I think you'll agree it's better the other way around."

Her voice is quiet and calm. This is grief, I think, that sound is grief. I feel as if I'm participating in that documentary film again, *My Own Life*. An award winner. Berlin Film Festival. We're now in the divorce segment. Camera will track me as I go to the phone, call a hotel, while I'm on the phone the kettle will boil and I'll cup my hand over the mouthpiece and call out, "Ellie, sorry, could you turn off the kettle for me?" and then say into the phone, "Sorry, go ahead—uhm, American Express. Hold on." I take out my wallet, read from the card: "That's 3710. 0529. 728. 10008. Right. Uh-huh. Expiration January 03. Okay, thanks." And then, this is the part so many people who see this film will remember: I make myself and Ellie each a cup of tea (Ellie is in the bedroom now, I take it in there), then come out again, pick up my cup, and go to the computer, where I sit down and write out a short document. I print it, print it again, and take the two pages to the bedroom.

"What is this?" Ellie says when I hand her one. She's sitting on the edge of the bed. Staring out into the night.

"It's a preliminary agreement of separation," I say. "Nonprejudicial. Won't affect the final agreement, that means. It's so that we have an agreement that I can see the kids two nights and a weekend day, and that I'll pay the bills and provide cash for living expenses until we have a final agreement." If I were her lawyer, I wouldn't let her sign such a thing, but she doesn't have a lawyer. She hasn't thought that far ahead.

"Wouldn't spoken words have done just as well?" she says, looking up at me.

"No," I say.

She reads it, gets to the bottom, her eyes go back, she reads it a second time. Then she lets it fall to her lap, and looks again out the window, a framed black space in the room.

I go to get my bag, put on a lightweight sports jacket. I almost say, Ellie, will you take this suit to the cleaners for me and see if they can get the blood out? but I catch myself. I roll it up, open the bag and stuff it in; I'll have to take it to the cleaners myself now, a fact which, because it is utterly symbolic, seems more sad to me at that moment than the dissolution of my marriage, the disappearance of my commitments and my decency, or the orphaning of my children.

"Are you going to sign?" I say, coming back into the bedroom. My bag and jacket are by the door.

"Sign?" Ellie says.

"The agreement," I say. "If I'm going I want to get going soon. It's late, I'm tired."

"Why should I sign this?" she says, looking at me. Her eyes are red-rimmed, blazing.

"Because if you don't, I won't go."

She stares a moment. "Then I'll sign," she says. "I'll sign anything to get you out, out. Go. Just go." She jumps up, takes a pen off my bureau, scratches her name across the bottom and sails the paper toward me.

"One more copy," I say, passing along the second sheet. She signs this one and flings it, a little less forcefully. I take it, align it with the first, and sign them both and fold them into thirds, handing her the one, pocketing the other.

"Okay," I say then. "I'll be back at some point, I guess, to pick up the rest of my things." I stand there; she has turned and gone again to the window, her back to me. The cameras are still rolling. They never stop. Ellie says nothing. I wait a time calculated to be decent, to give her a chance to speak, but she doesn't, and I leave her.

[7]

The usual evasions work and they don't work. When I was little, a boy of the Irish-American working classes in polo shirt and shorts, dragging some kind of lid of a can, I think—I think it was a late-summer day, a warm day, but nearing evening, in the cooling time after supper when the light turned thin—I chased a wounded sparrow into a corner where two walls met, the space between the back wall and a big incinerator chimney, behind the garden apartments near where I lived, and having chased the bird there, I killed it. I didn't mean to but I did; the bird couldn't fly, it was injured somehow, which was exactly what drew my curiosity, what made the bird available to me; it tried to hop and hobble away, but I wanted to see it, control it even; I may have had some idea of picking it up. I cornered it on this little hill, a mound, really, that sloped up into the corner where the walls met, and when the thing tried to get away I put my foot out to block it and stepped on it by mistake. I was wearing soft-bottomed moccasins I'd bought when we'd been on vacation in Maine; I could feel the contours of the bird's body through the leather, soft and round: I felt the life leaving it. Somewhere my parents were waiting in their separate rooms, all that death. I lifted my foot. I was horrified, the bird lay there, obscene, brown and gray and black feathers, lifeless, ratty, coal button of an eye shining up blankly at the sky, a convex reflection of a world it could no longer see. The bird's body looked germ-ridden and terribly dead. I wanted it to stir—as if it were playing at death—but I couldn't bring myself to reach down and touch it (and now I'm thinking of my teacher, the young nun, I loved her but I've forgotten her name, she left in the middle of the year; and the eggs, with the blood-spotted yolks, fertilized, although I'm not sure I understood what that meant besides that they might be born; the rooster fertilized them? How did it do that? We didn't ask, we would not ask; perhaps one of the girls asked, privately, but we would not . . .), so I nudged it, the still bird-body, with my foot, I bumped it an inch or two away from me, *bump bump*. It was so clearly dead, and a moment before had been living. The universe shifted in a sharp, painful, immediate way, and I was aware of its transformation, of God's presence there to escort this small soul out of the world of the living and usher mine into a new order of guilt. I have never forgotten this.

I stay in a hotel for two days, then take a room in a weekly rental studio, suitably squalid, on West End Avenue, in a euphemistically named "hotel," so called, I guess, because there's a guy in an office in the lobby and a cleaning lady twice a week. It is actually not that cheap and not that squalid, but it has about it the air of a place no one would permanently live in, a lack of certain structural and nonstructural components that leaves it open to depressing interpretations. The bed is not mine, the furnishings not mine, nor are they of a type anyone I know would purchase. The television is bolted to its stand and the stand is bolted to the floor. Several other pieces of furniture are similarly battened down. This is my place until I can find something, a one-bedroom on the West Side. Near home. For the kids, I tell myself.

Just after lunch on my second day away a letter arrives at the office from Ellie. Hand-delivered by some kind of messenger.

> Dear Ex-husband,
>
> Well, since you haven't called me I don't know where you are but I presume you are at least still working. You'd better be. We are already happier here without you. When are you coming to take away your things? It would be best to arrange this

in advance so we can *not* be here. Think about Saturday. Think also when you will want to visit Henry and Sam. For now I think you should visit here, take them out if you want, and I'll go elsewhere. There are plenty of movies I'd like to see.

No signature. Attached is a separate page, which is a typescript, Ellie must have taken it down as he spoke it, of what I recognize to be a set of Henry's "monster stories," tales from the ongoing adventures of a group of characters he has made up.

> There was a crocus who lived on a crooked. And then a woof-ff-ff turned into a hunter. And then another woof turned into a hunter. And then another woof and another woof and another woof—a lot of woofs—
>
> This is a *big* story about woofs turning into hunters.
>
> Here is a story about Peeney Piney.
>
> Peeney Piney had sharp teeth. Peeney Piney ate all the cows up.
>
> Himbong has sharp teeth. He went to Spain. The bad cows were scared of Daddy who got mad and ate up Himbong. And the cows were mad at Stromboli. They *were* mad. Daddy ran away.
>
> Peeney Piney is hiding Mommy in Spain.
>
> Real monsters wear hats.
>
> Cookie monster came into a box and ate all the cookies from the bus floor. Yucky yucky.

Scrawled across the bottom of this, some kind of orange marker, Ellie's handwriting: "Yucky yucky to you. Yucky yucky yucky."

*   *   *

Ron Adamson: the man, the wife, the violence. For the million and a half he will be spending on us we are expected to arrive at the Metropolitan Correction Center in groups of two or three with some frequency. On this day, in a wide-body Dial Car, it is Gerry, Jack, and I, grim faced across town, snaking through the streets of lower Manhattan. Downtown at midday you feel trapped deep in the plumbing of the city. MCC, wedged between the courts and Chinatown, vast and sterile to an almost lethal degree. A tower of glossy cream paint protected by wire and listlessness. Gate upon gate, door upon door, empty-faced and inefficient personnel move us along, glancing in boredom at us with their blank reptile eyes.

Inside, we wait in a greenish room lined with boaty plastic seats, aluminum legged. Three men, silent, briefcases open on their laps. Finally a steroid-enhanced guard with hair epoxied almost straight up and back, Bensonhurst style, escorts us to the gray cell room where we've been before, where prisoners meet with counsel.

It's a pro forma meeting when it happens. Our whole strategy at this point is to stand by the not guilty plea, of course, use the fact that Ron is in jail to force a trial date, and gamble that the U.S. attorney has fucked up big time, and doesn't have enough evidence. This is not as irrational as it sounds because there is no indication yet, in any of the documents we are receiving about depositions and witnesses, that they have anything we don't know about. We believe they are stalling for time, waiting for something to come along. We are preparing a challenge of federal jurisdiction but will surely not prevail. Nor are we that interested in prevailing, because it only reopens the case to the locals. We want a trial and we want it fast. This is Ron's strategy for staying in jail. After our retainer has been paid he will not have the liquid capital, he claims, to make the $10-million bail, which, given his overseas resources and contacts, no bondsman will touch. We have filed a motion for reduction of bail but, again, don't hope to succeed. With a defendant sitting in jail there is a great deal more pressure on the judge to move things along.

Ron enters through the prisoner doorway, looking hip-hop in the prison gear, like a teenager getting ready to go to Mickey D's, except even now, in his middle to late forties, he has not lost the air of utter uncoolness he must have brandished in his youth, as one of the wire-rimmed-glasses-achiever types. The face is grim, heavy lipped, resentful. He is not for the most part a casual-clothes kind of guy, and this shows in his face, where, it strikes me, he has always looked like a prisoner.

He sits down. "They've got me in here with some of the biggest drug guys going," he says by way of hello. "Big, big guys, Metina, Abuenos, Tiron. Have you heard of any of these guys? Apparently, they're celebrities down in fucking Guatemala or wherever the fuck they come from. Who brought me some cigarettes?"

"That's me, Ron," I say. I take two cartons of Newports out of my briefcase and slide them across the table. He puts them in his lap.

"What happened to your fucking face?" he says.

"I fell and cut it." I say.

"Looks more sordid than that," he says.

"You have a great eye for the sordid, Ron," I say.

Gerry, cutting me off, says, "Ron, we've just filed two motions, which we discussed with you on Monday, one challenging federal jurisdiction claimed in this case, there being little direct evidence the body was killed in Connecticut and then moved from Connecticut to New York. We have also filed a motion requesting reduction of bail to two point five million dollars, based on your current liquidity, and on the fact that you have children and a good deal of property and financial interests locally and would be unlikely to flee." Gerry passes copies of both documents across to Ron, who takes them, lifting up their pages lightly, and glances through them.

"Mental and physical suffering, uh-huh, children in need of reassurance as well as day-to-day management of care, uh-huh, mmmm, mmmm, mmmm." He looks up.

"I have to tell you that we don't have high expectations from either of these things," Gerry says. His voice, I notice, like those of many fat men, grows ever more rich and gurgly, like grease going *glub glub* in a deep-fat fryer. Every once in a while he coughs up the deep juices. "Federal judges very rarely decide they don't have jurisdiction. Ahhhuu-umph. Plus, the carpet is a rather solid suggestion, if not direct evidence, of the movement of the body. As for the bail request, the court is likely to suggest liquidation of assets to meet bail. We tried to be discouraging about that possibility, as you'll see on page three of the motion, but there is room within the financial statement for, uhm, other interpretations. That pretty much brings you up-to-date. Jack, do you have anything?"

"Well, Ron," Jack says. "We've hired a private investigator."

I sit up at that. It's the first I've heard of it.

"The reason being," Jack says, "that we want to be sure—"

"I bet you know a lot of good private investigators, Jack, in your line of work."

"Right," Jack says. "In any case, we want to be on top of whatever new evidence or theories might emerge from the FBI investigation. This guy is very good, very up-to-date on the new technologies, he was a district agent in southern California for the FBI for a number of years, so we feel it's a good move."

"Costs a bundle," Ron says.

"He's not cheap, no," Jack says.

"Are you billing at a profit?"

Jack puts up his hands. "Not at all. We'll pay his invoiced expenses and fees and pass along copies of those to you. You'll be completely informed along the way of what's going on."

"Suppose he finds something, Jack?" Ron says. "Have you thought about that? That noggin of yours is going to be bursting with conflicting principles, like sodium in a toilet bowl." Ron throws up his hands. "*Boom!*"

"Ha ha," Jack says.

"Someone I know did that in high school," I say. "During the Regents exams, to create a little confusion. There was so much water it came bursting out under the bathroom doors and covered the floors over the whole hall. Sodium in the toilet, I mean."

Gerry just stares at me, then looks slowly around the table. "Well, do we have anything else?" he says. "I hope everything is going as well as can be expected in here, Ron. If there are any problems please let us know."

"Yeah," Ron says. "Like when Tyrone wants me to be his girlfriend, right, I should call you up?" He gives me a smile. "And, hey, cigarette boy," he says to me. "Next time Newport hard box, okay? These are soft pack, and soft pack tend to get crushed around here. You get twenty cents more on a trade for the hard packs than the soft. Okay?"

"Sure, Ron," I say.

"Gentlemen," Ron says, rising. "Always nice to see you. Visitors to break the routine. Take good care."

subject: ineluctable modalities of v., 2

in jersey, the nice man again, the nice helpful firearms supplier, the cheerful checkout clerk of death. she fills out all the paperwork, the id's, the long forms with many questions. he tells her she will qualify, no doubt about it. her father, bless his heart, her father approves of this; he would. he's taking care of the new york city permit, which is a show-cause deal where you gotta prove you *need* a handgun as if anyone actually needs a fucking handgun for chrissakes, but daddy has connections and is taking care of all that, the new york permit, the reasons she needs one. the true reason: she really really really wants to kill someone. a particular person, though if he can't be found she can picture circumstances, a certain state of mind that she has come close to reaching in the past, in which an anonymous substitute would do. reason: applicant seeks a hot sliding proximity to death and destruction. she writes not that, of course, but, as per daddy's lawyers' instructions, of the crime against her, the continued threats (she says), her feeling of vulnerability as a known person of wealth (she says), her father being a public figure (she says). this amuses her, that her riches can be construed to make her appear vulnerable. in fact it is when you are poor that your ass is hanging out there, that your chances of getting shot to death are quite high; but it is being rich that gets you the right to own a firearm because someone might try to take away your shit, perhaps even PUNISH you for the privileges of your life, and a rational society cannot allow that to happen. no fucking way.

ten days later she has her gun. she spins out a little bit in her mind on fucking the salesman who is a well-built latino with a nice face and a bad haircut, and who she imagines has a large cock and balls that she will squeeze like the grip of a pistol to make him go off. bang.

at the range, the nine is a more imaginative weapon. your typical urban situation— this is how the gun people talk, the euphemism being necessary because what they really mean is "when you need to kill a hostile negro"—makes it the weapon of choice and vastly more reliable than a rifle. in bed, it is vastly easier and more plea-surable to manipulate. she uses the gun, the tip—no, mr riordan, she doesn't keep it loaded, the imagination has to do SOME of the work, please—then drops it and it lies between her legs pressed a little against her ass and she switches to the vibrator, which is structured along similar lines but with a more specific attachment. she gets the big arc as she always thinks of it, like the lightning arcs jumping from pole to pole in those bride of frankenstein movies, bolts of electricity zap zap zapping across five feet of open air, wisps of burnt ozone. it goes dark, then light, then blood—explosions in red behind her eyes. she can say this: she understands herself in a wordless kind of way, and maybe god is good because slowly she is losing her sense of horror at the knowledge, but—how much of it can ever be communicated to someone else, mr riordan? why is the world organized in such inhuman ways, mr riordan? you are among the organizers so explain it to me. is speech possible? mr riordan?

Right now, with the occasional cigarette, I'm big on Coke, cookies, M&M's—I play my blood sugar like an old pipe organ in daylong con-trapuntos of jagged highs and deep, devotional lows. I see God in his mercy and anger—blood-pressure visions.

"You're putting on weight," David says later in the week when I en-ter his office. He hasn't looked up before saying it.

"But with my large frame I carry it well," I say.

"Wrong," David says. "Incorrect response." I sit, flick a white thread off my trouser cuff.

"Twelve-thirty Mass," David says. He looks up. "You coming?"

"I don't think so."

He makes a little gesture with his head, dropping the point, and goes back to his chart.

"Gerry wants you into the Adamson case," I tell David. "Did he speak with you?"

David picks up a thick textbook from his desk, brandishes it. *Collection and Analysis of Dispersed Organic Fibers and Materials.* "If they get him, it's going to be on the carpet," David says. "They can't do much with hair, epidermal material, which would be there from common use anyway. Of course, there could be blood but I doubt it, I mean she was strangled, right?"

"Right," I say.

"But the carpet is very interesting, it's a real oriental of course, and very old, an antique, quite valuable. Azeri, not Persian. I've only seen the photos, but I'll be getting a look at it on Friday, making a little visit to the exhibit chambers. Extraordinary he or any other killer would have disposed of her in it, you could even make a case that only a rich man would casually throw it away. Or someone totally ignorant, I suppose. In any case the slight bloodstaining from contusions indicates that she most likely fell right there and the killer rolled her up in it without giving much thought to its value. It's hard to contend a house thief would do that."

"We don't have to contend anything," I say. "We only have to convince the jury that the government hasn't proved its case."

"Right," David says. "The materials are very particular, very easy to match. Most likely it was delivered after purchase, and cleaned in place. There would be records. Absolutely no reasonable explanation for finding fibers in the trunk."

"One can be thought up," I say.

"Yeah, lame ones that wouldn't convince anybody. But here's the thing. There are remarkably few ways of collecting and retrieving that kind of material. If he cleaned the trunk, and he would have, then anything that's left would be absolutely organic, tiny. Basically, if they try sucking it up into a filter they have to soak the filter and break it down, then particularize the elements that aren't the filter. This is very iffy work on a sample as small as what we're talking about when the material is organic. If it weren't organic, if it were mineral fiber or metal or something very stable, everything else could be baked or burned away and the remnants examined through an electron microscope or something—that would be doable. But with organic it's much more hit-and-miss."

Chin is in his element here. There is data, specialization, a mind running up small creeks of ephemera, he's deep in the woods. Everyone wants to be special.

A call comes in on Friday morning. I know it's a special call because Anna gets up and comes into my office to tell me about it. "It's someone who wants to talk to you about the Adamson case," she says. "He won't give his name. Says it's very important, you know, and he has a ratty little voice like in one of those forties detective movies."

I look at her. "Maybe he's calling from the booth near the soda fountain at his local drugstore," I say.

"Or the pool hall," Anna says.

I pick up the phone.

"William Riordan," I say professionally. It's like using your name as a depersonalizing wall, a zone in which you can't be touched.

"Mr. Riordan, uh, I'm calling about the murder."

"About what murder?"

"How many you got?"

"I don't *got* any. Who is this?"

"Look, for obvious reasons I can't tell you my name."

"Okay, well, how about the reason for this call? I'm very busy."

"I know, I know, you're a busy man. I called a couple of times and you weren't in so I didn't leave a message. Listen, it's about the guy who they got on charges of killing his wife, you're defending this guy?"

"The Adamson case?"

"Right, the guy who killed his wife."

"That hasn't been proved."

"Right, whatever. Listen, the thing is, I have some evidence you should know about. I saw his picture in the paper, and I'm pretty sure, hell, I know, it's the same guy I saw one night off a Hundred and Twenty-fifth Street near the river shampooing out his car trunk. I remembered it because a lot of people wash their cars over there but I never seen anybody, you know, with a Jaguar like that over there, a green Jag, Connecticut plates, and I never seen a guy washing out his trunk before, so it stuck in my mind, you know what I mean?"

"Hmmm, interesting," I say.

"Yeah, it is, it is interesting, see, that's exactly what I thought when I read about this guy. I think maybe you and I should meet."

Now this is a tricky situation—what I should do, I should blow him off, tell him to go to the police if he has evidence. A case could be made, fairly easily, that having received such a call, as an officer of the court, I should now go to the United States attorney myself. But for some reason the phrase "knowledge is power" runs through my mind, although this particular knowledge could be unethical, illegal, and a whole lot of trouble.

"Okay, that's fine," I say. "Tell me when and where."

"How about Tuesday? Is that good? Tuesday, say at John's Diner? That's right down on Rector Street near your office."

"You've done your homework," I say. "What time?"

"I would say afternoon, you know, after the crowds and whatever. This way we won't be crowded."

"Right, right. How about three o'clock?"

"That's good. Three o'clock."

"How will I know you?"

"I'll find you," he says. "It's usually pretty easy to spot a lawyer in a diner, if you know what I mean."

"I'm glad you're so interested in seeing justice done," I say.

"Look, justice, justice is a dream. I just want there should be something done to even things out, balance the way I feel. He was a tall man, dressed very well. This has made me feel very badly, the things I'm reading. This woman, the two fine kids, you know what I mean. I'm not sure, you know, that new evidence against their father, that might be the last straw for them. I could probably, you know, identify him. Looks like the guy in the paper—he's your client, right? The one I saw in the paper. That was the man I saw. Definitely." He takes a long suck from a cigarette, exhales in a fast blow, it's like a strong wind through the phone.

"Definitely," he says again.

That afternoon I'm out with Jack for an informal lunch: burgers and soup, he insists we take a cab up to a nice old remodeled and expensive bar and restaurant near Franklin Street.

"I want a Coke too," Jack says to the waitress when he hears me order one. "I haven't had a Coke in a long time. Do you serve Coke in cans or from the fountain or what?"

"From the bar, sir," the waitress says. She has tucked our menus under her arm like a true professional. Jack is sitting with his hands folded before him, a Catholic schoolboy pose.

"But it's got enough fizz in it, right? I mean, it's not flat?"

She looks at him, dull incomprehension like a pall. "You want some kind of special glass?"

"Huh?" says Jack. He was cruising right along, totally missing that the waitress didn't have the foggiest fucking clue what he was asking her.

"Coke with lemon," Jack says. "Plenty of fizz."

The Coke comes. No lemon. Jack shakes his head.

"Do you want to ask for the lemon, Jack?" I say.

"No, forget it," Jack says.

"We can just tell the woman."

"No, forget it," Jack says.

"Just say, 'Ma'am, I asked for some lemon here,' she'll bring it on a little plate. Like three pieces, in fact, more than you can use."

"Exactly, and that will depress me. Forget the fucking lemon," Jack says. "I don't want it now."

"She was concentrating on the fizz thing," I say. "So she forgot the lemon."

"Shut up, Will."

I take this opportunity to tell him about the informant, the guy who called me.

"What?" he says. His eyes are big. "He's claiming he saw Ron washing out his *trunk?*"

"You got it."

"But that's something he could easily be just making up," Jack says. "I mean any two-bit operator—"

"'Two-bit operator,' that's nice, Jack," I say. "I haven't heard that since my father ranting about insurance salesmen when I was a little kid."

"Yeah, right, but anybody with half a brain could come up with that story just by reading the papers. I mean, Christ, what's next?"

"He mentioned a Jaguar," I say.

"Really?" Jack says. "I don't think the Jaguar was in the papers, that's weird. Shit. Fuck."

"I'm going to meet with him."

"Look, be very careful of what you say. Don't promise anything or even hint at anything because it could be a setup and it could get you in a lot of trouble, all of us in a lot of trouble. End of your career there, boy, if that happens."

"Right-o," I say. I mock-salute.

"We can have this investigator, Larkin is his name, I'll be introducing him to you at some point—we can have Larkin look into it, see if there's anything there. You should try to get his name."

"It's going to be hard to get his name."

"Well, try. Maybe we can have Larkin or one of his people or whatever, you know, be there, scoping it out, follow the guy. I'll make the call this afternoon and let you know. Jesus, it's like a fucking comedy. This guy's gonna look like Woody Allen or some fucking thing. Total fly in the ointment. I can't believe this."

"Yeah, it's insane."

We eat our burgers in silence. The fat and blood and bread and mayo and ketchup enter the system like a drug, soothing us.

"What do you see as our course of action when we come to trial?" Jack says after a while. He's asking me this as an exercise, the way you go over and over spelling words before a bee, and popping two, three fries at a time into his wide mouth and masticating rapidly. Like they're peanuts.

"Well," I say, "the aim of the prosecution will be to exploit the obvious absurdity of robbers who would cart the body upstate. In a seventy-thousand-dollar carpet no less. None would, it only means more chances of getting caught. But this is not evidence—it's very difficult to introduce, it calls for speculation, and we'll be all over them with objections. They'll get it said, but it's circumstantial and we will be sure the jury understands what that means, what the limits are of any assumptions. They'll say it in opening arguments, closing arguments, and ask the investigating officer, first whether he has ever experienced a case where this has occurred, then follow up with whether he can imagine it happening or has heard of it happening—he says no before any objection we make registers. Then of course we get the judge to tell the jury to disregard the testimony, which will have a slight modifying effect, we hope."

"It will have no effect, but okay. What about on the defense side?" Jack says. "What else are we going to do?"

"Well, on the defense side, there is the duct tape over her mouth—we can bring it up in cross that this a pointless effort if she was strangled in a burst of marital hatred and tyranny, as the prosecution believes. It only makes sense if she was taped up ahead of time, as in a robbery attempt. That little gesture may have been the stroke of genius in this crime."

I don't say outright that the gesture was *Ron's* stroke of genius, but of course only for Ron would it have been genius. Jack looks at me like a child who has been wounded and needs love. For a moment, oddly, I do love him. Then he starts eating fries again.

Home life: the beat-up TV and VCR and "hotel-style" cable selection (they actually advertise this as an attraction), I keep them on through the night because suddenly I'm panicking on silence. I'm on the burlappy early eighties sofa, hardly listening, waiting for sleep to come, avoiding the bed, the altogether too-storied bed, a rejecting lover, a missing father. Everything feels hollow, quivering.

Tuesday at 3:00, or 2:55, to be precise, finds me at John's, a funny old-fashioned diner with U-shaped counters, perfectly in keeping with the tone and style my new friend displayed on the phone last week. Except for the lone souls drifting through for takeout and two guys sitting across the waitress's well from me, the place is empty. I order an iced coffee, pick up an abandoned copy of the *Daily News*. The two men across from me are traders by the look of them, grabbing late sand-wiches, middle-level guys in cheap suits, talking about going down to Atlantic City.

"We're renting a helicopter," one of them says.

"I wouldn't go up in one. That's where I draw the line. I heard too many of these tapes with the traffic reporters going down screaming in rivers."

"What, you think we're going to crash? Because these other fucks did, the traffic people? They go up in small things, whirly-whatevers with, like, burnt-out alcoholic Vietnam-era pilots, forget about it. Anyway, we're taking the helicopter down there, it's like the marines drive this thing, full luxury, a forty-minute ride compared to what is it, two and a half, three hours driving. They're giving us one of the best suites in the hotel."

"Really? You got a suite?"

"We got a suite. Trump Plaza, Celebrity Suite."

"That's nice, probably a lot of comps with that."

"A lot of comps, the fully stocked bar and fridge, whole bit. My wife's gonna be queen for a day."

"That's good, she should show you her gratitude, right?"

"Exactly." They laugh.

"Nice."

Then I sense him beside me—a little cough. As I turn he puts a hand on my arm.

"Mr. Riordan?"

"Yes," I say. He's not as old as I'd expected, and surprisingly handsome, dark hair, slightly pocky but dashing face, kind of Italian-looking but possibly not. Nice haircut, polo shirt, jeans, and new sneakers. Salesman on a Saturday. "And you are?"

"My name is Harry," he says. "Why don't we leave it at that?"

"Fine, Harry."

"Now, uh, I'm gathering since you're here, Mr. Riordan, that you understood the import or impact or significance of the thing that I told you over the phone?"

"Harry, I am just here to find out what you have to say. In the spirit of healthy inquiry. If you were to suggest anything illegal I would be shocked and dismayed and professionally speaking required to go to the authorities."

"Right, well, ahum, I think I can be discreet. As I told you on Friday I would like to put my conscience to rest. Perhaps there's some explanation for what I saw. Perhaps your client doesn't own a Jaguar, Connecticut license UEM 687? It might have been someone else. In which case, you know, we'd all feel relieved."

"Hmmmm," I say. "I'm not sure about the plate."

"Well, whatever, you can look it up when you get back to your office. Here's what I'm going to do. I'm going to give you an address at a mailing service here in Manhattan. Perhaps you can messenger me there? I'd like to get some information about that car by Thursday. There could be fifty thousand cars like that, you know what I mean? As a matter of fact, there could be a hundred thousand cars like that, you could let me know about half of the story on Thursday, the rest on the following Thursday? I know you have a lot of work, does that sound doable?"

"Hmmm," I say. "I tell you what. Leave me that address, I'll find out. I'm sure you'd feel better just knowing whether your information requires you to take further action. Give me a call on Thursday."

"That's a good idea," Harry says. He takes out a card, a Chinese restaurant card from a place not far from here, and writes the address down on the back. I take it.

"Well," I say, and stand up. I can't get away from this guy fast enough. It feels like the first time I had sex, with Debra Hanratty in the basement of Joey Dougherty's house in Flushing, the couch was scratchy and smelled of old beer. She seemed eager, but not altogether conscious. We'd all been drinking Seagram's 7. The Saturday after Thanksgiving in my senior year in high school. I was happy to be wanted, happy to be getting laid, but terrified, shaking, and so surprised that I didn't really qualify as present. "I'll talk to you on Thursday."

Harry nods vigorously.

Wednesday night: I've just come home from visiting with the kids; true to her word, Ellie lets me into the apartment and leaves for two and a half hours. She is civil, even friendly in a bizarre, like-we're-just-neighbors sort of way. I bathe the kids and put them to bed. Sam, who is too young to know time, seems nevertheless to be delighted to see me, or perhaps just cheerful, dry, without the stomach ailments that come in infancy and later, adjusting to the world. He takes a bottle from me and dozes off. Henry is a little more ambivalent, cloying one moment, collapsed in tantrum the next. We're trying to work all this out, I want to tell him, but it wouldn't make sense. I hold him in my lap, small quaking anger and life.

*   *   *

subject: the development of a personal aesthetic

mr riordan this is not about art, what I'm doing, what i'm sending you or not send-ing you as the mood strikes. art sucks. art reminds me of an open mouth, mr rior-dan, a wet devouring hole—something that feeds and then turns slack and stupefied. SCHLUP SCHLUP SCHLUP, as the good doctor said. cock and cunt im-agery. let me try again. NO THERE ARE NO SECOND CHANCES.

yes, let me try again, i'm free, i have a will, willriordan.

here it is: art is not as LEAN as what i want. art is static, slack, quiescent, latent, re-pressed. michelangelo found a way to avoid that, in the SLAVES, to keep it perpetu-ally moving, to keep it hard, to keep it muscular, in the flesh, unbounding, exploding, less than a moment, a hint of a moment, but absolutely fucking eternal, not in the sense that art should last forever because fuck it, blow it all up and start over as far as i'm concerned we live in a goddamned pathetic limp curatorial age; what eternal means is that the thing steps outside time, it's gone, not part of time and death any-more, and when you have it in front of you, or in you, so are you.

if art could be like a lightning flash, then this would be art.

Finally I locate an apartment, three weeks into my separation, an undis-tinguished but pleasant one-bedroom in a brownstone building on West 106th Street, available immediately. It's only half a block from Riverside Park, which soothes me, as if I'm taking this place for my children's sake. After I signed the lease I drove out near Newark Airport to IKEA, where socialism has been turned to a profit—sensible Scandinavian fur-niture that measures in the metric system and suggests the region's fa-mous long winters and suicide rate. It's a modern consumer experience, a vast warehouse of things you don't really want that much but feel obliged to buy because you came all this way and the check-out lines are like a European train station. And now I have to confront the process of putting my furniture together. Somehow I believe if I can make a rea-sonably legitimate-looking home out of the apartment I've rented—

$2,250 a month, more than $4,000 out the window to the real estate
agent—then I can stabilize my life, create some kind of rhythm with
work, the kids, and what? Something else. Something flimsily promised
in the display sections at IKEA, the Jersey Turnpike like a scene from
Blade Runner outside. The fast purchase, at low cost, of a new life—a
futon, a bed, both of which I've already put together, and these other
trappings, modular pieces of dining table, chairs, et cetera, which I
brought home on a roof rack and then piled nicely against the walls.
They have since remained there. The whole ensemble folds flat as a
tabletop and requires lots of assembly.

So here I am at nine-thirty cross-legged on the floor sweating and
getting pissed off, cursing the democratic impulses of this bullshit furniture, which ought to be put together by craftsmen and delivered by
Teamsters and put in place by servants, if the world were really arranged
properly, when the doorbell rings—a shattering electronic buzz that
leaves me jumpy and drained. It's David Chin, unannounced, bringing a
casserole to my ridiculous apartment. A strange sense: friendship, come-
on, mourning? He slides by me into my tiny kitchen.

"You do this when people die," I say. He's the only person at the
firm—or, not true, there is Anna too—who knows Ellie and I are separated. Ellie wants me to keep it a secret until after partnership, which is
shrewd of her.

"I've been thinking about the so-called inscrutable Asian personality,"
Chin says, putting the casserole down on the counter. A green bowl with
foil across the top. "My father was head buyer of men's haberdashery for
Lord and Taylor in Garden City. He was about as inscrutable as you or
I—which is pretty fucking inscrutable when you think about it."

"Is that bowl microwave safe?" I say.

"You don't want to microwave the whole casserole at once—that
would take like fifteen minutes and dry it out. You just microwave a serving at a time."

"That's sad," I say, looking at the bowl.

"You can freeze it in single-serving containers. What's sad?"

"You know, the image, the man sitting down with his single serving. I mean, why bother? Do you carry it in with silverware and everything to a table out in the living room, and then come back for your drink and the place mat and whatever, or do you just stand in the kitchen wolfing it down cold, the light from the fridge a triangle across your abdomen?"

"Do you really need me to answer that?" Chin says.

"Gulping from the orange juice container," I say. "The carton rises above you like a chalice, your Adam's apple bobs. In the background, the noise of the television or stereo, which is never off. The phone doesn't ring. All your clothes are hanging neatly in the closet, plenty of space between the items, still in their dry-cleaning bags. Six pair of shoes. Two pillows. One bedspread. A high-tech clock radio. Nobody cares where you live, or how."

"It's bad," Chin says. "Nobody's saying it's not bad."

"Do you want a drink?" I say.

"What have you got?"

"Some bourbon. And this little bottle of rum the real estate agent gave me. Part of some complimentary thing she got at a luncheon that day."

"Bourbon," David says. We drink to the new place, to bright tomorrows and partially revised yesterdays. We drink to China, to Ireland, to the United States, to brutish guys with hairy stomachs for him, to lithe and self-sufficient art-director ladies for me. It makes me nervous, I have to admit it to myself, having David here in the apartment. I'm fond of David, but something in me wants to keep him at bay, some demon faggot out of my unconscious that I beat back like Aquinas driving out the prostitute with a poker. The issue being not so much that I would want to sleep with him as I would want to *be* him. We have our drinks, sit, him on the futon/sofa, me edged away on a straight-backed dining table chair; we talk about the office, the Yankees, which he is only marginally interested in, for his father's sake, and fly fishing, which he loves all on his own. He looks around the apartment and seems excited by the possibilities of offering advice, which he then thinks better of offering, or so I guess, because after the first salvo he says little but keeps looking at the detailed woodwork and nooks. He leaves after a comfortable time, not rushing out but not lingering either, and I wonder whether he knows I was tense about him being here. Just after closing the crunching steel door, I have a moment of almost unbearable loneliness.

Here's what I turn to, not just tonight but every night: bare wood floors, white white walls, and a fascinating new television (bought in the neighborhood, not a major shopping expedition because TVs, let face it, are an impulse buy), sleek and black, no buttons to speak of, a small remote-control unit like the radio Kirk used on *Star Trek*. I cashed in on some introductory offer that gives me three months of every available channel, eighty-three in all; I cruise through them like a road-test driver on a Lexus commercial. I'm stretched out on my wood-frame sofa apparatus, the single man's urban life center, with an open bag of corn chips, munching, grazing, my eyes glassy with the narcotic effects of idle consumption. We know images now, they signify faster than letters. Somewhere literally inside the first second it hits my screen, I can tell a made-for-TV movie on Channel 7 from a real one on TNT from a fuzzy, divorcée-finding-herself on Lifetime. In less time than I can form the words I can tell the comedy from the drama, the new from the old, the possibly interesting from the unmistakably dull. I don't linger. Handsome men and women in forties outfits on American Movie Classics. I stay there for forty-five seconds, perhaps a minute, then keep going. Concerned, gray-faced men and dykey women deploring something on CNBC. Some kind of weird indoor football on ESPN2. A hearing in stupefying suspension on C-SPAN. Legislators conferring with their hands over the mikes. Down in the post–public TV regions an image looks new, arrests me: NY1 is covering new construction and renovation in Harlem. Colonialization: the beast never dies. I am with my corn chips, a new item, Wise "Authentic Style" Tortilla Chips. They've made authentic into a style. What happened to the bonfires on 116th, the

Bruegel landscape of melancholy and lawlessness? I am thinking about getting up and looking around the fridge for some kind of dip or some cream cheese or something to go with these chips. I am considering beverages. Via live remote, less than a mile away from this spindly halogen floor lamp, from this futon, and from this pair of broad bare feet propped over its sandy wooden arm, people with mysterious sources of capital try to nudge back the apocalypse.

And then Jack calls my cell phone—*twirrrrp twirrrrp*. "Will?" he says.

I say, "Jack." This is the number everyone in the firm has for me, an effort to keep work separate from home, which is now more fortunate than ever, considering there is no home.

"It's Jack," he says.

"I know," I say.

"Right, you said," he says.

"Right," I say.

"Will, I'm concerned—can you hear me?"

"Loud and clear."

"I thought I heard a dead spot," he says.

"We're fine," I say.

"I'm concerned about the Ron Adamson, uh, the Ron Adamson case, which is moving very quickly, too quickly. We're gonna get our balls cut off." Jack is drunk. His words are tumbling all over themselves and his voice has gone over to some higher, panicked register. I feel like Bob Woodward with John Mitchell on the line: *Katie Graham's gonna get her tit caught in a ringer . . .*

"Jack, don't worry," I say.

"HE'S GUILTY AS SHIT," he yells. "THIS LITTLE FUCK, THIS FUCKING HARLEQUIN, WHAT'S HIS NAME? HARRY ELLICAN, FUCK. RON IS GUILTY AS FUCK AND WE'RE PUSHING AHEAD THE FUCKING TRIAL." His voice comes down then. "I mean, it's bad enough, trying to get him off when we know he did it, but anyway we're taking big chances, big chances, and we're gonna look like a bunch of assholes."

"Look, Jack," I say. "I agree with Gerry on this. If they've got enough to convict him then they've got enough to convict him. Nothing we'll accomplish over time is going to change it. He's pleading innocent all the way, turning down the plea offers, et cetera, because that's the kind of fucker he is, and there's nothing we can do about that. The only thing we can do is force their hand, not let them sit there until something more, more than whatever they've got already, comes rolling into their laps. Besides which, even if he's guilty, he's entitled to a trial, and he's entitled to a trial now, not later."

"Let me ask you something, asshole," Jacks says. He's slurring all over the place. "Let me just ask you one goddamn thing. Are you comfortable with this? I mean, are you living with what *the facts* are here? I'm not talking about strategies, I'm not talking about the seventh goddamn amendment to the Constitution of the fucking United States, I'm asking you what the fuck you're telling your wife, your pretty, intelligent wife, every night when you get home? What are you saying, 'Hey, honey, with just a little more hard work and ambition I can spring this creep and make a million dollars for the fucking firm'?"

"I'm not telling my wife anything when I come home," I say.

"How is Ellie, by the way?"

"Fine, Jack."

"Give her my love."

"Sure," I say.

"I mean, look," Jack says. "Just answer me, how do you feel? How the fuck do you feel? I'm not satisfied feeling badly about it out here all by myself. I want to make sure you're suffering too, you young fucking asshole."

"I feel great. I feel fine. I never felt better in my fucking life. How do you think I feel? I don't like what he did any more than you do but somebody's got to defend him because that's how things work. So I'm doing it. You're paying me to do it. I'll suffer in silence, a spiritual way of life that I recommend, by the way."

"All right. All right. As long as you're happy. Happy happy happy.

He tortured her for years, then he strangled her to death, and either we're going to get him off or ruin ourselves trying. Not to mention his kids. Look, I'll see you out here at the party, right? You and Ellie?"

"Absolutely, Jack. We're looking forward to it."

Finally I get it all together, past one in the morning. Now there's a bed in the bedroom, with sheets. There's a table in the dining alcove, with four chairs. There are two low-slung chairs to go with my futon. I feel virtuous, having arranged this thoroughly predictable, replaceable lifestyle.

But what's missing? No sex. When those circuits get burned out . . . I am a man and can say nothing of lasting value about what having two babies does to a woman's body. It certainly did something to my psyche— sex is loaded now, it's not the free-spirited gruntal joining it was once.

But who am I kidding? It was never that anyway. Our problems started long before the children. When I finished law school we had to move out of the biggish apartment on Claremont Avenue (for married graduate students only) into a smaller place on West End. I suppose we could have waited for a bigger apartment to make itself known to us— we had an extra month or two—but looking for an apartment in New York City, especially at that particular time of real estate hysteria, of as-tonishing prices and people lining up at dawn, people paying insiders to get them the Sunday real estate listings the Tuesday before, of going day after day with stupid dreams of lovely spaces to see dingy little inhos-pitable boxes in the sky—it feels like a journey without end, it drains you of your identity, the small optimisms and visions of yourself that keep you going. The process is a formative passage toward becoming a New Yorker, a final journey to the side of New York everyone glimpses and can never quite forgive, the ungenerous, suspicious, status-starved side of the place.

Anyway, we moved into the place, and Ellie began getting edgy about me, about us and our life together. There wasn't enough room, it seemed. We were overfurnished, rubbing against the corners of things, bumping shoulders in the hall. Space as irritant.

I end the night at two-thirty, snipping toenails, digging for ingrown nails. Medieval self-torments at night, late: digging at toes with implements, cutting them too close, droplets of blood, digging for ingrown manifestations, signs of demons. Foul body, self-mutilating sweat. Or the other forms of damage: dental floss, wicked as razor wire. I wrap it around my fingers, slide it up the smooth side of a molar, push it deeper and deeper under the gum line, I want to get the floss over the ridge along the submerged tooth and down deep, I slide it back and forth. The iron taste of blood. A rinse of hot saltwater, tissue shrinking, shriveling, pulling away.

[8]

Saturday evening, the party Jack mentioned, at his house in Sagaponack, a self-conscious gray-clapboard neo-colonial. The architecture—perfect mid-eighties, with its oak-framed windows, its oversized post-and-ball stanchions and black-shuttered dormers front and back—is a series of exaggerated gestures to a past no one ever lived, certainly not Jack. Most of the partners are there with wives or husbands but among the associates only David Chin and I, rather pointedly, have been invited. David's come alone. I'm with Ellie. We three are staying out in Montauk, at the famous old inn there. The kids are with Ellie's mother in New York.

It has been strange with Ellie, we are undercover as married to protect "My Career": we have behaved well, and it's been rather oddly relaxed, even fun, but beneath that, infuriating. Why won't this woman have me? Her face is blank and girlish; I assume she is enjoying watching me suffer.

The party is saved from the boredom of an all-lawyer fest by the frisson of Jack's society friends, the marginally famous people who are constantly divorcing one another. Everyone seems to have a house out here. Ellie reads *People* and the society columns and can translate the faces from their glowing press photos to the saggy, always older, smaller or larger, fatter or thinner, less impressive versions of real life. She points out Arthur Tucker, the publisher and real estate developer, and Sandra Sondhaus, an actress who makes films a notch above the usual and so is considered "interesting," and Donald Appleman, the financier who catapulted himself into the limelight by running the fiscal entity set up to save New York in the money crisis of the seventies. A throng of twenty-eight-year-olds are busy setting up the money crisis of the next decade and perhaps Donald is positioning himself now to run that one too. Ellie has her figure back for the most part and she's wearing new clothes, a short white skirt with a sleeveless orange linen blouse, and sandals. The slight thickness added by two children, the softer shape of her hips and stomach, looks on her like a form of completion. Her hair is short and black and it sets off her white skin and red lipstick, a kind of Mary-Pickford-at-the-beachfront-property look. Her outfit is just a tiny bit too dressy for a Hamptons party, where everyone is casual in a studied, Jaeger-ish way, but she's happy, pleased with herself being out and looking good. Something about the party lights her up. I am nervous and vaguely angry.

Jack's place has a long stone patio edging a short cliff of six or seven feet that drops down to the beach. The caterers tend three large barbecues, shrimp and mako and chunks of marinated tuna, skewered vegetables, soybean burgers, London broils lined up like bricks. Jack's face is edgy, overanimated, as if he's lost his confidence in this display of prosperous ease. From inside the bright house, small children escape—they belong to guests who live out here— bursting onto the patio and disappearing among the forest of legs. The two baby-sitters Jack has hired, a tall slender girl and a friend slightly less tall and less slender, both in shorts and expensive blouses, pursue, pushing long hair off their faces as they bend to sweep the children up.

Jack comes over. He's wearing baggy shorts and a white shirt, flip-flops, dressed almost exactly as his baby-sitters, who are sixteen-year-old girls. A drink in an oversized cocktail glass with a napkin wrapped around it, southern style. "Jesus Christ, Will, stop making grim eyes at the help and have a drink. How are you, Ellie?" He puts an arm around her, gives her a quick kiss.

"I'm fine, Jack. Thanks for having us."

"Ellie loves parties," I say.

"Where are the kids?" Jack says. "Are they here?" He looks toward the house.

"We left them in New York, with Ellie's mother."

"Should have brought them!" Jack hollers. "Run around with the other kids, they'd have a great time."

"No, we shouldn't have," Ellie says.

Jack throws his head back and laughs, gives us a view of his many fill-ings. "Yeah, right, who needs it, right? Ellie, I want you to have a good time tonight. You deserve it."

"Thanks, Jack," she says.

Across the patio, David Chin is talking with a long-haired boy, per-haps seventeen or eighteen years old, dressed with lavish simplicity—wide square silk shirt, ripped denim shorts, loafers. David takes a joint out of his pocket and lights it. Next to him I spot a small mop-headed woman, talking to a bearded West Side type whose bad clothes say he's here on the basis of his intellect. He does not notice the smoke but she does, glancing up at David, who doesn't see her, with an expression that is supposed to be jauntily ironic about the weed, but is in fact intolerant and annoyed. She is in her early fifties I'd guess, but trying for a look much younger; she is glossed and frosted and, like Jack, dressed in the clothes of a teenager. Something about her looks familiar.

"Who's that woman standing next to Chin?" I ask Jack.

"You don't know her? That's Charley Nevins."

"Ahh," I say. Charley Nevins is in publishing, an agent. She was in-volved in some kind of epic divorce played out simultaneously in the publishing and society pages. Jack represented her.

"Why does she have a man's name?" Ellie says.

"Charley has taken three phone calls here tonight," Jack says. "Prob-ably more to come. I mean, there are people here involved in *major* money who aren't going to get a phone call. It takes ten years to write a goddamn book and another year to publish it, but she has to take calls on Saturday night, everything's a crisis, everything's this minute."

As I'd expected, he doesn't notice David's joint. Officers of the court, we are. There is something in David, maybe one of his peccadillos or maybe all of them in combination, that makes him invisible to Jack. He's been invited because of his star qualities in the firm, a political gesture, but at the personal, street level Jack can't even see David, can't bring his eyes to rest on him. David is strictly litigation, specializing in the gnarly long-term cases that involve lots of technical research and battalions of expert witnesses. Documents heaped on conference tables, long lists of codefendants broken down by region. Defense conferences up and down the eastern seaboard, occasionally as far west as Pittsburgh. David is one of the country's best-informed attorneys on issues of dioxin in the workplace. He keeps up with the studies on the health effects of electromagnetic fields. He knows airborne fibers, gases, insecticides. Cases like David's make Jack's eyes cross.

"Are you in the famous softball league, Jack?" Ellie says.

"I tried *like hell* to get in," he says. "Arthur says maybe soon. Arthur says do me do me do me. Like I'm supposed to throw him pro bono nuts to get in the fucking softball league. The guy's worth about six and a half billion, I mean, for Christ's sake." Ellie clucks disapprovingly. "I hear three or four people are going to be away in August," Jack says. "I'm monitoring the situation."

"Sounds like it could be fun," I say, lamely.

"Nothing these people do is fun," Jack says. "Arthur wouldn't know fun if it came up and blew bubbles in his face. But those games are a fucking gold mine. Can you imagine?"

We nod gravely. Jack says, "Listen, I want to show you two the bar, then I have to talk to some people." We move among the people, across the flagstones, Ellie slightly ahead, Jack and I behind. "Can you spare me a minute later?" he asks me.

"Sure," I say.

"Come find me after the food, like around ten. Just horn in on whatever I'm involved in."

"Sure, Jack," I say. He brings us to the bar and makes a point of ordering for us. Then he slants off toward the barbecues.

From behind Ellie, Sue appears. "Ellie!" she howls. "You . . . look . . . so . . . great. I can't believe you, after two kids."

"Thanks," Ellie says.

"I haven't even lost all the weight yet from Emma, and she's four."

"Don't be foolish," Ellie says. "You look fine. Wonderful."

"Well, not like you," Sue says. Her face shines in pastels of blue, burgundy, pale green from the lights. A harlequin with an Hermès scarf. Over a T-shirt no less, with linen shorts and loafers. Total lawyer on holiday. "So how is it? I haven't seen you in ages."

"Fine," Ellie says. She smiles. Sue smiles. After a while Ellie realizes it's her turn. "How are things with you?"

"Busy. You know. I hardly see Emma or Roger, I mean it's ridiculous. Some days I ask myself, why I am doing this?"

"You do it for money," I say.

Sue hits me on the shoulder. "I know that. I'm talking about worth. Quality of life, stupid. As in what matters."

"I just thought, you know, in case the question really needed clearing up."

"Right," Sue says.

"I'd love to get out of the house every day, go to work," Ellie says.

"Right," Sue says. "How has it been, at home?"

"Mind-numbing," Ellie says.

"Right," Sue says, as if she understands. "Climbing the walls."

"This is the first time I've talked to actual grown-ups in weeks," Ellie says.

"Except Will," Sue says, flashing me her face.

"We hardly talk," I say.

"He's so busy, I'm always tired," Ellie says. "You know how it is."

"Absolutely. Wasn't I just saying? I keep thinking, is this what it's going to be like, until I'm sixty-five? And then what?"

"At some point," I say, "you start to slow down. Fear and exhaustion take their toll. Your children go about wrecking their lives, and you look on benignly, eyes watery behind your bifocals. You plan vacation trips, to Portugal, Hawaii, Switzerland, Asia." I raise my glass to my lips but it's empty. Just a puddle of watery vodka and a few slivers of ice. I must have drunk it very fast, but I didn't notice. Behind Sue's head two middle-aged businessmen are talking. One of them says, "Windsurfing instructor . . . ," but I can't hear the rest and I'm left wondering whether he has one or is sleeping with one or his wife is sleeping with one.

"I mean, what did our parents do?" Sue says.

Ellie just shakes her head. Her drink is about half full. She hasn't taken a sip from it for so long I think it's fair to conclude she doesn't want it. I put my glass down on a red oak bench, behind which stands a wall of red oak rails topped with red oak planters, riotously abloom. One senses they are always abloom. I reach over to Ellie and gently loosen her drink from her grip. She doesn't seem to notice.

"We know what our parents did," I say. "That's why we're the way we are."

Ellie turns to me. "Give me my drink back," she says. I fork it over. "On the other hand," she says, to Sue again, "just what the hell is the matter with us? Look at us here, on a terrace by the sea, pretending we're suffering. Having children and making a life, why are we all so convinced this is suffering?"

"Because it's so *fucking* hard," Sue says. She overdoes the "fucking," as if it's some fashionable new word.

"Because nobody told us," I say. "Or they told us and we didn't listen."

"I think there's something seriously wrong with us," Ellie says. "And you know what, dahling? We need more drinks." She hands me her glass. Together we've emptied it.

"How about you, Sue?" I say.

"I'm fine," Sue says. I move off toward the bar. Sue and Ellie sit down on the bench. Waiting for the drinks, I watch them. It looks like a conspiracy. But that's just ego, I tell myself. You think they're talking about *you* but the world is larger than that, larger than you and everyone else. Blend into it. Disappear a little. By the time I get back Sue is getting up to leave.

"I have to go find my husband," she says to me. She taps me with a painted index finger. "Don't forget to come talk to me before you leave."

I hand Ellie her drink. She takes a sip, looks at me. "Talking to Sue is like dragging blocks of sandstone up a half-finished pyramid," she says. "I don't know how her husband takes it. I'm exhausted."

"He stands mute," I say. "Like Christ under the whip."

"Where's my bag, by the way?"

"It's in that small bedroom, remember?"

"Oh yes," Ellie says. "Yes, yes." She stands and puts her drink down beside me. "I have to go and express some milk. My breasts hurt and they're about to start leaking."

After dinner, served on white china plates which we balance on our knees, I spot Jack talking with Sue and her husband, the bald and timid man, looking thrilled to be here. I wander over and stand at the perimeter of their conversation, my back to Arthur Tucker and a man who, I think, writes for *New York* magazine. A DMZ between two regions of pointless social discourse.

My presence seems to lead the conversation with Jack and Sue to its break. "Will," Sue says to me. "You remember Roger." Roger and I nod and shake.

Jack puts his hand over my shoulder. "Have to talk to this man," he says to Sue and Roger. "You'll excuse us?"

"Sure, Jack," says Sue.

"If this were a Fitzgerald novel, or an episode of *Falcon Crest,* you'd suggest we meet in your study," I say.

He looks at me oddly. "I do have a study," he says.

"That's fine, Jack. Let's meet in the study. That will be perfect."

We pass through the silent corridors of Jack's house. I wonder what has happened to the children; the house looks thoroughly fresh and impersonal, as if every room and every object in it had come wrapped in blue sanitissue.

Jack has brought me here to meet with the detective, Paul Larkin; I have noticed him, I realize, at the party, talking with some kind of feverish energy to Charley Nevins. My thought was, You'd better be rich, and interesting, and awful, or you don't stand a chance. He's tall and muscle-thick, in his fifties, with sandy hair just going gray and the standard-issue Republican oversized wire-rim glasses. He dresses younger than his age—cream-colored slacks, Italian-looking loafers, blue blazer, black shirt—a kind of Miami-Beach-meets-Pentagon look. Jack introduces. We shake, sit.

"Let's start with the shakedown guy," Jack says.

"Right," says Larkin. He takes a folder out of an expensive briefcase. "Your man," he says, "is one Bernard H.—Harold, Harry—Ellican. Small-timer all the way. Served two and a half in Ossining for defrauding three companies on some kind of computerized payroll scam. Parole finished last January. While he was on parole he was a good boy, worked in the financial district as a messenger, unbonded, needless to say. Since then no visible means, which translates probably to running numbers or selling dope or chopping cars or some other kind of small-time operations. I took the liberty of creating some documents which place Mr. Ellican undeniably out of town over the period in question, in Phoenix, Arizona, where, as a matter of fact, his father and two of his sisters live. His mother is, uh, deceased."

"Mysterious circumstances?" I say.

"Excuse me?" Larkin says.

"The mother—her death was on the up-and-up?" He's such a spook I feel required to throw in this red herring just to see how he'll react.

"I, uh, do not have that information. Let me get back to you on that."

"Never mind," I say. "Just a thought."

"So let me get this straight," Jack says, though what Larkin is suggesting couldn't be more obvious. Jack goes dense whenever he hears something that upsets him. "You've concocted evidence that this guy was out of New York over that week or whatever?"

"Ten days, actually," Larkin says.

"What kind of evidence?" Jack says.

"Documents," Larkin says, with a passion for the word. Documents as biblical scraps, flaking remnants of the scroll, holy scripture. "Airline tickets, used. Car rental slips, charge receipts, we even managed to create a record of phone charges that we can then request from AT&T, which is, by the way, his long-distance provider. Very strong, very clean documentation."

"Wow," Jack says.

"As I say, we took the liberty, having access to that route."

"Will," says Jack. "Why don't you take care of those, keep them in a file somewhere in case they're needed."

"Sure, Jack," I say. "I'll just put them in the bag with my wife's breast pump, nursing pads, you know. Then they're sure not to get lost."

"You have a new baby?" says Larkin.

"Hmmm," I say.

"Congratulations. We had four. Laurie, my youngest, just finished at Berkeley in the spring. She's going to veterinary school in Montana."

"That's great," I say. "Horse country."

"Exactly. She's crazy for horses. We thought she'd grow out of it when she was three. Now she's in vet school."

"Life," I say. "It's funny."

"You're right," Larkin says. He trains his large, thoroughly unironic eyes on mine. "Life is funny." Then he hands me the envelope of false evidence. I put it in my back pocket.

"So," Jack says.

"We are pursuing the other lines of the investigation at this time," says Larkin. "Apparently the U.S. attorney has hopes of making something out of fibers found in the trunk. We don't have a line on what all that is. Our microevidence group is working down the possibilities, running things through the computer. We should have projections in a few days."

"Microevidence group?" I say.

"You wouldn't believe the size of this operation," Jack says. It makes him happy, hiring the best and most expensive outfit in the country. Like buying a suit on Bond Street. Childlike joy.

"Frankly, from the informal talks I've had with my people, this is really a needle-in-the-haystack-type thing. They will be very lucky to find anything that would pull this case together."

"Well, let us know," Jack says. "I'm going to be out here for a few more days, until Friday, then I'm flying to Italy for ten days. Call Will at the office. He can reach me if there's a problem. Do you have a card, Will?"

"Actually, no, Jack," I say. "I left them in the beach bag back at the inn."

"You're a lawyer, Will. Always carry your card."

"Right, Jack."

"I have the number," Larkin says.

"No doubt," I say. "Plus, it's listed."

"Right," Larkin says, rising. "Information is my business, right? Ha ha. I'm going to get back and help myself to some more of your booze, Jack. Wonderful spread here tonight."

"Fellows," Jack says. "All the joys of the Flemming estate, yours for the asking."

On the terrace, my wife looks flushed, interesting. Larkin has made a beeline for Charley Nevins, who looks as if she's about to give him the shake, but flirtatiously.

"Let's go for a walk," Ellie says. "On the beach."

I look around the party. "Let's walk straight out into the ocean and never come back," I say. She gives me a look, like, What's wrong with you?

"Don't look at me that way," I say.

"What way?" she says.

"I don't know," I say.

We go down the steps and pull off our shoes and start to walk. Soon we are out of the light, it takes a minute for our eyes to adjust. We are moving along, slowly, into the night. The ocean is regular and at first incredibly loud, then somehow less loud as we add it to our lexicon of things-that-are.

"Where did Jack take you?" Ellie says. "Are you two lovers?"

"No, we're not lovers. I could never sleep with anyone bald."

"That's mean. Suppose you were bald?"

"I'm not bald. Never gonna be bald. *I'm* gonna be fat, that's my plan."

"Like a big snorting rhino," Ellie says.

"Exactly," I say. "Someone with enough goddamn mass everyone else better get out of my fucking way."

"You'll stink. There'll always be some kind of moisture gathering in your folds. You'll have to shower twice a day and lavish yourself with scented powders."

"I'll have someone to do it for me."

"So where did he take you?"

"To his study. You should see. Floor-to-ceiling bookcases. I admire him going out and getting all those books for his goddamn summer house, even if he doesn't read them."

"*He* didn't get them, silly. The *designer* bought them."

I stop in the cool sand. My shoes, old leather deck shoes, which I've been carrying in my hand, I am now tempted to fling into the sea. "You're kidding," I say.

"No," she says. "What do you think? He went out and picked out five hundred books, scoured the used bookshops, went to the Sag Harbor Library sale?"

"That's inconceivable to me, living with designer books."

"Don't be so naive."

"I'm going to do my authenticity rap," I say.

"All I can say is, you'd better get on the ball, buster, if you plan on moving ahead in this world. You're supposed to become one of these guys, aren't you?" She turns from me and starts walking again, slowly, though, almost waiting for me. I reach for her and take her hand.

"Suppose," she says, "you're making half a million or a million a few years down the road? What do you plan to do with yourself?"

"Wouldn't you like to be there to share in the loot?" I say.

"We'll leave that question aside," she says. "According to my lawyer I'll be getting my share either way."

"Your *lawyer?*"

"Forget it. Pretend I never mentioned it."

The numbers she's tossing around are not, it strikes me, beyond the realm of the possible. If partnership goes through at year's end I'm probably in for a $75,000 bonus, on top of the $195 I'm making now. That's the opening bid on me as partner. A half million is near and a million isn't that far off. Money both obscene and breathtaking. Nine percent pretax is being moved into pension vehicles, and somehow, after taxes, and Henry's nursery school, and our car with its insurance and garage, and the rent, now it's my rent and her rent, and my college loans and law school loans, and the credit cards (what the hell am I buying, anyway?) and the doctors and the dentist and her phone and my phone and her utilities and my utilities and her food and my food and the dry cleaning and the lunches and the toys and the clothes and everything else, the occasional weekend and the goings out to dinner with that awkward moment about the check, which I pick up, there never seems to be much money around. There wasn't much money around before I left the house and there are real problems now. At least I think so. Envelopes are piling up, waiting for attention. I suspect the worst. We're not planners. Or I guess I should learn to say *I'm* not a planner. *I* don't like to go away on trips. *I* enjoy a glass of wine every night with dinner but I eat very little bread. I like blue in the bathroom or I don't like blue in the bathroom but my wife always hated yellow in the bathroom except I don't live with her anymore so why does it matter? It matters.

And the program, Ellie is reminding me, calls for me someday to be rich. "You know," I say, "I'm going to feel much worse doing nothing useful with five hundred thousand a year than I do now, wasting a hundred and ninety."

"You got it, baby," Ellie says. She sounds oddly happy. Night, wind, the spray of ocean and sand. Her hair floats and whips like flags outside the UN. "Every time your income goes up, a little more of your conscience has to die."

About thirty yards down we can make out David's white shirt low to the ground, almost phosphorescent in the darkness, and beside him a darker shape, probably the ponytailed boy. The sand is tinged with light from the stars and, distantly, faintly, the houses. Ellie begins walking slowly toward them, as if she's merely strolling. I follow. She reaches back for my hand.

"Suppose they're doing something," Ellie says. "You know."

"Approach in stealth," I say. "Watch for rhythmic movements. Rocking. Anything spasmodic."

In fact, they are only sitting together, staring out toward the water, which really can't be seen except for the occasional long whitecap, but it can be *sensed* in an immediate way. The night is clear but there is no moon. As we near them, David looks up.

"Ah, Riordan and Riordan," he says. We plop down about six feet away, a compromise distance between intimacy and separation.

"This is Jarrett," David says.

"Hi, Jarrett," Ellie says. She sounds like a college girl, ready for anything. We shimmy our bottoms to smooth the lumpy sand. Knees up, arms around shins.

"This feels like a seventies moment," Ellie says. She's right, it's a TV commercial from the mid-seventies, we're four sensitive friends, sitting on the beach at night, listening to the invisible sea. It's an ad for vinegar douche. Or recyclable paper. Or decaffeinated freeze-dried coffee. Or one of those beers thought of as "premier" in the seventies, like Michelob. Handsome young consumers. In the face of a troubled world, we demonstrate how to make a secret obsession of lifestyle. We are leading a scarred country back to the comforts of unabashed consumerism. A moment's silence, each of us wandering off with the thought, unbordered as sea and sky.

David looks up. "The rest of our lives," he says, "will be a series of seventies moments, progressively more disjointed and absurd."

Above us the dense and faintly backlit sky. Ellie is running her hands through the sand, letting it sift across the backs of her open fingers. Her legs are curled beneath her; she leans against me.

"The stars," she says. "You can never really see the stars in New York. When I was at Barnard I was taking this astronomy course at Columbia and we were supposed to have star-mapping labs out on the plaza in front of Low Library at night, and it was pathetic, you could never see anything."

"The sky uptown is always purple at night," David says. "At least when I'm up there. A kind of murky violet. I can never figure it out."

I find myself gazing up into it. "The universe is made up of strings of stars with enormous empty spaces and double black holes in between," I say. "And these galaxies of stars, they're expanding, pulling apart, at an increasing rate as a matter of fact, which doesn't make sense. Physicists are puzzled by these spaces, by their accelerating growth. Somehow no model of the universe's formation satisfactorily explains them. Yet they make sense—densities so great everything kind of caves in around them, rapidly, the way water going down a drain seems to go faster near the end of the process." I am lying down flat now, looking up. *La noche, boca arriba* . . . "Vast pockets of dominant nullity. The Jansenist view would be to take these as expressions of God's anger. The first monumental explosion, a paradox, an annihilating force of creation. The world is charged with the grandeur of God. All that. Except now there's a quality of *spent* and *enraged*. Have you been keeping up with this in the *Science Times*?" No one needs to answer. We've all had enough to drink. They know I'm rambling. My hands are under my head, I'm staring over Ellie's lovely pale shoulder toward the sky. I am aware of the sand's coolness under my back.

"It's so beautiful here," Jarrett finally says.

"Where do you live?" Ellie asks him.

"Brooklyn Heights," Jarrett says. "My mother's a *friend* of Jack's." The sarcasm isn't exactly bitter, but then it isn't exactly not bitter either. "Anyway, I came out with her this weekend because I'm, like, so tired of the city right now. It's so horrible."

"It is nice here," Ellie says.

David shifts. "The beach is nice," he says. "The house I could live without."

"The house *is* way too impeccable, isn't it?" Ellie says. This is a New York thing, it happens at every party, a postmod moment of retrospection about the experience while it is still going on. Subcategory: trash the host.

"I think if the house is beautiful, and a lot of people would call it that, then we have to accept that there are two basic kinds of beauty," I say. I'm still down flat on my back, a few feet farther away from the center than everyone else.

"Shut up, Will," Ellie says.

"Yeah, shut up, Will," says David.

Their shapes, Ellie, David, and Jarrett, are abstract, like large living stones in the muted moonlight. "No, really," I say. "The main kind of beauty, the one that's being foisted on us all the time, has its seductive powers, but essentially it's stifling. Just a triumph of cosmetic design. Trivial and godless. It's about stirring consumption. What's interesting is that here you have the other kind right on hand to compare it to. The gray, relentless ocean. Frightening and beautiful. Like sheer rock cliffs, or thunderheads gathering at the edges of the plain. True beauty that is awesome and abrasive. There's anger in it, a kind of murderous intent."

David says, "Oh man, Will. You are *so* full of shit."

Ellie laughs at that and can't seem to stop, flopping down beside me eventually. "Oh man, Will, you are so full of shit," she repeats and this sends her into another round, which makes David and Jarrett laugh too. I start things off by kicking sand onto Ellie because she can't stop laughing. David sees this.

"Don't kick sand on your wife," he says. "This is the new millennium. That's abuse," and he starts letting fly with his two feet in our direction and Ellie yells, "Hey!" and she starts too and soon the four of us have worked up our own small storm, a personal sirocco. By the time it's over the sand is in our mouths and in our eyes and filling our hair. Standing around, the four of us, slightly embarrassed, slightly postcoital, brushing ourselves off.

"Who has a comb?" David says. "Ellie, c'mon, where are the beauty aids?"

"Didn't bring any," she says.

"That's so butch," he says.

"That's me," Ellie says. "What can I say."

"Oh man," says Jarrett. He unbuckles his ponytail and shakes out his hair, sand spinning out like a dusty halo, the hair and sand both catching slivers of the low light. We all stop cleaning ourselves to watch. It's kind of a dervish moment, his head shaking back and forth, the hair flying.

We make our way back eventually, chilled slightly by sea air and night, to the wide plank steps up to Jack's patio. There's a woman sitting at the top of the stairs. We squeeze by her going up. Long wooden stairs, gray-brown and pale from salt winds. A woman bent over, her pose suggesting tragedy and defeat. It is Charley Nevins, hunkered down with a cell phone, the stub of antenna peeking out from her hair. She has it pressed up against her ear, listening, like a kid with a transistor under the covers. Her face betrays a twelve-year-old's doleful yearning.

"I can't believe this, this is *not* to be believed," she says. Then: "I know, but what is she thinking?" We edge our legs around her. She looks up sharply at us, as if we are in the way and not she, then bends again to her phone. "Tell her to fax it to me in the morning." A tone of doggedness and boredom.

"Yuck!" Ellie says, a summary statement that may or may not be audible to Nevins. David and Jarrett laugh. At the top of the stairs Ellie plunges into the crowd on the patio. David and Jarrett fade into some private space of their own. I look back, seaward. The beach is a pale blanket, stretching into the darkness.

Driving down the Montauk Highway, a dome of light running before us. We are alone because David, delicate seducer, soft-nosed as a dog nuzzling for some bit of carnage buried in the loam, has stayed behind to pursue young-man-with-ponytail. Ellie and I sit in the blue glow of the dashboard lights, listening to the engine whir and the wind; perhaps she is thinking, as I am, back to this afternoon, when we were checking into our room at the inn. We eyed the two beds. I was distinctly aware of it, glancing at the beds, seeing Ellie glancing at the beds, separate, but probably not separate enough for her, though she had told me to get us only one room because David would be around, and anyway someone might call or pay attention, she being if anything more determined than I to keep our split from becoming public for now. We talk about it in terms of the partnership but I wonder if that's really it; in my case I'm not ready to accept it as reality. It may have been underhanded of me not to tell her that David already knew. When I'd called the inn and requested that the room for my wife and myself have two beds, I'd been tempted to make explanations to the clerk on the phone—my wife has a bad back? I have a bad back? We both, can you believe this, have bad backs, you see—but ultimately, it was easier to say nothing, just proceed with New York monied arrogance through the conversation, knowing that whatever reason I might have come up with, this young woman, the clerk, had heard it before and couldn't care less. She had her life, her friends, her days at the beach and her nights in the packed oval barrooms of local joints with names like Salties II. The colossal liberating force of our times, that no one gives a shit what you do. So on our arrival we found our two beds waiting, flawlessly in keeping with the arrangements we'd made, answering no questions, telling no lies, and we looked at them; I saw Ellie look briefly, her thinking who knows what, the air thick as a butcher shop's, and then watched her pick one of the beds, with random-seeming care, and I foresaw the night, the undressing and the pulling down of bedclothes, her bare feet and legs, settling in, the awkward motions and displays—which now we are moving toward, in this car, through this night, but lingering first, feeling our way.

And to complicate our movements: the fifteen or twenty minutes we spent on the beach, complicit in the atmosphere of David's sex life, which wisps around us in the car now like the air rushing in the windows. I reach for Ellie, touch her bare arm. "You are my wife," comes out of my mouth. I couldn't have chosen a more provocative and absurd sentence, as if I am laying claim to some kind of nineteenth-century authority over her.

"Good-bye, city life!" Ellie sings. I run my hand down to the inside of her elbow, across her forearm, into her hand. We clasp fingers, watch the road, stare into the shifting halftones. Thick, pink-gray clouds have closed in over the sky and the darkness here is real—no stars, faint moonlight. I want to sleep with this woman very badly, that's how I feel, that she's a difficult new woman in my life and I want to sleep with her, one of the rare ones, and touching her arm, just touching her arm, is giving me a hard-on. This is childish greed, I know that, for the thing taken away, I know that, for the thing withheld. I am aware of that.

"None of them knew the color of the sky," she says, with alcoholic forcefulness. Ellie's voice is mischievous and pleased.

"Hmm?" I say.

"A line from a short story. 'None of them knew the color of the sky.' That's the way it looks right now. Imagine if you were at sea."

"I am at sea."

"Ohhh," she says. Then she darts in a new direction, like a minnow, or a drunk. "Would it be facile to say the kids are fine, Henry is having a blast with his grandma, Sam is sound asleep and will sleep through the night even without me, they're both asleep now, lips parted, faces slack and pale? Would this be transparent denial?" She turns toward me.

"Probably," I say. "But it's also possibly true." We are alone with each other's voices, a rare sensation even before we were separated. We are alone; we have left the world behind, we're on a potted lunar landscape looking back at the distant radiant globe we live on. Behind us a car rises over the crest of the grade, its lights like stars in the rearview.

"You are so glib," she says. "Nothing touches you." I say nothing to that.

"I've been flirting with boys on the beach," she says then. "Oh, I've had too much to drink and I'm wearing a new blouse and skirt and all in all indulging my fantasies of youthful sexual adventure and incipient glamour and meanwhile my children miss me, wonder where I've gone and why I'm not with them."

I sit silent, like a teenage boy confused by a girl more intelligent than he is.

"Things used to be harmless," Ellie says. "Nothing is harmless any-more. For some people this"—she sweeps her arm around, as if the scrub brush and sanded soil and gloom sweeping past us on the road, the east-end landscape itself, were the same as the evening's other events, the large party fueled moistly with the peat of so many individual dishonesties—"for a lot of people this is a life. It has meaning for them." She means to say she cannot be one of those people. She means to say she doesn't have the stomach for it. But instead she just stops talking. She shifts, leans her head against the glass on her side of the car and closes her eyes. Her face is pale and empty in the light.

"I wouldn't do that, if I were you," I say.

"Do what?" she murmurs.

"Close your eyes," I say.

"Hmmm," she says. A minute later, she sits up. "Can you stop the car please? Just pull over?"

I roll slowly onto the gravel and she's out almost before the car has completely stopped. She goes in small uneven steps across the weeds for a few feet, then leans down, daintily pulls her hair back from her cheeks, and throws up an impressive volume of liquid. Three tosses. I get out on the driver's side and stand there and wonder, as I always do when some-one is sick, or weeping on the subway, or unconscious on the street, What am I supposed to do? Am I really needed here? For instance, it might be a woman to whom I am married, but from whom I am cur-rently separated—does she want me in such a scene? The smell of the sea. Distant headlights. My wife retching in the prickly sand grass. I walk over slowly.

"How are you?" I say.

"I'm sick," she says.

"Right." I put my arm around her waist, walk with her—her walk is steady, surefooted, and I am surprised and impressed by this—back to the car; we lean against it. I give her a pack of Kleenex and she wipes her mouth and chin. She hands me the dirty one because she doesn't want to just drop it on the ground, she's well brought up even in these moments; she takes a new one and wipes her eyes and forehead. She wipes the back of her neck. She wipes the front of her neck, she wipes between her breasts. Crumpled tissues gather in my hand, they feel like little treasures.

"Never, ever, close your eyes when you're drunk," she says. "Do not close your eyes. That's the rule."

"That was my point," I say.

"I recall you mentioned something."

"That's me," I say. "I'm full of helpful hints. I'm just not very good at getting them across in a timely way."

Inside the Amagansett line there is a diner where we stop for coffee. The waitress asks us if we're having something to eat and we say no, just coffee.

"Well, you know, honey, there's a four-dollar minimum per person. It's a summer thing, with all the weekend people."

"That's all right," I say. "Just put us down for the four each. Maybe we'll order something later."

"I'll just leave the menus then," she says.

"Fine," I say. She looks at us a minute, then leaves.

"I think she likes us," Ellie says. "She wants us to get our money's worth out of this."

"I don't know," I say. "This is worth eight dollars to me." Separation is strange, being out together and so far away from the children, with no deadline to get home; I feel as if we are on a long and difficult and not entirely unsuccessful date, getting to know each other in the extremity of odd and funny circumstance—David and the boy with the ponytail, the woman with the cellular phone, Jack's head reflecting the Chinese lanterns, zones of pastel colors across his skull. We are creating a private humor, a catalog of buffooneries, as young couples do. Every small thing, the Kleenex, the four-dollar minimum, seems to bring us closer.

"I remember the diners we've gone to much better than the restaurants," Ellie says. "The one in New Jersey we used to stop in on the way to Philadelphia, the one that looks like an old rail car or like the rail-car diner in a monster movie. The one in King of Prussia that was like a combo diner and doughnut shop. That one always reminded me of Carolyn."

"Why Carolyn?" Carolyn was a college friend of hers.

"Well, when she was in grammar school her parents bought a doughnut shop, a Dunkin' Donuts franchise, and it obliterated their family life. The kids were left to raise themselves pretty much. Her parents were real weirdos, really strange, and they moved to the South, where Carolyn didn't really fit in. I mean of course she didn't fit in, it's so highly coded there. Her parents, you know, they go on and on about the ancients."

"Have you talked to Carolyn lately?"

"No," she says. "No, I should really give her a call. Her husband lost his job."

"Oh." Silence then. We sip coffee.

"Can we drive to New York?" Ellie says then, looking up. "Now, tonight?"

"No way."

"I miss my children," she says. "I have to see my children. They are small and helpless and alone in the world. Sam is just an infant. I should never have left them. They miss me. I can't stand it."

"You're talking two and a half hours. I'm too tired, you're too drunk, and we paid a fortune for the charming quaintness of our room."

"I'll take the train," she threatens.

"There is no train," I say. "Not at this hour."

"I miss my children, little Henry, can you see his feet? His face? What about Sam? He sleeps all rolled up in a ball, sideways in the bassinet if he can manage it. Can you picture this? It's unbearable. Of course, you feel nothing."

"I feel plenty," I say. I believe this.

"You're incredible, you're like stone."

"Don't turn on me, I didn't make you come."

"You're like a statue of yourself. Dead and gone. The granite is etched, 'Loving father, committed assemblyman.' I can't even see you."

"How did you know I was running for assemblyman? I'd barely made the decision. You're uncanny."

"Are you really?" she says, eyes widening. I can't tell whether she's drunk and gullible or playing the joke one line further.

"No."

"Oh, of course," she says, "you're not running *for* anything. You run *from* things."

"This is galling coming from the person who's thrown me out of my own home."

"Oh come *on*," she says. "Drop the aggrieved shit. You just forced me to make the decision for you. You were gone already, except we still had your socks on the floor and your piss on the toilet seat to contend with."

I am the compromise candidate, smiling and waving between two incompatible worlds.

"I have a raging hard-on right now," I say, "I've had it since the car."

"I'm past hearing about your hard-ons, your woodies, your throbbing tool. Mention it again and I'll call the cops, I mean it."

"Forget I ever said it."

"You mean you've had it all the way since the car? From before I threw up? That's sick."

"I said forget it, we won't speak of it. Just a few moments discomfort, an optimistic strain against unyielding khaki."

"At what point exactly did you get it, I mean, what were we talking about?"

"I touched your arm."

"You're an arm freak," she says.

"I am not an arm freak. I like your arm, your hands, your neck and stomach and legs and feet. I like your skin. I like your hair. Your face."

"What bullshit."

"No bullshit," I say. Clearly, she's pleased.

"Do you still have it?" she says.

"Talking about it has made it go away a little but I think it's still there." Actually it has gone away a lot but I'm trying to will it back into existence, usually a futile effort.

"Such an amusing physiological event," she says. "When I first heard about it, I guess I was like eight, the girls in school were talking about it, I thought it was a lie. A girl named Amy Wasserman told us about it. We used to call her Washerwoman. Anyway, I remember saying I didn't believe it, it was like saying your arm would suddenly get really big and stick straight out from your side. It sounded stupid."

"It is stupid," I say. "A man with an erection is the stupidest thing that ever lived."

"A phenomenon which I have often noticed," she says. Outside the big plate-glass windows of the diner, a car goes by with a lonely whoosh. Its tires ring faintly on the macadam.

"Do you want to get something to eat?" I say.

She's staring out the window, or perhaps at her own reflection in it. "Hmmm?" she says.

"Are you hungry, do you want anything to eat? Four-dollar minimum?"

"No," she says. "No. I mean I feel a slight responsibility to the nice waitress to get something to eat but I just threw up and all. Let's have a little more coffee."

I make eyes at the waitress when she passes by. She has the look of a woman raising a child alone, about forty years old, weary but still slightly amused by life's possibilities. "Did you find something in there you like?" she says. "Or just the check?" she says.

"Two more cups of coffee," I say. "Then the check I guess."

"More coffee, huh? You two are gonna be up all night. I suppose there are worse possibilities." She goes and gets the pot, pours our coffees, and then disappears.

Ellie is looking out the window again. "What are you thinking about?" I say.

"I suppose I look very moony," she says. "What I'm thinking about actually is Eliot."

"Why Eliot?"

"'A phenomenon which I have often noticed.' You know, what I said before? It's from *The Waste Land*. Or from the notes to *The Waste Land*, actually."

"You should really go back to graduate school," I say.

"Oh Christ," she says.

"No, I mean it. You should really go back for a Ph.D. You have a passion, you should pursue it."

"You should you should you should," she says. "You don't have any fucking idea what you're talking about."

"It seems like a fairly simple idea."

"And who takes care of the children? Who raises them?"

"We can get help, Ellie. That's what I've been saying for a long time. I make enough money. I'm going to be a partner at the end of the year, there'll be a nice payout and there'll be enough money."

"Do you have any idea how much work it is, to get a Ph.D.? You don't know what you're saying; it's as much work as law school except it takes seven or eight or ten years. I'm thirty-five years old. By the time I'm finished the kids would be ready for college almost. And this idea of hiring someone, you'd have to hire someone from dawn till midnight. You don't even know what you're saying. There's more to having kids than going to Lamaze classes and then *hiring someone*, Will, goddamn it. Goddamn you. If you want the kind of children who are raised by a series of someones and go to these precious schools and will never fit in with the rest of the universe except the fashionable neighborhoods of Manhattan, then fine. It's not what I want."

"Look, that's not what I said. I could help, I'd be home in the evenings to take care of them."

"That is such bullshit. I can't believe you're even saying this. No, I take that back. One thing I realized recently is that men—you, all men—you mean this shit when you say it, you mean all the nice stuff you say. This is what women have so much trouble understanding, or living with. You actually mean it. It just has no effect on you when it comes time to do what you want."

"That's not true. What you're saying is that people have no capacity for change or improvement."

Ellie leans forward, her eyes large and bright. "C'mon. Wake up. Children need love, Will. Just because you didn't get it doesn't mean they don't need it."

"I know that," I say.

"You know that, you know that. You don't know it, or if you do, you only know it in theory. The economy of love is attention and you don't have any."

"You haven't given me much of a chance,"

"I gave you a lot of chance. Time ran out. We have to get on with life. You have no idea what it's like to live with you. There's a difference between doing without your presence and attention and standing around waiting for them to arrive. One is progressive and the other debilitating. It's easier not having you there."

"Look," I say. "The whole way I've lived my life is, I've pictured what it would be like to do a certain thing, I mean really imagined and gotten to know it, if you know what I mean, or else I've watched others doing it for a long time, and *then* I've done it. It's a process of imitation. That's the way I learned to play baseball and to swim and to be an English major and a law student and finally a lawyer. Up until now, I've just imitated being an adult human being, or that's what it feels like. This other thing, being a father and a husband, I don't have any real role models for this. The men when I was growing up, nothing was required. They were supposed to bring home a paycheck and not beat everyone too badly when they got drunk, that was it. So it's taking me a little time."

Ellie sits back. "Oh, fuck," she says.

"What?"

"Nothing," she says. "I'm tired."

"I mean," I say, the feeling of righteousness and self-pity washing over me like a fine mist of chemicals, "when I said you should go back to grad school I meant it as a compliment, for Christ's sake. I thought of it as a sign of respect."

"It's a sensitive topic," she says.

"Yeah, I guess so."

The waitress comes up with the check and a white take-out bag. "I packed you some doughnuts," she says. We look up at her. "I mean, since you're paying the minimum and all. They're from this morning already, they would have been thrown out. You can eat them later if you're hungry."

"Oh, aren't you nice," Ellie says. "That's really nice, thank you so much."

"Don't worry about it, really. They're from this morning, like I said."

"Thanks," I say.

"Enjoy," she says.

On our way out to the car, stumbling a bit on the sandy gravel of the small parking lot, I put my arm around Ellie's waist. She spins gaily away. We get in the car, I stick the key in the ignition. Ellie puts the radio on, a classical station, but for some reason, the later it is, the more jarring and modern the music such stations play, so she begins switching around, looking for something else. We listen to the Allman Brothers, some long jam recorded live at Fillmore East, that I recognize instantly but can't name. Lots of drums. It seems perfect for the road, the rushing night. When it's over the announcer comes on with the station ID—soft rock.

"Since when did the Allman Brothers at Fillmore qualify as soft rock?" Ellie says.

"Everything's soft rock," I say. "They just want you to feel secure that you're not a metal freak or a gangsta or a skinhead. Otherwise, anything goes."

"I'd like to shave my head sometime," Ellie says wistfully.

"The hell you would," I say.

"No, I mean it. A kind of Sigourney Weaver/Sinéad O'Connor thing. With earrings and lots of makeup. The totally ambiguous message. Head like a dick." She laughs.

"Is this your idea of keeping up with youth?" I say.

"Listen, it's my head," she says. "You have nothing to say about it."

We get back to the inn and park behind it and walk slowly around to the front entrance. Ellie staggers a little, ends up against me, permits my arm to stay around her. We climb, a cumbersome four-legged animal late at night, up the steps. Behind the antique front counter, a young man looks up from a book. He smiles as we go by him. "Good night," he says.

"Good night," I say.

"What are you reading?" Ellie asks him.

"*Heart of Darkness*," he says, holding up an old green paperback.

"Oh, that's such a great book!" Ellie says. "Perfect for sitting here reading all night." She seems to be genuinely enthusiastic on his behalf.

"Yeah, it's great," he says.

"Are you in college?" she asks him.

"No," he says. "I mean yeah, but not now, I'm off for the summer."

"Oh, wonderful," Ellie says. I apply almost undetectable pressure on her back with my arm, hoping the idea of forward movement slips into her head unaware.

"Yeah," the boy says again.

"Well, good night," I say, smiling.

"Good night," Ellie says.

"Have a nice evening," the boy says. The evening's long gone, but I'm grateful he believes it is something, for us, still in development. We start up the wide stairway to the second floor.

"And this also," she says in a low voice, "has been one of the dark places of the earth."

"I'll say," I mutter, practically pushing her up the stairs. "I can't believe you were flirting with the hotel clerk. Right in front of me. Ouch."

"Don't ouch," she says, and pats my head. I open our door. "I just wanted to know what he was reading."

"Right," I say.

In the room, we turn on a single lamp and begin to shed our effects, ready ourselves for bed. She goes into the bathroom, I hear her urinate, flush the toilet, brush her teeth. Meanwhile, I take off my clothes. After she comes out I pass by her, in my boxers, and I take a leak and brush my teeth. When I open the door she is standing at the foot of her bed, bare-chested, unzipping her skirt.

"Is that all you're wearing to bed?" she says.

I look down at myself. "Yeah," I say. "I guess so."

"Then that's all I'm wearing too," she says. Her skirt flops onto the floor and she steps out of it. "I mean, if I can take it you can take it." She stands there, looking wonderful, looking like the most beautiful woman I've ever seen, almost naked in my room, which she is. I walk toward her. She watches me, amused.

"You still have that hard-on, I see," she says.

"It's a new one," I say. I put my arms around her and we kiss, the familiar thing, I know her, I know this woman. And then our hands are all over each other, and we're kissing for real, big deep breathless kisses, and we get each other's underwear off and touch each other and it's a kind of an electric feeling of dissolving toward each other, butter and Baker's chocolate and sugar melting in a pan, touching her, having her touch me. We get in the bed and roll and buck and kiss each other's bodies and have a fine time, with the one small lamp on across the room giving a warm haze of light. I'm willing to do this for a long time, I really can't believe she wants to have sex, it's been so difficult for so many months, years even, since she was pregnant with Henry, but she's got me pinned down and climbs on top of me and is ready even before I am.

"Do you have a condom?" she says.

"Of course I don't have a condom," I say. My hand is on her and she is rocking gently back and forth against it, very wet. I am sliding the hump of my thumb and hand into her and the back of my wrist brushes her clit. She reaches around behind her to grab my cock. "How would you have felt if I'd brought condoms along?" I say. "Wouldn't that have been presumptuous? Besides, it never even occurred to me, I'm the sexless single man."

"Oh shut up," she says, still grinding against my arm, rubbing my cock. "You should have thought of it," she says. "You should have thought of it, you should have thought of it, you should have thought . . ." And then she is settling herself down on me and as I enter her, her body changes, goes fluid, and I rise toward her like something tidal. She comes down; we come together and pull apart and come together and pull apart like two bodies of water rushing along beside each other. I have my hands on her hips and ass and legs, holding a living thing, and she has her hands on each of my shoulders with arms straight, propping herself up. Then she bends the arms and lowers herself toward me; I close my eyes so I can feel her black hair and her breasts brush against me and disappear. After a while I open them again. The room is lighted in gold and gray. She is propped up again and there is her face, her eyes closed now, I can tell she is far away, so very far away, and the look on her face is tremendous, a thing of great beauty, sculpted and shadowed in the light. I try to imagine where she is, I try not to make a sound, rising up into her and back down again, up and down, trying not to touch her anywhere but where we are joined, so that she can be alone wherever she is, thinking whatever it is she's thinking, with her keyed to this rhythm and slowly bringing herself to meet it each time. Then I bring my hand up from my side and and rub her gently around her clit with my fingertips, kind of grazing against it more than rubbing it. She almost collapses on top of me then, and bucks and bucks again and comes, not at length, not a big one, and then we find our slow rhythm again. After a minute we turn over and almost go off the bed because it's a single bed, after all, but we right ourselves and I'm on top of her, still fluid and slow, and I'm concentrating on feeling her entire body, the entire surface of it, my arms stretched out on top of her arms, the pose of a double crucifixion, and my legs vee'd out along the insides of hers and my feet rubbing hers, and we're just like that, two crabs or clams or images. Her skin is like warm, living stone. And then over we go again, we know the terrain now and compensate for the size of the bed, and we're hugging tight, we're tight together and speeding up, pounding at the hips and then she rises up above me and really rocks, jumping and twisting and I pull down on her hips until I'm as far inside her as I can go and I push it a little more—then I let her go and she's up again, way way way up and far off and I pop out of her for a moment and we both say, "Umph," which is kind of funny, and then she grabs me fast and pushes me back in, and we start slowly again, building up to where we were, and then she slows it again and I don't think I can stand it. But then it's okay and I'm able to slow down, until we're almost stopped. She leans far to my right and gives herself enough room on the other side to twist her leg around, careful not to separate us, and then she leans heavily to the left, to swing around the other leg, so that she's sitting on me very heavily with her feet pointing up beyond my shoulders, resting on my middle, and my pelvic bones, my cock, everything feels likes it's going to snap—I'm not as young as I once was, I want to tell her, but I don't say a thing, and once it's done and she's reversed the direction of her legs she takes my arms and lying back pulls me over, a neat flip. Her legs are open and I'm over her, high above, holding on to the short end of the bed frame, down at the foot of the bed, the brass cold in my hand, and I'm just using my hips, we're not touching anywhere again except the one human thought-less dreamy place, doing it just with the organs, the full sliding length of the thing we do together, until she starts to come and pushes hard up toward it, grabbing me around the ribs and then she wraps her arms around my back hard and pulls her whole body up off the bed and against me and I take one arm off the bed frame and hold her suspended body and slowly I lower us like a big piece of equipment. She is holding me tight to her with her legs around the small of my back, making rela-tively small noises because it's an old inn and who knows what you can hear and she's coming, or so I always think but one is never certain, is one, and me with my arms around behind her head to keep her from getting a concussion from the brass stanchions, with my teeth gritted and growling like it's some form of agony, banging in her and banging in her and banging in her and banging in her until the fire flares and balls up and explodes, torching its only pathway out, and I thrust and thrust and push up into her as far as I can until it's over.

Afterward I stay inside her as long as I can, sinking slowly, like a cruiser going down in the South Pacific, an inevitable disappearance, but long-winded or so it seems to us as we breathe and breathe, her clench-ing and clenching and clenching against the softening piece, with it still pulsing in a rhythmic memory mimicking the heart. When I came the tip of my cock felt like it was being dipped in liquid oxygen, something frozen and scorching at the same time, the world behind my eyelids absolutely bright red like a wound or the thermal center of a nuclear explosion. Slowly this sense of heat subsides. We are holding each other and still slowly rocking, kissing big wet orchid kisses. I'm whispering nonsense. She is kind of humming, kissing my skin and emitting a low animal sound. And then finally we are lying still and I've slipped out of her; she turns her back to my front and snuggles against me on the single bed. We lie like that for a good while, skimming across the surface of sleep like two blue herons over a glassy mountain lake. A distant voice-over: *These rare and beautiful birds, free from all predators but man, will mate for life.*

Finally I wake a little and I'm considering how to pull ourselves up to the head of the bed and get the blankets up around us, vaguely wondering also about the meeting of our loins where there is a great deal of moisture, almost too much to consider going to sleep with, a mess.

"Will?" she says after a long time.

"Yes?"

"I'm not feeling that great all of a sudden."

"I'm sorry," I say, and I really am; I feel immediately that I've done something terribly, terribly wrong. This is the first available emotion of every Irishman who has ever gotten laid—I'm sorry, I'm sorry, oh God I'm so sorry. *Quis hic locus, quae regio, quae mundi plaga?*

"What I'm thinking is," she says, and already I'm alert, something's coming, "is that I wonder if you could, if we could, you know, sleep separately."

"Oh," I say. "Sure. If that's what you want."

"Yeah," she says. She turns, looks at me. "Don't be hurt," she says. As she's turned she's drawn the covers off me, to herself.

"No, it's all right." I sit up and shake my head, swing my feet around to the floor, and I stand, holding on to the bedpost, which is catching what light there is in the room and seems to be ablaze. It's surprising, a tribute to the sex perhaps, or just a sign of age, how thunderously dizzy I am, and how weak in the knees. "What a quaint country inn," I say, swaying slightly.

"Really, I know you're hurt, but you shouldn't be," she says, sitting up herself, touching me again, on the leg—how gentle they are with us after we're spent, how wary before.

"I'm feeling sick and that wasn't exactly safe or smart and I'm on the verge of screaming all of a sudden. It's complicated," she says.

"Absolutely," I say. "Complicated is the word." I stumble over to my bed and manage, rather gracelessly it seems to me, to get myself into it. It's been made up as tight as a bed in a prison camp. By the time I accomplish this she has flipped herself around and gotten her covers rearranged.

"You're not angry?" she says.

"No, no," I say. No no no no no. Enraged, devastated, vanquished and vanquishing, who knows. I'm heaving around the pillows, which are the size of small automobiles, and I crack my wrist on the bedpost. "Yaaah," I say.

"Oh," Ellie says. "Are you all right?"

"Fine," I say. "Fine. Only a little discombobulated."

"Good night," she says.

"Good night," I say. I turn off the lamp and listen for her breathing. *Goonight Bill. Goonight Lou. Goonight May. Goonight. Ta ta. Goonight. Goonight.*

Good night, ladies, good night, sweet ladies, good night, good night.

NEW YORK CITY, AUGUST 15

TODAY THE HEAT BREAKS. It has been six and a half weeks of ninety- or ninety-five- or ninety-nine-degree days. Six 100-or-more-degree days. In the early weeks of this equatorial onslaught the city seemed slowly to be losing its definitions, melting and fusing into itself, and by the third week the same phenomenon was occurring to each citizen personally. People on the subway looked haunted and drained, sleepless, paranoic, as if they were in touch with a part of themselves they hadn't known existed, some primal sector of consciousness ready to kill with hands and teeth and lap the blood in grunting satisfaction, drought-suffering lions on the baked savannah, jowls running long strings of tinged mucus into the sand. The streets were like the murky, haloed glare of a nasty dream, an unfocused ghetto-scape, the air thick with rot. You get into your office, onto your air-conditioned train car, home to the whirring window machines, and the sweat won't stop, it's running off your forehead and over your eyebrows, down behind your ears, sheening along spine and breastplate. A shower in the morning, a shower in the afternoon, a couple of shirts a day. The sprinkling of powders against fungal armies, grotesque outbreaks.

Finally, today, it just comes apart like so much blockage washing out of the pipes. About noontime I go out and I can feel a breeze coming up from the harbor and above me the permanent gray wash of sky is giving way at last in a roundish line before the forward push of limpid blue. A high is moving in, pulling in winds off the ocean, from the north. Right now it's running up some channel in the harbor, and I am walking down lower Broadway with the wind fresh upon me, beyond the gaudy old custom house, into the park. Numbers of us, moving toward the water like drones to nectar. Along the promenade, businessmen, postal workers, retirees taking a break from the Battery OTB office— we all stand against the balustrades, with the wind, the miraculous wind, pressing our shirts flat—two dozen versions of Moses, in terror and faith, accepting God's power over the waters. Couples sit on benches, men stretched out, women clasping their shoulders. The giant-sized word-processing ladies, veterans of the seventeen-dollar meal allowance, trod fat-ankled toward the cool.

Tourists, weary and oblivious in their bright clothes, stand like escapees from a Midwest shtetl, *lined up to board the boat to Ellis Island, individual reversals of history. Their skinny children, uniformly in long, loose shorts and tank tops, suggestive of an entire nation, beginning somewhere in western Jersey and running uninterrupted to the Pacific, that wears nothing but gym shorts and tank tops and cuts its hair, boys and girls alike, short on top and scraggly down the neck, dash in and out of the forest of legs; the out-of-town parents fret after them, fearful of the city, the authorities, various unnameable dangers. The wind lifts the grit of the ages from our pores. Lapping harbor water swirls and rises and falls, one can almost see the cooler waters from below being stirred after long stillness to the top, from there to be blown in fine mist over us. The ferry departing for Staten Island tacks around Governors Island and sends out a fan of spray. Gulls scavenge in its wake.*

All around us is sound: birds, children, buoys, bells, and water.

This is where Walt Whitman walked, staring with exuberant lust after the stevedores.

I find myself in the shadows of the snack shed, near the ticket windows, as if in a dark wood, here in the middle of the journey of my life. Before me a bank of public phones. I've left my cell back at the office. There is something miraculous about the emptiness of consecutive phones in this crowd, so much so that I presume they're not working. But I check; dial tone audible, mouthpiece active, coin slot clear. I drop the coins, dial the familiar number that my fingers can run through without me thinking, calling home.

PART II

OCTOBER / NOVEMBER

[9]

Poker at Jack's apartment, a monthly partners' ritual to which I've been asked for the first time. Until I score this invitation, I'm not absolutely certain (though I'm fairly certain, I must admit) that I'm actually slotted to make partner. This is the final test, a sense of can-we-really-deal-with-this-guy. Right now we're about an hour and a half into it, I'm up about a hundred or a hundred and fifty. Jack's down and enjoying it because it's only a hundred bucks so far and there's a big pot built up for a hand of high/low. My hand is nine-high, which is very weak for lowball, but I'm sure Sue is faking low and going high.

I have two kings out there with the nine and the ace, and a two, four, and seven underneath, so who knows what I have. You'd have to think I look strong high. Jack's probably got two pair but not very high pairs, queens and nines I'm guessing. Sue's showing a two and a three, which she took on third and fourth streets, looking powerful low, then an eight and then a jack. The jack, eight, and three are all hearts, of which there are only two showing besides hers, which means there are eight potential hearts for her to fill out her flush, out of thirty cards not known to me. To beat me low her three cards not showing would have to be pulled from among the sevens, sixes, fives, fours, and aces: there are twenty such cards in the deck, out of that thirty again, but I have seen eleven of them, which leaves nine out of thirty. Roughly a one-in-three chance, multiplied by two, because she needs to have done it twice. I think she has the flush, and my two kings indicate I might have a full house, which would beat it; my betting only suggested this once, when I raised big, forty dollars, on a ten-dollar raise to me, from Jack, as if the raise struck me as an affront. Otherwise I've bet the hand medium-high, moderately, though confidently, trying to keep all the high hands in, since I'm going low. Her hand drove the other lows out early. I have the check after the announcement of high or low, so I can get away with seeing her forty-dollar bet at most, and probably less, in an $800 pot, minimum. This means, as a bettor sees it, I'm getting a twenty to one, maybe fifteen to one, payoff, on something that has a five-to-one shot, so it's a bargain bet. Besides which, and this is why I've followed along to start with, I'm pretty sure she's got a flush.

I pick up two chips, put them with both hands under the table, shake them around a little, stash them in my left and leave my right empty. The empty hand will announce I'm going low.

"You ready?" I say.

She looks at me, leans over the table. "You want to split the pot?" she says.

"Right now? No bet?"

"Yup," she says.

I think about it—there's very little way for me to make more money out of her because it's just the two of us, and whatever she bets, she's scared now; she thinks I have her high hand beat; if I say no she'll panic, I can see it in her eyes, and go low; in such a scenario theoretically she might go low and I could beat her at that and win the whole pot, except she almost certainly has a better low hand than mine that she's not paying attention to, all dazzled with a goddamned flush or whatever it is. Outside of this fairly remote possibility I'm only looking at a split anyway. It's a sweaty pot, the kind you perspire over. But I came into it looking only for the split, and somehow, as I'm about to push her over the edge, it comes to me: humiliate her and you've got problems at work. She's trying to look tough, on her face, waiting for me to answer, but there is something peculiar in her eyes. The thought flashes through my mind: she can't stand to lose this, not to me, in front of them, and she is incapable of deciding whether to go high or low.

I bring back my empty right fist, which has been pointing out over the table like a cannon nosing out of a fortress wall. "Sure," I say.

"Hey, wait a minute!" Gerry says.

"Yeah, what the fuck is this?" Jack says.

"We're splitting the pot," I say. "Which we are perfectly entitled to do." I toss my cards into the mess in front of Gerry, as does Sue, then we start the counting.

"What did you have?" Jack says, looking at me. I just smile. He looks at Sue. She looks back at him and challenges him to ask again. "Jesus Christ," he says. He gets up and goes into the kitchen. This half pot puts me up near six hundred for the night.

"It's getting pretty late," I say tentatively.

"Don't even think about it, asshole," Gerry says.

Things look good for me.

In negotiations with Ursula's case. The opposing firm is Kreishaw Whitney, a heavy-duty litigation firm with expertise, among other things, in insurance defense. Sue was to be here but she was beckoned instead to Los Angeles to an "emergency"—though undoubtedly capricious and unproductive—meeting with a bigger and more fabulous client, a well-known Italian-American film director with a wife in New York whom he wants to shed while still preserving his assets for the next project, or perhaps it is the project after the next project that he is looking to. In any case, he is one of those clients where to put him off is to lose him. He has some other all-purpose attorney on the West Coast named Barry whom he insists participate in everything. When Sue called me, nine-thirty A.M., which is six-thirty A.M. in California, she did not sound well rested and just back from her morning run. She had that slate hardness that she gets whenever Barry comes into her outer atmosphere.

"You can handle this," she says. "Take David so we don't look lean. And don't say anything, just act self-confident, put forward the case as we've written it, and listen to what they have to say. Don't say a word besides that."

"Okay, Sue," I say.

"I mean it, Will," she says.

"People are always saying that to me," I say.

"Yeah, well, there's a reason. Get a clue," Sue says. Then she hangs up.

The meeting is at the usual law offices with the usual rare and expensive wood lining the walls and corridors. Tulipwood, I'm guessing. Pale gold and elegantly grained. We are in a conference room in midtown with a view almost biblical in scope, looking down on all the kingdoms of the world in their magnificence. *All these I shall give to you, if you will prostrate yourself and worship me.* Suddenly, everyone in the room looks like a demon; we are hell's middle-management team, at a midday meeting.

"I want to thank you and Mr. Chin for joining us," Kreishaw's ranking partner on the case, Francis Downey, says. "I'm sorry my old friend Sue couldn't be here." His hair is slicked against his skull; I want to tell him this look passed out of style with the last explosion of destructive wealth, more than ten years ago. He pulls motions and discovery notices and notes from a Redweld and stacks them with military crispness to his left. Manicured hands.

"The reason I thought it might be beneficial to have a discussion at this point, rather early in discovery, is to explore the possibilities and test the waters before we really embark on what is going to be a lengthy and costly process," Downey says. "And I think to do that, I'd like to lay out what we feel is a fair and reasonable assessment of the range of potential, umm, interpretations that might be put on the evidence and claims in the case thus far. I hope that's an agreeable starting point."

"Well, we're here to listen to what you have to say," I reply. As I speak I cease writing on my pad and look up at him, as if I've taken a moment off from an important task that he has interrupted. I've been tracing out the words "When a Man Loves a Woman by Percy Sledge" in different hand-drawn letterings, over and over and over in the yellow spaces between the blue lines. I look down again and go back to it. "Our own interpretation is manifest in the original motion for relief."

"Right," Downey says. He then proceeds to lay out, with many words, a patchwork narrative of excuses and mitigations in which the building management company and therefore its insurers of course have no real liability for security in the building. I point out to him that under this ramshackle interpretation, there is no reason for the management company to provide security at all, since clearly it isn't needed and no one wants it and the management company isn't responsible for it in any case.

"It's a very tenuous argument at best," I say. "Not to mention unlikely to be compelling in front of a jury."

"Let's consider that jury," Downey says. "Do you want to bring this case in front of a real jury, Will? On behalf of a client whose, shall we say, proclivities—"

"'Proclivities'?" I interrupt him. "'Proclivities'? Are you seriously interested in taking that road? It has such a sweet, heavy smell, like some kind of National Socialist cologne. No one, Mr. Downey, not a single human being, has used that word in this *century* in an honest or credible way. If you take that direction in front of a Manhattan judge and jury we will leave you and your client sliced, hollowed out, and dull-eyed, like a roasted carp at a Chinese banquet hall. My advice is, don't go there."

"Mr. Riordan—"

"You know, Mr. Downey, I must say, hearing what you've just said, that I suspect you believe a bisexual woman, or '*practicing bisexual*' as you so enjoy putting it in your motion to dismiss, *deserves* to have her apartment broken into, herself tied up for six and a half hours with a heavy-gauge extension cord, be beaten, and, among other acts of horrific sexual aggression, have a telephone receiver inserted in her rectum—"

"Mr. Riordan, I seriously object—"

"While, I might add, the half-assed security guard who isn't really needed in any case is in the basement smoking dope and watching porn videos."

"That is an outrageous lie, and I seriously object to your tone with me and my colleagues—"

"It's an interesting point of view that you have, Mr. Downey, and I

can assure you that we look forward to arguing it with you in court. I'm
not at all certain we have anything further to discuss."

After the meeting, David says to me, "Roasted carp?"

"I know," I say.

"Chinese banquet hall?"

"I know, it's insane."

"Where did that stuff come from?"

"I don't know, it was just the image and language that came into my
head at that moment, I apologize."

"No," he says. "I think it was very effective."

"No, really," I say. "It was unnecessary, I apologize. It didn't help the
case one bit. I suppose we're going to have to tell Sue."

"My guess is, you get your first settlement offer within the next four-
teen days," he says.

"Why do you think so?"

"No one can bear seeing himself as a roasted carp in a Chinese banquet hall for long. Take it from me."

And sure enough, the following Monday, I get a call from Downey.
He is snide, dismissive, and, behind all that, totally ready to be plucked.

"They made an offer," I tell Sue.

"Who? Kreishaw Whitney? How much?" she says.

"I just got off the phone with Downey," I say. "Seven hundred
thousand."

"In his dreams," she says. "You didn't say anything?"

"I said I'd take it to my client," I say. "To which he said, 'Your partner, you mean.'"

"What an asshole," she says. She leans back in her throne of leather,
swivels, taps a pencil. "What did you say?"

"I said of course I do like to keep my colleagues informed, though
perhaps he encouraged senior associates to act unilaterally in his firm.

If so, perhaps we could talk about me taking a position there."

"And why did he call you and not me?"

"You're so vain," I say.

"No, really, did he say?"

"No. He didn't say. Maybe he thought I'd utter something stupid, give him a handle. He's had an edge on for me from the start."

Sue zips forward in the chair and clicks an address book icon on her laptop, leans back in her throne of leather, and says, "Okay, what should we ask for?"

"I was thinking about that."

"I'm sure you were. You're a very thinking boy."

"It's interesting they're making an offer so soon. They really seem not to want to go through discovery here, or the client doesn't. There must be some major shit they've got to protect. I say we ask for three point five," I say.

"Very *good*," she says. "I was thinking three, but the point five is kind of brilliant, it makes it sound like three but pulls up the whole back-and-forth by half a mil. I love that. Leave me now, darling, I'm going to call him and flirt and your presence will not be needed. Close the door on your way out."

The marriage/non-marriage is settling into a routine of ongoing ambivalence. On the advice of counsel and in the belief that a union bearing two incredibly young children demands at least some effort at salvaging, Ellie and I are seeing a therapist once a week, getting counseling, using an M.S.W. of the disappointed, of the overstressed, of those who have seen enough prosperity for deep and confounding melancholy and anger to set in. The office is nicely done to confirm middle-class longings. For Ellie and me the therapy is a grueling exercise in measuring the distances between us. I always leave the place feeling slightly corrupted, as if I've indulged myself. No matter what I say, how careful I am to speak honestly, the context of therapy is so unlike that of the life it attempts to reorder that the conversion of truths from one realm to the other is full of glitches and garbled text. Eventually you start acting, except the part you're trying to play is (or is supposed to be, or is your interpretation of, or has some tenuous connection to) your true self. And you realize that all life is just that, the same act of mimicry of yourself, and the therapy becomes just one more way of framing things, one more way of slanting the story. You come in, sit down, and the atmosphere is of the confessional, where you have managed to get the parish's easiest and most liberal priest. Almost every action is forgivable. The tremendous labored earnestness in our voices—*What I really wanted from Will in our marriage was his attention, his affection*—yes, that plus some magical power exercised by him to change your life, probably yourself. *No problema, mi hija, I do for you.* It would be nice if I were allowed to tell the truth: *What I want from Ellie is a faultless and bottomless devotion; she should take care of everything all the time just like Mommie, and send me out to play. If she asks me to wear clean underpants, I will. I'll stop in for meals and then, yes indeedy, bedtime, because we like that, at least on most nights. When I don't stop in, she should sweetly miss me. Since I'm not drunk and enraged all the time as my father was, as all the men in my childhood were, she should be telling me at every possible moment how fantastic I am and how happy she is to be married to a wonderful guy like me. She should be interesting and funny and good looking, and desirable to others and to me, except when I want to be alone, then she shouldn't be anything at all, most especially visible. That's it. Can I go home now?* In the simultaneous-translation business that is therapy, even saying things that are outrageously false is a way of communicating, albeit ineffectively. We will *work* on my ability to confront and communicate what I *really* feel. Then we can change it. Except, guess what, I don't want to change it and don't intend to change it and neither does she if truth be told, so why are we spending so much time and money here? Yet somehow when we leave we always feel a little closer than usual, bonded at least by the act of sharing our alienation with someone who is, essentially, a weird stranger.

After therapy we go for coffee at a café across Amsterdam Avenue—espresso, cappuccino in paper cups. Actually the system at this particular café encourages you to be an effete snot, because they actually have ceramic cups: just not enough, so you have to ask for them. Ellie is wearing a denim jacket over a wide pair of pants, and, because it's still warm enough, and because she knows I'll notice, sandals. Her hair is shiny black—I've been surprised and disheartened since we've separated to find that she's taking such good care of herself, that she looks so good. Getting rid of me, a new leaf. Not to mention the tug of desire—her feet in the sandals, skin still brownish from summer, strong and lovely. Her legs are crossed, one sexy-looking foot projecting out from beneath the marble-top table.

"I'm beginning to understand *why* you are the way you are," she is saying. "That doesn't mean I want to live with it."

At first I say nothing. It occurs to me that were you to open the heart of a saint you might well find a core of self-loathing, the last and most tenacious sin to overcome. The saint would be no less a saint, at least according to the rule book. "I guess there's something to be said for being able to come to terms with each other," I finally say. I'm trying to be responsible. "Being able, you know, to get along and arrange our lives around the needs of the children and not cause further heartbreak or tension or whatever."

"Yeah, sure," Ellie says. "Heartbreak or tension or whatever. Let's do avoid that." She takes a careful sip of the coffee. "The typical bullshit. It's better for me if I hate your guts, frankly. Gives me something to live for, to energize and focus my day."

"You look wonderful," I say, apropos of nothing.

"See? That's just what I mean. I can look good because I hate you, and I know how bad it makes you feel. I'd *like* to look good because I *want* to look good, for myself, not because it accomplishes or doesn't accomplish something with you. For God's sake. I want you out of my life, not there by absence. Right now it's the same as before, only with more leg room."

"I don't want to be out of your life," I say. "I don't want to be out of

your life and I don't want you to be out of mine and everything else that
goes with it, I don't want just the little notes with the check in them, the
brief informational phone calls, 'Henry's off from his play group on
Thursday and have you sent through the papers to get Sam his social security number.' I want to be let back in your life. Okay? So don't ask me
for advice about how to clean up your codependency problems."

"That's sweet," Ellie says. She's looking at me.

"Oh, screw you," I say.

"No, really, it's very sweet. Except you're not telling the truth. You say
you want to be part of things. Unfortunately you have no idea how actually
to *do* it and nothing you've ever done in your life indicates you want to. You
don't want to be cut off, certainly. But that's not the same as a voluntary act
that would include you in other people's messy, loud, intrusive lives."

"Uh-huh," I say. I go into a high voice: "'Uh-huh, uh-huh, I *like*
it . . . Do a little dance. Make a little love, Get down tonight. Get down
tonight.'" I sip the end of my coffee. Cafecito negro. I stand up. As the
seconds pass, she watching me, I grow angrier and angrier. She still sits.
I gaze down; her bright eyes. "So, what you're saying is that love—"

"Shhh," she says. "Not so loud. Does everybody at the café have to
share in the discussion?"

"—is that love, hours and hours and hours of conversation, the time,
the experiences of lives shared and recalled, a little travel, the extraordinary transformation of having children, discussing them, getting to
know them together, shaping our world, coming to conclusions about
the people in it, the choices we have had to make, and sex, touching,
sleeping, touching in dreams, all of this is not enough? Right? Right?"
I'm feeling marvelously pissed off. "Some deep essential part of my will
and consciousness and pain don't yet belong to you and may never belong to you, and that eradicates everything else? I'm withholding, cold-
bloodedly, in the protomale fashion. Well, to that I say, keep dreaming.
What you want to be married to is a woman, someone with no sense of
boundaries, only half a concept of self, someone for whom sin, darkness,
and despair are merely symptoms of a known, nameable, eradicable
malady—a malady that has been nicely identified in the Health section

of the *Times*, it's actually viral, you know, and can be overcome by eating more green leafy vegetables and getting lots of exercise. Jane Brody's written about it, plus there are also certain herbs, you're tracking that information down now, it's part of the new Asian thing, all over the city women are throwing the names of ancient herbs around like they actually know what the fuck they're talking about—"

"What women?" says Ellie.

"—shut up and don't interrupt. You think euphoria, home organization, slim legs, and the grace of God, they all can be had in one holistic regimen. Life is a problem of what fucking gym to join. Lots of other women on the West Side are on to this, there will be discussion groups, thank god, support and information, the new nexus of womanPower, one word in a precise, fashionable type, with a capital *P* in the middle and a 'TM' after it. Women of your generation and caste believe the whole goddamned dilemma of selfhood properly ought to be blamed on someone else, in any case. Worst of all, this is what I find appalling and men in general find appalling, you actually think we ought to address these concerns of yours in *hours* of frustrating, leading-nowhere, ostensibly-empowering-but-actually-the-opposite fucking talk."

Ellie is still calmly watching me squint down at her. "NT," she says.

"What the fuck does 'NT' mean?"

"Nice try," she says. "And it was, it was a nice try. Unfortunately, I'm talking about the desirability of living with someone who comes home every night with a dead face and dead eyes and whose silence and alienation and barely contained anger fill up the room and choke everything in it. When he speaks, it's to be nasty. When he fucks, it's to dominate, or to exorcize some foul demon. Not my idea of fun."

"Thus you have indicated," I say.

She stands. She puts three dollars down, for her coffee and biscotti. We look at each other, eye to eye. She is beautiful, goddamn her. The three dollars is a fucking power move on her part and probably a dollar short, too. "And there we are," she says. "So, sweetie, see you next week? We can talk about how hard it is to *date*."

*   *   *

I grab a sandwich and take a phenomenally expensive cab back to the office: in addition to the lawyers we've each put on retainer, and the hundred and thirty a session for the counseling, these weekly confabs are costing almost forty bucks in transportation. At my desk, sandwich, Arizona medicinal tea, a small package of nuts. Two bites and I check my e-mail. The modern attention span. And here it is again, from Ursula. The text hovers and blinks, little glyphs and scratches on a glowing white Etch A Sketch panel.

subject: "on rape"

if you were to give this some susan sontag bullshit title that's what you'd call it. "on fucking rape" might be better. here's my point, in a nutshell, mr riordan—you've got to tell it from the other point of view. tell it from the rapist's point of view—maybe that's you, mr riordan. maybe you're the abusive type. my experience—well my experience is a little wider than i'd like it to be, but in my experience these men don't show it on the street as it were. gentlemen, gentle men, all elegant and calm you know. and you probably DO know, somewhere in that grim locked irish psyche of yours, covered up with a forever graying Sunday winter sky, right? the rapist's perspective? you can see things that way. why not use your voice? tell it the way you know it. here's what you might say—that rape is fucking someone who doesn't want to be fucked, and i want you to know that people DO things and furthermore that what they DO has MEANING, so it's stupid to pretend that every bad thing that happens is a coincidence, that every crime is an accidental convergence of random energies—when somebody rapes another person he fucking means it.

here is a fact, ladies—to commit a rape you have to have a hard-on. i'm not talking the new bullshit version of rape where if somebody says something you don't like they've RAPED you for god's sake. i'm talking we-make-money-the-old-fashioned-way, we-fuck-it-out-of-you kind of rape. the rapist just before the rape is standing somewhere, we envision darkness, but life is more complicated than that, isn't it? it could be fluorescent-lighted, "cool white" is the market name of that color; it could be on the linoleum floors of a federal office getting rehabbed—wherever it is, he is standing, waiting, with his dick in his hand. this is what really IMPRESSES one about rape—as opposed, say, to murder, which just possibly CAN be accidental, or im-promptu, can be due to certain biochemical overloads, the twinkie defense, although it's not likely. rape, though, rape, now, rape—well, rape needs to have an erection. and don't let men fool you, an erection is evidence, it means something that a word doesn't. it's an expression of desire and malice and will, a man's oh-so-special-way-of-saying-I-love-you. without an erection it's not rape, not in the real or the legal sense, the police they call it something else, the police call it sexual assault, molestation, groping in the stairway, felonious sodomy behind a tree (why don't some of the vic-tims just bite that soft dick they're told to suck right off?); without the hard-on the attack becomes a symbol of sex rather than sex itself—nasty talk.

the hard truth (no pun etc): plenty of you would rape if you could, if it weren't too dangerous, IF THERE WASN'T THE DANGER OF BEING CAUGHT and humiliated by the woman you are victimizing (isn't that right mr riordan?); it's romance in a cer-tain sense, just it's against the law. animals DO rape each other—their world doesn't include what we'd call justice; or it's a justice founded on purely physical and genetic laws and one of those is, IF YOU HAVE DICK, YOU SHALL ATTEMPT TO USE IT. mr riordan don't avoid the rapist's story—he can tell you about a world without human justice. he can tell you something like you hope the dead would be able to tell you about a state that you fear and that you're bound for.

here's what mr riordan says, up there on broadway on the yupper west side of manhattan incorporated NY. he's got his dick in his hand right now and he's say-ing—mr riordan you should know that i'm drinking a lot of coffee and not eating a thing, so that i can go a little crazy and risk going a lot more but pull back at the last minute so—THERE'S NOTHING REALLY TO WORRY ABOUT, for instance i can keep numbers and prices and lists in my head and still write this—café bustelo over on first avenue—have you ever noticed this?—is $2.89 a can and on lexington it's like $5.99 or $6.19 or some shit, have you noticed? which means that on lexington this particular coffee is an import of some kind, priced for the white people, like a fucking artifact of a culture that happens to live, breathe, work, sleep, fuck, eat, shit, piss, piss again, and climb back into bed maybe 800 feet away.

fuck society, fuck responsibility. do i misread the times? we should admit that the suffering in the world, the violence and victimization, is our will in action, our hearts' desire. what happens happens because we want it to, it's no mystery, it's not PUZZLING or COMPLICATED or ANOMALOUS or STRANGE. the real mystery at work in the world is decency. the real mystery is respect; the real mystery lies in the nearly invisible expressions of kindness and love that you find in the world—yes, in new york, more often in new york than elsewhere, i've noticed—you can find it every thirty feet or so like circles of light from the yellowing street lamps. it's like light but it's a more dangerous light than that. when christ said "i am the light" there was no such thing as "cool" light; it was understood that he meant something hot, something on fire.

i am astonished by my own selfishness.

whose voice is that?

The next day, she is in the office, an appointment with Sue and me for an update. She is capable, apparently, of a wide range of styles. She looks more elegant than the last time, black slacks, brown loafers, a loose, deep-red cardigan, and pearls, a kind of Katharine-Hepburn-meets-Pam-Grier-lesbian-rich-lady thing.

"We have had a very successful, at least we feel, series of meetings with the attorneys from Kreishaw Whitney," Sue says.

"I read your letter," Ursula says.

"What I haven't reported yet, because it just happened," Sue says, "is an initial settlement offer, a kind of let's-see-how-serious-they-are kind of offer, of seven hundred thousand dollars. I will need authorization from you for a response, which I recommend be a flat-out turndown with a counteroffer for a settlement of three point five million."

"Three and a half million?" Ursula says. "Dollars?" Her face looks like she's sucking on a wad of tinfoil. Sue's hands are flat out on the table, ten digits radiating from the center line of her torso like guns covering the room. Her nails are the color of raw steak.

"I think it's a reasonable starting position. In all honesty I had to consider whether four or five might not have been better, but the higher the number goes the longer it takes to negotiate the ultimate settlement. I'm aware of your concern for the timing of these negotiations in terms of their rapid closure."

"Yeah, their rapid closure," says Ursula.

"These conversations with Kreishaw Whitney have been very re-
aling. Underlying their opening offer is a fundamental admission of
ostantial liability. Now it's just a matter of how many dollars they'll
in the pot. We have the upper hand because we're willing, even ea-
, to go to discovery and trial, and they're not. That gives us power."
says this last in a chipper tone.

"Shit, woman, we don't have power," Ursula says. "Don't fool your-
nobody has power. But go ahead, get all the money you can. I don't
need to hear about it until it's over. In fact, that's what I prefer."

We'll send you a confirming letter on that," Sue says.

New York is about being late, about rushing, about scheduling twelve
things in a day that fits four. Movie talk, the rush of footage that we live
in, the constant extemporaneous cinema. At the Forty-second Street station on my way home from work every day, the subway doors shush
open, and flashing before us within the narrow frame of the doorway is
the essential movie screen, filled with stone-gray light and shadow, swift
legs and droll, anguished faces. St. Petersburg, Dachau, Beirut, Calcutta,
Manhattan. Men, women moving through the tunnel like prisoners, a
forced march toward what they've chosen or more likely what they've
been handed. Sometimes there is music, musicians playing for loose
change on the platforms, a sound track never really captured by actual
movies, in the moist resonant acoustics of the subway.

Right now I'm in my apartment, up early though I didn't get to sleep until late—I was out wandering again. It's a little after six and I'm puttering
around, feeling charged up but in a patient way, or I want to say penitent
way, which is the truth but beside the point. My regret has no bearing on

today's chemical forecast: a nice mixture of insomniac energy, slight nausea, tremendous guilt, and yes, there it is, a thin strip of self-confidence, a sense of endurance I haven't felt for a long time. Where does love come from? Something is clarifying for me, I can feel it happening just below the surface consciousness, like a trout taking bugs just before they reach the surface and hatch, the trout's dark nose and back dimpling the film. Standing at the refrigerator an image comes into my mind, clear as water, of Ron's son, Friar. I don't see the little girl but I feel her there. With the fridge door open, and me not remembering what I opened it for.

And I think: *one of my babies, one of my own children . . .*

There is really no risk for the firm if we lose Ron's case, and of course each of us secretly wants to lose the case; everyone believes he's guilty; he has no friends and no supporters and there will be no attention in the press to anything about us or the way we handled things; and, of course, we will be paid. Yet we move inexorably forward toward winning, conditioned by training, by professional vanity, by all the habits of our knowledge of jurisprudence. We are carried along on the current of our knowing that there is too little evidence, that the prosecution does not deserve to win, that they've made too little effort in not enough time. And I see the justice in what we'll do, I actually believe in the necessity of forcing the state to prove its case, regardless of the circumstances, because guilty men going free pose far fewer risks than innocent men going to prison. And Ron's children—they're already doomed. No matter how it goes they have to shape lives out of the smashed crockery and jumble of singed wood their parents have left for them, an impossible task. But they shouldn't have to deal with him anymore, it seems to me. I'm not certain of the law on this issue, but if he's acquitted I don't see any clear or simple way to loose them from him, and I know he won't give them up on his own. That would be an offense to his well-developed taste for tyranny and possession. His children, my children, a simple notion, really, a duty you can put your arms around, a deep instinct: don't let bad things happen to children. But we do.

As for this morning, who knows? You can't predict the electrical events in the brain that change you, that move your life a little closer to what has been known for it since the beginning of time, a spark's leap across various neuroreceptors and zones of grace. An entire plan falls down like a scroll in front of my eyes.

And I think, *milk*—I have opened this door, which is letting out the frosted richness of refrigerator air to chill my shirtfront, for milk. I take the milk. On the radio, the man stops talking and then they're playing Bach's concerto for two violins; I pour milk in my coffee. Extraordinary the sound of Bach, an old recording, not remixed, brutal and raw, gut strings and horsehair bow, offal as art, the first movement a question, a request perhaps, to God; and then the second, an answer, a conversation of infinite tenderness. For each of us, salvation undeserved. I lie down on the futon to read the paper and now mildly happy, suddenly relaxed, I doze off. I don't leave for work until nine.

Outside, it's one of those slant-lighted mornings of October, an edge to the air, dusty blue. Down at the end of 106th Street the valiant horseman stands, before a spiny field of orange and brown, the fall branches of New York City just reaching their muted color, already half bare. The statue's bulk of verdigris bronze trembles in the air before them. What political vanquishing earned this horseman his paralyzed heroic moment, head toward the river, ass toward the sidewalks and streets, on the end of 106th Street in Manhattan? I keep promising myself to notice on a walk who this horseman is. I'd like to be the kind of person who would know that, like knowing the names of trees, the predominant mineral constituents of local rock face, the bird species, but apparently I am not that kind of person. I turn again, as always, in the opposite direction, toward Broadway, toward commerce and purely human interaction, away from history. On my way to the subway. First, though, I stop in the bagel place at the corner to get a coffee. Ahead of me a girl, she looks like a student, in jeans, ordering a poppy bagel with cream cheese. I feel too alert, too sharp, like a hangnail, all adrenaline and nerve ends, no one can bear this for long, like after taking very speedy acid, but more cruel because more functional. She puts a glass bottle of raspberry iced tea on the counter. It makes a *clunk* sound or a microseconded series of sounds as the edge comes full weight onto the Formica, a glancing *thunk*, a sound full of the precise weight of the thing and the dull-thudded thickness of the counter. I am drowning in the details.

"Could you make the bagel without too much cream cheese?" she says to the counterman. "Put it on thin?" This, too, is unbearable; I have to watch the man, and of course he doesn't put it on thin, they never put it on thin, that would take too much concentration and a most daring divergence from the conventions of the daylong lathering of soft cream cheese on bagels. Oh, I want to tell her (farther up the line now, unmindful, moving with smooth grace and lovely hanging hair toward the register, where the wrapped and too thickly spread bagel will be delivered), it's not thin, it's not thin. You wanted it thin but in fact it's going to be oozing out from every side of the bagel, since the warm bagel, which would have been nicely served with a touch of butter, by the time you get to it will have turned that mound of cream cheese into a revolting white slime-edged mess. Just try to take a bite of that bagel, I dare you.

I'm not getting enough sleep . . . I'm delirious . . .

They give me my coffee and I leave my seventy-five cents. I carry the hot container with a napkin wrapped around it, angle across Broadway. Down in the subway, on the platform, I open the coffee by peeling a small triangle out of the lid. And suddenly I am weak in the knees with shame—I want to run out and up the stairs and go to my family's apartment and find my children and hold them close to me, hold them all day and into the night. It's a feeling along my front, a molecular desire in the skin, something heavy and unbearable behind my eyes, with a sickness, an actual nausea and sinking of the stomach, and I feel as if I can't stand it, that I will be weeping soon, and I have to run, but I stand there frozen, shallow-breathed—and then slowly, slowly it abates . . . The girl from the bagel shop comes onto the platform carrying a backpack over one shoulder and the brown bagel-shop bag. She has the iced tea in her hand, is close to finishing it already, a starter for the rest of it, the bagel and coffee.

She stands by the trash can and gulps the last of the liquid with her mouth nicely but not too roundly opened to meet the wide neck of the bottle. My breath is coming back to normal depth, I'm calming down.

I'll call from work, make sure they're all right . . . I'll take my love and desire and worry and need and I will phone it in and if I'm properly dead and work-obsessed I will be fine.

When the train pulls in, the girl and I get on the same car; I maneuver slightly to be across from her. So much for my grief. The male heart, never right, always too small or too large, too hot or too cold. The morning's gone over to the late side now, it's almost nine-thirty, there are seats, and so she has enough room to settle herself and put her backpack beside her with little proprietary gestures, making sure it leans onto her side and not toward the Latino young man in the seat beyond; and then she opens the wax-papered bagel and lays it out on the brown bag, which she's flattened in her lap, and eats with unconscious relish, licking all that extra cream cheese she didn't want, surreptitiously and lightly from around the edges of the bagel . . . Over her head, an AIDS awareness ad, featuring various couples. One hetero couple, one gay, one lesbian. The gay couple is a tall black man with modified dreadlocks nuzzling a shorter white man; similarly pious culture-mixes prevail among the other couples, Asians, Latinas, whites, blacks. Isn't that nice. The last panel in the series, to the left of the girl's head—she eating her bagel and reading her book, oblivious—displays an array of important tools, a condom, a tube of lubricant, and a rubber surgical glove, a grouping that transforms quickly, through engagement with the imagination, into the most sexually explicit photo I've ever seen on a public conveyance. Five fingers in the glove. Snap. Where does love come from?

I am staring at it, I suppose, because the girl looks up, the way you will look up to the sky if someone else is doing so, to see what's there, and indeed she turns and does see what is there, her face moving visibly through the phases of analysis and comprehension and some harder thought, and at that moment I understand the barriers we face between us as humans, the impossibility of knowing what another person is thinking, what another person experiences internally, in the silence of home base, the skull. We can glean the contents, the basic narrative line, sometimes; if we're good we can hear a little of the language of it and empathize through that toward the emotions, but we can never comprehend the shape and color and flavor and feel, never see the pictures themselves or share the sense of time and memory feeding it. What each of us comes up with on seeing this sign, this last panel with its latex and jelly, the multimedia show it sets off in our brains, will never be communicable to anyone, except perhaps in the act of sex itself, a momentary vision of the other that is rare and that even more rarely translates into larger understanding. The guy who gives you two singles in change when it should have been $1.98 and says, "Don't worry about it" when you struggle to find his two pennies beneath your keys, a standard-looking guy with a Texas Rangers cap of all things at the newsstand, that same night finding himself transported as he lies across a gym horse in a downtown club with someone's forearm up his ass: from an evolutionary standpoint, or doctrinally, why we even have such a realm of shadows and want is a mystery. What I see on her face then reflects that mystery. *What seas, what shores.* As always on a woman's face, this thing is enormous and seductive.

After that, the first half of bagel done away with, she opens her cup of coffee, not too hot now, but still hot. She does the little peel, sticks the plastic lozenge it leaves in her pack, sips slowly across the top. She lifts from her lap her paperback: the title flashes, *Crime and Punishment.* At this I remember the young woman killed by a falling chunk of cornice on Broadway when I'd been, what, a freshman? Sophomore? The headline on the *Post*'s second-day follow-up story, long thereafter a joke among my friends: "She Loved Dostoevsky . . ." Raskolnikov in his rooms, sweating, impoverished, immobile. His fine, frightened sister, worn to a nub, his mother failing, the slow construction of rage. I remember those scenes in his rooms better than the killing, better than the psychologically famous interviews with the policeman who knows but can't prove Raskolnikov's guilt, better than the ending, which in fact I

can't remember at all . . . Raskolnikov, similar to raskalni, raskal, the outsider; in English, rascal and rake, for the nasty and dissolute, and there's
a French word, raconteur, one who tells stories as I am telling myself a
story now. She's a sweet-looking girl and I wonder what it would be like
to take up with a sweet young girl now, I view it from on high, lascivious
and high-minded like J. D. Salinger but with none of the cultural cre-
dentials; there is all that water under my bridge, the deepening commitments and drear of adulthood, *and men shall trod and trod and trod*—I
suspect I wouldn't have the patience to wait out the neuroses, all the
phantoms in possession, which can be counted on from someone in her
early twenties, the big despair pierced by fleeting electric hopes, inde-
scribably unattainable, yet near, near; and the frequent antic depres-
sions—just this momentary dwelling on it brings it back, that warpy
age, not knowing but desiring with intense desire, and so little power.
All the vacuous flirtations. The engineer hits the brakes too hard, we all
in the subway car lurch toward the front of the train, then back, and
both the girl across the aisle and I absorb the shock and keep our beverages level, my coffee now just cooling enough to sip without peril, I'm
holding it a bit aloft as if it's on a bouncing arm, and none spills, one of
those little skills you develop in New York unconsciously, a small piece
in the puzzle of survival. We see each other doing the same maneuver
and she smiles at me.

Ahh, she smiles at me.

At work, I am clearing away certain lingering cases, handing things over
to younger associates, preparing for discovery and trial. The depositions
begin soon. David is at work on the whole fiber and microbe side of
things, DNA samplers, preparing even though the DA has yet to show
any sign such evidence exists.

Despite our early efforts at secrecy, everyone knows now that Ellie
and I separated; the reaction ranges from the surprisingly emotional to

the oddly matter-of-fact. Jack was nearly in tears, Mr. Separation Agreement. Anna has been motherly, never mentioning the thing directly but tuned to the mood swings, which run from edgy to exhausted to bellicose. She brings me herbal tea in the afternoon and murmurs aphorisms. I don't like hot herbal tea that much and tell her so; it's good for what ails you, she says. I doubt that, I say. Somehow she has it in her mind I'm madly in love with my wife and now am sick at heart. I am sick at heart, but otherwise the story doesn't match hers; a nice, simple, romantic story, in which the man, uncharacteristically, proves capable of a strong, expressive emotion.

In the daily mail, invitations from the organizations I belonged to in law school, the fraternity, Moot Court Society, Lawyers for the Environment. Dinners, banquets, honorary luncheons, cocktail parties. I'm tempted by each in turn before I throw it in the trash. I have never been tempted before, even for a moment, by these horrifying events. Meet the female law students who populate these affairs, laugh loudly, expose the dental work, tell myself I am "networking." I remember the tenor of this action from my time, middle-aged Italian lawyers leering at the twenty-three-year-old first-years. Everyone's hair the same length, nicely layered, gray and black, combed to an immovable and unnatural perfection.

subject: les mémoires d'une grande dame

i remember certain things, i am a person with memories. i remember coming to new york as a kid, this isn't you mr riordan, THIS IS ME, walking with my mother and my grandmother, i liked everything about new york, we had moved up to new rochelle by then, the negro greenwich, but i liked the city, it felt all gritty and historic to me and infused with the stories of my parents and my grandparents, the stories they told of big snows (1947, they all talk about the snow in 1947, at christmas) and hard times, rationing during the war, working in places downtown when there was work, all the troubles with white people over the years, all the nuances of color. i liked even the parts that scared me. i had a dream one time that we had to move from the house where we lived in the suburbs into a tenement building—we had NEVER lived in a tenement or anywhere near one even in the harlem time, we had a house on 137th st.—but i dreamed about a tenement, a crumbly looking broken-down place with sooty walls and windows giving on to an air shaft filled with brick and fire escapes and other windows and a web of disturbing clotheslines. people hung out the windows shouting at each other. the dream frightened me, i was afraid of the feeling of sliding, of losing our grip, of moving down, down, down. and then later, after college, i wanted to be on my own, i wanted to live free of the stink of my father's money, the sweet smell of all them jellies and conks and the phone calls on top of phone calls from the people at the badly written tendentious bullshit newspaper and from the money guys talking about the radio stations and the cable options and every other fucking thing he owned. they invariably hired all black men ostensibly to run things and then they had these white guys, these other white consultant guys on the side, did you know that? that's how all the rich ne-groes stayed rich mr riordan they hired white men, preferably jews, they loved the ultimate arrival of having jews on the payroll, watching over the black folks they've hired, to make sure the black folks don't fuck things up too much with their sense-less inefficient colored-people ways. nowadays there are black men and women who have forged themselves white enough, in the heat of cultural transformation, to do this job, but in them days, no sir. the way i lived then was not the way i live now, obviously, but at the time it meant something to me, the chimera of indepen-dence, and so i had a number of apartments like the one i had dreamed about. i moved down—and i came to understand that what i had feared wasn't the eco-nomic disaster, which always loomed close in my mind, even while daddy was mak-ing his fortune in hair oil—you know he still conks his hair? like the tobacco company men who all smoke—what i feared was the exposure, the release from the monastery of childhood and our home out into the crowded, windowed world, trapped in a place that is myself, with all the phantoms of anger peering out of my own windows . . .

and so i remember walking in times square holding my mother's hand and looking at all the pictures in the peep-show storefronts. nude women, ladies, mostly white but a few light-skinned colored, their breasts hanging down, you could sense the weight of a woman's breasts the way these women were posed, and i thought someday i will have those on me, they will be mine and i will know what they feel like to touch; i liked the colored ladies, i was pleased to see them, yes, we were rep-resented there and that was ALWAYS the important thing, unless it had been all black women, which would have been bad in the other way, there they were, bent forward toward the camera-eye. i remember peeking at them and thinking that since they were right out there on the street i HAD to be allowed to look at them.

i could hardly believe it yet i knew it was true that someday i would be like those women. i didn't know exactly what it was they were selling but i knew it was SOMETHING and it had to do with men and things men did, very frightening, awful feeling, oh they twisted us, this is the way i thought about the things men liked about women, which as far as i could tell began with seeing them naked and which i knew i would never allow, never ever. even my husband wouldn't be allowed to see me naked, that's what i thought. my mother was embarrassed, i could feel how embarrassed she was; my grandmother was oblivious, she moved through a world inhabited by her family and friends, the holy ghost, and seagram's old-fashioneds in the evening, two or three, and she didn't see anything else at all. all the feeling about those pictures was between me and my mother. i wondered if my father had anything to do with all this, came to such places and did things there and looking back now i would not be surprised if part of my mother's edge was formed from her thinking roughly the same thing, only what i wondered about, she knew. what amazed me about those photos was that no one forbade them; it belied everything my mother and my grandmother and my aunts with their downturned frowning mouths and black lacing shoes had tried to teach me about the world, about its rigid moralities and its high expectations, about stockings and gloves and the way a lady in the talented tenth carried her handbag, it made them into liars, especially my mother—

she was a liar—that's it, she lied to keep things pretty, to pretend life was under control. i remember when i told the people i was staying with after school, it was kindergarten or first grade and my mother was working at my father's company, she always said how much she LIKED to work, but later i realized she wanted to keep her eye on him—i told them, anyway, that my mother had slept in the hospital waiting room the night I had my tonsils out—this was very important to me. they laughed at me, said, "girl that's what she tole you." the girl, della, was my age and her mother said absolutely that my mother did NOT stay in the hospital overnight, that she wasn't allowed to, even the white people were not allowed to, and nobody did, that this was only what mothers SAID. della's mother had assured della that SHE would be staying but she hadn't and i couldn't figure out how della could live so comfortably with that, and smirk so too, how the awfulness of that lie could be so casually accepted between them, a lie so big it could explode you. i remember telling them that in my case it was different because my mother and i had an agreement that we would never lie to each other. i remember the girl's mother looking a little abashed then—realizing she had taken the truth too far—but della wouldn't relent. "of course that what she tell you" this wise-ass little girl said. oh how I despised her, she had cornrows and little bows. my hair was straight, after all, my father insisted on that. her father was a doctor, which made them our class, but the mother and the girl weren't very educated, which i remember my father complaining about from time to time. talented tenth, child. the father had his practice in mount vernon and he had all the colored people from there and some of the poorer ones in new rochelle, or that's what they said, but looking back they couldn't have been doing very well because my parents were paying them to take care of me after school and why would they take in children if they didn't need the money . . .

mr riordan i lost your voice but don't worry. i am writing a little story about you.

On Saturday morning I stop into the apartment to pick up the boys. Ellie doesn't have them ready yet and I stand in the hallway waiting, not knowing whether to pitch in or keep my place, the outsider, the uninvited. A small mess, the detritus of Henry's wanderings over an hour or two. I'm arrested by a toy, a small shoe, the remembered sounds of home. Henry has run to greet me with a yelp and I have hugged him and now he is gone again, into the Something Else that is his constant motivation. In a minute or two he will bring me whatever he's found, to show. I will say, Do you want to go outside with me? and he will go for his jacket, hanging on a hook by the door, pulling at it until I help him get it down and put it on. Where are your shoes, Henry? Do you remember where you put them? I feel the thing and it makes me afraid. Love as desire, love as annihilation. Ellie comes out of the kitchen carrying the baby. "Do you need any help?" I say.

"No," she says. She takes him past me into the boys' little room, where she'll change him. I pull back—I always pull back. Otherwise who am I? Do I even exist? I'm a boy in his bedroom, reading. His brother down the hall. Somewhere mother and father crouch, ready to spring. Lie low, lie low. Silence, exile, cunning. That's love as far as I'm concerned and I may never learn any other. Women are different, or some are. Ellie is ready to risk everything; she's like Quixote riding Rosinante, some tired overfertile beast, out, out into an unyielding and overimagined landscape.

And then the boys and I are out the door and there is a moment, as we hit the sidewalk with the cool new air and sunlight, that I can feel their sense of freedom. In the stroller, Sam closes his eyes and lets the passing breeze wash over his face. Soon he is asleep. We go down Broadway, Henry runs short distances ahead and runs back, adults watch him with nervousness or small smiles. He runs right at their legs. I say, "Henry!" and they dance to keep from knocking him flat. Near the corners I make him stay with me. Bus bus. He points at them. At the bus shelter we stop to look at a poster for the aircraft carrier and planes; we go on from the bus stop finally, he happier now and staying closer, more traffic and more to look at that is new, moving, never to be seen again. On the avenues, he heels. Down toward the river he runs again, then waits, and by the time we get down into the quiet part of the promenade, along Riverside, Henry is less wild, less an escapee, happy to stay near, and the baby is asleep in the stroller. I pick up the stroller with him and the diapers and water and wipes and provisions in it and carry it, a contained ecosystem, down the stone steps into the park. Uneven rough steps, slightly greasy with dried urine: I sidle down them gently. At the bottom, lowering the stroller wheels onto the stony pavement, I notice in the mortar cracks around the stairs at my feet and above me a sprinkling of tiny nodules in children's colors—plastic caps to the clear crack vials, which are littered among them like corpses amid the skulls. The crack vials strewn in the crevices and mortar. I look up the brown-shadowed stairway—a nightly graveyard, the dead and the dying gathered here sucking pipes, bones, and the last remnants of flesh; flesh and bones, sitting, leaning, crouched, at the turning of the stair. We walk down the paved pathway for a long time to the big playground at Ninety-seventh Street, under the peeling sycamore trees. Henry climbs onto one of the small platform-and-slide sets; Sam in the stroller wakes up, at first I think he won't, but that's just hope, as always wrong. He fusses, and I change his diaper, looming over him, humphing a little from having to stand bent in half, manipulating his little legs, hoisting him and turning him and cleaning him and dusting him. He's unhappy about it, because I never do it well, with the gentleness of his mother, or so I think, but maybe it's just his knowledge that I am not his mother, period, which has him unnerved. They know their mothers, their little pulse rates go wild and they emit special small odors and burrow with a surprisingly muscular intensity when they're held in their mothers' arms. As soon as I'm finished I snatch his bottle out of the bag and lift him into my arms, hold him and sway for a minute to calm him, sit on the bench, and give him the bottle. Henry goes down the shallow slide and lands on his rump, picks himself up, runs around to the steps at the back of it and begins his labors to climb them again. Sam's little arms make stabs at the bottle, but he can't get it together to grab on to the thing in any organized way.

Henry is standing in his red-striped shirt on the platform, rocking himself and holding on to the bar. Sam, wrapped again and dry, watches. The darkening blue of his eyes: they will go to hazel or green, I suspect. In two months, or three, or six. He sucks, mechanically, deeply, and his eyes close and he goes dozy again, but he's working. The yellowing sycamore leaves blowing softly above me. Dappling light; I look up, up, leaning back as far as I can, like a kid making himself dizzy, staring into the vaulted web of half-peeled branches, yellow leaves, mosaic sky. Holding this child, the first foreign sense of being with another in my life; not being alone is more than a situation—Ellie is right about this— it is an elusive task, an act, and of itself not enough. Leaves flutter and turn in a field of azure and light.

Perhaps in this frozen moment I have fallen asleep for a second. I don't know, I've lost the thread of the here and now for just a moment, a synapse failure, brief general shutdown. When I bring my head down

again—how long could it have really been?—I do the automatic check for
Henry, then do it again. I'm not quite taking it in, that's he's nowhere in
sight, not on the little nice slide, not on the big dangerous one, nowhere.
Out to the south some older schoolboys are playing soccer, kicking the
ball around, goals set up with two jackets marking a net's width. Not that
way. To the north, a high wall overlooking the playground—a walkway,
actually, there are two kids on it, older too, but not Henry. And then I see
him; I'm standing now, the baby is still sucking, flopping a bit in my arms,
Henry, with his little independent determined walk is climbing the distant pathway that leads out of the park and onto Riverside Drive. I take
off, the baby bouncing, crying. I stick the bottle in my jacket pocket and
fling the baby up onto my shoulder, and run, shouting *Henry Henry
Henry*. I catch him only a few feet from the gateway to freedom. He turns
around just as I near him, and comes running with a big smile, now that
I'm humiliated and ready to kill him. And I pick him up in my other arm,
hug him close, make that split-second decision not to yell but to be firm
and to get it across to him that he should never, never, never go away
from Daddy or Mommy. His arms around my neck, the two of them bun-
dled in my arms, slightly precarious. Never, never, never. Never leave us.

Another endangered child—Friar. His sister. The state-appointed coun-
selors, the experienced prosecutor from the Child Action Center on
Livingston Street in Brooklyn, where all the child experts reside, a bee-
hive of ineffective good intentions, the combined state/federal Child-at-
Risk Project (CARP is the acronym, a lucky word for me these days), a
kind of tactical command center for investigations, prosecutions, and in-
terventions for crimes of abuse against children. I get fifteen minutes of
time with a legal expert in wresting custody from a dangerous parent.

    Then back into Manhattan to meet Chin at the federal offices, the
Jacob Javits building; going in we pass the wretched-looking green-card
supplicants lined up outside. Five hundred feet of hope against hope.

The workers here, years back, protested the work of aggressive, feder-
ally sponsored art on their plaza: awash in the pink glow of Ronald Rea-
gan's promise to undo all that had changed over the course of their lives,
they took on the enemy art and asked to get rid of the liberal art, which
was a strategically rusty, black, steel, prisonlike wall by Richard Serra, a
rather moving and brutal piece like much of his work; but now they have
this, another permanent sinuous wall, more fluid, of humans throbbing
waiting.

I am back at he office. It's funny what starts you off—late afternoon, an
image comes as I'm resting at my desk, my head bowed over motion papers. I see in my mind a moving picture, a three-second cinema, of a man's
hips nested in a woman's on beautiful pale grainy film with slow movement, curve kneading curve, soft skin, dusty light and shadow. He plunges
and her leg opens and rises and slips to the side; her hips come up for him
and push forward. The two bodies, bellies and loins, come together with a
kind of shiver and a tiny sound, a sharp female intake of breath. That's all.
Light and skin, dark hair and shadow on marble. A suspended moment
and then it's gone, but in that small bubble of time the world explodes. I sit
back, wait a moment, breathe, and actually shake my head, as if to toss the
thought away like a bronc shakes a rider.

Then I get up, go out the back door, and use my key to get into the
men's room. Empty. I choose the second stall, farthest from the door. I
can't really get that image back so I think about Belinda, a younger associate at the firm: I've never thought about her before, but she has been
looking very good lately, skirts that cling, shoes and fine stockings, one
pair with just a hint of green. It must be the way she said, "Hey, Daddy,"
to me when she stopped in my office yesterday and asked about the kids,
cooed over the picture on the desk. After a certain age and still looking,
there's a scent they pick up when you're vulnerable. A kind of warmth in
her voice. Stroke my vanity. So now I'm thinking about her, that unreal

face always composed and projecting, and her long, stretched-out body, in a dress, slip, high heels. A woman takes off her shoes and sits with you, always a first moment, a move of the clock toward the eventual striking of the hour. Hands on stockinged legs, bodies together suddenly, the artificiality and awkwardness of the beginning, the smell of another person, oddly right or oddly wrong; and the thinking that goes with the kiss at that point, the self-consciousness, the self that you are conscious of, suddenly foreign to you as you offer yourself and prepare for decline or acceptance; so that it is not merely a foreign body close to yours but two foreign bodies, perhaps switching places. The hand has its own thoughts: strange clothes, strange hair, strange bones, every inch of it feels uncataloged and alien, desirable and frightening.

My dick in my hand, dry, smooth, heavy, half hard. I enjoy it dry, having rejected all the unguents of youth and finally the proletarian spit, just a soft dry touch on soft dry skin, two pieces of rice paper sliding easily past each other. Thoughts wandering, wandering. Red lips, black hair. Lips, lips, lips. Handfuls of that hair. Fast-forward to her mouth on me—that.

Affirmative, Houston, we have a go.

Then, no go. It just leaves me, the whole thing, except the forward-forcing ache of the groin that now must be dealt with, the knowledge that no one gets out of this stall until one of us is dead. I think about first kisses. With Nina, whom I dated one summer just after college, I was very suave, I remember telling her, "Come here," and she did, and I kind of pulled her face a little closer and leaned in and did it. We were in her tiny apartment with the nice view, it was near sundown and I could see a small church tower against the Hudson, and she had just changed her clothes right in front of me (she put a skirt on over her jeans, then took the jeans off, turned her back and changed her shirt, facing into the open closet, very lovely). We'd spent the afternoon together and now she had to go out with some guy, she had a date, which actually pleased me in some perverse way. It was a long, jawboning kiss, lots of swirls and eddies to it and our bodies twisting to get closer and press on each other.

We kissed and kissed and meanwhile the guy was waiting downstairs. I put my hand on her beneath the skirt, she was warm and very damp and she trembled a little and her muscles tightened and she trembled again, and even as she pulled back I thought she was falling in love with me and I enjoyed that, for I was not falling in love with her, and this was a first for me, the power position, and I was sending her out with someone else knowing she was going to be thinking about me. She had long, beautiful legs and light brown hair. I'd heard that she'd kept her virginity for years by giving her boyfriends blow jobs. We knew such things about one another in those days. And sure enough, she was very good with her mouth, which kind of takes me someplace and then it doesn't, and I think about her ass, which was beautiful, but that image just dissolves and fades away after a few moments too. There was Lila. One time, late at night on a dark road in Connecticut, where her parents lived, I'd picked her up there in a borrowed car, me driving it, one headlight out and who knows where we were going, she leaned in front of me and started kissing me, her hair flying all around my face in the wind from the open windows. I couldn't see a thing and finally I had to push her off or we would have crashed, which is why she did it then and not some other time when it might have led to something. I concentrate on how her tongue felt, she was very active with it and soft in the lips, she had wonderful lips and amazing, luminous skin, I can see her there, her lips and face, the smooth brown hair flying, what you could do with that hair, soft and straight, her dark eyes, her mouth and her tongue . . .

After that I lean back and rest. Shake down the arm. I could use an ice bath on it, like a pitcher after a tough nine innings. I lean back harder and the flush handle gives way and I accidentally flush beneath myself. A cool breeze then, briefly. Reach down, just fiddle, let images slide in and out of my head, don't push, let them vaporize before I even try to get hold of them; I am committed now, no rush. Of course if I had a piece of pornography I could make short work of this. When you have the photograph your mind is anchored down, you can focus, you kind of sink into it and work at its narrative edges, the suggestions of before and af-

ter, until you have a scenario going, held concrete in the photograph—
and there you are. Without that you have to write your own story top to
bottom and of course then your characters are unpredictable and do
what you don't want them to and the visuals are inconsistent, some as
real as memory, many others fuzzy, amorphous, altogether too made up.

Then I'm thinking of a black woman, slender, hair straight and
pulled back, red lipstick. Large, hanging breasts, nipples dark as asphalt.
That uniformity of tone that makes their skin look so solid and deep.
Tight-coiled pubic hair, face in cunt, hands on belly, tongue in ass, long
fingers wrapped around my prick, lips on it, the feeling of that . . . But
here's where that story goes wrong: when I was a teenager I came into
the city from Queens one evening by myself and went with a black
whore on Seventh Avenue to a room in a "hotel" somewhere in Hell's
Kitchen. It was a horrible little place, a man behind a scratched acrylic
partition who took five dollars for the room. A bowed, bleak stairway up
to a dim hall. The room had an opaque dirty window and a bed and bed
stand and lamp, an awful room but not really what you'd expect, more
like a nasty flop for a broken-down salesman to stay in, or the space a designer would come up with for a play about such a salesman, or such a
salesman having been quite done, some other broken-down character,
William Burroughs in Panama City perhaps. Anyway, we got undressed
and she said for twenty dollars she'd go around the world and I was seventeen so I said what's that, and she got on top of me and let her tits
hang against me and graze and engulf me and then she started fluttering
her tongue down my chest and belly. Then she started giving me head
and was about to rim me but at seventeen I was spooked by that; I
stopped her and said what about sixty-nine, the stupidest thing I could
have said because next thing I know she was blowing me and had turned
herself around and squatted over my face and to this day I have never
seen or smelled anything quite like her cunt, it was huge, with hundreds
of layers, a Georgia-O'Keeffe-on-acid image, lurid pinks outlined by
shades of old and crusty brown. The thing was about as wide as my head,
a crack in the universe. She was tough and black and a little bit mean and

between her and the room I could no longer get it up, never mind come, and eventually she just rolled off me and lay there, looking very bored and giving me a handjob. I managed to get through the handjob by closing my eyes and thinking of England, and when it was finally over she got up off the bed, very quickly, pulling her clothes on from the pile we'd left on the chair, and while I was still getting my underwear on she walked out. When I went to get my pants I found them twisted up on the floor and my wallet, empty, nearby. Some of my money was strewn way back under the bed. I yelled "Hey!" when I saw the wallet, and "Hey!" again when I saw all the money was out of it, but nobody paid attention. In another room a woman was screaming. Some other black whore, looking big as a lineman, came in and made a furious, disgusted sound when she saw me crawling around in my underwear looking for what was left of my money. I should be remembering the way that woman's tongue and breasts felt against me, her red lips pulling at my dick, but instead all I can think about is all that humiliation, the soft dick, the money on the floor, and fear at that wide orchid cunt in front of my face, like some deep-dwelling sea plant, flaps pushing open and closed, tiny mouths in the soft currents—or like the desert when you're flying over it in an airplane, brown and red, fissured and ancient.

After I subdue this image, I remember the Dostoevsky girl of the subway, the smile of the girl, with her paperback and bagel and clunky shoes and jeans and sweet lovely graceful hands, those hands, with a loose, wanting grip, and white skin; there is something so shocking about girls with very pale skin, naked they offer almost too much of themselves—*what whiteness would you add to this whiteness, what candor?* I see her for some reason in an open flannel shirt and bare-legged in a house somewhere, very domestic scene, and her, suddenly, I love; we are living together, it is peaceful, so free, nobody's wearing any pants, how nice is that? I am older but she loves me. I see her beautiful feet on a wood floor. I read to her in the evenings . . . This is getting me nowhere fast.

And then someone comes in and takes a leak: bang of door and zip of zipper and the stream in the urinal, a faint *sssss* at first, then silence as it tapers down. I feel very relaxed just sitting here, listening. Finally a flush, steps to the sink, a quick run of water. I cough.

"That you, Riordan?" says David.

"Yup," I say.

"Hmmm," he says. "Need any help in there, lad?"

"Absolutely not," I say.

"Just thought I'd offer," David says.

"Very kind of you, but no thank you. Perhaps some other time."

"I'll keep my hopes up," he says.

"Fuck you," I say.

"Ta-ta," he says, and is gone.

I review the possibilities in the images he has left me with, am properly horrified, and get back to my business. I'm almost sleepy. For a minute I don't even remember what the impulse was that brought me here, and then I do, those thrusting hips. My hand again. Barbara: a woman I never slept with, she told me every which way she could that she wanted to, but I wasn't interested. I was back with Ellie then, we were on the verge of deciding to get married. Barbara was beautiful, I'll say that; I think about her figure. We worked in a small office together, for a photographer. Randy, the photographer, had hired her to go around and represent him, a leggy blond in nice clothes carting his portfolio around, that's the kind of thing that made him feel better when he wasn't making any money. She never made one sale. She was an early yuppie, just out of college as I was, she had a small apartment on the east side and was the first person my age I ever knew who belonged to a health club. She presented this, the way all fads are presented, as the most exciting thing, which everyone had always known about and done forever and ever, except it was new and great. There was some crisis while Randy was away and I had to go to her place to drop something off, and she was in tights, working out. There was a mat on the floor. She leaned against the wall. I had just gotten back from Long Island, where I'd learned that my aunt and uncle on my mother's side, the Italian side, (it is insane to remember this now, with this task, this duty ahead) had been murdered. It was Thanksgiving Day. My aunt and uncle were supposed to join the rest of the family that afternoon but they never showed up, and finally someone went over there and that was that. They had been killed with a hammer. One of them was in the bedroom and one was on the couch. I remember driving many times that day from an aunt's house in Malverne, where everyone was waiting, to the apartment in Rosedale, where the corpses were; the TV van was parked on the sidewalk and the cops had a rope up. I remember standing in front of the building waiting for another one of my uncles to come down, I was allowed inside the police line because I was a family member, and the cops going in and out kept asking me, "Are you with the force?" because I had the right general build, ethnic looks, and a mustache, and I had a long coat and looked like I was packing. Then the TV reporter, a lanky, elegant black guy (they'd sent him out on the "drugs equal murder" story, the story of "a tragic Thanksgiving in a neighborhood gone bad"), asked me, "Officer, is there any news about what's going on inside?" and I said, "I'm not with the police, I'm a member of the family," and he said, "Can you give me any news at all about what's going on?" and I said, "No, I don't really know anything." But I did know a few things. I knew there was blood spattered all over the simple, elegant apartment they'd kept for forty years above the barbershop and beauty parlor that they ran together, blood all over the glass bookcase that held *The History of Civilization* series by Will and Ariel Durant; I knew that my uncle, with blood that had run in lines and dried now down every part of his face, with his eyes opened looking at the absolute nothing that our lives and the world had become for him, had been a student in Italy before Mussolini and had actively opposed the Fascists, who he thought were thugs. Eventually this became an unhealthy opinion to hold and he left for the United States. I knew something valuable that he once told me, that to be young meant to think constantly of the future, but that for him, an old man, he spent his days thinking of the past, and that the key to a happy life was to work on creating a past that will bring you pleasure.

And by the time that day was over, I just didn't feel like dealing with

Barbara. She was intent on seducing me, I heard later, and was hurt that I paid her no notice in that way; what I remember is, even after telling her briefly about my day, she seemed forcefully not to have taken it in, that I had just arrived from a murder scene; she couldn't grasp it. She went right past it, as if I'd told her I'd been stuck in some pretty bad traffic. So I gave her whatever it was and left. Now I imagine it differently: the day is different, no one died, my life is different, I haven't fucked anything up; I'm standing in close to her, feeling her softness against me, peeling those Danskins off her and fucking her down on the mats, her long white body and the skin and its dampness from half-dried sweat, her long, long fingers gripping my back, digging in a little, those arms and breasts and shoulders. (Things are going along nicely now, I'm hard to the point just short of pain, jumping with the pulse, my sight starting to tunnel down, down, tinged with red, my head a little woozy.) That fine, bony face, those breasts and legs and her broad back and her broad round backside and that white, white skin. Peeling those tights down her body. Her sweaty matted blonde pubic hair. The smell of it, the absolutely perfect distinction of another human being. Sweat pooling in the depression on the plastic mat. Sounds. Legs wrapped around my face. The taste of warmth and salt, her arched feet laid softly on my back. She jumps a little when she comes, I can picture it, one of those women who seem to be electrocuted, all the muscles go so hard and the movements that jump so out of time. Then I slide up her body and look down into her face, I can see it all sweaty, and I plant my knees and go in, glide in, slowly, slowly, all the way to the back where that small and immensely powerful conversation takes place, the tip of cock and wall of cervix speak, and then out, the feeling along the wet wet walls, and then in again, pressed in, pushed in, holding it there, taking her hips and ass and pulling her deeper onto me, grinding, feeling the muscles grip. Then the back and forth, balls bouncing on her backside, her legs up high now, over my arms, over my shoulders, in, out, in. It's important not to rise above and see the scene, which is two sad mammals mating; it is important to be in it, to remember what the thing actually feels like at the molecular level, the rising of a ball of fire at the bottom of the gut, slowly, slowly, like an explosion captured and re-played a frame at a time; it is important to remember that warm tight wet sliding feeling, it's actually dicey trying to keep that in your mind, like pain, it is difficult to remember. But I'm getting it . . . There she is, her face contorted and blazing with light; the hips within hips, wet hair along the pubic bone rubbing against her, the labia opened and lightly touching the shaft, I'm going red, red, red, the warmwetfuck, a fire building and burning upward, fuck fuck fuck. Wet. Red. Fuck. There. Fuck. Red. Fire. Cities burning, shattered glass, melted steel, thousands die, metal death descending, boom boom boom, fuck fuck fuck, there, fuck, there. There. Fuck. There. There. The muscles slowly, slowly loosen, relax, except for the one which still runs through its private cycle of clench and drip, clench and drip.

And then he come to some kinda awful climax . . .

The toilet paper is too tight on the holder and it won't roll. I can only get one sheet at a time. Goopy mess, that ever-so-slightly greenish-gray, and silver. The smell in my hand: warm brine and protein: life. *I will show you fear in a handful of dust.* Eventually wiped and down the toilet. Long breaths. Flush and away, thousands of encoded copies of myself, swirling in the water and disappearing, spent on an autumn afternoon.

Our pretrial hearing is set for October 28. As the date nears, it becomes obvious that the prosecution has a slender case. List of witnesses: two SUNY Albany kids who jostled the carpet . . . completely unnecessary, in my opinion, and Gerry's too, but who knows. The two officers called to the scene. Pathologists at the scene. Albany coroner. Diane's boss, three women friends from her office. Ron's neighbor. Ron's ex-assistant. All character stuff. One expert on microscopy . . . there's the thing, what do they have there? Gerry is convinced they have nothing, or they wouldn't be stalling for time. If the judge doesn't grant them an extension, Gerry believes, the case is over.

*   *   *

From Henry's first year onward, as I've seen him with his mother, I see my mother and me. Ellie is more active than my mother, but less observant. Ellie loves to play, she gets Henry very excited; my mother wasn't like that. Ellie bounces Henry on her legs and I remember riding my mother's legs like that, playing horsey while my mother sang a song or we sang together. All mothers and children do things like that—they sing together and cling, lovers in love like that, absorbed in each other, learning each other, tingling and warm with it, and *I do not think that they will sing to me*—an obnoxious bit of self-directed pathos, but sometimes it feels that way.

I look at pictures now from when I was very little, the year when my parents experimented with separation, and my mother looks ghastly; she weighed under 100 pounds then, she wasn't eating and probably was drinking a good deal. Her face looks haunted, her hair lifeless and often set stiffly into some unnatural wave or curl that she hadn't worn before and never wore again. He came back or they got back together a year and a half later but I suppose she never really surrendered to him after that, a stony silence rested between them, and across that consuming terrain, like two figures in a desert landscape, they shouted at each other. Of course they must have talked sometimes even though I only remember the fighting; I seem to remember they talked in the front seat of the car, they got along nicely on drives and long trips, in the dark chamber of the front seat with the dashboard lights and my brother and I quiet and sleepy in the back.

I remember little from the time they were apart. Just images . . . Sunday afternoon and she is napping on the couch. Her legs. I go to the bathroom and moisten a bunch of Kleenex—no, I put water in a little pail, a bath toy, and bring it back with the Kleenex to the sofa. My mother is sleeping. Her legs. Her feet first, I put wet Kleenex on her feet and on her shins. How old am I? Four? Three? I'm certain I'm not five yet. It is long before school age. My mother wakes up with the wet

Kleenex being applied to her shins like compresses. How cold they must have been. The water must have dripped onto the upholstery. She didn't complain or make me stop; no, she seemed very, very grateful I was doing this—for some reason I believed she needed these ministrations with the wet lumps of pink tissue. It was like our secret and wonderful thing, that I'd decided to do this and gotten the water and the tissues and begun this project on my own while she was sleeping. Her shins were stubbly, except for a ridge of gleaming, smooth skin along the shinbone, from years of shaving. My mother was in her early thirties at this time.

I put lumps of wet Kleenex along each stubbly shin. Then her knees. The wobbly muscles around the ridged kneecap. Her thighs—so much softer and less marked by shaving than her calves.

I remember lifting and turning her legs as she lay there. She moved them just enough to assist me, no more. I could feel all their weight. The flesh of her thighs sank as her legs rose, then flattened again when I lowered her legs back onto the sofa. Soft soft. It was the softest flesh I'd ever felt, except my own, which I had no sense of, no memory for. I raised her skirt a bit, I'm sure I did that. She probably controlled how high I raised it. Or, likely even then, a child, I knew the limits of the hemline, the skirted leg, how high to go and no higher: where the flesh was softer and softer, and whiter and whiter, and then the terrors of the dark.

[10]

Out walking, at Eighty-first and Riverside Drive, I see a tall young man, just turned fifteen, sitting on a stoop, after midnight in New York. I know he is fifteen before I know that it is Friar; the fact of his age comes into my consciousness a split second ahead of the rest of his identity. He is filling out; he is sophisticated looking, in a white hip-hop sort of way. But he is still fifteen and fifteen-year-old boys, even the most disadvantaged, are not out on Riverside Drive after midnight.

I sit down beside him without any of the "What-are-you-doing-out, does-your-grandmother-know-where-you-are" preliminaries.

"I have friends," he says, himself without preliminaries. "I have friends who are down in the park right now, partying with homeless guys. They think that's cool. They're getting stoned and drinking Bud 40s." In our day we graduated from Boone's Farm to Mogen David to Southern Comfort to vodka with orange juice in fairly short order: making inroads toward the extinction of personality that adolescence seeks and adulthood clings to as a hope unfulfilled. On the Drive. Occasional cabs go by with the wet *whoosh* of rubber on tar. The limestone walls of the Riverside buildings hang suspended, almost phosphorescent in the moonlight. The surrounding colors you'll need for this painting are dark umber and green, for trees; silver and white, for light; and charcoal, for everything else.

He pulls out a pack of cigarettes; Parliaments. He is fifteen years old, I think anew, every time I look at him. I take a cigarette when he offers it.

"There's two guys, I swear to God," he puffs, holds it in a second, as if it's a joint, "who let the homeless guys blow them just for kicks."

"Jesus," I say.

"He's not there," Friar says.

"How do you know?" I say.

"I sure as fuck ain't seen him, blood."

"That's not definitive," I say.

"So what's your deal, yo?" he says after a pause. He shifts around, raises a leg and plants his foot on the stoop wall opposite. "What keeps Mr. Normal Joe Q. Citizen up on the streets so late at night? You looking for action?"

"Just out walking, taking the air," I say.

"Yeah, testing death," he says. A puff and an exhale, like a pro. "That would resolve some shit."

"Can't do that right now," I say. "I'm way underinsured."

"Right," he says. The subject of money temporarily silences him, as it does most people who are accustomed to having vastly more of it than others have. He changes the subject.

"Are we, like, *allowed* to be talking?"

"You mean with the case? It's probably not a good idea."

"I won't say nothin'," he says.

"That's good," I say.

"You realize, right?" he says. Then he doesn't finish it. He takes out another cigarette, offers one to me. "Don't give me no shit about smoking, okay?"

"I would already have given you shit about smoking if I were going to give you shit about smoking. Smoking's the least of your problems right now. At your pace it's clearly too late for me to do anything about it anyway."

"I don't know," he says. "I mean, what to do. I mean, I have no *idea* what I'm doing. My sister, she's like fading into this dream-world thing where all her dolls are named Mommy, okay? And I don't blame her, I . . ." He pauses. "Whatever. For missing everything. The life we used to have. I mean, it sucked but it was better than now. At school, everyone is like, yo, what's up, how's it going, but beyond that, it's like I have cancer. The teachers are treating me like, you know, I'm one of those retarded kids with no legs and I got some kind of machine to breathe with. My father's fucking picture was on the front page of the fucking *Post*, man—can you even begin to imagine? With like that whole *other* angle to it. I just want out of here, man. And I'm like the star witness pulled from the sky, you know, on some episode of fucking *NYPD Blue*. So like, what am I supposed to do?"

"I can't tell you what to do," I say. "Even if I knew what you should do, I'm not allowed to tell you what to do. I'm your father's lawyer and you, potentially, are a witness in his prosecution. Besides, I don't know what you should do."

"My father's sick," he says. At first, I think he means his father is mentally ill, a psychopath. But then I realize he means actually sick, ill.

"What does he have?"

"I don't know, they wouldn't talk about it. He's been sick a while. Probably some kind of cancer. Actually, probably AIDS. I don't know." He snaps the cigarette butt out over the roofs of the cars lining Eighty-first Street. I'm trying to imagine what it would be like at his age to have his kind of knowledge.

"Here's what I can tell you," I say. "If he's sick, it only confirms what I think, which is that you shouldn't be walking around, with all the other problems you have, your life, your sister, your grandmother, school, et cetera, believing that your father is your problem to solve. I can't say any more than that. But your job is to remember that you don't have a job. All you have to do is grow up. Do what you think you need to do, what your conscience says to do."

"If I don't testify, I mean, if I don't have like anything to say, then does he get convicted?"

"I don't know. I don't know what else they have. I suspect not. I shouldn't be talking about this."

"I don't want to live with him again," he says. He has put another Parliament in his mouth but not lighted it. "And I don't want my sister to."

"Then don't," I say, and stand up. "And, Friar?"

"What?"

I lean down to him. "Go home. Go to bed. Don't hang out here at this hour. It's bad, period. You know it is. Go home."

"Yeah, right," he says. But as I step down, he rises.

The deposition of the police officers is upstate; this at the request and convenience of the local lieutenant, busting the balls of the defense lawyers, an automatic gesture. Gerry and I early one Thursday morning in the back of another hired car, $1,000 from 8:00 A.M. until 5:00 P.M. and $250 an hour thereafter, plus gas and tolls, we need a driver because *we are working* and charging $800 an hour combined, plus the car for the day, plus expenses, meals, gas, tolls, every receipt an asset, photocopying at 60 cents a page. It's all on the clock. Long-distance calls, from firm cell phones, phone number, tone, case code, client code. It's all charged back by the mainframe. If I or my secretary is working on a document on the computer, to get to the file we have to identify ourselves, give the case number, and from there the mainframe tracks the work time to the thousandth of a second and processes the billing. Anything over two minutes idle it subtracts. I have to file computer time manually in green, so it can be checked against the network logs but won't be double charged. Tick tick tick. In the backseat of the car, I move systematically again through my notes and the major discovery documents, police reports, the pathology report that was generated by the hick ME. As soon as they found out in New York that they had a suspect and the suspect was, publicity-wise, a *major* lode, they did a second autopsy, running to twenty-three pages, against four for the guy upstate. Basically, no matter how you string it out, certain high-tech chemicals of a prescription nature in the bloodstream, all matching scripts she had, but the barbs in slightly excess quantities; inconclusive small contusions, chipped teeth, a broken arm postmortem, etc. She was strangled, by hands, probably gloved. The upstate county ME is part of a volunteer corps from among the local doctors; they get a stipend of less for the year than we'll charge for this day, a lot less. The New York guy, on the other hand, probably makes $280,000 a year.

"Look at the colors," Gerry says. This is an odd comment because he has his head down, he's reading. He has some papers out on his lap and has been sitting still in the profound way men his size can be still, gravitationally held immobile.

"How can you look at colors through blue-tinted glass?" I say.

"I assume the blueness, or account for it. They're quite vibrant." He hasn't looked up.

I lower my window, push my face out into the passing wind. I had been aware of the colors as Autumn Scene, but hadn't really looked at them. They are loud; brackish fuchsia maples, burnt orange and electric-yellow oaks. Every fifteen or twenty feet, trees show the red posting signs; a remnant, from British law, of that most basic of property laws, which posits that owning the land means owning the food that resides thereon. And to whom it is entailed it shall be entailed with only the most eminent domains claiming contrary possession. I imagine men and youth of the manor, riding the woods; wardens trapping for the kitchen.

We are on one of those minor roads that for the region is a main road, off to the county capital; we've instructed the driver to get off the thruway earlier than need be to take this more local artery, ostensibly to enjoy the best weekend of the year in the country but also to avoid passing the rest stop in question, I suspect; when I suggested this to Gerry I saw a significant look pass through his distant, bright eyes, a look more suggestive than the prospect of a nice drive would evoke. We've just taken a long curve onto the downside of one of the big hills that border the Berkshires, and alongside the road suddenly there is a brown stream, sizable, sparkling, a decent-looking trout stream, though you never know nowadays what crimes have been committed, killing off the fish. That river color, in the east, one of the few shades of brown that can be translucent, a darkening amber, the color of certain beer bottles, running to silver at the edges of the riffles and also where the sky reflects and the sunlight hits, in a jagged pattern down the center channel. Once

I start watching the water I can't take my eyes off it. The stream is big enough for a couple of interesting-looking divides, decent little feeder streams, everything down near the bank glistening with mud or bony dry rocks along a beach where some spring's freshet made a turn that's since been straightened. A fisherman stands at the upstream edge of one of these, casting up into the tail of a broad, flat pool. As we go by, an easy flip of the line across the top of the water, the soft dropping of the tippet onto the surface. We drive on, toward the county office building somewhere down the mountain.

Houdacek is the state police lieutenant. He got the investigating officer assignment the night of the call-in from a man with a raspy voice, on a pay phone at the rest stop, who naturally split the scene. The SUNY connection didn't actually happen until almost an hour later, when one of the two kids, back at his dorm, freaking out, called in to say he had seen a rug, a woman's foot, had left. They sent someone to interview him, but he hadn't seen anything beyond that. By this time the place was crawling with cops. Houdacek: a Czech name. Big hands, knobby fingertips, fidgeting, fingers almost too large for all their small, nervous motions.

We ask useless stuff just to ask it, a kind of probe. "You didn't take the call, did you, Lieutenant?"

"No, sir, the call went in to country 911."

"Counsel, do we have the name of the operator who took that call?" The assistant United States attorney on the case is an albino, oddly enough, named McCarthy, in a good gray double-breasted summer suit, of Italian provenance, I suspect.

"I'm not sure we have it here, but we can get it."

"I'd like to request that."

"For what purpose, may I ask? Are you considering a deposition?" He is quietly, confidently hostile.

"We'll consider a deposition if we think there's evidence pertinent to our defense, yes."

"Is this pertinence or lack of pertinence something that's going to be revealed to you by the name?" he says. "Or what?" He's busting Gerry's balls.

"When the pertinence makes itself evident we will have the name on hand because you are legally obliged to provide it, and if you do not wish to provide it I am happy to take the matter before Judge Skurnic."

"I'm certain that the name is in the original arrest documents, which you have," McCarthy says. "If you are unable to locate it I will provide it again. Whatever good it will do."

He can get away with comments like this at a deposition. We can move to strike this remark, but in fact it will be there in the reporter's transcript until we actually go before the judge to remove it, which no one ever bothers to do. The whole discussion goes under "Colloquy: Provision of 911 Operator," and amounts to nothing at all. There will be many hours of this before we get to trial.

"We also request copies of the tape of the call," Gerry says. "Are you doing a voiceprint of that tape?"

McCarthy looks up, his Day-Glo eyebrows raised. "Not at this time," he says.

"But you stipulate as to provision of the tape."

"So stipulated. Can we move on?"

Back to the stolid lieutenant. "So you were called to the scene by the emergency operator?"

"The 911 operator contacted the state police headquarters. SPH contacted mobile units"—he looks down at some papers—"3756, 3281, and 3429, which responded. The first officer at the scene," still reading, "mobile unit 3429, Sergeant Bill Culcas, contacted me. I was the ranking investigations officer on duty at that time."

"How long did that take, between the call and when you were notified, if you know?"

McCarthy interrupts. "All these calls are in the record."

"About five minutes, maybe six or seven."

"And how long after that did you arrive at the scene?"

"Another ten minutes or so."

"Can you be exact?"

He looks at the papers. "Records indicate I called in my arrival at nine thirty-nine, which is, uh, twelve minutes after the nine twenty-seven call from Sergeant Culcas." He puts the papers down.

"And when you arrived at the scene, what did you discover?"

"I verified the report of Sergeant Culcas that there was a deceased female in the Dumpster, wrapped in a rug or a carpet."

"Did you move the body?"

"No."

"How could you tell it was a female?"

"Enough of the corpse was showing to indicate it was a female. It appeared either that the body was poorly wrapped or that someone had partially unwrapped it."

Why do they all talk like this? Who teaches them? *Enough of the corpse was showing to indicate it was female in nature, due to its genitalia and other indicators such as hair, face, nails, in addition to but not exclusively a certain, shall I say, delicacy to the hands and feet.* Gerry starts using the same language, something to put the good lieutenant at ease or something to get at precisely what he wants or just because the jargon's catching. *And you notified the medical examiner on duty at what time? And what, if any, details did you observe about the carpet or rug? What marks on the body did you observe, if any?* Later: *Were there, in your observation, any bruises or marks on the body?* The federal: *Asked and answered, Counsel.*

Finally it is almost four, and everyone is thinking about wrapping up. An off-the-record on how late we'll go. Gerry has just a few more questions, he says. We reserve our right to call Lieutenant Houdacek for further discovery; we all make our little calendar arrangements for our next get-together, as if it's going to be a dinner party; and all we've managed to unearth so far in six and a half hours, with lunch, is that this particular Dumpster was seven and a half feet high, which means whoever got her over was very strong, with her cascading from her unrolling sheath in the process—and that, if this summer evening was any indicator, people are rather frequently willing to climb up with some degree of difficulty to look into a giant Dumpster just to see what's around. As if life isn't hard enough.

Meanwhile, back on the record, Gerry goes to his long-pause routine—a glancing through papers, a make-the-hitter-wait-getting-nervous-in-the-box strategy. "Forgive me, Lieutenant Houdacek." Shifting things around, reading snips of documents, putting them aside. These gestures are like punctuation marks, ellipses and white spaces in the narrative, denoting movement to a new section, a new track.

Finally, he looks up. "Lieutenant, you have investigated murders, homicides, before, I assume?"

"Yes."

"And we who are less familiar with such crimes, we often hear that the most common culprit in a homicide case is someone close to the victim, someone who knows the victim, especially a boyfriend or girlfriend or spouse. Is that common knowledge or mythology an accurate—does it accurately reflect the reality of your experience and knowledge, investigating and solving homicide cases?"

Houdacek doesn't know where this is going. Gerry's voice, his approach, are soft and sincere, he seems to be playing into the prosecution's hands, even, and the big state trooper just stares at him. It takes every muscle to keep himself from looking at McCarthy, who is just watching, waiting to pounce as soon as Gerry reveals his direction. "It's often the case, yes," Houdacek finally says.

"Why is that, Lieutenant?"

McCarthy breaks in. "We have not qualified this witness as an expert in criminal behavior or family violence or pyschopathic motivation, Counsel. Inappropriate line of questioning."

"Let me put it this way," Gerry says. "Such crimes are known in the common parlance as 'crimes of passion,' are they not?"

"Counsel, this is totally beyond the expertise of the witness—"

"I am inquiring into the investigating officer's experience and opinion in shaping his judgment in this case. Which experience and opinion led, you might recall, toward his conclusion, in apparent agreement with other, subsequent federal investigators *and* prosecutors, that my client committed homicide in the second degree. It was a judgment based on mere shards of so-called evidence—if I cannot inquire into that judgment, then you, Mr. Prosecutor, are proposing that the criminal justice system is little more than a charade. I doubt that Judge Skurnic is quite the cynic you apparently are, or that he would agree with you as a point of law. The lieutenant placed my client at the top of his list of suspects and I want to know why. We can settle the question before Judge Skurnic tomorrow, if you'd like."

"Why don't you get to the point, Mr. Rorjak."

"I was at the point, Mr. McCarthy, before you interrupted. Lieutenant Houdacek, how many homicides have you investigated, approximately?"

"I don't know," he says. "Maybe twenty, twenty-five."

"And would you estimate that the majority of those involved someone who knew the victim or was close to the victim?"

"Yes, the majority, I'd say that's probably true."

"And in how many of those homicides has the murderer, that is, the homicides where the perpetrator is someone known to and close to the victim, in how many of those cases has the murderer taped the victim's mouth, or carried the victim to another state, or both?"

There is a pause, so short you might call it a bump and then simultaneously McCarthy says, "Objection," and Houdacek, bless his heart, says, "None."

"Did you get that, Mr. Reporter?" Gerry asks.

The reporter reads, in his uninflected way, "*—and in how many of those homicides has the murderer that is the homicides where the perpetrator is someone known to and close to the victim in how many of those cases has the murderer taped the victim's mouth or carried the victim to another state or both counsel objection witness none.*"

"Thank you, Lieutenant, very much, for giving us your time," says Gerry.

McCarthy says, "I will move to strike that answer."

Gerry is already packing his briefing bag. "You do that, Counsel," he says.

At this point, I whisper to Gerry. He looks at me, turns back to Houdacek. "My colleague, Mr. Riordan, has just a few questions for you before we close, Lieutenant, if you don't mind."

"Deposition tag team," McCarthy says.

"I move to strike that remark," Gerry says.

"Fine, fine," says McCarthy. "My apologies. Go ahead."

I say, "Lieutenant Houdacek, I just have a couple of questions about the night Mrs. Adamson's body was discovered. You arrived at the scene at, you said, nine-forty or so P.M., first investigator on the scene, and then other investigating officers and the medical examiner on duty all arrived thereafter, that's right, isn't it?"

"Asked and answered, Counsel," McCarthy says.

"Are you instructing him not to answer this incredibly simple establishing question?" I say.

"On the basis that he has already testified on it, yes."

"All right, I'll presume my memory is correct on your testimony, Lieutenant, since the Assistant United States Attorney for the Southern District of New York wants to spare you the pain of reassuring me. Now, at what point that evening was the Dumpster examined?"

Houdacek looks at me. There is a cloud in the vision, a kind of gap in the look, that sets off bells in my head. I feel like it's Final Jeopardy! and my chief opponent has just been revealed to have wagered everything on "Who was Grover Cleveland?" when I know it's supposed to be Garfield. He says, "Do you mean, when did we look inside it? As soon as I arrived."

"No, that's not what I meant, Lieutenant. I meant, at what point, presumably after Mrs. Adamson's body was removed from the Dumpster, were the Dumpster and its contents examined for evidence? They *were* examined for evidence, weren't they?"

"Yes, they were examined," he says. He's undeniably glum.

"They were examined. And what was found?"

"Nothing. Nothing was found."

"You mean the corpse of Mrs. Adamson and the carpet were the only items in that large Dumpster?"

"No, there was garbage in it, you know, refuse from the rest area and such."

"Right," I say. "Like what?"

"Refuse. Garbage, papers, food, food containers. That sort of thing."

"And you made a list of the contents of the Dumpster?"

"Um, no, we didn't make a list."

"Well, did you file a report on the contents of the Dumpster?"

"No, we didn't file a report."

"Who examined the Dumpster?"

"Do you mean which officers?"

"Officers, forensic experts, yes. Who looked through the Dumpster?"

"I don't recall who did that. A number of officers were involved. I don't know who they were."

"So, you're telling me that no written report exists, and we don't know who did the examining, but somehow we *do* know that *nothing* was found—nothing relevant to this case was to be found in this nearly eight-hundred-cubic-foot Dumpster that had Mrs. Adamson's body in it?"

"Well, you have to keep in mind, if it's an eight-hundred-cubic-foot Dumpster, then we had at least three or four hundred cubic feet of garbage there, so there was a limited amount we could do with it. Anything relevant to the case would have been removed and become part of the evidence kit."

"Was the Dumpster examined for blood, for Mrs. Adamson's blood or anyone else's blood or any other human organic material?"

"Yes."

"How do you know that, Lieutenant?"

"Well, that's standard procedure."

"Okay, that's standard procedure and so you assume it was done?"

"Right."

"But who would actually know? Who could testify about what was or wasn't actually done, what was or was not actually found?"

"I don't know."

"How long did the examination of the Dumpster take?"

"I don't know."

"Were there big lights that were brought in, did they go back in the morning, what?"

"Well, we had lights there, set up before we removed the body, and they stayed up for most of the night, I believe. We sent an evidence crew out to do a complete sweep of the area the next morning."

"How far did that sweep extend?"

"Quite a ways, actually, because at that time we had no idea who the body was or where it had come from. We searched the full rest area and the woods beyond it and some sections of the roadside leading in and out, how far I couldn't tell you."

"And what did you find?"

"Nothing that proved relevant to the case."

"Meaning nothing?"

"Well, you send that many guys out, male and female officers, plus, you know, dogs, and you search that big an area, you find stuff. Ah, we found a Japanese World War Two vintage bayonet, as it was later identified, in the woods behind the rest area. For one example. But since the victim showed no signs of stabbing, and the bayonet was quite rusty, we concluded it was unrelated to the case. Condoms, underwear, you name it. Liquor bottles. Stuff like that."

"You found liquor bottles?"

"In the general area, yes. Many."

"Were they examined or dusted for fingerprints?"

"No."

"Why was that?"

"Because there were so many that they were like part of the landscape. It would have been like dusting the leaves and tree trunks for prints."

"Not exactly the same, though, is it, Lieutenant? I mean, the murderer or murderers of Mrs. Adamson could have brought a liquor bottle or more than one liquor bottle into the area but he or she or they presumably could not have brought a tree, correct?"

"Sure. There were still too many bottles to examine, too many to be able to pick one out as potentially coincident to our case."

"Okay, fine. In terms of the Dumpster that day, do you know what occurred, how that specific search was handled?"

"No, I don't have, um, details on that. I know general procedure."

"And there's nothing in the records that indicates here what was done with the Dumpster, how it was handled?"

"Not that I've seen here today. I could go back through."

I turn to McCarthy. "Mr. McCarthy, I'm sure you realize that we do in fact request that the lieutenant 'go back through,' as he puts it, and that anything related to any search at any time of the Dumpster be forwarded to us. We further request that whoever took charge of this alleged search of the Dumpster be produced to be deposed."

"Duly noted," McCarthy says, clearly pissed off. He knows as well as I do that a major hole has just appeared in his case, a procedural fuckup of a high order, and whether he's pissed at the state police or at himself for not thinking of it sooner, or both, he's getting pink in the forehead.

"And I object to your use of 'alleged search,' Counsel," he says. "The lieutenant testified under oath that the Dumpster was searched, so 'alleged' is uncalled for."

"Fine," I say. "He *assumes* it was searched, but for now we'll retract 'alleged.'"

"Anything else?" McCarthy says.

"No, I don't think so," Gerry says.

"I have the time as 5:06 P.M.," I say.

"Agreed," says McCarthy without looking at his watch. The court reporter clicks off his machine.

The car and driver wait, engine idling, in the parking lot of the diner; Gerry and I are inside for a quick bite. We offered to buy a meal for the driver, who it turns out is a former cop, also named Gerry, but he assures us he ate during the afternoon deposition.

"I bet you anything you like," I say, "that they're going to go to that Dumpster and search it now. Dust it, put lasers on it, the whole bit. If not tonight then tomorrow or maybe the next day." I'm staring out the window at the houses across the main road.

"Hmmm," Gerry says. A moment of silence. He is working through a meat-loaf sandwich. "We could go there, you know."

"I don't want to go there," I say.

"Of course. I don't want to go there either. But we shall. It's our job, isn't it?"

Gerry the cop is happy with the OT: once a cop, always a cop on that as well as other fronts. We sit in the rest area and shoot the shit and watch. Gerry, my Gerry, gets on the cell phone with the office, we have staff still waiting there though it's almost seven; Jack is still there too, and, always resourceful, he gives us the number of a detective agency in Albany. We call, leave a message. In a car nearby a man gives another man a blow job; we watch in failing light the head rise and descend; the recipient's arms are back in the reclined front seat. Gerry looks where I indicate, observes for a moment or two, says, "Hmm," noncommittally, and then puts his attention back in his briefcase where it's nice and safe. Eventually the blow job ends, successfully I gather, and the agency calls back. They will send someone, absolutely; expect his arrival in forty-five minutes to an hour.

And forty-eight minutes later, this is a good sign, we're dealing with pros, our man shows up. His name is Artie, a big, fake-cheerful powder-keg type, pure heart-attack build, all chest and belly with thin ass and legs, white hair in a DA, a smoking, drinking, fifty-eight-year-old still doing the Elvis look. He's got a seven-year-old Lincoln with a phone and bar in back, since he drives in between security and surveillance jobs. Gerry the cop looks this rig over with professional interest. Our detective will stand in for the night, we'll have a replacement there tomorrow. He's well supplied. We make it back to New York a little after ten.

*   *   *

The next day, around eleven, a phone call from Artie. "They're heeeeeere!" he says. Cheerful, he is. "They came at six-thirty A.M., big crew, they clean the Dumpster out, they go through piece by piece, they sweep, then vacuum the bottom. Can you believe that? Now they're in there examining the metal. I took about forty shots from the car."

"What do you know," I say.

"I tell you what I know. They got major equipment in here to turn the thing sideways. I got a little conversation going with trooper here, nice young fellow. Like I'm just a tourist. 'Used to be on the job,' I tell him. 'What's up with this?' I ask him. 'Murder scene a while ago,' he says to me. 'I guess they're still looking for stuff.' '*I guess they're still looking for stuff*,' can you believe that shit? Yeah, I'll say they're still looking for stuff. You need me to file a paper report on this?"

"Yeah, we probably need that for the files. Maybe an affidavit, I'll let you know on that."

"Fine," he says. "Give me a fax and you'll have a write-up by the end of the day."

"Send me the fax, then put the original in the mail," I say.

"Yeah, sure."

I can hear it in his voice: lawyers. The files grow and grow. Faxed copies, originals, photocopies, each stamped, dated, initials of the secretary stamping it into the flow, on each copy the initials and markings of the attorneys working on the case. You lean to toss something in the can, stop yourself, consider the shredder, and then, what's easiest, you drop it in the box for the files. Storage spaces on several levels, reinforced shelving, structural engineers come in every six months to check the weights and stresses on the flooring. An archive center in a warehouse in Yonkers, shared space with Cravath, Swain & Moore. I wonder how many pieces of litigation have seen stipulations regarding sealing of archived material between firms sharing warehouse space. The paper game.

Gerry will want the news, and I'll give it to him in person if I can.

Before I head upstairs, though, I go to the kitchen for a cup of coffee. Jack's machine: gleaming in the slanted light through the window on the far wall. Knobs, nozzles, appendages, a Rube Goldberg challenge to the basic need for a cup of dark caffeinated beverage. A pot on the burner has some old-looking stuff that I pour into the cracked Dilbert mug that always seems to be the only one left when I want a cup of coffee. I've never known of a cartoon whose fans are so invariably unfunny.

Gerry's in. "Pay dirt," I tell him. "They never did a full forensic check on the goddamned Dumpster and, like schmucks, they went back today to cover their fucking tracks."

"Good lord," Gerry says. He's on some new diet all of a sudden and has a forty-six-ounce water bottle beside him on the desk; leaning back in his chair, taking a slug, there is a moment when he is a grotesque baby, in a high chair, having his ba-ba, weighing in at 350 pounds. Off the charts.

We spend the rest of the day drawing up a list of people and issues for discovery to give to the federal prosecutor, McCarthy, and his people. He calls back completely confused. I enjoy letting him in on how boneheaded the New York trooper boys are.

"I'll get back to you," is the last thing he says before hanging up. One can almost hear teeth grinding.

"You know," Gerry says later, in a meeting with me and Jack, "I'm not sure we should even have gone to McCarthy at this point, it tips our hand. We could have trapped them later into falsifying evidence, getting the whole case thrown out."

I say, "Yeah, well, consider this—if we get the whole case thrown out, which is a long shot that doesn't exactly clear Ron Adamson's 'good' name, he inherently won't be happy with it. More important, they fucked up, but why let them ruin their careers and lives? I can see that guy Houdacek right now. The other guys. I mean, sure, they screwed up and they're maybe willing now to screw up worse to save their asses, but let's just go ahead and press our advantage and maybe also spare them losing their fucking jobs."

Gerry looks at Jack. "What a pussy," he says.

Jack smiles. "Yeah, but he's my pussy." He's perspiring heavily, though it is a typically temperature-controlled day here at Reyner, Paul, and Jenrette.

Working late with Anna. I offer to take her to dinner. She declines. She gets a $26 voucher for dinner when she works late and usually cashes it in and eats later at home, and before I go to sleep, with my dick in my hand as a matter of fact, it occurs to me that while she probably had no desire to go to dinner with me she didn't have to think that hard about it because she mainly reacted to protect her twenty-six bucks. I cannot usually masturbate successfully thinking of someone I know well or have actual feelings for, and this proves so tonight, thinking of Anna. She is too tangible, too much present with her voucher that will add $26 to her paycheck, with her quick, automatic calculations of overtime, giving some of her salary every month to her mother, probably helping her sister too, who has a child with cerebral palsy, no husband, one of the disappeared. The boy is a sweet, maimed child with extraordinary, dense black hair. I've seen him twice, and his picture is on her desk, a face filled with divine ignorance and incomprehensible love. It is more a received love shining through its containment than a love extended by will outward—or that's what I believe. He is one about whom no one will ever know much. His face is roundish, ill constructed, odd in the eyes, with that thick black hair, that shining hair like the black bristles on an expensive paintbrush. And who could come thinking of all this? I am soft now, my hand moves slowly through my pubic hair, clean and damp after a shower. The ceiling I stare up at is white and newly painted, but in the bright, cheap halogen light I can see the plastering repairs, the thicker, less reflective places where the joint compound was laid down and sanded, under the paint. If I were rich, I wouldn't see such things, which is not to say I wouldn't be lying here unable to arouse myself, staring at the ceiling, but that, gone soft, the ceiling I would be staring at would be flawlessly plastered and painted and would perfectly absorb the soft light, light as soft and unpenetrating as I. I don't regret it, not being rich; I can't imagine that I will manage to be rich even when, fiscally speaking, I am rich; I don't foresee that perfect, no-visible-extension-cords life. I like seeing the thick patches, I like seeing the work of them, picturing the scene of their making, before my time here, an empty apartment, a splattered radio, Pall Mall cigarettes, joint compound and tape and primer and paint. A buckling battered brown van double-parked outside, a ladder lashed to its side.

David comes to see me. He sits, which is unusual. He looks at me across my desk.

"So?" I say. "What, what, what? What could bring such a serious look to your usually bland, unreadable, might I even say inscrutable eyes?"

"I have a friend," he says.

"I'm glad to hear that, David."

"Her name is Deirdre Considine."

"Oh, sweet Jesus. Get thee behind me, Satan."

"Look, she's nice, she's in her mid-thirties, she's attractive—"

"What kind of word is that? 'Attractive.' If you're gonna play hetero matchmaker you gotta upgrade your thesaurus. We say 'good-looking' or, better, 'fantastic-looking.'"

"She's totally excellent, babe-a-licious, with a great ass and big tits, how's that?"

"Over the top. Is she intelligent?"

"Very. She's a reporter for the *Daily News.*"

"You mean, intelligent in a 'Liz-Furious-at-Barbra' kind of way."

"No," David says. "Actually, more intelligent than that."

"'Rebs Accuse Salva Prez in Nun Slay.'" *Daily News* headlines from my youth. "'Bridge Hits Span,'" I say. "'Ford to City—'"

"Shut the fuck up, will you, and listen?" he says. He hands me a card. "Here's her number. I was out with her and some other people on Saturday and I was talking about you and she seemed interested, so I asked if you could call her and she said yes. In fact, she said, absolutely. I'm serious. You'll enjoy each other."

"'Whayyyy you doo 'dis to me, Deemy?'" I say.

The Exorcist," David says. "Followed by, 'Can ya spare a dime for an old altah boy, faddah?'"

"Amazing," I say. I pull out my sheet and mark it. "That's when the demon says it. He means to freak the priest out. It's from earlier when the priest is with his mother, but then there is no next line, as I recall. The priest just stares at the mother, bumming. I actually meant, though, why are you doing this?"

"She's smart, you're smart, you're both available, et cetera."

"I'm available?" I say. "It's only been ten weeks."

"You're separated, aren't you? It's time to shit or get off the pot. Old Chinese expression."

"That's such a nice way of putting it, I'll be sure to tell her your exact words."

"Don't you dare," he says.

I pick up the card, look at the *Daily News* logo with the old box camera next to the banner. "New York's picture newspaper," I say, to no one in particular, since David's already left.

Leaving the building, I find my old pal and favorite blackmailer, Harry Ellekin, waiting for me on the sidewalk.

"How are you, Harry," I say. Like the song.

"I ain't that good, actually. I been waiting here for you."

"Really?" I say. "We didn't just run into each other by accident?"

"No, no. I been waiting. Actually, I was waiting inside, it's fucking cold already out here, but they threw me out. I told them I was waiting for you, but they told me to wait outside, can you believe that?"

"Yes, actually, I can believe that," I say.

"Look," Harry says. "I need some money. I got a problem and I have to solve it, tonight. I need three hundred."

"I don't have three hundred, Harry," I say.

"What have you got?"

I take him downstairs into the subway, stand by the token booth, and give him $160.

"I have a problem with this, Harry," I say. "It's getting to be a little bit too blatant a shakedown operation for a rising midsize law firm to bear."

"I got a fucking problem too, pal," Harry says. "This fuck that you sent around threatening me. I should go to the fucking cops. Tell this guy to lighten up already and negotiate something fair in terms of a deal here."

"I thought we had done a deal. The deal was done."

"The deal is reopened," Harry says. "There are, what do you say, unresolved issues."

"Good-bye, Harry," I say. I wave my fingers at him, like playing bye-bye with a baby.

"I still got a problem," Harry says, turning to leave. "And if I have a problem, then you have a problem. Think about it. Tell Larkin to find me."

"Bye-bye," I say. "Bye-bye, Mr. Harry, bye-bye."

Deirdre. Thirty-six, divorced. Works the city desk. Welcome to the new club, the Irish-American marital failure society. I pick her up in front of the *News* building, red hair and a long blue coat she has told me. She is wary, I suspect, of my being a lawyer, believes I will be some boring ass-hole. I know enough of her field and downplay mine sufficiently to loosen her up.

I have had relatively little experience with grown-up dating and so find myself interested, in an altogether too detached way, in the tightly packaged fragments of information that get passed back and forth. Job: happy or sad. College: Fordham. She wanted to be an actress originally, got involved on the paper. Grew up in Brooklyn. It turns out she is a fe-rocious pool player, though it takes a while to find this out. She plays with her sister out in some billiard hall in Brooklyn where her family mostly lives; they win money at it, some kind of Irish and Latino mix on the scene, gambling and drinking in the old style. Every Thursday night.

"But this is a Thursday night," I say.

"Duh," she says, looking me straight in the eye. As "duhs" go, a fairly mild one. Somehow, disastrously, I figure, we end up talking about children, but we only stay on mine briefly, pointedly. "How old are they?" she says, taking in a forkful of grilled tuna.

"They are almost five months, and two and a half."

"Wow," she says.

"Yeah, wow," I say. I look away from her, across the restaurant full of New York faces, the fakers, the grotesques, and the sufferers, this last being the smallest group and the only one you'd want to know. Something in my own face, a kind of hot twitch, tells me I could weep; and I know I should weep, for what's been said, for the large fact made palpable in a few small words. But that should be later: not here, I shouldn't do it here in a restaurant with a strange woman, because that would become one of the watershed moments, one of the red markers on a downhill course.

So we end up talking about women having children but no husbands; like many unmarried women her age, Deirdre has been tempted to try it that way. What I want to know is, so many women like Anna's sister, why do they do it, with all the trouble it brings, with the no money and no prospects.

"You overestimate the rate of upward mobility out of the working class," she says plainly, fork gentle in the fish. "There are rarely husbands anymore," she says. "Even when the guy sticks around they end up living together on and off. And women often don't want much more than this because they know the guy is going to end up being a problem at some point, or at best a pain in the ass. They have visiting rights, and the grandmothers on both sides are heavily involved." She coldly discounts the sex, where, of course, I have focused. In the case of Anna's sister, I imagine it this way: sister a Brooklyn tough, slept with a Latino guy, thrills and chills, and had a baby at nineteen.

Dinner ends, we walk to her apartment. And then her soft lips on a good-night kiss. A very promising grown-up kiss all of a sudden, from this stranger, full of knowledge, resignation, history. Later I will think of that indescribable moment before, that hanging air, the weight of it; and our bodies move together but not much, we are not well enough known yet, but during the—what? three seconds?—time of the kiss they move slightly closer, a bit more and the kiss is about to go somewhere, our arms reaching farther around each other, the front of her body softening and pressing, and then, of course, she guides it down, and we are apart.

"You're good at that," I say.

Her eyes have none of the cloudiness you would see in a woman who has *really* been kissed. "At kissing or stopping kissing?" she says.

"Both."

"I had a nice time," she says.

"So did I," I say. "Absolutely." I will call her. She will call me. There are no rules on that front anymore. One of us will call the other. That is the intention.

The next day, David the Chinese yenta is in my office early. "So how did it go?" he says.

"It went fine," I say. "She's intelligent and good-looking. We had a nice time."

"No real spark there, eh?" David says.

"My dick was about an eighth of an inch long all night and fortunately I was not called upon to display it."

"The mushroom cap effect," David says. "Common on first dates."

"Even for you guys?" I say.

"Okay, not as much for us," he says.

"Fuck you," I say. We end up talking about restaurants. Restaurants are a safe thing to talk about. Needless to say, David knows infinitely more about restaurants than I do. I am not fond of restaurants, there are about five I like and this one wasn't one of them, but David, he loves restaurants, the newer the better, he talks about specific specialties of the house and half the time I don't even understand the food he is naming. I am constantly stunned these days to find myself in the orderly and highly artificial-seeming world of no children.

"You should know restaurants," David says. "People who know restaurants are always in demand."

"I can't be bothered keeping up," I say. "I like old restaurants, I'm suspicious of this new shit. I'm suspicious of these soft-voiced guys telling you every ingredient in the cooking of every dish on the specials. I remember going to restaurants where the dishes had a name, and you would say what's that, and they would say it's in a butter sauce, it's in a cream sauce. You didn't need to know every goddamn herb and what part of the Americas north and south the protein slab came from. At this point, where can we go with this? What can be newer than the last thing? Maybe a new restaurant in Central Park. *Restaurant dans le parc.* The waiters will all have that voice, the everything-is-a-question voice: 'Hello, my name is Kurt? I'm your waiter for tonight? Tonight's special appetizer is fresh Central Park frog slightly roasted over chips of old Upper East Side furniture, mostly walnut and fruitwoods? For entrées, we have Harlem bass from the Meer, in a Dairy Queen vinaigrette, with fresh chervil and California garlic, or blackened squirrel, also from Central Park, skewered with giblets intact, dipped in a light tempura batter and crisped over an oil-can fire by three homeless men? Would you like to start off with a drink?'"

"You're never going to get laid at this rate," David says. He heads for the door. "Which is probably your intention."

It appears that the Adamson defense will be an expert-witness defense, shedding doubt on the likelihood of a husband killing a wife premeditatedly (i.e., with gloves) by hand; the unlikelihood of his disposing of the wife's body in the carpet (we might add, we might not, *with the children inside the car . . .*).

David is our expert-witness man, the guru of expert witnessdom inside the firm, and he is doing the research and going through the case law to find psychologists, psychiatrists, former FBI serial-killer guys who have testified, roughly speaking, for the defense in a spousal murder trial. It is slim pickings. There is, too, the psychoanalytic/forensic literature. He is in hog heaven with the effluvia, the detail, the slow, tenacious movement through documented history, clinical reports, scientific speculation. I assist, he gives me lists, I move through material, go online, scroll up, scroll down, suspecting always that he is saving the best stuff for himself. Of course, he has no interest in actually speaking to any of these people. He wants to avoid contact with others. Actual human exchange. Being the poet that he is. Which is where I come in, articulate salesman. It is a delicate matter, suggesting to the three, four, then five potentials we find that the case is "interesting," that it presents "certain anomalies," that, for example, it occurs to us as laymen and purely in a commonsensical sort of way that our client, being arrested in ladies' underwear, would hardly have threatened that vital identity by enacting such an aggressive and hypermasculine killing; well, you can't really conclude anything until you have more to go on, yes, of course. And then, ever so subtly, I convey the deep-pocketed nature of things in this case, that unfortunately this could mean extended time in New York with expenses paid and a nice fee, plenty of time to service their careers, their dicks, or both. *Of course, this could mean a day and two days at a time in New York, away from your practice and/or classes and/or research in Tempe, but of course the firm pays all accommodations and your daily retainer.* Each of them is very busy, quite busy, but on this note each volunteers to review the case and give an initial report. A thousand, fifteen hundred, one of them even twenty-two hundred a day, and they will invoice with the first report.

subject: a long story about mr riordan

mr riordan my litigation attorney has come to the house to explain the fine points of how to make as much money off misfortune as is legal and possible when some

accidental shifting and a forgotten fly combine to reveal his erect cock—spring!—
shaft through trouser opening, and nigger princess she descends on it as if it is an
ice cream cone, licks those red lips, says needs more sprinkles baby. a multicultural
extravaganza. diversity galore. she uses lots of teeth. WHEN I THROW BACK MY
HEAD AND HOWL . . .

that girl LOVE to put things in her mouth. when she older she going to get fat.

How old are you child? How old? Who's your mommy and daddy? Do I know them
girl? They must be decent folks, I am sure of that.

mr riordan brings groceries, staples and a few small treats, sugar, flour, a box of
doughnuts. how are you my dear?

the public is greedy for mystery. example: mr riordan trapped in the city at night
ponders the following: if the universe is of finite but expanding dimensions, and is,
conceivably, but one of a distinct series or even an infinite series of universes, into
what domain, what space, does it expand? is it a subuniverse within a larger, similarly dynamic superuniverse? therefore can we imagine it as swelling into the empty
spaces within a larger structure, like ivy crawling through lattice? or an airbag,
blown at the moment of impact, surrounding and taking the driver's torso into itself, a polyvinyl pietà? is that woman wearing a bra? will i be able to see her breasts
through the opening at the front of her blouse? bare breasts? a nipple plain, from
the side. pressed softly against shirtfront. are the breasts of the woman that amazing white, or brown? come to me.

it is night. mr riordan drinks coffee at the greek diner and considers his misdeeds.
he attacked a woman today—not badly, no permanent damage, a loving assault. it
was in a quiet subway station, in the middle of the afternoon, because nobody was
there, because nobody could see him, because nobody could see a thing. it was a
situation where, upon realizing he could do this thing, the doing of it became necessary, compelling, seizing her at the foot of the stairs and trying to pull her
around to the side, into a little corridor that was hidden from the street. (i know
your comfort at thinking yourself incapable of such a thing, but you're not. it's in
the eyes.) she fought him. she fought mr riordan and he didn't like that. he grabbed
at her breasts. she was alive, it was surprising how alive she was, watching her on

the train from thirty-fourth street down to rector mr riordan hadn't realized she actually had a tangible existence and personality as forceful and real as his own and this made him very unhappy, to be surprised by it like that made him feel shocked and humiliated and that wasn't nice. she was a hard, strong, struggling body, an animal fighting for survival. her resistance, her animal fight, shocked him, outraged him, hurt him. why he had thought she would simply succumb he doesn't know. but that's what he'd thought really, that he would grab her and frighten her and she would surrender. her fighting took something away from him. it disappointed him. it was just another rejection. it played out in strange silence, a struggle with no voices. scuffling, a movement of air as each lunged and grappled; there may have been, must have been, some grunting. mr riordan was seeing and hearing with an unusual clarity; things were slowing down. she did not scream. in all likelihood she merely forgot, she just yanked and pulled and hit at him and kicked backward at his legs. he was behind her, pulling on her. he tried to bring his hands down to her crotch but she kind of bent over so he was caught in the fold of her stomach. her hands reached back for his face, for his hair. her hair, which had looked so beautiful on the train, so many shades within one body of reddish brown, her hair was a mess now, flying in every direction. she twisted like a dervish or a concrete mixer, back and forth hard, she grunted and kicked. it's stupid to talk about it, how hurt he was by that, by her hatred and fear. from behind her he began to lift up her skirt, he wanted to touch her ass and her pussy, that's what he'd been thinking about on the train, the human softness, but the second she felt him there she twisted even harder, a real bolt, strong as a horse and kicking like one. at this moment or perhaps even earlier his body began to feel heavy, began to lose resolution and strength, it happened very fast, he turned to lead, he lost his edge. he had not known what it is like to be defeated physically, just defeated, overcome, the resignation that precedes the rage, which is longer lasting. and so he let go of her. as she pulled away she sent a fist flying back that caught him in the temple. then came the sound of her shoes as she ran up the stairs, a very rapid scraping/clapping sound. he stood there, he felt confused and separated from himself, although he was not even as self-conscious as that implies: what he felt like was a collection of random molecules—no, he had moved out of consciousness into the biological present of body, the metric of his pulse and breathing, so what he felt was his own randomness at the cellular level; he was a collection of organisms, and the organisms were chaotic, overheated, frantically bumping against one another. he understood cancer, then, though perhaps not consciously, the cells overstressed and hyper-procreative. perhaps some small tumor formed inside him at that moment, in those few seconds, a dna trigger was pulled in some tiny spot inside him. boom.

on the exterior he was wrinkled and askew, not ready for the world. and then he came back to himself (he wanted a cigarette), and it was in his memory now, not in his blood; what had just happened, five seconds ago but across a wide chasm of some internal time—how she'd felt, her dress, her body, and he hated the stabbing disappointment; he wanted her again or someone like her, he wanted someone who would just take it, who would just LET HIM—or some situation that would make it impossible for her not to let him.

when he reached the top of the stairs he saw her across the street, staring at him. all her composure was gone, as was his; she'd lost her stance, the pose she took toward the world was interrupted, it was shot to hell. she was reduced to her animal state, spine slightly curved, muscle, bone, sweat, adrenal alertness and strength, unblinking eyes locked on an enemy over the hood of a car, bright, fearful, mad with survival. he stared back at her. she turned and ran down the street, and then slowed to a very fast walk. he stayed on the other side of the street and followed.

why she didn't scream, look for a cop, or ask someone for help, he would never understand. it amazed him. here he was following her and she didn't want anyone to know. even in the brutal immediacy of an attack she didn't cry out, didn't want to draw attention to herself. i could explain it to you mr riordan but what's the point? you'll never get it. sufficient to say there was a pride in her shame; she PREFERRED to think herself guilty rather than acknowledge he was brutalizing her on a whim, by chance, because they happened to cross paths, five minutes or two either way, on a tuesday afternoon near rector street, and that for him she hardly existed at all, didn't deserve the fullness of creation—how a man can think of a woman, and how a woman, instinctively denying certain ugly truths in the situation, can reroute the thought to something else.

in any case, they made their way up toward broadway, with the deranged roles casting him as innocent and her as criminal holding more strongly with every passing moment. he had composed himself; she looked wild. he had on an expensive nicely fitting suit, on his side of the street he was that official thing, the white man in jacket and tie, walking fast, on his way to a meeting or back to his office or even to one of those quiet whispery stores you all go to, where the salesman gives you his card and tells you his day off is thursday. the hints of madness and violence in his face, the tautness of expression, the fire in the eyes: standard issue to successful men, certainly nothing to be suspicious about. she however was openly disheveled, crazy-eyed, noticeably perspiring—one of those people on the streets you assess and avoid, give clearance to, her affect just exceeding known boundaries of the immediately sane. from where he was she looked like anyone, which is to say she'd been separated from herself, leaning far forward and walking way too fast, heading up the hill toward trinity church and wall street. from time to time she looked back. he smiled at her: HERE I AM.

you have children, don't you mr riordan? think of it this way, from an early card you've seen of mine: this is a story about rape; this is a story about insemination; this is a story about fatherhood.

let me tell you mr riordan about a woman i know, or knew once. this is something you can understand. she was working in a good office, in a respectable office building that was being renovated on its lower floors. one night, not late at all, a little after six, she was leaving her office. going home to a salad, a few phone calls. she was alone on the elevator. it stopped at an empty floor, the doors opened and a man was there. he pulled her out of the elevator and attacked her. she resisted and he beat her, quite badly, and then raped her. that's all I actually know, all i was told. when i heard that story, of course i felt sorry for her, although it doesn't sound as bad as my incident and i felt the hardness i feel about that. but also, the story being distant and familiar at the same time, i thought this: how lucky he was that night, to have the doors open and reveal an attractive woman (and she was—is—an extremely attractive woman, like some kind of roman cat, striking and explicitly sexy). AND she was alone. the scene just could not have conformed more tangibly to what he had imagined, had always imagined and wanted. it must have filled him with rage when she fought him, when she destroyed his fantasy.

you see your situation mr riordan comes to you in my telling of it accidentally, you weren't looking for it. suddenly there it was and as soon as it was in his mind it was done. he knew he could try it and probably get away with it and that put him over the edge, that excited him a great deal. they walked down the platform toward the exit, toward the steel spike revolving doors, the opposite end from the token clerk and the token booth, a mistake for a woman but she did it, toward an exit-only set of stairs that was closer to his office and, apparently, hers, since they both chose to go that way. he was a white man in a suit and so she wasn't too nervous about him. he had about thirty seconds to watch her, to think about it, to think about how it would be. he watched her ass. thinking about touching her, because that's really the first and great thing he wanted, to touch her, and thinking about that as they walked gave him a hard-on. he had a hard-on when they started but not when it was over, not after she fought with him like that. you see, the person who attacked my old friend, he must have been standing there in the dark with his hand in his pocket working it. it has taken me a long time to begin to understand what can happen to a man when he gets that way. your blood, everything inside you is boiling, vile. you start to sweat, that really acrid-smelling sweat, that high-anxiety stuff. he must have been ready just to explode, explode. it probably started as a fantasy. you have had that fantasy; a lot of men have had that fantasy. it depends on how good at fantasizing you are, how much you need to make it better as time goes on. for some people the fantasy gets more elaborate, you work it into the material world somehow, and then it reaches a level where you've got to take it out and test it because you want it just to keep getting better and better, the way it has been. so he must have really seen it, being a stalker the way he was, finding a place, staking it out, watching, sneaking into a building, working the elevators. i bet you he had his dick out, his pants open and his dick in his hand. i bet you when those doors opened his dick was right out there. i bet you it was the best hard-on he'd ever had in his life. and all he was thinking was fuck, fuck, fuck,

"How old are you, girl? Are you lost? Are you lost honey? We've got to see if we can find your momma and your daddy."

yes, your honor, we realize that mr riordan is a milder type. let us admit that he is at heart nonviolent. he felt the skin of her leg, her thigh, he felt her underwear, there was a second where his hands passed over her face and down onto her breasts. then he was going in under her blouse from the bottom, his hand in the fold of her stomach. then trying to move down, but no. so he held her like a frozen image of someone tackling another person, having the opponent around the waist and about to bring her down. he used the other hand to pull up her skirt, feel her leg, her panties. he wanted to get through them right there, through them, he wanted to have that, have it in his hand. she was kind of a big woman. her skin was soft, like some treasure he'd found, he couldn't stand not owning it, he couldn't stand that—she fought him and fought him and then she broke away from him.

last time i visited i picked up on a few little facts about you. wifey's not around these days, is she mr riordan? getting any?

she turned at broadway and for a minute he lost her in the crowd beyond the spiked fence of the cemetery. when he reached the corner he saw her running, RUNNING, because she knew she had those few seconds where he wouldn't be able to see her, she was a clever bitch, but pathetic, and he hated her. he wanted her. he hated her. she crossed broadway and scooted down wall. he followed. she turned, he smiled, and until he smiled and saw what it did to her face he didn't realize fully what an evil pall had come over him; it shocked him. she walked, faster. they were on the same side of the street now so she really had to turn all the way around to see him. he thought: when i can't see her she runs but when i can she walks. that's the way it was. he thought: she's putting on airs, she's playing games. so all right.

so he followed her to her building, went back to his office, then came back at four, making excuses on the way out. he waited outside her office for four hours, moving from a newsstand to a magazine shop to a coffee shop, all spots that gave view of the doors. he felt like an assassin, and he liked it. four hours; that's commitment. that's love of a kind. or hate, the other name we give it. finally back to the newsstand. he bought a pack of cigarettes, a candy bar, and just stayed close to the newsstand and the subway stairs, kind of in a swirl of people most of the time, a brainless rush of humanity that protected him from being seen. she may have been watching him from inside. it seemed to him she could have called the police anytime, anytime, and that would have been the end of it, finis, all over. but she didn't. he was willing to risk it, to stand there and be arrested. fuck it. that's the way mr riordan was feeling. he was on fire, he was burning, burning, he was already dead, so what could they do to him? he was the white man, so highly developed, so steeped in irony and mechanical living he was beyond human. he was dead to the world. what is death like? mr riordan thinks, death is nothing, it's the sudden stunning absence of everything, it's the final emptying out, a swoosh, a rapid loss of pressure, like a voice saying—

WARNING WARNING

—a feeling of something-is-dreadfully-wrong-here, the moment we've been afraid of all along, the whole time, this is what we feared, an awful but intimately familiar feeling of loss, of dread—

AT A HUNDRED AND FOUR THOUSAND FEET AND TEN NAUTICAL MILES

—a collapse, a cave-in, an implosion—

THERE WERE NO ANOMALOUS INDICATIONS PRIOR TO LOSS OF DATA

"A nice stick," he says.

"It *is* a nice one," I say.

Then comes a silence that feels comfortable and full. Our hands touching seems to be enough to communicate, we stand for a while where the walkway runs along the turnaround for cars passing below the road and coming up again on the downtown side—they come at us dangerously fast, or so it feels, then *whoosh* and hum on their tires, the sound of a string against cardboard, as they make the long, circling turn, just missing us, disaster passing us by, blessedly, once again. We are lost in a sudden sense of the river close up, on this scale, the breadth and iron-gray strength of it. Small waves pushing tree branches and bits of trash, odd things; out farther there's a tire, closer in a large wood pylon, cut loose from somewhere on the ruined docks, floating now in a rise and fall under the swells, looking heavy and lethal and dark with water.

On such days it is a brave and beautiful world. The scent of autumn, of dampness and earth in the park, a lone runner on the dirt path; a squirrel or rat, so fast you can't tell (so you assume rat), dashing from beneath the roots of an oak; families, bicycles, three girls and a father on their way to a soccer game. Overhead, the delicate lacework of branches and remaining leaves are backlit against the sky. The Hudson lies there, massive, flat, molten, gray. It reflects the sky, which hangs low and vague, a computer-screen white, an empty file.

When I think of the children I think of their feet for some reason, Henry's little feet pounding down the hallway *dum-dum-dum-dum-dum* because he is on the run, driven by an idea which is followed in some sequence by another idea and another, each leading him to the next small exploration, his mind expanding like a muscle continuously and repetitively exercised.

subject: 7

can you name the seven dwarfs? i mean right off the top of your head? there's dopey, we all remember and identify there. sneezy, the allergic cokehead. Was it grumpy or grouchy or moody, the closet gay one who wanted only the world of men and was horrified at the prospect of having a beautiful young woman around? what was HIS name? irritable?

    After a time we head back up again to the main promenade and north to the playground with the slides and sandbox at 110th Street. Henry plays in the sandbox, moves to the slide, the baby fusses in the back of the double stroller. Once again, like that other day several weeks ago, when I look up from dealing with Sam, Henry is out of sight. A middle-aged Latina caretaker, who seems to be very nice, watching a three-year-old in the sandbox, smiles at me.
    "I think I'm missing a child," I say. "Will you just keep an eye on the stroller?"
    "Sure, sure, I do," she says. She pulls herself over, starts gently rocking, happy to be active in her child-care duties. I walk out to the promenade and look both ways: and there he is about 100 yards south of here, walking away with his right hand planted in the much larger hand of a grown man whom I do not recognize. The image is squared and framed, absolutely incorrect in every way: Henry in some stranger's possession. His small, toddling, absurdly self-confident walk. To the nice woman I say please watch my baby, *uno minuto solamente*, and take off; she stands up to watch. The run brings an odd kind of focus. I am moving without any physical sense of feet and legs, without any up and down; I'm flying, off the earth. My forward movement registers as camera movement, a closing of the focal length on my object, small child and man, a cheap brown leather jacket, jeans and sneakers, coming closer, larger, clearer. My breath is calm, my steps almost silent; I accomplish these things with instant application of the brain, which at this moment has powers it will never again possess. Closer, closer. When I am near, the thief begins to turn his head. Since I am aimed at the center of his back this only moves the target slightly; I duck my shoulder at the last second and hit him like a linebacker taking down a receiver who's on the descent with a short pass in his arms. He tumbles down; Henry falls to his knees and makes not a

sound, just looks up at me. I take his hand, pull him to his feet and drag him behind my legs. At the periphery, exclamations, movement quickly away from the violence developing at the center. I recognized him as he turned: the famous Harry of the night scene at 125th, the Jaguar and license number, the oily shakedown. He rolls right out of the hit and comes up at me low; I step away, keeping Henry on the lee side; Harry rises and we are in close on each other. He has something in his hand. I am in the realm of fury however and don't care and pop him under the eye with a right. "Fuck," he says, giving only a little. And then, *click*, a knife. The word "shiv" suddenly becomes available in the mind's thesaurus.

"Look," he says, and with that I know I am all right. Alpha position.

"Doing some baby-sitting in your spare time, Harry?" I say. "Supplementing the blackmail business?"

"We have a little compensation problem here," he says. "I don't know if your friend told you." Behind me, Henry is struggling to get his head loose from the grip of my hand pressing him against my legs.

"One," I say, "my friend didn't tell me. Two, what the fuck are you doing with my kid? And three, which fucking friend are you talking about?" I must be screaming because there is still more sense of people fleeing at the periphery.

"The pasty-faced former fed, the fuck," he says. The knife close to his ribs, held out at me, but not obvious. "He seemed to feel there was really no room for negotiation in this sensitive area."

"He's awfully full of himself, isn't he?" I say. "'Pasty-faced former fed, the fuck' was very nice alliteration by the way."

"What?"

"Never mind, asshole." Henry is pulling on my shirt, saying, "Daddy, Daddy." I let go of him and feel him move off behind. "Henry! Stay here," I say over my shoulder. I don't dare glance to see if he's listening. "There's always room for negotiation. But not over a kidnapped kid. So put the knife away and get the fuck away from me and my children, okay, asshole? Because if you so much as call me on the phone, never mind come near me again, I am going to have so many cops up your ass you're going to feel like you got fucked by a bridge."

"Mister, mister!" We both look then, down toward the playground. It's the nice Puerto Rican lady, she's waving something that I think at first is a gun, like the whole city is secretly armed to the teeth, until I realize it's a cellular phone. "Mister, I call the cops. I call the cops, they coming!" What a magical statement—*click* and the knife is away, and old Harry is beginning to move off.

"We still got us a little problem, you and me," he says.

I have Henry by the hand, he seems to be quivering a bit. "I'll have the pasty-faced former fed the fuck be in touch," I say. "I'm sure you two can work it out splendidly." Harry is at the stairs, turns and runs down them, into the main section of the park below. Henry and I start walking back to the playground. "Are you all right?" I ask him, bending down. He looks at me, doesn't answer. "Henry," I say. "Are you okay?" He nods, we walk again, maybe three steps, and then he turns and clings to my legs, a hug from the depths. I pick him up and carry him, which I should have done from the moment we started back, but was too dazed to think of. He throws his arms around my neck and puts his head down on my shoulder, and we walk back that way. At the stroller, Sam is sound asleep. The Puerto Rican lady is wide awake though, pacing in short bursts around the stroller, a knot of other parents and caretakers kind of milling, keeping watch. A few others, I notice, are packing up and leaving.

"That man took his baby, took his boy," she is saying, seemingly over and over. I walk up and they turn to me. Is he all right, is he all right, but I nod at them, I put my finger to my lips and they quit that stuff. "Everything's fine," I say. "We are all just fine." Henry doesn't need to be any more frightened than he is already. The man is someone I know, I tell them, a misunderstanding.

"That's quite a misunderstanding," one woman says.

I have a bit of the shakes as the adrenaline wears off, and my shoulder where I hit him is starting to ache.

"You got to call the police," the Puerto Rican lady says. "This phone no really work, it's a toy, you know?" She demonstrates by pushing the button, and out comes the Taiwan-microchip-imitation-phone-ring sound. I look at her, amazed. The other parents are smiling, shaking their heads.

"Thank you," I say. "You're wonderful." Henry, meanwhile, unwilling to lift his head until now, rises suddenly and turns to see the toy cellular. She rings it again. He is looking at it, with a standard air of wanting that fills me with relief.

She hands it to him. "Here, you keep," she says. "That one"—indicating her charge, coming a bit wildly down the slide—"he tired of it already."

I put Henry down on the bench, where he plays with the phone. One of the other parents, a small, balding man, another weekend father, perhaps, says, "You hold on to that, son, it did good work for you." I assume the other kid is going to discover we have his toy and we'll have to give it back, but I hope not: absurdly, I want very much to have it, a kind of sacrament of Henry's return to me. I pull together our things, bending over the benches, packing the stroller, then pull up straight again. The lady is standing beside Henry, still looking over him in her mind. "I want to thank you again," I say to her. "You did a great thing and I'm very grateful to you." The words are awkward and unreal, like a politician's, but she gives me her hand and her smile anyway.

9:05 Monday morning. Larkin sits in my office; in before me, Mr. Full Access. I had called his office that Saturday afternoon, we had made an appointment for 9:15. "Where's my security?" I say to Anna. "Can just anyone get into this office?" She looks up at me and raises her eyebrows, a what-do-you-want-me-to-do-about-it look.

I go in. "Mr. Larkin. Good morning."

He stands and extends his right hand with almost military precision. I shake it. We sit.

"Well," he says. "I have to admit an error here. I thought Harry far too much the putz ever to try anything like that."

"It was upsetting," I say. I wonder: who is this man sitting here masquerading as me?

"I'm sure it was. Of course, I'll deal with it. The question is, do I deal with it at a cost or at no cost."

"We should ask Jack," I say.

"Well, that's a problem, actually," Larkin says. Uncharacteristically, he moves, shifts a little in his seat. "Jack is in the hospital."

"What?"

"He had a heart attack on Saturday morning."

"Jesus."

"He's going to be fine, they stabilized him and rushed him in for a bypass, and now it's just recuperation and then a regimen, some meds. Look, it happened to me. He's going to be fine."

I call out: "Anna!"

"Yeeees," she says from her desk. "No reason to shoouuuut."

"Did you know Jack had a heart attack?"

"It's one of your messages that you haven't looked at yet. You're supposed to call Gerry."

"You know those things you're supposed to tell me no matter what else I have going on? This was one of those."

"Sorry," she says. "He's at Columbia-Presbyterian."

"Mr. Larkin, I tell you what," I say. I am standing up now. "Let's give my friend Harry one more chance and seven hundred and fifty—no, tell him it's a thousand and tell him it's from me. Can you get your hands on a thousand in cash? It's a little difficult here today."

He nods once.

"Okay, and tell him that's going to be my money, not the firm's, not the client's, and that is it, period. Call it a day. Make sure he understands the well has run dry."

"Nice seeing you again," Larkin says.

"Likewise," I say.

Jack in the hospital: disorienting modern technology as an agent of spiritual change. He is surrounded by machines and he has that funny elastic tube sock on, with the hole in the sole, on his left foot. I've always wanted to know what those things are for but now is not the time to ask.

"Will, hell, good of you to come up," he says. He looks and sounds weak, but clear-eyed in a certain way, his face shining with some light that is softer and more benign than what I'd seen haunting it before.

"How do you feel?" I say.

"I feel like shit. They cut my chest open with an electric saw. I'm under but I'm convinced I could hear that thing buzzing and eating through the bone. Christ." He tries to move, pain shoots through his face like a bolt of electricity.

"You know they make you get up and walk the second fucking day?" he says. "Is that cruel or what? Hand me that contraption over there." He is indicating a plastic canister roughly the size and shape of a bong, with a breathing tube attached. He takes it from me, breathes into it, and a small plastic ball rises about halfway up inside the body of the thing. Three of these and he stops and closes his eyes and rests.

"You know it gets better every day," I say.

"That's a philosophy to hold on to there, son," Jack says in a near whisper. Eventually he opens his eyes, rejoins me in the room. He uses the electric device to raise the back of his bed and grimaces through the worst of the rising.

"Well," I say.

"Yeah, be well, get well, do well. That makes a life," Jack says. "You know what's interesting? I'm in my apartment on Saturday morning and, let's face facts, my life is totally fucked up and I've wrecked just about everything that I ever came near that was worthwhile, out of sheer boredom and destructiveness, but there I am on another Saturday morning and I'm going to have brunch with this lady friend and I'm feeling like shit, like I have been, and suddenly everything tightens up and there's a pain, the fucking actual size of which you would not believe, it's like someone just put a Mack truck inside your chest, and I fall to my knees and down I'm going, and the lady friend screams and goes for the phone right away and I'm lying there in unbelievable pain and I can't breathe and you know what I think? I think, I want to live. I want to live. Now, ask yourself, why should I want to live? What have I got to live for? More fucking money? This lady friend? That lady friend? A thousand lady friends? That some sleazy miserable fuck like me says, I want to live, it's a miracle."

"A conversion," I say.

"Yeah, something like that," Jack says. "Something like that, only more fucking brutal. It's like your life has a certain lightbulb and then pop! it goes out and then they come and put in a new bulb and everything looks different. That's all. Everything and nothing is changed."

Pop.

Back in the office, I wander down the long hallway, carrying a file folder, going to see Sue, making a few stops along the way. You get out of your own square footage, do the social thing, it keeps you sane and grounded. Have you seen such and such movie, such recent film? The game. A certain bizarre example of the kind of world we live in, on television last night. The president, the president's strange wife, why are they all so fucking weird, the wives? We talk about the partners. Jack, the heart attack, can you believe it? He's calling in already, handling some issues, what an animal. Bill Samuelson, the litigation guy, is trying to get his daughter into a good school, she's kind of a cute kid, shy, but she's tested low and he's acting all desperate about it, hitting on everyone with kids in decent Manhattan schools to put in the word for him. A four-a-half-year-old on the brink. The unspoken angle here, the ugly thought everyone nurtures but will not say is that he married this Carmen Miranda type who's sexy but a dolt; it made him feel macho. He's a doofus himself about most things in life except litigation, and the wife is missing the litigation gene. His marriage matches a career in law, in that way: it made him feel good at first. He named the daughter Sarah, and likes to picture her, I think, as some kind of sandy-haired character from the periphery of *Franny and Zooey*. Meanwhile, he has Carmen Miranda's daughter.

Gossip, cheers, greetings as we meet up at Jack's new copper god, the multiarmed coffee urn.

Finally, delicately afloat, carrying coffee and folder, I make it to the far end of the hall. I raise my eyebrows at Jeannie, Sue's secretary.

"She's in," Jeannie says. I poke my head around the door. I think, as always, corner office.

"Hello, Will," Sue says. She sits enthroned on her high-backed black leather swivel. I walk to the desk.

"So, Sue, do you want to have some fun?"

"No," she says. "I only like to toy with you."

"I don't mean that kind of fun," I say. "I mean real fun."

"That is real fun," she says.

I give her a bland look.

"Irishman," she says.

Onto her desk, from my folder, I drop my typed, untitled custody agreement: what I have in mind for Friar and Susan. Sue looks through it, looks up at me. "Ron Adamson?" she says.

"Bingo."

"You're a bad, bad boy," she says. "This will drive Jack nuts."

"I think Jack is seeing the world in a different light, actually."

"Really?"

"I think so," I say.

She reads my pages more carefully. "Pretty good," she says. "There are a couple of minor points, but basically you're ready to go."

"Good, thanks. I'd appreciate your help. I have to see him tomorrow."

"Hey, thanks for giving me so much time," she says. "I don't want my name anywhere near this. If the question arises, you did this all on your own, agreed?"

"Absolutely."

"Actually, I can give you what you need right now." She goes through the document, makes notes in various places. "You can find the templates for all this," she says, and hands the document to me. "Jeannie has them on her machine if they're not on the network drive already. And notice how pointedly I'm not asking you what you have on the guy that's going to convince him to sign this."

She sits back in her CEO-meets-Captain-Kirk leather chair. I envision her, moving offices, reviewing with avidity and lust the special catalog for super-luxury executive office furniture, picking the main pieces and accessories, enduring a few comments when the expenses are examined at the quarterly partner's meeting.

"Will," she says, "what did you have in that poker hand?"

"It's not what I had that matters, Sue. It's what you thought I had and what I thought you had."

"What did you think I had?"

"You had a flush; queen high probably. You could easily have had a very decent low hand too. You were worried I had a full house."

"What did you have?"

"Nine-high lowball."

"Shit!" she screams. It must carry through half of the office. "Goddamn motherfucker! I had an eight-high low hand *and* a goddamned flush, I could've taken the whole goddamned pot!"

"Such a mouth you have on you. I had nine, six, four, three, ace," I say, goading her.

"I had a eight-five, a goddamn eight-five. You son of a bitch."

"Yeah, but you didn't know what I had. I hadn't let you figure it out. That's why I got four hundred and fifty bucks, because I played well. That's how poker works, and other things too. Like the law."

"Are you playing that well?" she says. She holds up my agreement.

"I'm taking a calculated risk," I say.

"Is the payoff worth it?"

"Absolutely."

*   *   *

At the grandmother's house: an Upper West Side brownstone, humble in comparison to what Ron might have (sixteen rooms on Fifth, specifically) but elegant and monied nevertheless. A calculation you make as you enter the domicile: current price, probable acquisition date, probable price at that time, minimum income then, minimum income now, rates of inflation, possible investments, and where is the furniture from? How old, how new? She is a well-kept woman, as the saying goes about monied women over sixty with decently but not overly trim figures and youthful haircuts and clothes. There is a tough, defeated look about her face, a look of tears fought off for decades in a battle that, imminently, she will lose. Her attorney is there; he has reviewed the papers (he called me yesterday to clarify a couple of issues on the money side, and then said, "I suppose I shouldn't ask why you're doing this, or point out the conflict of interest involved," to which I replied, "That's absolutely correct, you should not ask anything or point out anything.") and we go over them with her now; one senses she desperately wants the children, not in an acquisitive way but to keep them from Ron. She signs where needed; her attorney, a bit rumpled but clearly from old money himself, gathers everything together into the Redweld. I rise to go.

"Mr. Riordan," she says. "I have one question. What if he refuses?"

"I don't believe he will."

"Then you don't know him. I'm asking you, what happens when he doesn't sign?"

"Well, then, again, *if* that happens, we wait to see how things go at trial," I say. "Custody might end up a nonissue." Her attorney is watching me, a face wiped clean, many years ago by the look of it, of any vivid or telling expression.

"He will not likely lose at trial," she says, more a statement than a question.

"No, he probably won't."

"And then?"

"And then a protracted legal battle, if you choose to take it on, in which you would have a great deal of difficulty prevailing." Her man nods, though she cannot see him.

She puts a hand on my arm. "Then I shall hope you know something I don't, and that he will sign."

"Yes," is all I can say to that.

"Thank you, Mr. Riordan. Thank you very much."

"You're welcome," I say. I turn to go, and pick up my bag, the Redweld under the other arm. "I have two children of my own," I say, turned away and to no one in particular, or to myself. Then I walk from the room.

At the Metropolitan Correction Center I pass again through the outer rings and into the long, echoing corridors. Glass and wire mesh and cinder block and steel bars, woven into a unity of a kind by a multitude of locks, every kind of lock man has ever thought of.

Ron is brought in thirty-five minutes after I request him, something that does not happen when a group of lawyers, including older, more established-looking ones, arrives, as is usually the case.

"What the fuck are you doing here?" is his opening gambit. It is interesting, now that I know he is sick, I can see the lines of death begin to circle his eyes, to draw down his cheeks and mouth.

"I don't know, Ron," I say. "Just missing you, wanting to check in and see how things are going, how you are. You must be having the time of your life here."

"You wouldn't believe this place if I even began telling you about it," he says. "It's a tough question, if they ever throw *you* in here, which you'd lose the use of first, your mind or your asshole." He laughs and reveals his large teeth and unspeakably obscene, lolling tongue.

"Ron, I have some papers for you to sign," I say, and start piling up the documents on the table. I stand and open the door and lean out. "Guard? Would you be so kind as to come and witness some signatures for us please?" The guard, I presume familiar with this drill, steps into the room.

Ron is looking at the first document, titled "Adoption Agreement."

"This doesn't have to do with my case," Ron says.

"You know what?" I say to the guard. "I was premature. I have to consult a little more with my client. I wonder if I might call you again in a few minutes?"

He leaves again to stand outside the door, making sure I don't miss his clear "fuck you" look.

I turn back to Ron. He has put the adoption agreement back on the top of the stack and is staring at me.

"Actually, Ron," I say, "these very much *do* have to do with your case. Your case has encountered a little problem. It seems that a nicens little fellow whom I cannot name at the moment happened one night to be hanging around down under the old bridge of Riverside Drive over by the meat warehouses at 125th Street, you know where I mean? And he happened to witness a very distinguished man, he might even have said 'handsome, distinguished man,' I can't quite recall. And saw him very elaborately cleaning out the 'bucket,' as the English say, of his Jag-u-ar, as the English also say. Green it was. With beige leather interior. Just north of the Fairway parking lot. Know the location? So. Guess what? You know the man he saw in the newspapers? He seemed to own this car. He was throwing away much carpet from the trunk and replacing it with a new one. Very good visual memory, this fellow. Plus, can you believe it, he wrote down the license plate number. Then sometime later he sees your picture *again* in the paper, can you believe that? And you know what? His conscience has been bothering him."

"What have you done about it?" Ron says. He is taking out a cigarette. "You didn't bring me any cigarettes, by the way."

"No, I didn't bring you any cigarettes, Ron, that's true," I say. "As for the more interesting question, what we've done about it, well, with the utmost concern and kindness, we are trying to assist this gentleman, who is exactly the kind of fellow who might be hanging around at two-thirty in the morning under Riverside Drive at 125th Street, if you know what I mean—anyway, we've tried to assist him as best we can, to alleviate all this stress and whatnot, his heavy conscience. But somehow in the process, now, my conscience came into play. Isn't that strange? Isn't that inconvenient?"

"So what are we going to do about your conscience?" Ron says.

"We're going to sign all these nice little papers," I say.

"The fuck I will," he says. He looks away, like a pissed-off high school girl.

"I'm not going to bother you with the moral arguments," I say. "I'm going to put it in plain language, your language, actually, the language of utter self-interest, so I'm certain you'll understand it. This gentleman is prepared to testify against you unless we take care of him. He'd love the notoriety, the fifteen minutes—and he's already gotten just about as much out of us—out of you, I should say—as he's going to get. I will pick up the phone and call the United States Attorney's Office and get myself an immunity deal and then tell them name, address, phone number, anecdotal history, and all the rest, in a fucking heartbeat, if you don't sign these papers, turning custody of your children over to their grandmother . . . In a fucking heartbeat, do you understand? And then, Ron, you will be convicted, and out of Manhattan, and in some maximum security penitentiary from hell where they won't give a shit what you're dying of and will leave you to get sicker and sicker until one day they find you where you've been lying for hours, even days, in a pool of piss and blood and excrement reciting fragments of old song lyrics and broken nursery rhymes—"

"You'll be out of a job so fast—"

"Don't even waste your breath," I say. "Do you think I give a shit? Do you think I like what I'm doing? Throwing it away and being disbarred, returning to some version of my authentic self, that's just the kind of thing my wife tells the therapist she's scared I'll do—depress the plunger and watch the whole fucking thing blow, that's right up my alley, I'm very good at that. This"—I indicate the papers—"gives me a perfect excuse."

"And your precious—"

"Say another word and I'll beat you again like I did the last time. Just picture it: you're dying, Ron, on a cold cement floor. Shit and piss. Spitting up blood. Hold that shot. Then sign."

He shifts, looks at the papers, picks them up. "So, what, you believe in justice, schmuck?" he says. And then he is signing, with one of the pens I've laid out (they've been counted by the guard, who will count again before removing Ron, and search him as well), one page after another, lifting sheets to get to the little signature stick-ems. I open the door and the guard walks in. I will notarize. It is in Ron's face: the completeness of his self-interested analysis; he doesn't actually care about the children; he understands that few people will know he's been forced into this; and he won't, under any conditions, spend the rest of his life in prison. Thus he signs, and signs, and signs. Each time he puts pen to paper I feel a jolt of terrifying grace. He pauses, holding a page up to sign the one below. He just peruses, scowls, signs, drops the upper pages.

"You know dick about justice," he says. "Nobody knows dick about justice."

"You will soon, Ron."

"What, at some rat's-ass trial?" he says.

"No, it wasn't the trial I had in mind," I say.

"Fuck you," he says.

I hand the papers to the guard, he signs the witness lines, I put them in my bag, to do the notarizing later. I feel like I'm carrying some kind of liberating document and there will still be ten checkpoints before I get them over the wall to safety. I walk out, the wooden heels of my Aldens clapping on the hard government floor.

subject: street life

mr riordan, i am on the streets, why is everyone out on the streets these days? i have my mini camera and the nine, this separates me from most of the other negroes because the way i figure it some have the one, more have the other, but not too damned many have both. now that the weather is cooler i have the leather car coat to put the gun under; the warm weather makes your concealed weapon, your basic tidy but substantial handgun, a little problematic, mr riordan, don't you think? now i know why the men wear jackets even in the summer; another gesture signifying power.

truth is, mr riordan, i have seen my man again. i have seen him and followed him and learned his comings and goings as it were. he's uptown, the high nineties and second avenue somewhere though i lost him before he went home. an old Irish neighborhood i gather with the latinos coming in strong the last twenty-five years those poor folks do breed and they pack 'em into those old apartments too, seven to a room. there's a hardware store over there he seems to work at part-time, or just hang out, i couldn't tell which, but it's nice, isn't it, a hardware store? so all-american and suggestive too. i'm intending to make him more intimate with hardware than he cares to be.

so then i'm home, mr riordan, and on a bag of nuts, i read: "farley's bridge mix. don't forget the farley's . . ." the malt balls are my favorite. and don't you just love those little chocolate-covered raisins? i just love those. the other day I found two that had been covered together so it was like getting two for one! i was in heaven.

"farley's guarantee of quality:

"farley continues to offer you, the consumer, the finest products that meet your special needs. at farley we know the importance of consumer value and variety."

now mr riordan is this not complete non-english, or proto-english, making the right noises but fundamentally senseless? don't you agree mr r?

and i think to myself what the hell is that? what does that mean? i cannot stand all the bullshit. the world is filling up with it, with bullshit words that don't mean anything, mr riordan, like an unimaginable profusion, like viruses, organisms that steal meaning just by multiplying and taking up space, the hyper-breeding of senseless language with the aim of infecting people with dumb urgency . . . if farley's had hired me which they would not have BECAUSE WELL YOU KNOW WHAT I MEAN WE DON'T HAVE ALWAYS TO SAY WHAT WE'RE THINKING HUMPH HUMPH HMPPHHH i'd have sat down and told old man farley this won't go, my man, this is

a waste of ink and paper and the human spirit that reads it, it's a dangerous document and UNPATRIOTIC in the extreme because you're flinging things around that
you don't understand.

tell them what you mean, jack, I mean mr farley. tell them, "look—candy is an impulse purchase for the most part. if you go out and make a large consumer purchase, say a sofa, and it doesn't work out, if it's not as comfortable as you'd hoped
or if it doesn't fit the space as well as you'd planned, or if it's cheap and ugly, well
then you've most likely made a mistake, you haven't done your homework; but
when you a buy a bag of candy, and it sucks, you've been rooked. you can't open up
a bag of candy ahead of time and take a taste to see if it's a quality product, or what
you really want. you have to rely on us, farley's, to give you the full, rich flavor of a
fine confection—without disappointment or apology. and that, my friend, is what
this company, this great enterprise, is all about."

[Signed] RICHARD FARLEY, CHICAGO, USA [FLAG, YELLOW RIBBON, MAY
OUR BOYS, AND WOMEN NOW, THAT'S RIGHT, WE'RE INCLUSIVE, THE GALS
TOO, MAKE IT HOME ALIVE, UNSUNDERED, MAY GOD BRING THEM ALL
HOME SAFE AND VICTORIOUS FROM WHATEVER RIDICULOUS, MENDA-
CIOUS ENGAGEMENT WE'VE SENT THEM ON THIS TIME, TO GET THEIR
ASSES SHOT AT AND NUKED, WITH, WE MIGHT ADD, A SPECIAL EMPHASIS
ON THE POOR NEGROES, WHO ARE AS ALWAYS AT THE FRONT OF THE
LINE WHILE WE WORK ON LIMITING ACCESS TO THE PRESS POOL, EACH
ONE OF THESE BRAVE YOUNG MEN AND WOMEN MAKES AMERICA PROUD,
ETC. ETC. . . .]

It's getting to be like—and I realize that this means, clearly, that I have
to go back to my wife and family—I won't survive this, it's like I know
what she's thinking and I am thinking the same things, the same way.
Today's message came in and kind of entered my machine and my consciousness like a stored file whose language comes up for review on
every search operation. Electronic contact may be the worst. I have to
read every e-mail. So now, like some sort of hypnotism victim, I'm eating a bag of malted-milk balls (Farley's, as if she is programming me

from a distance, I'm the Manchurian Attorney and, yes, there is a bizarre patriotic statement on the back of the bag) and I'm watching porn on cable. Robin Byrd, naked talk-show hostess, a haranguing smoke-coated voice on a thickly built tired-eyed woman with dyed hair whose improvisations rely on a thorough and uninteresting foundation of vulgarity, is giving this guy what we're supposed to believe is a handjob with a rubber glove on as if he himself and not a virus is the disease; whatever she's doing you can't see it because it's kept just underneath the camera's scope. I wonder if Ursula is watching the same thing, given her state of mind it seems quite possible, and I speculate or project, really, the idea, whether Robin and the guy, he's ugly and old, if they're actually *not* faking it as they so clearly seem to be doing, if whether this is what sex *is* for people like them; it is the horror of a personality so stripped and narcissistic and without a shred of beauty that interests me, far more than the supposed entertainment. The two of them in the small wood-veneer-paneled studio going through the motions, he's got to throw his head back and roll his eyes and grimace and shake; she's got to pump that arm and make her breasts bounce, and issue that horrifying laugh and push her face at the screen; she looks less like a sex queen than she resembles one of your less likable cousins, come upon inexplicably and repulsively nude, and of course to the two "performers" and everyone around them, the crew etc., the whole thing is old, old, old. I imagine the crew, hell, with this show there can't be more than two or three, drinking coffee in white Styrofoam cups, sneaking out to call their wives and ask how the kids are doing, they should be home in a couple of hours, hold down the fort, honey, the whole thing from the performers' perspective a bad act and acutely, I would think, embarrassing. I saw a picture recently, can't recall where, of an "art" show in the early seventies, a gallery in which a white woman is stretched out on a black waterbed masturbating while people in turtlenecks and haircuts from the *Klute* period stand around with glasses of Chablis. She, there on the bed, she was the art. As awful as that was, it was not so bad as this—somehow in the art-gallery photo the woman seemed to be managing to masturbate in some kind of authentic way, the photo suggesting, in her body, that sinuous gathering, the involuntary and incremental muscle tension of actual arousal. These people, with the bad video values and the bad sound . . . impossible to imagine who might be aroused by it. The problem with what this tame American world thinks is dirty is that it's not nearly, not nearly dirty enough. We are getting to the point where nothing will be dirty enough, except bone-shattering injury and spattering death.

I am tired but I cannot sleep.

Every time I think about partnership, I think: Hello, asshole. I might write a little essay, after I have been a partner for a time. "WHAT I DO FOR A LIVING." I rely on the typical cash flow of six or seven normal American families. I put in a year, perhaps two, finding small cracks and handholds in the cliff face of the law, a minute process, while (if I am with the program, if my career has the purpose of those of my colleagues) I plan my next big purchase and my next big vacation. These vacations are self-confirming narratives (as are most of the purchases: I'll have no other way to prove I exist), each is a tale of How-I-Can-Afford-This. I will learn (and pretend never not to have known) the world of designer books. And oh, how proud I will be of my travels to well-advertised places. The high Sierras, a private sea, ravaged canyons with full-service hotels. A wonderful package offered by a creative travel agent promising some momentary electric contact with history; the travel agent's name is Terri and though she doesn't understand your longing to feel a part of the movement of time that is palpable in ancient cities, she does know that you want to go there with all your material comforts intact. Weeks upon weeks pushing the dollies on which power and privilege rest, to and from the loading dock, grunt work, and then a holiday on credit: to Turkey, Crete, Athens, Rome; to New Zealand, South Africa, Ceylon, and Mozambique; to Cairo, Jerusalem, Damascus; *to Carthage then I came, burning, burning.* The vacation of a lifetime until a few years from now when I take another vacation of a lifetime—this is what I have to look forward to, what partnership will bring.

In the meantime an unnecessarily large, pleasant home that surprises no one, with electronics galore, with the refrigerator set into the wall and always full, Sub-Zero or Sub-Sub-Zero or the newest, Absolute Zero, wherein the fucking temperature can stop fucking subatomic particles dead in their tracks—or whatever is the best at the time, because why not, that's what I'm working for after all, the meaning of my days; and, if I manage to be particularly enlightened, a couple of spots that indicate an effort toward beauty, an aesthetic fully informed by online access to the *New York Times* House & Home section . . . Something to be longed for and worth good money to maintain.

Your children—you are very concerned with reading scores, with growth charts. When they are small, how to explain their beauty? Secretly, one takes credit for it; then asks forgiveness for taking credit, and tries to grant the credit where it belongs. You pray first that they survive, second that they thrive, that they will be, in every sense, all right. On selfish or worried days, you pray that they will not disappoint you, and in all likelihood they won't. You pray you will not disappoint them, but you will and you know it. They will probably, like the vast majority of their friends and peers, step graciously into their heritage of privilege, competence, and prosperity, even if a few years late, because the alternatives in the world to come, the new Middle Ages, will be unacceptable. They will be forced to hold on to every protection and hope of stability against what is to come: which you envision as a tectonic shift, an underlying *thunk*, after which the gatherings begin on street corners. Isolated harangues will become political movements; in good time, only the priests and nobility will know how to read, this being the ultimate achievement of educational reform. The money people will be the best barometer, which is something your children will know because you will teach them; the money huddles like cattle before a storm. The property types pull in their interests, safe-haven their capital, protect themselves—literally, in a real estate realignment, out of the cities, they will isolate their interests, displaying the self-preservatory habits of a vulnerable genus; it's a profoundly reliable intuition they have. It hasn't happened in thirty years, so it is due to happen again, like the early 1970s only worse, faster, more precipitous and terrifying. Watch the streets, watch the markets. For a short time there will be a way to thrive in misery; play against the new inflation, the new unemployment, or both; you can bet on the burgeoning underclass, you can put money down on ever more restricted distributions of wealth, a gathering of all available net cash at the top of the economic ladder, you can be certain of government cutbacks, deficits, deep trade imbalances; all of it means money is changing directions, moving from one place to another, like the salmon runs, and if you get up ahead of where the money is running you can expect to siphon off a nice piece of the action; but when the trouble really breaks out watch the money hide; not a glimmer in the water. Does the word "overseas" mean anything to you at all? Euro, Swiss franc, yen. The fortunes of five hundred thousand men and women, the small-time casino players, will disappear in a couple of keystrokes. The big money moves away from the disturbance like a retiree who spots a gang of young men fighting on the street up ahead of him; literally like that. Crosses over. And the piddling mutual-fund investor and amateur trader, you, for instance, will be left holding the bag; the pension funds will get totally fucked because some of the money always has to get fucked for the other money to survive and grow, and, if the system works as it should, this means fucking the people who have actual needs; the dollar will sink, the markets will have no bottom; and the real people will have foreseen it all; they will have caused it, in the short term, so they're not surprised, and more important, they're not in it. They're long gone, baby. This is what you will protect your children from. Good-bye, New York, hello, Shanghai.

It seems to be getting a little better in the neighborhood—one of the cops says, "It's like a self-cleaning oven," then he laughs.

There's no point even trying to sleep. Around midnight I head up to

110th Street, to the all-night newsstand, the all-night groceries, the all-night bagel shop, the new café and bar on the corner that's open until four; I might go into any of these, depending on my mood, but I also like the walking, and usually keep on going, up to 116th and into the Columbia campus, a hazy white-lighted place at night, and David is right, the sky is always purple over Harlem toward the east. I wander the campus, watch the shadows, toy with a sweet nostalgia. The big McKim, Mead limestone buildings glow like sand in moonlight.

Then out and down Broadway: and there it is again, a man walking along behind me, I am faintly aware of the weight and shadow, a mumbling that keeps up and must therefore be directed at me. I turn and it is the cup: Aegean blue with the Parthenon on it, the take-out coffee cup, these cups being the last vivid icons of the West and its oft-lauded civilization. The Greek tradition, pride and futility. *Spare twenny cens? Spare twenny cens?* in a quiet, chanting voice. The visionaries and shamans who have chanted through the ages: altered states of mind in which God speaks, and snakes rise from stones. All over the city, the quiet moan, the blue cup, the broken Doric columns and rattle of coins. *How 'bout a little help tonight?*

I stop at the newsstand, I'm not sure why at first and then I realize I'm there to buy a pack of cigarettes. Ahead of me, a tall, thick-shouldered, prosperous-looking man in gray slacks and a pink Lacoste shirt, he is maybe fifty years old and he's buying dirty magazines, a goodly number of them too. I wait for my nicotine while the gentleman selects his pornography. With expertise, with apparent discernment, he picks out several sets of 4-for-$12.99s, the hardest-core stuff they've got, and negotiates the price down to $30 for the whole thing. The Pakistani guy packs them in a bag. The gentleman strides off with an air of absurd confidence and pleasure in himself, as if he actually is about to get laid.

"Pack of Marlboros," I say. My eyes drift overhead to the magazines, wander among the penises and open mouths. Ladies pose doggie style. Brown men with curlicues of black hair running down their middles in a thin vertical line. Invariably, these men have mustaches.

On the other side of the newsstand a bedraggled man with fierce eyes sits on the edge of a trash can. To his chest he holds one of those little ironing boards, the size, roughly, of a child, a toddler, Henry. We exchange looks. "Yo, big man," he says, brandishing the little board, waving it in my direction, "no more ironing on the kitchen table man." He holds it out like an offering, a little altar on which to perform the known rituals.

"No more ironing at all for me," I say. "It's all about the new casual."

He sets the board down and comes over. "Yo, big man, listen. Can you spare a hundred and thirty-nine dollars, you know, for a one-way ticket to Bermuda? I got a travel agent down on Forty-seventh Street, she gonna give me the ticket for a hundred thirty-nine dollars, man." His hand wraps around my upper arm, fingers strong as talons. "In fact, you know, you could just give me your credit card number, and she could charge that shit right up, give me the ticket. The warm air good for my lungs and whatnot. Charge it right to your American Express card man, Visa Gold, whatever. What you got, you got the Platinum Discover? Diner's Club? I need the exact spelling and the expiration date, keep in mind. Can't take any more of this New York winter shit."

"My cards are all above the limit," I say. His hands, his face, the crusty unliving look of his hair and his beard, like bunches of old wool. Too much intimacy, too many people closing in, I'm just watching them as if I'm a lizard, cold-blooded and slow, behind a glass.

"Just a hundred thirty-nine, and Bermuda is mine," he says. "Figure out where to go when I get there, you know, like the man says, definitely 'Better to Be Homeless in Bermuda.'"

"I don't know about that," I say. "New York is very understanding. It's very tolerant, we accept all kinds here."

"Fuck that shit, it's cold," he says. "You ever been cold? All night? No hope of getting warm?"

"No," I say.

"Makes *tolerance* look pale, man."

"You're probably right."

"Listen, my man," he says, "you know I'm just kiddin' around, right?

No disrespect. No disrespect. Here's the real shit, man, I got a problem down at the welfare. They give me a ID card, you know, for my checks, but it got stolen in the shelter and now I can't get my check. They givin' me the runaround. Here, look at this," he says, his grip loosening so he can pull from various pockets torn pieces of paper, gray and soft as chamois cloth.

"No documents," I say. "I don't look at any documents."

He folds the battered scraps back into his cracked palms.

I say, "This is a good story, by the way, a proto-narrative that comes up all the time, a major legend. I heard the same thing a while back at the hospital, you know, the stolen ID at the shelter, et cetera, et cetera. It works."

"Yo man that shit happen all the time," he says. "All the time. There's all kind of shit going on out there, people stealing shit just the tip of the iceberg, you got no idea, man, no idea what-so-fucking-ever. And not just among the lower classes either."

"I know," I say.

"No, you don't," he says. "Anyway, big man, it's like this see, I got to get down to Third Street to the shelter down there, they got a bed assigned to me down there. And in a few days I get my card back, you know, a new ID, and I get me a check and then hopefully I be off the streets. How 'bout a little help, man, you know, whatever. I gotta get downtown."

I give him a dollar. He moves on, I look down the block, three or four beat guys waiting with paper cups, a gauntlet I'll have to run to get, where, home? Can I even call it that? And beyond them Broadway stretches into the charcoal-lavender night, buildings loom black against the glowing sky, most of the windows dark, most of them always dark after nightfall although the apartments certainly aren't empty, who knows why, and down the gentle slant of the avenue hang the traffic lights, small red streaks, tongues of fire along the urban grid.

By this time of night the main thoroughfares are a Fellini dream sequence: gathered on the street corners, shifting like unquiet waters, a slow-motion flow of the lame and the halt, an Easter Parade, or gaudy like it, but also unavoidably grim; in the middle of 110th Street, literally on the yellow lines, a crazed-looking woman in a wheelchair, twirling toward the westbound traffic and then as quickly swerving back around like a mechanical drunk to face the eastbound, shaking her cup in midair like some kind of awful preacher of gloom and perdition—as if she believes the cars themselves are personalities on the scene, listeners, inclined to come to Jesus and give her some change. She shakes the cup at moving cars that are going thirty-five or forty or even fifty miles an hour, cars that have shown her an uninterrupted streak of kindness only in that she hasn't been flattened by any of them. She is there for many nights, but a night will come when she will not be there, and no one will see her again. EMS will have taken her away, or the cops; she'll do time in a hospital bed, be sent to social services, be unable to follow the dotted lines that keep her in the system, and be dumped back out again in a new spot, among some different group of horrified citizens, to harrow them for a while.

There are others, always ready to take the spot, a steady supply of men and women of few means but strong public presences. Silhouetted, they have strange postures and forward-leaning, bony walks; ones sees them either fleeing in a great and heaving rush to get to some probably imaginary appointment or else they are rooted to the spot. A ragged man seems half twisted, turning and turning, like one of Michelangelo's *Prisoners*. The ones who aren't lost yet to incoherence and rage will give you their stories. If a prayerful person were to pass by, he might phrase an address to the Almighty along these lines: *God, in your wisdom and mercy, what exactly do you have in mind for us out here on the street at night?* One believes that prayerful people are indeed passing by, at least a few; one believes this now because in the new medieval city there are essentially three groups—the powerful, the devout, and the bankrupt. And here in the glowing white darkness of night in autumn in New York City, near the river, smoking a Marlboro and going slightly woozy with it, I think the only possibilities are devotion or nothing at all, devotion like the poet felt when he fell to the floor in front of the *Pietà* in St. Peter's, the hope of a moment when the idea of a thing and the thing itself are so perfectly joined that your knees fold and your legs collapse and your face lies flush on cool marble. In that moment, thick woolens wrapped him and deep gravity pulled him to the floor. A cold coming, an impossible union.

It has not happened for me. It almost happened for Ellie once, also in Rome, and might have happened, I like to believe, if there hadn't been a German; or perhaps it did happen and it was the German who caused it. This was the year after we were married, and we went for five weeks with not much money to France and Italy—we were in Rome the longest because we had friends there, although there were friends in Paris too but not as close a set; we had friends all over in those days. We went one day to see the *Moses*, which resides at another St. Peter's, San Pietro in Vincoli, which means Saint Peter in Chains. We went for the marble and art but ended up captured by the chains. Ellie gave herself to the scene; she had done it in Florence too, climbing the abandoned scaffolds in the Brancacci Chapel where they were doing a chemical peel on Masaccio—*chiuso, in restauro*—up she climbed and pulled back the canvas that draped Adam and Eve, banished and in agony. I thought somehow we would be arrested for such a thing. I don't really know how to live. She takes things on as they come, a deeply bred, intuitive fearlessness. In Rome, in an open crypt before the glass-doored reliquiarium holding St. Peter's chains, she stood utterly still, just watching. Her stillness seemed to me a kind of prayer, or a shawl used in prayer, something she wrapped around herself like a shell of less demanding and cluttered light, something more silver-gray than the brown-gold light of the air around her; it was grace perhaps; and then quietly up behind her came a tall German with a camera, He was studious, careful, and dull; you could see it in his shoes, those awful German shoes. He wanted a picture of this, as of everything else that caught his interest, the chains in this instance because that church was about the chains, though Michelangelo's *Moses* loomed off to the side and above, a carnival of unnecessary ideas by comparison. The German raised the camera and she did not hear him, and watching from above her on the main floor of the church, I knew what would happen but could not call out to her, it being a church, and then came the rude flash—white, sudden, air-shattering light. It made her leap—like an explosion. Time collided with the infinite and she was thrust back into the blinding world. White flash and black silence; it was Paul's fear and blindness reenacted, he'd been struck from his horse all over again, and all over again he was hearing the irresistible voice—*Saul Saul why do you persecute me?*—on the road to Damascus.

Fear on the road now—among the many disciples on Broadway, late at night, hearing voices. I know the feeling, a small portion of it, that chill and stillness, and if I do not at this moment have actual belief, then I have the desire for belief. *He has risen, he is no longer here . . . Woman, why are you weeping? . . . Ich glaube mein Herr, hilfen mein Unglauben.* The frightening moments are these, finding the stone moved back and the tomb empty, when you are forced to recognize that God is immune to history. *Before Moses was I am . . .* The problem of course is that we get to see none of that; we live in the age of the invisible god, the age of flaming cities, mass human holocausts, gossamer surgery gently waylaying our avid search for death. *Why do you seek the living among the dead? . . . Go quickly, and tell the others.* He could be anyone, anywhere, anytime, and will be. He could be under the white and yellow streetlights, one of the women or men who live in this place, their figures moving slowly across the scene, shadows and memories of shadows. *Who is the third who walks beside you?* Shadows like the shadows that a child has seen, moving across graying walls as sleep escapes him, as sleep teases him and frightens him. He lies still, watching, making out patterns and reflections, and taking comfort from these and from the sound of cars, the soft hiss of rubber on pavement and the low, muscular sound of engines. All of it in time—real light, real walls, real tires—and out of time, the coded talk and semaphore of a different and supernatural side of creation. Distant in the house for that child—I remember this—is his mother at the sink; the pipes clink and shush when she turns the water on. Outside his window, a little bit of rain. A sweet wind.

There are drops on my face now, and the soft bite of a northern wind, on Riverside Drive, in the dark. *O dark dark dark, they all go into the dark* . . . The park below me is lush, black, a lattice of gray branches forming the roof to an eerie, shadowed cathedral. I do not understand suicide. Suicide is too difficult. It is insufficient; it has never been enough. I want to be knocked down; I want to be flattened, atomized, crushed; I want to be annihilated; I want to be absorbed; I want to be assumed.

I want to go home.

[12]

The bleep goes at 4:12 in the afternoon. E-mail—Notify *HIGH PRIOR-ITY* . . . With the signifiers I'm accustomed to: From: "Ursula Murray" <murray212@earthbird.com>. The subject heading is *re: all tied up.* I stare at it, a heavy feeling, than double-click to open. It says, IMMED RESPONSE REQUESTED. I open the file to a view box and save it, even as I am reading it.

mr riordan there's a man in the bedroom and rather roughly treated he's been, i must say. tied up with clothesline from THAT hardware store, the very one. not a very elegant-looking job either, because frankly there was too much cord and i'm not all that fastidious about knots and such. i don't gift-wrap very well, never mind bind a man to a queen-sized bed. i'm feeling a little wired to tell you the truth. to tell you the truth it's like being on a high slope or in the middle of a rough stream or up on a thirty-story ledge not quite clear on how you got yourself there—a dream maybe—and having no idea how the fucking hell to get back, which is where the dream always turns to panic . . .

in the bedroom right now even with the door closed and his mouth taped with sil-ver tape I can hear all the fuss he's making, a lot of fucking noise which INFURIATES ME. it infuriates me. i want to hurt him. i've already hurt him a bit but i want to hurt him some more, i just want to beat on him and beat on him with a pipe or a bat or a rifle butt, which is what i've already used on him, to tell the truth, the butt of the rifle across the ribs and back mostly, because—you know what's odd?—i don't want the mess, the blood and viscera and whatnot. i don't want to know from his goddamned liquids in my goddamned house. i just want him gone now. i'm done. he's in pain and he knows why and whatever i had i just got rid of it but you know HE'S still here. you realize at a certain point that it takes a shitload of work and it's very, VERY difficult to kill a man, and it's extra-special difficult to do it without him bleeding on your shit.

so it started from when I went to the store, up there on third ave. and he was there and I bought my stuff, you know, those critical items a lady needs to keep the house tidy and in good order, like two shrink-wrapped plastic packages of clothesline to tie a man up with or choke him with or hang his fucking ass out the fucking window with, who knows; and rat poison to stuff down the man's throat or grind into his eyes, and mineral spirits and naval jelly and brushes which are good for the eyes too or also to slather up his balls with.

all in all, just a few harmless household items.

the silver tape, I remembered that at the last minute. and there he was, which i knew, I KNEW he'd be. he grinned at me and leered and made a comment because I had put the tight shirt on and was showing a lot of bounce which caught his attention as predicted, plus the skirt and the platforms and I just acted like all flirting was fucking and this was fine with me and so we took it from there, him pathetic, trying to be cool in a tired elvis-goes-bronx-goes-rikers kind of way and me like the horny black ghetto chick in a van peebles flick from seventy-one. off we go, to one of the last of the old-man bars where the old men, not subtle types, assumed i was dat old-fashioned seventies whore as advertised, they hadn't seen much of that in a while, not since the spics and then the investment bankers came in, one after the other. they was seein' pink hot pants even where there weren't any you know what i'm sayin? he had three beers zip zip zip while I worked on my one which of course he didn't notice because why should he give a shit what i'm doing or thinking—he already knew he was getting laid, it was in his eyes, that ten-year-old's pleasure with his own mischievous success sparkling there. everything was clear to me as in a motion picture or photograph; like a three-dimensional map, fluid, improvisational, but utterly reliable. i had escaped feeling, i didn't feel anything except a perfect commitment to the performance. so he sits with his look of love such as it is, an unquenchable need of superiority and vanity and nastiness, and there i am on a different entrance ramp way farther on down the space/time highway and seeing it all in front of me, ahead of me really, the going through the lobby and up the elevator and into the apartment and everything he will say and how he will move and his frozen surprise and his suspicion that it's just a joke when i raise the rifle to him and tell him to lie on down on the bed. no, i will say (and ended up saying, having foreseen all, foresuffered all, as the man said), it is not a joke, except to the extent that life, particularly your life, is a BIG FUCKING joke. in the specific sense no sir this is not a joke sir. i will shoot your ass. in the meanwhile he talked at me about fucking stock cars and daytona and who knows what other shit, pure white people trash bullshit from when he was in the navy, until I said v. brazen look why don't we cut to the chase you know and just go up to my place? i like the way you look honey but i'm not that innarested in cars, you know? it's not far. sure says he.

he was really pleased with himself, mr riordan. i was in that zone, but looking back it was kind of touching if you can picture it.

anyway walking downtown with him I started getting the shakes and I really thought my head would explode. one thing led to another and the next thing you know he's naked and trussed and he's got a rifle barrel wedging its way up his asshole. life's funny isn't it, even in the nonjoke mode.

but the joke was on me there was nobody even there to bluff, as bob dylan once said. i've been stuck in the mouths of ten thousand graveyards . . . i imagine you liked dylan once upon a time, mr riordan, before you went to law school and thought better of it. there were negroes besides hendrix who listened to dylan, not many but a few. now you like what? NY Times preapproved prepackaged WQXR classical? Obscure and unerringly excellent old jazz and blues cuts? CD 101? something guaranteed not to frighten you in any case. you're amazed that white kids listen to hip-hop, aren't you? this is the same as it always was. let the negro sing. no one ever listened to louis armstrong or dizzy gillespie or coltrane, no one ever sat down and listened to nat king cole or jimi hendrix, and then decided not to beat up niggers no more. it's okay to listen to our music it's just actual participation in the civil laws, in leadership, and most especially in the clean-cut systems for the distribution of wealth that have to be kept safely distant from black people, except for a few, like the jews who cooperated. poor mr riordan: it's all escaping you . . .

and here is the bluff: now i got him i don't know quite how to get rid of him. don't worry he isn't dead. he is farting, actually, can you believe it? he's farted probably four or five times which makes me want to jam the barrel up there again and let go a round. of course, can you see the mess? in your mind's eye? i can. he farts wet, a gurgle, he's got some kind of condition i think, it's like a methane shift breaking the surface tension of the swampy insides. not at all healthy and i told him so.

i'm tired now. why don't you come to see me mr riordan and help me get the fuck out of this. you can charge me the usual hourly fees.

please.

*   *   *

When I get there, Ursula opens the door, recedes, sits at a desk with the laptop and some papers.

"Bedroom?" I say. She makes a gesture with her head in the direction of the door. I open it. He lets out a muffled growl or roar or mere shout for assistance, I can't tell. A mild fetid odor. Not pretty. I'll be right back, I tell him. Back out the door, another gurgled shout.

"Where's the gun?" I ask Ursula. She looks at me.

"The rifle?" she says.

"No," I say. "The nine-millimeter."

She opens a desk drawer, hands it to me. I look at it. I realize I don't have the faintest idea how it works. My panic subsides when I realize that this is just fine because I don't under any conditions want it to work anyway.

"Is it loaded?" I ask her.

"Yes, it's loaded, what do you think?"

I look at it and feel around the end of the handle, then give it to her. "Take out the clip," I say.

She takes it from my hand, clicks out the long clip, holds the eviscerated gun in one hand, clip in the other, double open palms, and looks at me. I take them both, empty out the clip onto her desk, the bullets fall with a satisfying, heavy little clatter, and then I try to slide the clip back in. "Here," she says. She takes it from me and does it.

I go into the bedroom, look at the catch of the day, tied and taped on the bed, an extraordinary presence of unhealthy-looking flesh.

"I'm here to get you out," I say. "Make trouble, and I will shoot you." He grunts. I decide to take it as an affirmation. I gather up his clothes, which, bizarrely, are folded neatly across the back of a chair. His beat up shoes stand below. I carry them out; he makes a ruckus as I go.

"Shut up," I say.

In the kitchen I find a shopping bag, place the whole slightly greasy and unpleasant pile in it, and walk it over to the apartment door. Ursula has to undo the complex series of locks. I put the bag out in the hall.

"Stand here," I tell her. "Where's the rifle?" She indicates it standing against the wall near her desk, where I should already have noticed it.

"Get it," I say, "and then stand here with it hidden behind your right leg and use your left hand to hold the door open when he comes through. If he tries anything, let the door go and shoot him in the leg. When he's out the door, close it and lock it behind him."

"Shoot him in the leg?" she says. "Shoot him in the fucking leg? That's easy for you to say. Which leg did you have in mind, I wonder?"

"Whatever," I say. "Shoot him somewhere if he tries to kill me is what I mean."

"Those are instructions a girl can keep in her head," she says. "I'll try not to miss him and hit you, you know, by accident."

Back in the bedroom, with a knife in one hand and the gun in the other, I start cutting away the insane profusion of tape and knotted cord. "As soon as you're free just stand and walk the fuck out. Make one move I don't like and I will shoot you. Your stuff is out in the hall. There's no one there. Throw some of it on and then go. We'll be dialing the police the second the door closes behind you." This is an absurd lie, at this late point in the day's proceedings, which he must know. He must also know, by smell if in no other way, that I'm incapable of shooting him and certainly not up to subduing him. What we're relying on here, gambling on, is his own volition, his wish to be gone rather than wreak more havoc.

I untie him. The flesh, pale, with pale brown body hair, large gnarled feet. A longish, skinny dick, nestled in a profusion of darkening unclean hair. A number of repugnant smells. Other humans again, that flash. They're horrifying, and they're all we have. He stands and bolts, stumbles from stiffness and pain, groans once, a wild animal look in the eye, muscled arms and legs, and bolts again, out the bedroom and outer doors into the hall, with the door slamming behind him and Ursula like a bank guard closing up at night, snapping locks and bolts across the thin strip of space that would allow him back through, to her. When she's done, she fingers the locks, keeps her back to me. I stand, watching her.

"Well," she says at last, and turns around. "Now that's done I'm glad it's over." This makes her laugh. She walks back to the desk, sits, stares at the screen saver, stars shifting across a plastic universe. She looks me in the eye. "You know," she says, "it was remarkable, really. I said to him, 'You don't remember me, do you?' and he says, 'Fuck you,' which means it's coming back to him and I say, 'C'mon, you don't remember a black bitch you tied up? And fucked? And robbed? I remember *you*.'" She lights a cigarette with a Zippo lighter. The *swang* sound as it opens, like a sword being drawn from a steel scabbard.

"Terrible habit," she says, exhaling. "Disgusting. You want one?"

"Sure," I say. She hands me the cigarette and lighter.

"So he's tied up on the bed there and I have the rifle stuck right into his asshole and I say to him, 'I'm going to get a little justice,' and you know what he said? He said, 'Go to hell.' Which struck me. Gave me pause, oddly enough, that phrase. I said to him, 'How many more people you going to rape, you goddamned fucking cracker.' And I was mad, still mad, but now it was like I was mad at a little kid. I prodded him with the gun but not that bad. I said, 'How many more?' And he said, 'Go to hell,' again. And I jammed him hard and he kind of gasped a big breath with his teeth all gritted and his face screwed up and I said, 'Let me make a suggestion—don't ever do that to a woman again because you never know when one of them might kill you.' Anyway, I walked away. I decided to let him go. I decided just to let him go. Fuck it. Of course, I needed a little help."

She looks at me again, as if for the first time. "How much money did you get for me?"

"They've offered one point six million," I say. "We'll call them in the morning and it goes into escrow before the end of the day. If everything goes smoothly and the judge signs on it, it will be delivered when all the papers are signed, a million plus for you, about five hundred for us, plus expenses."

"Good," she says. "Buy more guns and shit." I give her a look and she smiles, like a little girl.

"Lighten up, homes," she says. She looks around her apartment, stands up. "Well. That's a lot of money."

"Yeah," I say.

"I'm going to have to figure out something good to do with it," she says. "A burden of a kind. It all demands energy, which I don't have much of right now."

I stand up. "I'm glad you're all right."

"Nobody's ever all right," she says. "But thank you—*Mister* Riordan."

"You're welcome," I say.

Jack is back in the office, and Ron is back on the street. After nearly four weeks of delay just for the pretrial hearing, when we were finally in front of the judge and all prepped to argue for an immediate trial date, the federal prosecutor, McCarthy, in his quiet but still arrogant voice, put before the judge a motion to dismiss all charges against one Ronald Adamson for the murder of his wife. Ron smiled, briefly, and shook Jack's hand, but not mine. The judge chewed McCarthy out pretty well and offered his apologies. We put Ron in a cab. The following day, a letter went out bowing out of any further representation of any kind; and if my luck holds I'll never lay eyes on him again.

Ellie and I together, watching the news: a woman, seventeen years old, "blacked out" and her nineteen-month-old baby was found floating facedown in a tub of scalding water, which was overflowing, flooding the building lobby and disabling the elevators . . . In this strange, charmed, lethal city, I have moved back in with my wife and children.

It started on a Saturday morning, the usual pick-up routine. On the floor I saw a tag, like a clothing tag, the kind that hangs off the sleeve of a jacket in a thrift shop, with the same black Magic Marker writing you would see on it in a thrift shop, but instead of "$7," it says, "Just Relax." It's got the reinforced hole and the little string. I stand in the kitchen looking down at it. "Just Relax."

"It came on a shirt I bought from Yoga Express," Ellie says. "I keep trying to throw it away but it keeps making its way back out onto the floor." She pats my chest and passes into the dining room. "I think it's meant for you. Put it on your desk. It's a message."

"Yoga Express?" I say. "Isn't that a contradiction in terms?"

"You ask unnecessary questions," she calls out from the living room. "Put your mind into your twisting spine."

I take this to be some sort of yoga-ism, some exercise in displacement and the one true peace of not thinking—born in the East but always meant for America.

"You really could use to stretch and relax," Ellie says after she's come back into the kitchen. I am pouring a cup of her coffee.

The coffee is terrible. "This coffee is terrible," I say.

"I can't make coffee," she says, rather sweetly. "Only you can make good coffee. Will you make us some?"

So I do. And while we wait for it to drip through the filter she gives me a massage on my shoulders and neck: the muscles feel as if they've been petrified by a thousand years of wind and ice and heat and rain. And we look at each other, and we start exploring other things, (but here is Henry!) and after two thousand dollars' worth of marriage counseling we acknowledge that I need her hands and she needs my coffee.

Today is one of the first normal days since I've moved back home. Normal, that is, because it is without the sense of eggs underfoot, the delicate, overpolite process of getting used to each other again, the unspoken fear that our violence of feeling will arise again, unstoppable and sudden, as it has always been; the unspoken hope too of avoiding all that. At least for now. It is evening, we're watching television, the children are asleep, we breathe deeper, in the beautiful and short-lived state of no requirements, beautiful exactly in that it is so temporary; we're just sitting with two beers, her leaning into me, a kind of charged quietude. Making up is wonderful for sex; in these ten days we've made love on the living room floor, on the couch, in the bathroom standing up against the wall, in a warm tub face-to-face with her on my lap, legs around my waist. A constant state of arched readiness, a pushing back of boundaries. Marriage is like this, a long campaign, huge gains and catastrophic losses that come with casualties and death and also with glory, heroism, and grace.

Or it goes like this: we wake up with me pressed hard against her, insistent, and in seconds, it seems, I am on top of her and she is eager and it is fast and smooth the way it can be when fatigue isn't so much a part of the proceedings. When it's over I stay inside and feel her squeezing, squeezing, squeezing, the nicest thing. Then I start to soften and I shift and am out and we lie there, until the knowledge we should get up grows too harsh. Ellie showers, I wander through the apartment, Henry gets up and boom-boom-booms right past me on his flat, active feet for the living room and the television set.

"Good morning, Captain," I call out after him; he doesn't answer. Major bedhead, sweet pajamas. Ellie is finished, I shower, she dresses. When I come out Ellie is at the table and Henry is planted where I left him in front of morning TV, only now he's watching *Sally Jesse Raphael* . . . transvestites, abused wives. Abused husbands. Sitting mesmerized, he can turn on the TV but somehow is not inclined to change channels, just watches whatever channel it's been left on. I turn it to *Sesame Street*.

And we sit down to eat and put out cereal for Henry—the baby is blessedly still sleeping—but Henry doesn't want to eat yet, he's enjoying tooling around the living room by himself with the TV on. Finally he walks into the dining room and asks Ellie, "Are you having sex?"

"Not at the moment," she says.

"Am I having sex?" he says.

"No, dear. Where did you hear about having sex?"

He turns and walks back into the living room. Ellie looks at me. "We have to pay attention to what he's watching," she says.

"He doesn't know what it means," I say.

"He knows it means something," Ellie says. She's right about that—he said it and this little charge went off when we both looked up and in his eyes one could see it clearly: pay dirt.

"Besides which," Ellie says, "he might come out with that anywhere now. I can just see it: we'll be at the dry cleaner's or something, where the nice Chinese lady always says, 'Herro, rittle boy, herro, rittle boy,' and he'll be, like, 'Wanna fuck?'"

"Hmm," I say. I'm back into the paper.

"Don't ignore me, Will," she says.

I look up. "I'm sorry," I say. "You were frightening me."

"So be frightened," she says. "Don't read the paper, be actually frightened. Children are frightening."

"Where did it say that in all the books you bought?" I say.

"They left that part out," she says.

Chin comes to the apartment for dinner. I am making coffee. He is telling Ellie about the coffee machine at the office, which blew several gaskets and needed some special repairs only obtainable in France and has been scrapped in favor of a more modest though still elaborate machine with three regular pots and an espresso extension. In the kitchen, getting cups, spoons, milk, sugar, I hear David tell Ellie, "Steam absolutely *billowed* into the hallway, the secretaries were screaming and dashing out of the dining room like there was a bomb. And Jack came up, he'd only been back a few days at that point, just looking at it, you know, with that preternatural expression of calm he's been wearing since the heart attack—I think he met God and doesn't quite concern himself with merely mortal affairs anymore—and he just stares at it, you know, until the steam kind of begins to give out and then he goes in and pulls the plug. Then he stares at it some more and walks away."

I come in, the Melita pot on a stained but still serviceable oven mitt that I'll use as a trivet. I put the coffee down, start to go back for the crockery. "You know what he said to me?" I say.

"No," David says.

"We were in his office later, in the middle of doing some actually interesting work, and he looks up at me and says, 'What the fuck was I ever thinking about with that coffee machine? It looks like some kind of antique street-cleaning device.' Then he goes back to work."

"So, David," Ellie says. "Whatever happened to that boy on the beach?"

"Ah," David says.

"You're getting all dreamy-eyed," I say.

"A gentleman doesn't talk," David says.

"C'mon," Ellie says. "You didn't. Did you? He was only a *child*."

"He was *nineteen*," David says.

"How do you know that?" Ellie says.

"I made him show me his driver's license."

"You carded a guy for sex?" I say.

"You can never be too careful," David says. "Besides, it was in the spirit of the flirtation."

"How do you do that?" I ask him. "I'm genuinely interested, I mean, at what point do you do that? In bed, before the moment of truth, or in the car or what?"

"You guys are embarrassing me," David says. "I did it back at the house."

I do a police voice: "Do you know why I stopped you, son? You have a broken taillight . . ."

"He had a broken taillight, all right," David says.

"Shut up," Ellie says, slapping at his arm, which he pulls away.

Memories of sex that night in Montauk.

"He's an extremely sweet and slightly confused boy and it was very nice," David says. "Nicer for him perhaps than for me."

"Do your parents know?" says Ellie, a little weirdly.

"That I slept with that boy? Or that I'm gay?"

"That you're gay," says Ellie. "Obviously." She's projecting ahead in her own motherhood here, I can see. One day Henry comes home from college: "Mom, Dad, I have something to tell you . . ." It occurs to me that if this were to happen, Ellie would blame it on the college.

"Yeah, they know," David says. "They're beginning to live with it after seventeen years. My mom doesn't really talk about it or anything that might lead to talking about it. My dad, he's big on old Chinese sayings like 'Listen to your heart, and proceed with confidence . . .' I say to him, yeah, only your heart says spend money and run away. Then he looks disappointed." David makes an older, more Asian-looking face, a particular kind of stoical glumness written on it, that makes us all laugh.

The next day is a Saturday. I go down to the firm early, do three hours of work, call it a day, head back home. We go for a walk in the park in the afternoon, come back, the kids take a nap, Ellie and I in the dining room, each reading part of the Saturday papers.

"Jefferson," Ellie says suddenly, "was a little cracked but he was a great writer." She is reading the *Book Review*, part of the Sunday paper that they deliver on Saturday.

"Why's Jefferson in the paper?" I say.

"A new biography," she says. "Here's something. He's talking about Washington. Jefferson says, 'His mind was great and powerful, without being of the very first order. His colloquial talents were not above mediocrity, possessing neither copiousness of ideas nor fluency of words.'"

"He's falling in historians' estimation, you know," I say.

"Who, Washington?"

"Yeah," I say. I'm in the kitchen now, pouring water for coffee. "I mean no. Jefferson. Jefferson. They emphasize now how confused he was, gave no speeches, never appeared in public, kind of a President J. D. Salinger kind of thing. Wrote thousands and thousands of letters, like, about gardening. He's on the way down. FDR and Truman and Eisenhower are rising."

"That's good about Truman," she says. "He was such an American."

"He also dropped two atomic bombs on Japan and started the cold war."

"That's fine," she says. "Level gaze. Empty conscience."

"It's just that some people still find these things problematic."

"I like his face," she says.

I am married again.

Later in the afternoon, the baby has woken from his nap and I've changed him and he's in that splendid mood, clean, rested, not hungry yet, eyes full of fun. Ellie is dozing on the couch. His eyes are a wide and oceanic blue. I have him on the bed and I'm standing over him ducking my head into his tummy and up again and he is laughing: something about the top of my head always amuses him. He laughs, and his arms reach and recede, reach and recede. He is searching the world, looking for the one who made him—a search he takes up now and will later forget, until finally, feeble and old, incontinent, silenced, as he is now, he will search again, back where he began, a child with eyes opened but hardly seeing the world. The words will be there, already spoken, common among the dialects: *Father, Father, why have you forsaken me?* He will be nothing more than an infant, as I will be, as we all will be. I can see Sam completely at this moment, his whole being, Samuel John Riordan, the span of years. He will not die young; I can see this, impossible to say how, like a vision or a voice or a quick message to the center of the mind; I am grateful for it and hope for its truth. I lean over him and I watch his arms stabbing, reaching. I watch his eyes and his eyes watch mine, and I am praying again, as I did in the taxi those months ago, because this is important, life or death, I pray for what seems like a long time though it is probably less than a minute, and after that one message there is no further answer, and I don't feel any different. *I want to do the right thing*, that's what I'm asking for, because on my own it is beyond me, way past what I know. And then Henry comes in—I hear him, he pounds into the room running toward the-something-new; he sees me there and stops. I turn, and there he is, at a different stage from Sam, so much larger, but the same. They are the same and I am the same. We look at each other, he breaks into a goofball grin. That smile, that smiling face. Perhaps I've embarrassed him, but it's all right, he's happy to see me. He waits, he is a moment of stilled energy, of alertness, of wanting—a boy in sneakers. His eyes shine. Behind that light there is a tunnel to darkness, to mystery, and behind the veil of all that's visible, everything I can see, the same darkness, the same mystery. His eyes say, Who is this I am looking at?—stranger? criminal? father? Yes, father. Sam gurgles, grunts. Henry watches me, expecting something, ready for my first move, ready for the world; he's standing there looking at me, looking at his brother, these days coming into his first contact with willful love, actually loving us of his own volition, and he's asking the question that is the only question that matters until the day, the hour, the minute you die: What's next?